YAMADA MONOGATARI:
THE WAR GOD'S SON

BOOKS BY RICHARD PARKS

YAMADA MONOGATARI:
THE WAR GOD'S SON

RICHARD PARKS

PRIME BOOKS

YAMADA MONOGATARI:
THE WAR GOD'S SON

Prime Books
www.prime-books.com
Germantown, Maryland

For more information, contact Prime Books:
prime@prime-books.com

ISBN: 978-1-60701-457-7 (print)
ISBN: 978-1-60701-465-2 (ebook)

For Carol

CHAPTER ONE

THERE WERE THREE of them standing near the foot of the
bridge that joined what had been Kuon Temple to the shore
of a mountain lake. They looked almost human, but there was
a slight shimmer in their outlines that spoke of their tenuous
connection to this world. The temple itself had been abandoned
for nearly a hundred years, but the bridge was of stone, and so
had not *quite* fallen to ruin. Kenji and I had spent four days
tracking our quarry, and I was feeling a bit impressed with
myself for finally running him to ground, but that was before I
saw the creatures waiting for us.

Shikigami. Of course.

Now I not only knew who the culprit was but how he had
made his attempts on Lord Mikoto's life, twice entering locked
gates and guarded rooms. We were dealing with an *onmyoji*,
a magician of some skill. Dolt that I was, if the assassin had
managed a third attempt, chances were that my client would
already be dead.

"*Shikigami*," Kenji said, and he sighed. "I really do detest
those things, Lord Yamada."

The priest, like myself, was badly in need of a shave and a
bath, though he had the added disadvantage of a stubbly head
that by rights should be clean-shaven. Still, four days of rough

pursuit in the mountains north of Kyoto hadn't allowed for even the bare minimum of hygiene.

"It does explain a lot, though the fact our quarry has studied Chinese yin-yang magic surprises me."

"Any more such surprises and *we* may turn out to be the quarry," Kenji said dryly. "What do you think? A strategic withdrawal?"

"I think turning our backs to these creatures would be a serious mistake. Besides, it would have been easy enough for their master to arrange a potentially far more effective ambush farther along the path, and yet they meet us openly at the bridge."

"So you believe their purpose is primarily to delay us, assuming they cannot kill us outright?"

"Their master knows, if he did not before, that he is being tracked. Right now there are three of the creatures. Give their master enough leisure and there will be dozens."

"I was afraid you'd say that." Kenji took a firmer grip upon his staff as I drew my *tachi*. "If there's no help for it, let's go," he said.

We crossed the bridge at a quick trot. We had one advantage— the *shikigami* were armed only with clubs rather than swords, but I had dealt with enough of their kind to know better than to underestimate them. Yet as we got closer, the creatures' human appearance grew even more tenuous. They might fool anyone at sufficient distance, but closer than a bowshot no one would mistake them for people. Frankly, I had seen far better work.

Almost carelessly done. Or perhaps hastily?

I didn't have time to ponder meanings, for in a moment we were on them. Or it might be fairer to say they were on us. The bridge was too narrow for all three to meet us at once, but two took the lead with the third close behind as they charged out to meet us. With no room to maneuver, Kenji and I were stopped well short of the end of the bridge while the creatures seemed perfectly content to keep us there. I had no room to swing my *tachi* properly, and pressing forward would bring us into the range of their cudgels.

Kenji deflected a club blow with his staff. "It seems your assessment was correct, Lord Yamada," he said.

This wasn't working. I retreated a half-step and glanced over the side of the bridge. "Kenji-san, are there reeds on your side as well?"

"Yes," he said through gritted teeth as he dodged another swing of the club.

"Jump in the water on my signal. Don't worry—they can't follow us."

"And this will accomplish what?"

"Just do what I say . . . now!"

Kenji held his nose and jumped. I merely stepped off the bridge, aiming for the closest patch of reeds. I heard Kenji's splash from the other side just as I made my own and found myself chest-deep in the freezing lake. Spring had arrived, but winter was not yet completely done with us. I almost lost my breath in the cold water and knew I could not remain there for long before my fingers would be too numb to grip my sword. I held my *tachi* above my head and waded toward shore as quickly as I dared. I glanced through the supports of the bridge and glimpsed Kenji doing the same on the far side.

After a moment's apparent confusion, two of the *shikigami* left the bridge and guarded the shore against me while the last one went after Kenji. My two crowded the shore, waiting.

Perfect.

I continued toward shore with my *tachi* raised to strike, but while I was still out of reach of their clubs, I raked my palm against the water's surface and raised the biggest splash I could. One jumped back out of reach but the other was caught flat-footed by the water. For a moment it merely stood there, looking confused. Then it began to shimmer and dissolve like mist in the sun. Another moment and there was nothing left of it but a slip of paper lying in the grass. I smiled and made another splash, driving the second creature back even farther. It was just far enough to let me reach shore unimpeded. I almost slipped but recovered in time to dodge the club. I heard another splash from the other side of the bridge but didn't have time to see what was happening. I had removed one attacker, but the other was quite capable of killing me without any assistance, and it seemed intent on proving this fact without further delay.

Kenji, for both our sakes you better not have lost . . .

I got my answer when Kenji's priestly staff smacked down hard on the creature's head from behind. The staff passed through the more insubstantial portions of the *shikigami*'s anatomy and I heard a ripping sound. In an instant the last attacker was reduced to a torn piece of paper.

"Thank you. I gather your opponent was no problem?"

Kenji picked up the paper. "Not once I realized why you were splashing so much. I'm guessing it made the writing bleed off the paper?"

"Just so. The ink was still fresh, which helped." I found the other strip of paper that had embodied the first *shikigami*. The ink had completely run, turning it illegible.

"I managed to catch mine on the end of my staff and threw it into the water," he said, and showed me the final piece of paper. "This is the only one left?"

It was as I'd feared. While I was grateful to Kenji for dealing with our last opponent, the blow of his staff had ripped the paper into shreds, rendering it as illegible as the first two. "I was hoping there would be more left."

"Don't you already know who we are hunting?"

I did. The problem was that, considering who our quarry was, my word would not be enough. I needed proof, and I said as much.

"We're on an island," Kenji pointed out. "Unless there's a way off other than this bridge, our proof is here."

I hoped he was right. We followed the path to the abandoned temple as quickly as we dared, using movement instead of dry clothes to try to stay warm, knowing all the while there could be an ambush waiting for us along the way, but we reached our goal without further incident.

Kuon Temple had lost its patron almost a hundred years earlier when a wealthy cadet branch of the Hata Clan had made enemies of the powerful Fujiwara and been all but annihilated. Now all that was left of their power and influence was what had been a very fine stone bridge and a temple complex slowly returning to the earth. It was easy to see what it had once been— what roof tiles remained were of baked clay rather than split wood, and the remaining woodwork and carvings were very fine. There were even some traces of the old garden remaining, but it was clear the abandoned shell of the once magnificent temple would not last much longer.

"If he's gone to ground on the island, our proof is here," I said softly. "Be on your guard."

Kenji smiled, though his teeth were chattering. "A-a-always, Lord Yamada."

We both needed to get out of our wet clothes and make a fire before we took ill, but there simply wasn't time. I drew my sword again and stepped through the doorway. Even so, I waited a moment for my eyes to adjust to the gloom before pressing forward. This turned out to be a wise choice, though even then I didn't quite believe what I saw.

Sitting in what had been the main hall of the temple was Lord Otomo no Tenshin, brother to Otomo no Mikoto, head of the Otomo Clan, and the man Kenji and I had spent the last four days in the mountains hunting. Yet if our pursuit had been of consequence to him before this point, the man did not show it. He was just a little younger than Lord Mikoto, who was about forty, and the family resemblance was clear—he had the same slightly flattened nose and piercing eyes as his brother. He kneeled in the center of the large hall wearing immaculate formal robes of green and gold and a high-peaked cap. His dress and demeanor might have been appropriate for the Imperial Palace itself, except that he held a *tachi*, sheathed in an ornate scabbard, in his left hand. When Kenji and I stepped into the room, he calmly drew the blade and rose to his feet.

"Yamada no Goji," he said, "you really are the most inconvenient person."

I wasn't inclined to dispute the point. The Crown Prince's own uncle, Prince Kanemore, had said the same thing of me on more than one occasion, and he was my friend. I could not say the same of Lord Tenshin. From the expression on the man's face it was plain he intended to insure I would no longer be an inconvenience to anyone.

"You plotted the assassination of your own brother, your rightful lord," I said. "You almost succeeded." I wondered if he would attempt to deny it, but that question was quickly answered.

"A minor set-back," he said airily. "Soon to be corrected. After all, so far as Mikoto is concerned, I remain his loyal and obedient brother. You followed me on your suspicions—well founded, I do admit—but you have no proof. Kill me, and your patron, my dear brother, will personally demand your head from the Emperor himself. Is that not so?"

"It is," I admitted. "But then, it was never my intention to kill you."

"Honestly, Lord Yamada . . . Perhaps your reputation is somewhat overstated. Did you think I would hand my confession to my brother like a love-knot letter?"

I thought nothing of the sort, but I was finally starting to think of something else. "If you intend to kill us—and you know you will have to do so—what are you waiting for?"

He smiled. "*Baka.* Rather I should ask you—why are you in such a hurry to die?"

I understood the point of the *shikigami*. They were trying to delay us. But why was Tenshin doing the same thing? Were there really more *shikigami* crossing the bridge even now?

"Kenji-san, do you have a spirit ward close to hand?"

"Always," he said. "But . . . oh."

Kenji took a slip of paper from within his robe and slipped it through the rings on the head of his staff. This he held out toward Tenshin, who had been watching him with a puzzled expression on his face all that time. When the head of Kenji's staff was at full extension though still out of the range of the man's sword, Tenshin's outline shimmered like a heat-vapor in summer.

Baka is right—

"*Shikigami!*" I shouted, but Kenji was a step ahead of me. His staff shot forward just as the image of Lord Tenshin attacked with unnatural speed. Kenji's ward didn't stop the attack, but it slowed it just enough for me to counter and return the stroke. I sliced through the creature's robes just at the neck, and it was only by sheer luck my blade found the slip of paper that bound its master's will to the creature's insubstantial form. In a moment the creature who had appeared to us as Lord Tenshin dissolved and disappeared, leaving its empty robes, sword, and high formal cap to fall to the dusty floor.

"Follow me!"

I ran to the opposite end of the hall and through the empty doorway. The back garden had long returned to the wild, but there was still the fishermen's path, and I followed it, Kenji close behind me. We reached the crumbling wall surrounding the temple. The gate doors hung askew on their hinges, and we slipped past them and kept running.

When we reached the opposite shore of the island, we found a fairly new fishing dock and the rope that would have tied up a boat, or rather the sliced end of that rope. Someone hadn't bothered to untie it. There was nothing else. We looked out over the water, saw nothing, not even a speck on the water, in the distance.

"Chances are he's been gone for hours," Kenji said. "He could have put to shore at any one of a thousand places. It'll take us days to pick up the trail again."

"If our luck has changed, we won't have to. We'll search the compound, but I don't think he's here."

We first checked the path to the temple, but there were no more of the creatures to be seen. Kenji and I did a thorough search of the remaining temple outbuildings and grounds. When we had satisfied ourselves that Lord Tenshin was not still hiding somewhere on the island, we returned to the main hall, where everything was as we'd left it. Kenji picked up the sword and returned it to its scabbard while I inspected the robes.

"This bears the Otomo family *mon*," Kenji said, indicating the scabbard. "And the blade is very high quality. I think this is Lord Tenshin's sword."

"I'd be amazed if it wasn't, just as these robes are his as well. He sacrificed both to buy himself more time to escape. Now we know why the first three *shikigami* he created were done so hastily—he focused most of his efforts here. The building's gloom aided the illusion, but you have to admit this last *shikigami* was a work of art. It was only after I realized it, too, was trying to delay us that I suspected we were not dealing with Lord Tenshin directly."

Kenji sighed. "But now we have proof he was here!"

I smiled. "Yes, and so? A nobleman makes a pilgrimage to a remote, obscure temple for some pious reason or other, which he would gladly fabricate. It's not a crime, Kenji-san. Before this is done and over, I'll have to give Lord Mikoto sufficient reason to execute his half-brother. I'll need something more than a pile of clothes and a sword. I'll need . . . ah!"

I held up the slip of paper I'd found in the now-empty robes.

Looking at it now, I realized I'd been even luckier than I'd first believed—the tip of my sword had snagged the paper just enough to tear it clean through. A *shikigami* was a creature as much of will as magic, with the words written on a slip of paper no more than an anchor to tether the creature to its master's bidding. By damaging the paper sufficiently, I had broken that tether and rendered the creature back to the nothing from whence it came. I unfolded the paper, careful not to tear it further.

"We were never able to recover one of these pieces of paper before. In the first two attempts, they were completely destroyed. My water trick and your rather enthusiastic staff blows did for the three at the bridge. But this one—" I held it up "—still has its writing on it. I cannot read this script. I fancy you might."

Kenji sighed. "I am a priest of the Eightfold Path, Lord Yamada. Whatever my faults, I do not dabble in Chinese magic."

"Fair enough. But it's plain Lord Tenshin did. This script is clearly done in his own hand, which I have no doubt Lord Mikoto will recognize. This, together with Lord Tenshin's personal items and our own accounting, will be more than enough proof."

"Then we've won, and Lord Tenshin can drown in a fisherman's net or get eaten by a mountain ogre for all I care. I am ready to return to the capital."

"Bluntly stated, but correct," I said. "Chasing Lord Tenshin any further would be pointless. My charge was to identify Lord Mikoto's secret enemy, and I have done so. What Lord Mikoto will choose to do about it is a clan matter and not my concern."

Kenji frowned. "True. And yet you sound like someone trying to convince themselves of something they do not believe. What is bothering you, Lord Yamada?"

"The same thing which has been bothering me ever since we left the capital—why did Lord Tenshin run in the first place?"

"Why . . . ? He knew you suspected him, and he also knew you intended to question him. He panicked."

"Possible, but unlikely. When he left Kyoto, I merely assumed he must have believed I had proof. My assumption was reinforced by the fact he chose to travel unescorted—any clan *bushi* he could enlist would owe first loyalty to the clan chief, and that is Lord Mikoto, whose proxy in this matter I am privileged to hold. A word from me and they would have arrested him themselves."

"Then what has changed your mind?"

"The *shikigami* itself. Remember when it said we had no proof? A *shikigami* knows nothing its master does not know. It is, in essence, a projection of the magician's will. So if the *shikigami* knew we had nothing but my suspicions, then Lord Tenshin knew it, too. There was no reason for him to panic—and even less to run."

"Unless the *shikigami* was lying."

"As much as I would like to do so, I do not believe it was."

Kenji shook his head. "But then nothing makes sense! If Lord Tenshin wasn't running from us, who was he running from?"

I considered, but not for very long. "Perhaps he wasn't running *from* anything at all. Perhaps he was running toward something else."

"Such as?"

Kenji had cut straight to the heart of the matter. "I don't know. Perhaps it's not important."

Kenji looked at me. "But you don't believe this, do you?"

" 'It is not the snake on the rock that kills you. It is the one in the grass you did not see.' Yes, Kenji-san. I think it might be important. But for now my duty is to return to the capital. Yours as well, if you want to collect your fee."

"I want nothing more than to do both and as soon as possible."

By the time we had concluded our business on the island, the sun was already setting. Despite the promise of better shelter among the temple ruins, we decided against making camp on the island in case Lord Tenshin—wherever he had gotten to— sent more *shikigami* against us, and if he did so it would best not be where he might expect to find us. Barring any incidents, two days' travel southwest would bring us back to Lake Biwa and the road to Kyoto. I wasn't a big enough fool to assume there would be no incidents. We had no sooner set foot on the bridge than I was proven correct.

There were *bushi* waiting for us at the end of the bridge. I counted five armed men, four of them carrying bows in addition to their swords.

Kenji swore softly. "*Shikigami*? So soon?"

"No. I am reasonably certain they are human. But I don't understand what business they have with us. They are far too well-dressed and equipped to be bandits."

"I don't suppose we could swim for it." Kenji said wistfully.

"Not if they know how to use those bows, and I'm guessing they do." I sighed. "Not to mention the water would freeze us before we made it to shore. The sad truth, Kenji-san, is that we are trapped."

"So what are our options?"

"Well, we can go discover their intentions or try to hide on this tiny island. If they mean us harm, our only real choice is where we die."

Kenji shook his head. "Sometimes the clarity of your mind is really annoying. Let's go greet them then, shall we?"

I considered that, if the *bushi* did mean us harm, from a tactical perspective the halfway point on the bridge was the perfect time for them to draw their bows. We would be well within easy range and both too far from shore to charge them and too far from the island to retreat before their arrows found us. When we crossed the halfway point with no sign of movement from our visitors, I knew better than to relax, but it did make me all the more curious about our situation. Moreover, at least one of the men seemed familiar to me. By the time Kenji and I reached the end of the bridge and stood before the *bushi*, I was certain of it.

"Fujiwara no Tadanobu," I said. "Greetings."

The young man smiled and then, to my considerable surprise, kneeled in front of me and bowed. "Lord Yamada, I am very happy to see you."

At that moment, the sight of a member of the Fujiwara Clan bowing to one such as myself worried me more than the potential of another *shikigami* attack. "Lord Tadanobu, first of all, please rise. Second, it's good to see you again, but why are you here? We're a long way from Kyoto."

He got back to his feet. "Indeed, which is one reason I am glad to see you. These gentlemen and I have been searching for you for days. We knew you left the capital by the Demon Gate heading toward Lake Biwa, but little else."

While the northeast gate to the city was commonly referred

19

to as the "Demon Gate" because it was believed to be the favorite method for evil spirits to enter the capital, for most people it was simply the most direct exit for that particular direction. That Lord Tadanobu had managed to track us with no more information than the gate of our exit spoke well for his skills. I had once helped him with an issue relating to the death of his uncle and found him to be a brave and capable young man. In truth, he was the only living member of the Fujiwara Clan I could imagine being glad to see. Yet his appearance here was puzzling, and I repeated my question.

"My apologies. Prince Kanemore sent me to find you—or rather, I volunteered. The capital is a rather . . . unsettled place at the moment, and I was glad for the chance to get away. I would say more, but Prince Kanemore gave me strict instruction to say no more than I must. He wants to see you as soon as possible."

This was clearly going to be a day which bred more questions than answers. "I am at His Highness's disposal."

Lord Tadanobu whistled, and three more *bushi* appeared from out of the forest, leading horses. Struck with a sudden and horrible suspicion, I counted them, and it was exactly as I had feared—there were two extra mounts, doubtless intended for Kenji and me.

Kenji smiled a wicked smile. "It appears we will not be walking back to Kyoto after all, which suits me perfectly, but I do know how much you hate horses."

I sighed. "For your information, I do not hate horses, Kenji-san. I only hate riding them."

At this even Lord Tadanobu couldn't suppress a smile, but I ignored both of them. Prince Kanemore was as aware of my aversion as Kenji was. If his business could not only wait for my return but also required him to send riders after me as well, there was more to be worried about than even I had imagined. And I prided myself on my ability to find the worrisome side of anything.

"Let us be on our way, then," I said. "I have the feeling there is no time to waste."

CHAPTER TWO

MY BUSINESS with both Prince Kanemore and Lord Mikoto had to wait, despite its obvious urgency. When we arrived at the capital it was too late in the day and we were far too exhausted to attempt either obligation. Lord Tadanobu and his escort departed to arrange our audience with Prince Kanemore for the following morning. Kenji withdrew to whichever of Kyoto's abundant temples had not yet thrown him out, and I immediately returned to my rooms at the Widow Tamahara's establishment to arrange a bath and whatever she could manage for a late meal. I found the formidable old woman in a rather foul mood, and for a moment I wondered if I'd forgotten to catch up my rent again, but she quickly arranged matters to my satisfaction, so it was clear to me the heart of her grievance lay elsewhere.

It was Kaoru, a young woman in Widow Tamahara's employ, who brought me a bowl of cold rice and two rather sad-looking dried fish shortly after my bath, but in truth I hadn't expected better considering the hour. I also didn't expect to glimpse a bandage showing at the edge of the girl's kimono at the shoulder. She winced as she placed the tray in front of me.

"Are you injured, Kaoru-san? What happened?"

She looked away. "It is nothing, Yamada-sama."

"It is indeed something," said someone who wasn't Kaoru.

The Widow Tamahara stood scowling in the doorway. "Kaoru was attacked the day you left here in my very compound. She has only today been well enough to return to any of her duties."

This was both unusual and disturbing. An establishment such as the Widow Tamahara's was always subject to disturbances of various sorts by its very nature, but her livelihood depended on keeping everything in order and—relatively—calm. Security was as important to her as discretion was to her patrons, but there were always free-lance or down on their luck *bushi* available for hire, and she normally had a minimum of three in her employ for security.

"What happened, Kaoru-san?" I asked.

The young woman glanced at the Widow Tamahara, who grunted assent. "Tell him."

"I was serving a group of gentlemen in the main hall, and we'd run out of saké. I went to the storeroom to fetch some and found Taka-san standing by the veranda just outside the storage buildings."

"Oh? And who is this Taka?"

"A *samuru* I had hired to replace one of my former guards who had preferred staying drunk to performing his duties," said the Widow Tamahara. "Taka was supposed to be on duty at the north entrance. Kaoru knew he wasn't where he was supposed to be and spoke to him."

"That's all? Then he attacked you?" I asked Kaoru.

"*Hai.* He grabbed my arm and twisted it. I don't know why, but his eyes were so strange. It was as if the only reason he didn't cut me down then and there was that he was too angry to think clearly. It made no sense."

"None at all," the old woman added. "It's true Taka was assigned to one of the entrances rather than within the compound, but it turned out he'd simply switched duties with one of the other guards. They do that sometimes and I don't mind, so long as both entrances and the compound are covered by *someone*. Of course Kaoru didn't know that, but there was no reason to attack her."

It was indeed strange, but I had the feeling it was about to get even stranger. "What happened then?"

Kaoru stared at the floor. "I screamed. He hurt me, and I was so frightened . . . then the other guards came running."

"They knew they'd damned well better," Tamahara-san said, betraying a bit of satisfaction. "What sort of reputation would I have if I didn't protect those in my employ? But Taka let Kaoru go and took off as soon as he saw them. They said they chased him down the alley between two storerooms, and Kaoru saw them, but it was a dead end. There was no way he could have escaped, except . . . "

"Except he did."

The old woman sighed. "They both swear that, when they reached the wall, he was gone. Only a monkey could have scaled the wall there, and Taka was more of a boar-hog. I fear I may have been harboring a shape-shifter or worse."

"What if he comes back?" Kaoru asked plaintively.

I was practically asleep on my feet, but I also wasn't averse to doing the Widow Tamahara a favor. I knew it might mean the difference between staying or going if I happened to be late with the rent again. In either case, I considered it might be in my own best interest to confirm my suspicious, if that turned out to be possible. "If it eases your mind at all, I will have a look."

"I would appreciate it," Tamahara-san said. Kaoru just bowed.

The Widow Tamahara had other business to attend, but when I finished my late meal, Kaoru led me to the spot where she had met Taka, as it turned out, five nights before.

"Here?" I asked, standing in the spot she had indicated.

"Yes, but he was turned toward the building. I believed he was watching your door, but maybe it was just the building itself. I would have told him you weren't there, but he didn't give me the chance."

"And then he fled between the storage buildings?"

"*Hai.* Which—which also makes no sense. He'd been here long enough to know it was a dead end."

Indeed it should have known. I'm guessing it did know.

The sun had already set, but there was still a good bit of light, probably enough for what I needed. I told Kaoru to wait outside while I entered the alley.

Dim as the light was between the buildings, I could still see clearly to where the back of the storage buildings met the wall. There was no gap between the rear of the buildings and the compound wall. It was simply cheaper to use the wall itself as the back section of each building, rather than use additional timber, and the Widow Tamahara was nothing if not a practical person. I was familiar with the alley. During the worst of my drunkard period I had once slept in it for two days, thinking it was my room. Fortunately the weather was warm. It was only when it rained and the overflow from two separate roofs was pouring down on me I finally sobered up enough to realize my error. Naturally, there was no good reason to revisit the alley since.

If I'm right, it will be around here.

Tamahara's two *bushi* hadn't found anything, but that was only because they didn't know what they were looking for. I did. It only took me a moment or two to spot it—a small slip of paper, undamaged, wedged into the planking of the building on the left. While I had dealt with the physical manifestations of the yin-yang magician's art more than once, examining an undamaged example was a rare opportunity.

The thing tried to avoid me. It had a sort of life, bestowed upon it by its master and the charm written upon it. Nor was I unaware of the danger—while its master's will had been withdrawn, it could return and refocus in short order, which is no doubt why the creature had been directed to hide rather than let itself risk being destroyed. There was a purpose to its presence in the Widow Tamahara's compound which had not yet been fulfilled.

The paper itself had been folded into a roughly human shape, and the characters written on it were strange, probably an older version of the Chinese writing used at Court. I could make out a word or two, but most of it was gibberish to me. I knew someone who could possibly interpret the script, and I put the thought away for later consideration. I had several orders of prior business to take care of but, in one regard, this discovery came first. I very carefully ripped off the part of the paper representing the head of the *shikigami*, after first making certain nothing was written there. The rest of the writing I compared to the example I possessed of Lord Tenshin's work and satisfied myself they were one and the same. Then I went back to where Kaoru was waiting for me.

"Kaoru-san, Tamahara said you were attacked the day I left on business. Do you remember when Taka was hired?"

"About two weeks before then," she said. "He was usually at the south gate, so you might not have noticed him."

It occurred to me I might not have noticed him if I'd walked past him every day, if the quality of his creation was anything like that of the *shikigami* who impersonated Lord Tenshin himself.

"Two weeks? You're certain?"

"*Hai*, Yamada-sama. I remember seeing him for the first time on the night of the Chrysanthemum Festival, just over two weeks ago."

If Kaoru was correct, then the presence of a *shikigami*, and specifically one created—as I was certain this one was—by Lord Tenshin, made absolutely no sense. Why would he send one of the creatures, either as a spy or an assassin, a full week before his brother had even hired me? Besides, I knew my involvement was not a decision Lord Mikoto had made at leisure or in consultation with anyone, including his traitorous brother.

A shikigami disguised as a bushi would make a credible spy but a better assassin. Yet the creature's presence here only makes sense if neither I nor Tamahara or any of her women were the target—the creature had plenty of time to act before it was discovered. Which leaves only a client. I know Lord Mikoto does not frequent this place, so who was it after?

Whatever the answer to that question turned out to be, in a way it was fortunate Kaoru had somehow triggered a defensive response from the creature. Otherwise it would still be roaming the compound with impunity.

"Yamada-sama? Do . . . do you think he will come back?"

I looked at the young woman and felt a little ashamed of myself for taking so long to realize how afraid she was. Serving the Widow Tamahara could not have been the best of all possible lives, but there were far worse options for poor girls of no family, and at least with Tamahara there had been some measure of safety and security. For Kaoru this was now gone, and there didn't seem to be any way of giving it back. I simply told her what I knew.

"I can, at the minimum, assure you Taka will not return, but there are others like him, and they may have a reason for coming here I have not yet ascertained. You're going to have to be careful, Kaoru, as is everyone here. Do you understand?"

"One such as I should always be careful," she said simply. "I learned this lesson long ago and was recently reminded of it. But I will tell the others."

"Good. There is one other thing, however," I said. "Please ask your mistress not to hire another guard until I have a chance to meet him. Perhaps I can stop this from happening again."

"I will be grateful for anything you can do, as I'm sure my mistress will be as well."

I almost smiled. While the old woman could appreciate the odd favor, Kaoru and I both knew real gratitude wasn't a commodity Tamahara-san dealt in, as a general rule, whether she actually used the word or not. But it was also true the formidable old woman never forgot a debt, whether owed or owned, which was almost the same thing as gratitude in practice.

I made certain Kaoru returned to the main hall without incident, then went to my room and surrendered gladly to sleep. At one point I dreamed I was being devoured by a thousand paper fishes, but otherwise the night was restful enough. When I finally awoke, the sun was already showing mid-morning. I had no sooner finished a bath and dressed in the best *hitatare* I owned when Kenji came to collect me.

I yawned. "For some reason I was expecting Lord Tadanobu," I said.

"I can't imagine why," Kenji said. "He's a Fujiwara. I'm amazed he even deigns to speak to us."

I smiled. "But he does. I gather you've spoken to him today?"

Kenji grunted. "He said Prince Kanemore had need of a Fujiwara, for some reason His Highness had not yet divulged."

Undivulged but easily imagined. As a Fujiwara, doors would open for Tadanobu which would certainly remain firmly shut to one such as myself. As for Kenji, the only reason he was allowed within the Imperial Compound at all was because Prince Kanemore had, on more than one occasion, expressly ordered it. This would be the aegis under which we doubtless appeared there today, assuming this was where we were to meet Kanemore. I soon learned this assumption was in error.

"The mansion in the Sixth Ward," Kenji said. "We are to call upon His Highness there this afternoon."

Royalty and the nobility alike had mansions scattered about the city in favored locations in addition to whatever housing they claimed within the walls of the Imperial precincts, but the Sixth Ward was no one's favorite location. The Sixth Ward Mansion served mostly as temporary quarters for the sick and infirm. "Is His Highness ill? I hadn't heard anything to this effect."

"Nor I. Doubtless he has his own reasons for meeting there."

One possibility was it was a bit more private than the Imperial Compound. Fewer witnesses to our arrival and departure. And to the prince's own movements, for that matter.

"You've spent more time out and about than I have. What have you heard?"

"The war against the Abe Clan is apparently not going well at the moment."

That was old news. The Abe Clan were the hereditary military commanders of Mutsu province, which included lands claimed by the Emishi, a northern barbarian tribe vanquished by the Abe in the previous century. But the Emishi were never entirely quiet after their subjugation. The Abe Clan chief, Yoritoki, had a mandate to keep the barbarians in check and maintain order. The problems arose when he assumed full control, supplanting the rightfully appointed civilian governor. Worse, he took on the role of tax collector for the province and kept all receipts for his own uses. The disobedience was bad enough, but withholding revenues was such a dangerous precedent it left the government in Kyoto with no choice but to act. The Emperor had appointed Minamoto no Yoriyoshi as the new military and administrative governor of the province, and all he had to do to assume his post was to push Abe no Yoritoki out of it. This had proved to be very difficult. Including three years of temporary truces, the war had been raging back and forth for eleven years, with first one side and then the other holding the advantage. Even the death of Yoritoki some years before hadn't ended the conflict. His son, Sadato, held the upper hand at the moment and this was unfortunate, but not a disaster. I said as much.

Kenji sighed. "You don't understand, Lord Yamada, and if you had bestirred yourself earlier you'd have noticed the tension. People aren't just afraid Yoriyoshi is going to be defeated for good and all and the Emperor be forced to appoint some other ambitious warrior to take his place. They're afraid Sadato will take his clan's treason to the capital itself!"

"This is not possible," I said. "He's on the far eastern part of the country with dozens of loyal provinces between himself and the Emperor. He can neither defeat nor suborn all of them, even if he does take the Minamoto Clan's measure."

"Normally I would agree," Kenji said. "But you don't think Prince Kanemore recalled us to the capital because he misses our company, do you?"

"No, I do not."

Kenji nodded. "Lord Yamada, I tell you something is in the air, and it's a great deal more ominous than the petty succession squabbles of the Otomo Clan."

As much as I didn't want to believe it, I suspected Kenji might be right. That didn't mean our business with Lord Mikoto could be neglected. Since we would pass where Lord Mikoto was currently residing on our way to the Sixth Ward, there was no reason not to settle it as soon as possible. On the way I told Kenji about what had happened in the Widow Tamahara's compound while we were gone.

"Kaoru? I know that one."

"You know all of them, unless I'm misremembering your reputation."

Kenji scowled at me. "I am not *quite* the scoundrel you think me, Lord Yamada. I merely meant that she is a very sweet and gentle young woman, as I recall. I'm glad she wasn't seriously harmed."

"It was serious enough to her," I said dryly. "But I agree it could have been much worse, and I still don't understand why one of Lord Tenshin's creatures should have been there in the first place. Apparently it had nothing to do with me or his plans for his older brother. At least, not in any way I can as yet divine."

" 'The brightest light casts the darkest shadows,' " Kenji said.

"Which means?"

"I have no idea," Kenji said. "But it's something my old master once said to me, and it sounds profound, doesn't it?"

We crossed the Tama River at the Third Street Bridge and proceeded toward the Sixth Ward. Lord Mikoto had gone to ground in a well-defended mansion in the Fifth, and there he nervously received us in audience.

Lord Mikoto kneeled on a cushion on a dais in his reception hall while Kenji and I kneeled in front of him. He was about forty, I knew, though the black hair showing under his formal *boushi* was already showing gray, and he looked older. The man was tired, frightened, and—unless I missed my guess—tired of being frightened.

I told him what we had discovered, and produced the remains of the final *shikigami*. I didn't name the creator. I didn't have to. Lord Mikoto stared at the writing as one in a daze.

"I gather you recognize the hand, Mikoto-sama?"

He closed his eyes and nodded. "I'm guessing you do, as well," he said. "Where is my brother now?"

"He fled north, but if north was the direction he originally meant to go, I could not say. I was charged with discovering the culprit and this I have done. You can understand why I wished to take no further action."

I didn't think Lord Mikoto had heard me at first, but he finally tore his gaze from the writing. "Hmmm? Oh, yes. Certainly. This is a family matter now, and I will . . . deal with it. As for your reward, everything will be as we have agreed." He sighed then and rubbed his eyes wearily. "I should thank you, for you have done me a great service. Yet it was information I really did not expect . . . or want."

There was nothing more to say. Kenji and I took our leave then and continued toward the Sixth Ward. The city was not so bustling toward the southwest where the mansion in question was located. There were other people about, and bandits and footpads were common in this part of the city, but if any of the folk we passed were of such inclination, my sword and Kenji's staff were enough to dissuade them. The mansion would have guards posted at all hours, but even so it was easy to see why it served as the sickroom for the royal family and others of the greater nobility. And, it was rumored, as a place of assignation. For both purposes, isolation and discretion were prime considerations. Yet it seemed to me the area was even a little more deserted than usual.

Kenji broke the silence first, as was his habit. "What do you think Lord Mikoto will do?"

"Petition the Emperor to declare Lord Tenshin an outlaw, I would imagine. Which would prevent his brother from having any claim to the leadership of Clan Otomo, even if Lord Mikoto were to die, thus removing his brother's reasons to harm him. That is what I would do in his place."

"What if Lord Tenshin's grievances against his brother are not merely dynastic?"

"Then the sensible thing for Lord Mikoto to do would be to put a very generous bounty on his brother's head. I suspect he may do this anyway, considering what Lord Tenshin tried to do to him."

"Is this what you would do?"

I took a deep breath. "Kenji, as you are well aware, my 'clan,' following the disgrace and death of my father, consists primarily of myself. My only brother died when he was twelve, so none of this, for good or ill, is a choice I'll need to make. What happens now is Lord Mikoto's responsibility, and I do not envy him."

"Yes, you do," Kenji said. "At least a little."

I scowled but did not answer, and Kenji, sensing my mood, let the matter drop. We walked the rest of the way in silence. Kenji could be annoying even at the best of times, but no more so than when he was right. As we got closer to the Sixth Ward mansion, I discovered he'd been right a second time. Also, it became much clearer why we'd seen fewer people in the streets—the area around the Sixth Ward mansion had been converted into an armed camp. We saw the first enclosures even before we could see the walls of the mansion compound itself. The clan insignia belonged mostly to the Minamoto, but I did see a few Taira and other military families among them. The outer enclosure was purely Minamoto, however, and served as a barrier to further progress. We were greeted by two unsmiling *bushi* who demanded our names and business.

"Lord Yamada no Goji and the Priest Kenji. Prince Kanemore is expecting us."

There was a whispered consultation between them, and one of the men hurried away to return with a young man I recognized as one of Kanemore's personal attendants. The newcomer looked at me and then spoke to the guards who, apparently satisfied we were who I said we were, allowed us to pass.

The attendant bowed. "Gentlemen, if you will follow me?"

We let the attendant lead the way, but I turned as much attention as I could to our surroundings. My first impressions were reinforced by everything I saw—the warriors present were not simply to guard the compound at a time of fear within the capital—there were far too many of them and from far too many clan families and with far too much equipment. There were wagons being loaded, makeshift stables, racks of armor, and bundles of fodder and arrows. What we were seeing was the staging area for a military expedition, and I said as much to Kenji.

"Which explains Prince Kanemore's presence here rather than the Imperial compound," Kenji said, "It would be one thing for a Fujiwara minister to order reinforcements acting on behalf of the Emperor, but this is the sort of thing the Emperor would need to approve directly, otherwise every family involved runs the risk of being declared outlaw."

Kenji did have his moments of astuteness, I had to admit, and now he had cut to the heart of it. While the Fujiwara—whether their titles accurately reflected their actual power and importance or not—were the real government in Kyoto, the Emperor's prerogative could not be ignored.

"And Prince Kanemore's mere presence in and knowledge of these preparations tacitly assures everyone involved this approval indeed exists. I see your point," I said. "Are these reinforcements for the Minamoto in the north, I wonder? If they were intended as defense of the city there would not be so much obvious preparation for travel."

"That would be my guess as well. One thing I do *not* understand," Kenji said, "is what any of this has to do with us. The more I see, the more I worry."

Time and experience had taught me, whenever I agreed with Kenji about anything, it was usually a bad sign, and I did agree with him whole-heartedly in this particular matter. There was nothing for it but to see what Prince Kanemore required of us. I had the certain feeling we were not going to like it.

As we approached the mansion, the servant led us around toward the northern entrance, past the boundaries of the military preparation, and into one of the formal, if somewhat unkempt, gardens of the mansion. For a moment I hesitated, so much so that Kenji and our guide were several paces ahead of me before they noticed. They both stopped and looked at me curiously.

"Lord Yamada, what is it?" Kenji asked.

I finally sighed, and hurried to join them. "Nothing. I just thought I saw something in the bushes near the north wall."

The servant bowed. "Lord Yamada, if there is an interloper within the grounds the prince will need to know of it. Please tell me what you saw."

"Obviously, I was mistaken. Unless the staff of the Sixth Ward mansion have taken to keeping foxes within the grounds as pets?"

"Certainly not, my lord," the young man said.

"No, I didn't believe this to be the case," I said.

Especially white foxes with more than one tail.

"Let's be on our way," I said, "I don't wish to keep His Highness waiting."

We followed again, but Kenji and I held back a step or two and Kenji whispered, "Did you see what I think you saw?"

"If I did, it's only because she knew I was coming and wanted me to know she is here. If that is true, we'll find out the 'why' of it soon enough."

I knew I was not mistaken in what I had seen, which meant Lady Kuzunoha was a long way from her territory in Shinoda Forest, and that is not something she would have done on a whim. Her presence added to the mystery of our summons and increased my apprehension. I was becoming even more convinced Kenji was right, and that great matters were afoot. I was not fond of "great matters," for all that I often found myself in the middle of them. When forces both unseen and powerful were set in motion, it was inevitable someone was going to get trampled, and this someone was just as likely as not to be myself or someone I cared about. I did not consider myself fortunate considering, since the death of Princess Teiko, the number of beings I did care about had shrunk considerably. I would count myself even less fortunate should the number shrink even more.

I had expected to see Prince Kanemore in the main audience hall, but as we approached the north veranda, the door slid aside and he came to meet us personally. We all immediately kneeled and then bowed low as protocol demanded. Kanemore bid us rise and dismissed the servant.

"The mansion is a bit crowded and noisy at the moment, gentlemen. As there is a matter we need to discuss, please walk with me in the garden."

Meaning he does not wish to be overheard.

Prince Kanemore was my friend and had been ever since we first met in the service of his late sister, Princess Teiko. He was one member of the Imperial family who could both issue a command with such force you wouldn't think of disobeying and again issue the same command with such gentleness it really did sound like a request, such as the one I'd just heard, but there would be no disobeying in either case. Not everyone had Kanemore's skill in this, even those who had the right of command.

We walked in silence for a short while, and I took the time to examine my friend. I had not seen him in over a year, but it was certain a great deal had happened in that year. He looked tired, and older, which was enough to concern me as I was a few years older than his forty-odd years.

"It's good to see you again, Your Highness," I said, after the silence had persisted for some time.

"And you. I ask your pardon for my reluctance to get to the matter at hand. Our first meeting gave cause for regret, for both of us, and I fear this one may do the same. Yet I must ask a favor of you, Lord Yamada. And Kenji-san as well."

"We are at your service," I said, shooting a hard glance at Kenji, in case he was tempted to say otherwise, but he merely waited, serene and innocent as a Buddha.

"It seems," Prince Kanemore said, "I must ask you both to go to war."

CHAPTER THREE

"You're saying the forces under Abe no Sadato are using magic?" Prince Kanemore reached into his robe and produced a torn bit of paper. "Which should surprise no one," he said dryly, "as the great Abe no Seimei was also of that clan, I am told. The potential to one in Lord Sadato's position would be obvious. So. Look at this, and then tell me what you think it is."

I barely had to glance at it; its presentation was a mere courtesy, I knew. Kanemore and I had fought *shikigami* together on one occasion. He knew what they were as well as I did. I handed the paper to Kenji, who needed even less time. "*Shikigami*. And of a high quality."

Prince Kanemore grunted. "During their last . . . setback, the forces of Minamoto no Yoriyoshi were attacked by several dozen of these things in a flanking maneuver while the real Abe *bushi* attacked from the front. Yoriyoshi's son Yoshiie was the commander in the field, fortunately. He kept his head and organized a retreat in good order, which is the only reason the entire force didn't lose their own heads—permanently. It was a bad business, but it could have been a great deal worse. If the Abe Clan can conjure warriors out of paper, all the branches of the Minamoto and Taira Clans combined may not be enough to defeat them."

"You said the *shikigami* force numbered in the dozens?"

"Such was reported. Only a few of the flanking force were killed, but every one of them who fell left just a bit of paper rather than a body."

"I know you are familiar with the creatures, Highness, but one thing you might not know is creating a *shikigami* is not without cost. Since they are not really alive, they have no motive force of their own. This must come from the *onmyoji*. Also, in order to perform anything other than a routine task requires at least some of the magician's attention. One could make, at most, a half-dozen or so, and then only if their sole purpose was limited, such as to attack on command. Even a good *onmyoji* could not keep them all active for long, because otherwise the magician would be quickly exhausted and break the connection."

Kanemore looked thoughtful. "Then the reasonable conclusion is the Abe Clan has more than one yin-yang magician in their employ."

"They must," I said, but my thoughts were already elsewhere. Kenji was clearly on the same trail.

"I think we know one of them, Lord Yamada," Kenji said.

"It would explain the timing of his exit and the direction," I said.

Kanemore smiled. I'd seen that particular smile before and knew better than to stay on the wrong end of it for long. "Gentlemen, if you have knowledge of this matter, I would ask that you share it," he said.

I quickly told Prince Kanemore about our pursuit of Lord Otomo no Tenshin, what had happened in the abandoned temple, the incident in the courtyard outside my room, and my suspicions about why Lord Tenshin had left the capital so quickly. "This would mostly make sense, if Lord Tenshin had already been recruited by the Abe Clan when he was plotting against his brother. He might even have meant to bring the Otomo over to the Abe cause, under his leadership. Only it does not explain the *shikigami* at the Widow Tamahara's establishment."

"Why do you think it reacted as it did when the girl challenged it?" Kanemore asked.

"On a guess, I would say it was because of the *shikigami's* limitations, which I touched on earlier. We both know how dangerous they are when under the magician's direction. But if the magician's attentions were necessarily elsewhere, the creature could only react to the most basic of directives, such as 'Do not let yourself be discovered,' or 'Defend yourself when necessary.' Kaoru-kun's simple question could have provoked either response."

"This is troubling news," Prince Kanemore said. "If the agents of the Abe Clan are already active in the capital, this could hint at his ultimate intentions . . . and there is something about this situation you may not yet know. I assume you heard this conflict began when the provincial governor of Mutsu first asked for aid because the Abe Clan was usurping his role and withholding taxes?"

"That was my understanding," I said.

"There was more to it. Yoritoki was the military commander of Mutsu, not its governor, but he began treating Mutsu as his private domain. Worse, he also led an army of Emishi south into Miyagi province and annexed lands there. He has also sent envoys to the Kiyohara and other great families of the area, suggesting alliances. He never planned to confine his ambitions to Mutsu. The traitor is now dead, but Yoritoki's son now continues his father's ambitions. This is why the Emperor's government is, shall we say, concerned, that the Abe Clan has not been brought to heel. The Abe may have Imperial ambitions."

This was certainly something I had not known before, since I did not usually concern myself with provincial politics. As matters now stood, the threat to the capital was not as far-fetched as I had originally believed.

"Possibly, Highness. It's also possible the creature's presence at the Widow Tamahara's was in some way meant to benefit the Abe cause itself, yet how they would so benefit escapes me at the moment. I have no reason to believe Lord Tenshin placed the creature there because of me. I doubt he even knew I existed at the time, and certainly he had no reason to care if he did know. So we know only that it was there, but we do not know why. The answer may be critical."

"Then you will need to find the answer within the week," Prince Kanemore said. "Yoriyoshi needs men with experience fighting these creatures and their masters, and *I* need representatives to assess the true situation in Mutsu. I will provide you with the proper credentials, and tomorrow you will meet Yoriyoshi and his son. Yoriyoshi will proceed with a separate force day after tomorrow, but his son Yoshiie will delay a week until all the reinforcements are ready and then follow. Neither will give battle until they join forces with the governor's clan, the Kiyohara, in Dewa province. When Yoshiie is ready, I want you both to travel with his forces."

"There is more to this, I think," I said. "Am I wrong, Highness?"

"No, you are not. What I've told you is true, so far as it goes—the *shikigami* are of great concern, but my greatest concern is for Lord Yoshiie's safety. This is the real reason you will accompany him."

"Yoriyoshi is the clan chieftain," Kenji pointed out.

"True. But it is Yoshiie who is the heart of the Minamoto cause. He's become something of a hero and rallying point for the clans who are inclined to oppose the Abe. Yoriyoshi is shrewd and fearless, but he is also an old man. Yoriyoshi's loss would damage the Emperor's cause, but losing his son would cripple it. My primary charge to you is to keep Lord Yoshiie alive at all costs."

I took a breath. "Understood."

"Well," Kenji said, "I've never been to Mutsu."

"No matter," I said. "I have no doubt you'll make your reputation known there soon enough."

We were given rooms at the Sixth Ward mansion since, under the circumstances, Prince Kanemore wanted Kenji and myself close to hand. I had no objection, though I knew this arrangement no doubt interfered with Kenji's planned nocturnal activities. He did grumble a bit but acquiesced, as there was really no choice. Our lodgings were not exactly peaceful, however. The mansion buzzed like a hornets' nest with servants and *bushi* and couriers scurrying about on some errand or another. With so many people passing through the mansion, it occurred to me that, if someone of malign intent wanted to place either a magical or human agent within the compound, it would not be very difficult to do.

There was much about the situation which concerned me, and

on the following morning I planned to take steps to either calm my fears or clarify them. For this particular evening, however, I had other plans. The rising moon was only just past its new crescent, for which I was grateful. No doubt a fuller moon would have required a moon-gazing party from the inhabitants of the mansion—even under their present circumstances—but when I walked out on the veranda long after sunset, I had both it and the gardens to myself.

Well, myself and one other.

I went out onto the grounds and found a convenient boulder to rest on about halfway between the veranda and the north wall. "I gather you want a word with me," I said aloud to the darkness.

The foxfire appeared first. Small glowing lanterns—without the lantern part. Just little dancing flames which appeared around an area of greater shadow near the chrysanthemum bushes by the north wall. Their presence didn't announce Lady Kuzunoha, since I already knew she was there. This made me wonder why she bothered with the flames. Despite our shared experiences, it was not likely I'd forget her true nature. Yet it seemed she wanted to remind me, and for a moment I expected her to appear in her true fox-demon form. But when she stepped out the shadows, she was in the human form I remembered— Lady Kuzunoha, once the primary wife of the leader of the *kuge* branch of the Abe Clan, Lord Abe no Yasuna. I knew, as a high-level fox demon, she could take almost any form she desired, but the one she chose was as I remembered her. A little older, perhaps—there was now a touch of gray in her long black hair— but no less beautiful.

The foxfire winked out and she approached to within ten feet from me and kneeled. "Greetings, Lord Yamada."

I stood and gave a bow. "And to you, Lady Kuzunoha. It . . . it is good to see you again."

She looked at me and smiled a little wistfully. "You may not think so once our meeting is done. I'm afraid I must once more place myself in your debt."

"Are you in some sort of trouble?"

"My trouble is one you well know, nor has it changed since our first meeting. It is for this reason I have come to you. While I do not pretend to know what your involvement in this gathering of *bushi* may be, you must understand what is happening—this force is being mustered to punish the Abe Clan."

"This was my understanding as well," I said. While I realized it was possible Lady Kuzunoha and I might be on opposite sides of the matter, I didn't see any point in denying the obvious. Lady Kuzunoha's interest guaranteed she would discover what she needed to discover, her discretion about my own part notwithstanding. "But what has this to do with Lord Yasuna? He is of the Court branch of the Abe. I have no seen no indication they are involved."

"Their name involves them, and the conspicuous fear at Court isn't bound by such nice distinctions. Lord Yasuna is a hostage in this very mansion."

This was something I had not known, and I said as much.

"The Emperor's government insisted Lord Yasuna be held as assurance of the Court branch's good behavior. Prince Kanemore assumed responsibility for him," she said.

The panic at Court must have been greater than I had

imagined. "The *kuge* branch of the Abe have no forces at their disposal—or at least no more than a few dozen *bushi* and those mostly for show. The only real threat they could pose . . . "

I stopped, and Lady Kuzunoha let out a sigh. "You see it now. They are not a military threat, but their presence and connections at Court mean they could relate every facet of the Emperor's forces' plans and strategy to their kinsmen in Mutsu if they so chose."

"I have met your former husband," I said. "I cannot imagine him being so great a fool. Except, possibly, where you are concerned."

Lady Kuzunoha smiled a very faint smile and blushed faintly as she did so. "But the one does not change the other."

I could see the potential threat, and from a tactical viewpoint it made perfect sense. Yet I could not see this benefit as being worth the risk of making an enemy of Lord Yasuna. He had a reputation as a wise counselor and a discreet confidant and friend, and those two attributes alone made him more of an influence at Court than even his family connections would suggest.

"This is indeed troubling, but I cannot believe Lord Yasuna is in any great danger. There are no charges against him, nor is he in the hands of his enemies. Prince Kanemore's custody of him is enough of a guarantor of his safety."

"For now," Lady Kuzunoha said. "But when the Minamoto reinforcements leave for Mutsu province, he will be with them. What about then?"

I let out a slow breath. "Would you mind telling me how you knew all this?"

"Oh, please, Lord Yamada . . . there are advantages to being a shape-shifter, and there is very little the servants do not know. My husband . . . my former husband, has few enemies, but this is not the same as none at all. Someone at Court, either out of fear or spite, persuaded the Emperor my lord has more influence with his distant relations than he really has. I can't imagine Lord Abe no Sadato caring a rotten plum about Lord Yasuna's safety, but if the Minamoto believe otherwise . . . "

She didn't finish. She didn't have to. "What is it you want me to do?"

"I don't know," she said. "I don't know what you *can* do. But whatever happens, I would like you to be Lord Yasuna's friend. He may need one."

I smiled. "I can do that."

We both heard voices. Distant but coming closer. Lady Kuzunoha rose. "You have my thanks, Lord Yamada, and my trust in your discretion, meaning you will not mention this meeting to Lord Yasuna."

"It is never my inclination to reopen an old wound," I said.

Lady Kuzunoha looked grim. "But there is one thing I probably should mention—I, too, will be traveling to Mutsu, and if the Minamoto harm my lord in any way, I will destroy them. I will personally tear out the throat of Yoriyoshi, his son, and any other progeny either may have. I will not stop until the Minamoto cease to exist as a clan. I promise you this." She turned to go.

"Lady Kuzunoha—" I began, but she turned back and smiled at me. It was perhaps the saddest smile I had ever seen.

"Lord Yamada, I am as my nature dictates, and I will do what my nature and my own inclinations compel me to do. This is no more than fair warning. I feel I owe you that much courtesy, even if there had been no debt between us."

In a moment she was gone as if she had never been there. Two slightly inebriated *bushi* came stomping through the garden on their way to the mansion. I watched them go.

Lady Kuzunoha has not forgotten what she is. She just made certain that I would not forget as well.

At least now I understood the foxfire.

OUR FORMAL AUDIENCE with Lord Yoriyoshi was scheduled for the following afternoon. When Kenji and I arrived at the audience hall, we found Prince Kanemore and Lord Yoriyoshi sitting formally on the dais. Fortunately Prince Kanemore had anticipated my and Kenji's relatively limited wardrobe and had seen fit to loan us clothing worthy of the occasion. My green brocade *hitatare* was the finest I had ever worn, and Kenji looked almost respectable with his freshly-shaven head and new surplice. Both Prince Kanemore and Lord Yoriyoshi were as resplendent as one would expect.

Lord Yoriyoshi's *tachi* stood beside him on a black lacquered stand brushed with gold. It was little inferior to Prince Kanemore's own weapon. While Prince Kanemore had the habit of keeping his sword close to hand, it was an unusual custom for a member of the royal family and revealed the prince's martial inclinations. For Lord Yoriyoshi, keeping his weapon on display was no more or less than what one would expect. I had, however, expected Yoriyoshi's son Yoshiie to be present as well, and found myself a little disappointed when he was not. As Prince Kanemore had noted, the young man's exploits during the war were already taking on the color of legend, and I was curious about him, as I was of his father as well.

Prince Kanemore himself made the introductions, and Kenji and I bowed low.

"Lord Yamada, Prince Kanemore speaks very highly of you. I hope and trust his confidence is not misplaced."

"As do I, my lord. My associate and I are at your service."

Lord Yoriyoshi studied Kenji and myself as if he'd found some curious creature dwelling at the bottom of a horse trough. I did the same with, I hope, some objectivity. The leader of the Minamoto Clan was at this point in his early seventies, still strong and active, but the years were taking their toll. His thin face showed one scar, almost lost in the wrinkles, though his eyes were clear and focused. Even so, it was my understanding that, as the war dragged on, by necessity his son Yoshiie was assuming more and more of the command obligations in the field, while Lord Yoriyoshi had overall command of the expedition.

"I think we should drink to our success," he said finally, and I almost winced. While saké no longer had the hold on me it once had, I had learned not to underestimate its power. Regardless, when the occasion called for a drink, I trusted myself to do what was necessary and no more.

A young male servant brought saké in a fine porcelain bottle and five cups, even though there were only four of us. Four was *shi*, and a symbol of death and therefore unlucky. As the servant approached the dais, Kenji's posture stiffened and he glanced at me, but I signaled him to wait. Prince Kanemore and his guest were served first, and it was only my somewhat shaky faith in my understanding of the situation that kept me from leaping to the dais as Kenji had doubtless intended to do. I waited until Kenji and I were served before I raised my cup.

"To your health, Lord Yoriyoshi," I said, shooting a sideways glance at Kenji who nodded almost imperceptibly. We both immediately dashed the contents of our cups into the face of the young servant, who expressed shock before turning into a writhing piece of paper, and then shriveling away.

Neither Prince Kanemore nor Lord Yoriyoshi, on the other hand, was shocked at all. I wasn't surprised to see both men break into grins. Yoriyoshi took his fan and slapped it across his knee. "Well done. When you allowed the creature to approach the dais, I admit I had my doubts."

"That did surprise me as well," Prince Kanemore said. "Surely you would not have risked both our lives? For a moment I thought my confidence was misplaced."

I bowed low to hide a smile. "I simply knew my own confidence had not been misplaced, Highness," I said. "Would the Prince Kanemore I know be fooled by the presence of such a one on his own personal staff? I should say not, so the only logical conclusion I could draw was this was a test, and neither of you was in any danger."

"Less a test and more a demonstration," Prince Kanemore said. "And we do have our own magicians at need. Lord Yoriyoshi, are you satisfied?"

The old warrior grunted. "More than satisfied. Impressed, I

should say. I gladly accept your offer of the assistance of these two gentlemen and shall so instruct my son."

"If it is not impertinent to ask, when will we meet Lord Yoshiie?" Kenji asked.

"This evening," Prince Kanemore said. "I would suggest you both get a little more rest between now and sunset."

I raised an eyebrow. "Oh?"

"My son," Lord Yoriyoshi said, "likes to keep somewhat irregular hours."

CONSIDERING THE CIRCUMSTANCES, a nap would not have been a bad idea, but there was no possibility of it. After giving the notion a fair chance, I finally rose and sought out Kenji. I found him lying on his back in his assigned space, staring at the ceiling.

"I see sleep is elusive for you, too."

"A clean conscience and a relaxed frame of mind are the best aids to sleep, I've found," Kenji said, "and since I seldom have the first, I have to depend upon the second. Today it has failed me."

"Then forgive me for not making the situation any better." I related my conversation with Lady Kuzunoha, including her final warning. Kenji sighed and swung himself into a sitting position.

"She really is the most charming creature when she chooses to be," he said. "But she is a fox-demon, after all. I think it was kind of her to remind you."

"She called it a fair warning, and I agree. But kind? In what way?"

"Because I think her fox-demon nature is something you are more inclined to overlook than I am."

I would have answered harshly, but I knew there was some truth in what Kenji said. "I have great respect for Lady Kuzunoha," I said. "But even if there were more to my feelings than respect, I know there is only room for one human being in her true affections. I am not that person."

Kenji looked thoughtful. "You would be wise to keep remembering that, but since you mention the one human she loves, I did see Lord Yasuna here in the mansion earlier today. I did not realize he was a prisoner. He certainly didn't act like one."

I smiled. "It's not as if Prince Kanemore would place him in a cage . . . unless he had to."

Kenji looked disgusted. "Nevertheless, I must share your opinion of the matter—keeping Lord Yasuna as a hostage is worse than useless—it is dangerous, and Lady Kuzunoha's potential wrath is only part of that danger. He has many friends in and out of the Imperial Court who would not forgive anyone who brought him to harm. There would be bloodshed before all is done."

"Fear makes people do foolish things," I said. "Though we have no authority over such choices, it is now our responsibility to make certain they do not lead to tragedy."

"Such burdens," Kenji said. "Once I was a simple monk, going where I would, peddling my spirit wards and charms, living as I thought I should. Then I had the misfortune to meet you."

I grunted to keep from laughing. "If you're trying to blame me for your lost innocence, Kenji-san, don't waste your breath. That bit of washing fell off the pole long before our first encounter."

"Perhaps, but it feels better to blame someone else. So, then . . . " Kenji rose and slid aside the screen separating his temporary lodging from the outside veranda. "Sunset. Time for us to go meet the famous Lord Yoshiie."

Due to the lateness of the hour, we had expected to meet Lord Yoriyoshi's son at the Sixth Ward Mansion, but instead a servant led us the east gate, where we found an escort of a dozen mounted archers and five saddled mounts waiting for us. Prince Kanemore arrived a few minutes later in the company of a man I easily recognized.

Lord Yasuna.

I had not seen him in nearly ten years, but he had not changed a great deal. He was older than I, perhaps in his late forties now, but he carried the years well, for all that he appeared a bit somber. He was a very handsome man, the truth be told, but I knew this was not what had led Lady Kuzunoha to him. Their relationship had started with a random act of kindness in saving what he had thought was an ordinary fox from a pack of hunters. In time her gratitude had turned into something more. Yet also in time Lady Kuzunoha's true nature had proved impossible to conceal, and Lord Yasuna's clan would have been embarrassed had the truth been revealed, so they were forced to part. The woman I had loved was dead, and I knew I would grieve for the rest of my life. Lady Kuzunoha's love was alive and well, and yet, despite their mutual desire for matters to be otherwise, they could not be together. I was not sure whose pain was the greater.

Lord Yasuna's face brightened in recognition. "Lord Yamada! It is good to see you again."

"And you, my lord. I trust your son Doshi is well?"

He smiled briefly. "Twelve years old and almost a man. He will be taller than I am within two years, mark my words."

Prince Kanemore grunted. "I should be surprised you gentlemen already know each other, and perhaps a story for another evening. Let it suffice for the moment that Lord Yasuna has consented to join us," Prince Kanemore said. "We should be going."

We mounted and rode northeast through the city. A suspicion dawned, and I reined in beside Prince Kanemore. "If you'll pardon my asking, where *are* we going?"

"We're going to the Widow Tamahara's to meet Lord Yoshiie. I would rather the meeting took place at the mansion, but apparently our guest has chosen the venue on his own."

I knew Prince Kanemore wasn't concerned about appearing at the Widow Tamahara's. This would not the first time an Imperial prince had patronized the Widow Tamahara's establishment, and Kanemore was willing to do so openly. That Yoshiie would choose it was another matter, and this did concern me a little.

"I take it Lord Yoshiie has not been in the capital very often?"

"He went to war against the Abe when he was fifteen," Prince Kanemore confirmed. "He's seldom been out of the field since."

"So I'm guessing he didn't so much choose the venue as make it impossible to meet elsewhere?"

Kanemore sighed. "A bit of carousing is to be expected, considering the circumstances. Yet it is still damned reckless of him. You know as well as I that simply because the Abe *bushi* are not in the capital does not mean there is no danger. Even so, Lord Yoshiie has been planning this excursion, I am told, since he arrived."

"I can see that the Widow Tamahara's reputation is more widespread than I had thought. I'm not entirely sure this will please her—" I stopped. "You say he planned to be out tonight? And this was known?"

"He's spoken of little else."

Damn . . .

Now I knew what the *shikigami* had been doing lurking in the Widow Tamahara's courtyard. I prayed to any *kami* willing to listen that I was wrong.

"Your Highness, Lord Yoshiie is in danger!"

I didn't wait for a reply. I kicked my horse's flanks, and it lurched into a gallop. I suddenly remembered how much I hated riding, but it did not stop me from urging the beast into a run. I heard the pounding of hooves behind me as the rest of the escort gave chase. When Kanemore caught up to me, he didn't waste his breath on questions. In a moment he had passed me and now I was urging my mount to greater speed. We reached the Widow Tamahara's to find the entire compound in an uproar.

I heard screams and the clash of weapons within. Prince Kanemore leaped from his mount before it even had time to stop. I was not far behind, mostly because I fell when my foot slipped out of the stirrup, and it was only my grip on the saddle that stopped me from taking a nasty tumble. The gate to the compound was open and we rushed through, followed closely by Kenji and Lord Yasuna. A lantern was on fire on the ground by the veranda; I saw two of the women in the Widow Tamahara's employ cowering by the building, and as we watched, a rather disheveled older man crashed through a sliding screen and fell face first onto the veranda. He staggered to his feet, and I saw he was bleeding, but whether from a cut or the fall I could not tell. His eyes were slightly unfocused but he wasn't armed, and I recognized him as a regular patron. He stumbled past us seeking the gate, and one of the escort moved to intercept him.

"Let him go!" I shouted, and the man half ran, half stumbled out into the streets.

"Swords!" roared Prince Kanemore. It took me a moment to understand what he was referring to, but then I saw the members of the escort, who had finally caught up with us, dropping their bows and drawing swords. Of course. We were about to go into tight quarters where bows were likely useless, and the escorts were the only ones properly armed. Even Prince Kanemore had left his *tachi* behind, but he did have a dagger and so did I. Kenji had his priestly staff, and Lord Yasuna picked up one of the bows and an arrow that had been dropped. There was no time to do better. Prince Kanemore directed three of the *bushi* to circle the building while the rest of us ran through the opening the escaping patron had made and followed the shouting.

We found a young man in the large wine shop wing of the building grimly holding off a ring of attackers with no more than a long dagger and battered stool. He swung the stool as one his attackers darted in and was rewarded with a loud crunch as the bludgeon connected. His attacker went down and, not at all to my surprise, disappeared.

"*Shikigami,*" Kenji muttered. "But *how*?"

"Later, if there is a later. Kenji, can you reach the casks?"

He understood my intent immediately and bolted for the long fixed table behind which the Widow Tamahara kept the saké ready to be served. Prince Kanemore and our escort engaged the attackers, and the prince took out two of the creatures with one sweeping cut, aided by the fact that the creatures' attention was all on the young man I assumed was Yoshiie. I used my dagger to decapitate a third, but even as the creature fell, I had the sick feeling it wouldn't be enough. Yoshiie was about to be overwhelmed—there were simply too many of them and not nearly enough of us.

I heard Kenji shout *"Kampai!"* at the top of his lungs, and suddenly it was raining inside the building. I smelled the saké. One entire arc of the attacking creatures dissolved to wet paper as the young man gleefully bashed two more of the *shikigami* with his improvised club, and now the tide had turned. Yoshiie was still on his feet, but he was bleeding at shoulder and thigh; there was no way to tell how badly he was wounded. Prince Kanemore rushed forward as Kenji sprayed a second shower of saké from a broken cask, but one of the creatures managed to tackle Yoshiie and raised the point of a sword over his throat.

I heard the twang of a bowstring just before the arrow tore out the *shikigami*'s throat. Lord Yasuna had found work for his bow after all. Yoshiie staggered to his feet.

"Come on!" he roared, but there were no more of the creatures left. There were shouts from the courtyard on the far side of the building, then silence. The remainder of our escort appeared on the veranda. We had lost two men to the creatures, but it could have been a great deal worse. Yoshiie grinned, then sat down hard on the floor.

"Kenji!"

The priest drained the last of the cask down his throat and discarded it. "At your service."

Prince Kanemore set guards at front and back of the room and sent the rest to scour the grounds. I did not think they would find anything else, but it was best to be sure. In the meantime, Kenji examined the young man who was still grinning, despite what he'd just endured.

"Your wounds aren't severe, my lord," Kenji said, "but they will need tending."

He grunted. "I've had worse dozens of times. It's nothing."

"Nevertheless," Prince Kanemore said. "I would be neglecting my duties as host and as your father's friend if I did not insist you follow Master Kenji's advice."

"I've fought those things before, I think," he said.

"Quite right, my lord. They were magical assassins sent to kill you," I said.

He frowned. "And who are you gentlemen? I mean, I was told who to expect, and Prince Kanemore I know, and I do owe you all my thanks, but aren't introductions in order? Isn't that proper?"

"Very proper," Kanemore said. "Lord Yamada, Master Kenji, Lord Yasuna—"

"The bowman," the young man said. "Well shot."

Lord Yasuna apparently only then realized he was still holding the bow. He set it aside. "Thank you, though it was no great distance."

"Too long for me to cover in time," Prince Kanemore said. "Now I think everyone does know each other. Gentlemen, this is Lord Minamoto no Yoshiie."

"And I am both drenched and parched," he said. "Master Priest, would you be so good as to open another cask?"

"Perhaps it would be wiser to withdraw to the mansion?" Lord Yasuna asked.

"Certainly," Lord Yoshiie said. "But considering what we've all just been through, I think drinks are in order."

Prince Kanemore consented to one round of saké while the dead were being removed and our wounded seen to. The Widow Tamahara finally emerged, along with what servants she could round up, and began putting the place to rights, though not without a few scowls in our direction. I felt certain I would hear more of the matter later, but she would no more create a fuss in front of Prince Kanemore than she would sleep on hot coals. Fortunately, more than one round of drinks was unnecessary. The battle light had long since faded from Yoshiie's eyes, and in the end we had to carry him out to the wagon we sent for to take him back to the Sixth Ward, along with enough additional escort to make certain he would arrive safely. Prince Kanemore, Lord Yasuna, Kenji, and I remained behind.

"An interesting first meeting," I said. "And, in its way, impressive. Lord Yoshiie had already been drinking, and yet he held off more than a dozen of the creatures for a minute or two before we got here, armed with nothing more than a dagger and a wooden stool."

Prince Kanemore shrugged. "He's been a warrior since he was fifteen. One who has survived to his current, albeit not advanced age, suggests a high level of both skill *and* luck," he said. "But none of it would have mattered if we had arrived any later. Lord Yamada, how did you know?"

I took a slow breath. "I didn't, at least not for certain. But I'd been puzzling over the matter of a *shikigami* planted at the

Widow Tamahara's. I know Lord Tenshin placed it there, and I know he did not do it on a whim. I'd already realized I could not be the target. What did not occur to me until almost too late was the creature's discovery and disposal was simply too easy."

Kenji frowned. "Are you saying Kaoru-chan was involved?"

"Not in the sense she had anything to do with the creature being there. I had assumed the creature's reaction was simply defensive, but if that were true, then the way Kaoru-chan described it made no sense. Why would the creature become enraged rather than simply kill her and walk away? There were no other witnesses—it could have remained at its post."

Now Lord Yasuna looked thoughtful. "But surely there would have been some sort of inquiry?"

"Exactly," I said. "The Widow Tamahara has her faults, but she does care for the people in her employ. I would have gotten involved, and all this would have brought unwanted attention. But if the danger was perceived to be past? Another matter entirely."

"So the creature created a fuss instead," Kenji said. "And when you found the ensorcelled paper, that would be the end of it. Danger past, whatever it had been. Or so everyone would have believed."

"Lord Tenshin didn't know about me, but he did expect *someone* to find the creature. That is what, in my arrogance, I overlooked. Once the *shikigami* had reverted, it would still have motive power. There are a thousand places it could have hidden between and within those storehouses, and none the wiser, including me. The creature was meant to be found and destroyed because its work was *already done*. Once I learned Lord Yoshiie's plans were commonly known, and assuming—with reason—that Lord Tenshin is in the employ of the Mutsu Abe, the real target became obvious. Then my original question—what was the creature doing there in the first place?—had an answer."

Kenji considered. "But why raise a fuss at all? Why not just slip quietly away once it had planted the other *shikigami*?"

I smiled. "When anyone voluntarily leaves the Widow Tamahara's employ, the first thing she does is a careful and very thorough inventory, as she trusts no one. There was a chance she would uncover the creatures too soon. My guess is Lord Tenshin knew that as well and decided not to take the chance. The planning was meticulous."

Prince Kanemore looked a little pale. "One assassin? Possible, but chancy. A dozen?"

Lord Yasuna smiled grimly. "It almost worked. And the loss of young Lord Yoshiie would have been devastating to the Minamoto—and by extension, Imperial—cause. It's unlikely Lord Yoriyoshi would be able to succeed without his son's help. You are as clever as I remember, Lord Yamada."

I sighed. "Thank you, my lord, but I have to disagree. I very nearly allowed the plan to work."

"Barely dodging an arrow is not the same as having it take up lodging in your heart," Prince Kanemore pointed out.

"Which may be, Your Highness," I said, "but there are a lot more arrows in that particular quiver."

CHAPTER FOUR

WHEN WE MET Lord Yoshiie for a proper audience the next morning, you could hardly tell he'd been in a drunken fight for his life the night before. Frankly, he looked in better shape than Kenji, who had overindulged a bit once the fighting was over. Lord Yoshiie did, however, appear a little bit uncomfortable. I had thought it might be related to his wounds but then realized he was pulling at the edge of his formal robes at the neck and waist as if he didn't like the feel of them.

"... *a warrior since he was fifteen* ... "

It occurred to me that Lord Yoshiie might have chosen a less formal venue the day before because he was simply not comfortable in formal robes and setting. Now he sat on a cushion on a raised dais beside Prince Kanemore, not bothering to pretend his heavily brocaded and stiff Court robes weren't making him itch. He bestowed gifts on Kenji, Lord Yasuna, and myself, which was only proper under the circumstances. He had clearly been coached on the proper etiquette. Matters only became more interesting when the formal part of the audience was over.

"Lord Yasuna," he said. "I have been instructed by the Emperor himself to take you with us as we return to Mutsu."

Yasuna bowed. "As the Emperor commands."

Yoshiie leaned forward. "You and I—and I'm sure the gentlemen present—know this is likely pointless, yet the Emperor will have it so, and I will obey, and thus so must you. You may arrange a personal escort and whatever attendants you require, I would suggest no more than six of each, as you will also be required to provision them yourself. We are both at the Emperor's command, and so I will not consider you my prisoner unless you make it necessary. Please do not do so."

"You are generous, my lord," Yasuna said.

Yoshiie grunted. "No, I am not. I am grateful to you, as I am to His Highness and Lord Yamada and Master Kenji. I am very aware that, without your timely aid, I would likely be dead. However, my gratitude does not lessen my obligations to my father and clan. We will be at war, and I cannot guarantee the safety of any of you," he said, glancing at Kenji and me. "I am also grateful for any assistance you may be able to offer. But I want one thing understood, Lord Yasuna—I must subdue the Mutsu Abe at all costs. If I am wrong and you do in fact have some influence among your kinsmen, I will make use of it. That is how matters stand."

Later, Kenji and I ate the noon meal together in the mansion's garden where I had met Lady Kuzunoha only two days before.

"I'm not sure if I find Lord Yoshiie's candor refreshing or troubling," Kenji said between mouthfuls of rice.

I sighed. "Why choose? It can be both. I found his honesty refreshing but his bluntness a bit worrisome."

"I would simply expect someone of noble family to be a bit more at home within the capital," Kenji said. "It's clear to me Yoshiie does not feel at home here, despite being perfectly willing to take advantage of its . . . diversions. I'm certain this is not what worries you."

"Actually it is, in an abstract way. I've been observing the young man, to the extent I have been able to do so. It's not his manners which concern me, but rather his mannerism. His entire bearing. Imagine, for a moment, that Prince Kanemore as a young man had no obligations to the Court and was able to follow his inclination. What do you think he would be like?"

Kenji pondered, but not for very long. "I think," he said, "His Highness would be a great deal like our young Lord Yoshiie. He has always been as much *bushi* as prince."

"Now consider all the provinces, not just Mutsu: Miyagi, Eichizen, Oe . . . all of them. There are provincial noble families who share responsibility for both governing and enforcing the writ of the Emperor. And they are all producing sons just like Yoshiie— more at home in armor and on a horse than sitting through the New Year's poetry competition. Fighting for their lord and clan first of all and the Emperor as a distant second, if at all.

"Probably not exactly his equal," Kenji observed dryly, "but I take your point."

"Many have *kuge* branches, such as produced Lord Yasuna. A worthy man, but as we have seen, his kinsmen outside the capital look to their own provinces, their own holdings, and seek to expand them. Do other governors and military commanders, like Lord Sadato and his father before him, see those places as their personal possessions and not held in trust for the Emperor?"

"No one would dare—" Kenji began, then stopped. "A foolish thing to say. They already have, haven't they?"

"Yoshitoki and his son Sadato are proof of it. I don't question Lord Yoshiie's loyalty, mind," I said. "But one does have to wonder how deep a particular stream runs. The Minamoto have been fighting the Abe for almost twelve years because the Emperor told them to. He also promised them the military governorship of Mutsu province if they succeed. Do we really wonder which of the two is the greater inducement?"

Kenji took a deep breath and let it out slowly. "If there are greater matters afoot it is even more important we tend our own garden, Lord Yamada. So. What do we do now?"

"We go see Master Chang Yu, as I have been wanting to do since we arrived here. I have some questions I believe he can answer."

MASTER CHANG'S shop was near the Karasuma section, which was a bit of a walk since we were not mounted this time. Not that I minded terribly. Horses had their place, but I was used to walking, and I liked it—less chance of being thrown or trampled.

The shop was deceptively small, not unlike Master Chang himself. The front part of the building was his alleged real business, selling Chinese medicines and herbal compounds. There was a pungent blend of ginger and lemongrass and a dozen more smells I could neither identify nor avoid. Master Chang's compounding table was not in use, and his chair was empty. A girl of perhaps fifteen was watching the shop.

"Gentlemen, how may I assist you?" she asked.

"You can tell your master Lord Yamada is here to see him.

You may also tell him it would be useless to try and slip out the back door, so he may as well talk to me."

The girl frowned but quickly bowed and passed through a curtained doorway. There was a few moments delay, and then Master Chang Yu himself appeared in the doorway. He was about a head shorter than Kenji, who was perhaps half that much shorter than I was. He had a long gray mustache and wispy beard and he managed to look at once plump and tiny. Master Chang had kept the same shop in the capital since I had known him, and that stretched back twenty years or so. Over the years he had not changed at all—he still wore the robes of his foreign homeland, and I knew his clothing choice was driven as much by business concerns as nostalgia and habit. He still spoke our language with an atrocious accent, except when he needed to speak plainly and be understood, and not just play the role of aged Chinese merchant a long way from home.

Master Chang looked chagrined. "Armed men, Lord Yamada? Seriously? One would think these old bones were a danger to someone."

"I did inform your servant slipping out was useless, but you had to test me to see if I was bluffing. I'm not above such things, but in this case? No."

Prince Kanemore had insisted Kenji and I take a two-man escort into the city. Since they were there, I had decided to make use of them, in case Master Chang was in his usual uncooperative frame of mind, and so the matter proved.

"One should not blame an old man for trying to avoid trouble," Master Chang said. "And you are trouble, Lord Yamada. You do know that, yes?"

"I do not think anyone knows it better than Lord Yamada," Kenji said, "though personally I know it better than most."

"I need information, Master Chang," I said, ignoring Kenji's comment, "and once I have it, I will gladly take myself and my trouble elsewhere. This concerns a man named Otomo no Tenshin. I think you know him."

The old man shrugged. "I suppose. Members of the Otomo Clan have been my customers for years, as have Fujiwara and Minamoto and Taira and . . . well, nearly all of them. I even get the occasional royal transaction."

"You taught this one how to make *shikigami*. There are more than a few in the capital with the skill, but those at the very highest level? Nearly all were trained by you," I said.

"I suppose I should be flattered, but I'm an old man and far past such things," Master Chang said. "Assuming what you say is true, what crimes have I committed?"

"Many, I would assume," I said, "but none I care about. I said I came for information, and information is all I want from you. Nothing more. Do you recognize this script?" I produced the remains of the creature I had discovered at the Widow Tamahara's. Master Chang examined it, his face expressionless.

"If I answer your questions, do you promise to leave me out of whatever endeavor you're involved with *this* time? The last incident in which I cooperated with you nearly lost me my life."

"Not even close," I said, "but for what it's worth, I will settle for the information, as I said. Your personal involvement will not be required. You have my word."

"In that case . . . I recognize the work of Lord Tenshin," he said, "and yes, it was I who taught him the art, or rather a portion of it. He already knew a great deal when he came to me, but he wanted a few more shall we say . . . *specific* techniques."

"Such as a creature which can manifest already armed with a weapon? Steel, for all intents and purposes, but no less ethereal than the creature itself and returns to paper if the creature is destroyed?"

"Child's play," said Master Chang, looking smug. "Though the technique does take more concentration and preparation time. Lord Tenshin already knew that trick. What he wanted to know was how to make the creatures last, and how to create one with more sense than a rutting boar-hog."

"Please explain," I said.

"After your own dealings with lesser creations, isn't it obvious? The creatures are powerful but *limited*. Now take the example of my servant Mitsuko-chan over here—I'll wager you haven't yet gleaned her true nature, despite your wealth of experience. Am I right?"

I admit I was taken aback, and judging from the look on Kenji's face, he was as startled as I was. I took another long hard look at the girl, but I finally had to admit defeat. "You're saying she's a *shikigami*?"

Master Yu's expression passed smug and went on to extraordinarily pleased with himself. "Impressive, yes? Doesn't she make you wonder?"

"A servant you don't have to pay, feed, or house, who obeys your every command without question?" Kenji said. "Why would we wonder?"

I knew why, and so did Kenji, though I knew Kenji pretended otherwise to draw the man out. "I don't know how she managed to escape my notice, but there is a basic problem with the creatures," I said. "They obey your every command, no more and no less. She would have to be told everything you wanted her to do, or it would not be done. She would not notice, for instance, that the door had fallen off or a particular rare herb was in short supply, except if you remembered to tell her to watch for those things. She would sweep the floor at a certain time every day, whether it needed sweeping or not, if the building was on *fire* or not. They are decent agents and assassins when single-minded devotion to a task is required, but they make terrible servants. Managing one such more than a day or so would be exhausting and hardly worth the trouble."

Master Chang grinned, showing the gap of a missing eyetooth. "Now suppose I were to tell you my charming servant here has no such limitations, and that she has been minding my shop while I work, requiring no additional instructions whatsoever for the past three months?"

"I'd say your initial instructions must have been very thorough," Kenji offered.

Master Chang dismissed Kenji's comment with a wave of his plump hand. "Rubbish. Even I can't think of everything. Test her, if you doubt me."

"Very well." Kenji approached the girl, who merely watched him with big dark eyes. "What am I, girl?"

"You are a man. You are dressed as a priest."

"I am a priest," Kenji said.

"I will make note of that," she said. "I have seen priests before. They carried themselves differently than you do."

"Different how?" he asked.

"Like I know priests to bear themselves, all their mannerisms and actions. You bear yourself as a man."

A habit he has been quite unable to break, I thought but said nothing. I was curious to see how Kenji would approach the problem of Mitsuko.

"Let me ask you a question . . . Mitsuko, is it?"

"Yes, sir."

"What are the medicinal uses of a rug in traditional Chinese healing?"

I think Kenji expected the creature to turn to Master Chang for guidance. I rather expected the same; we were both surprised.

"None I am aware of," she said without a moment's hesitation.

Kenji frowned. "Did Master Chang tell you to say that?"

The *shikigami* called Mitsuko answered immediately. "He did not. How would my master know someone would ask about the medicinal value of a rug? It seems to be a silly question. Is that how you intended it, sir?"

I couldn't suppress a laugh. "Enough. Master Chang, I am impressed. And you taught this technique to Lord Tenshin?"

"He paid handsomely for the privilege, I assure you. Yet there are limitations, even with such a wonder. It pains me to say, but Mitsuko-chan probably won't last another week."

"Why?" I asked.

"Because volition still requires a living spirit. If I'm not supplying it, then it has to come from someone else."

Kenji scowled. "Did you—?"

"Please, Master Kenji. I am no murderer. I am of the Way . . . not your Way, but an older one."

"There is no older Way—"

I interrupted. "While I am not against a rousing philosophical discussion, gentlemen, we have more urgent business. Please go on, Master Chang."

"I was simply going to say that we understand the principles of universal balance, the yin and the yang. A ghost is a contradiction. It is a human spirit but it has no body. As long as it remains in this world it will always be incomplete, out of balance. My technique makes an artificial body, which will take on the appearance of the once-living person as soon as the spirit manifests within it. Naturally, if there is no available spirit to fill the void, the technique does not work. But to answer the question you have not yet asked, *this* is why you did not recognize Mitsuko as a *shikigami*. She has a human soul. She *is* human, in most ways that matter. So this is why she triggered no spiritual alarms in you."

"But why does it last only for such a short time?" I asked.

"Again, we're back to the balance I spoke of, Lord Yamada. While a void always wants to be filled, a human spirit was never intended to live in a house of paper, and the sustaining power of the initial charm is not unlimited, even with normal *shikigami*. I can already see signs of this in Mitsuko. Three months, I have found, is about the limit."

Whatever hints there were of Mitsuko's imminent dissolution, they were invisible to me. She appeared perfectly fine and healthy, but that reminded me of the question Master Chang had not yet answered. "But for a traditional *shikigami*—not one like Mitsuko—I believe Lord Tenshin spoke of a way to make them last. I'm guessing he meant they could be made less prone to being destroyed?"

"Indeed," Master Chang said. "In some ways a more difficult problem than the creation of Mitsuko. These creatures have many weaknesses, as you have discovered—physical damage, for one. Then fire and water for obvious reasons—one destroys the paper, the other ruins the ink which holds the charm in place. Even the most powerful *shikigami* can be undone by a simple spring shower."

"Or saké," Kenji said. "Though it broke my heart to waste it."

Master Chang smiled. "Ah, yes, I did hear about this. News does travel in my circles, Lord Yamada."

"Unfortunately one cannot always count on the rain or barrels of saké when fighting a *shikigami*," I said. "But fighting the creatures would be more difficult if Lord Tenshin has a way to overcome that limitation."

Master Chang sighed. "I'm afraid he does."

The technique Master Chang then described was one in which the ink could be mixed with the white of an egg in certain proportions, with one extra ingredient—blood. "The magician's *own* blood," Master Chang hastened to add. "The secret is to bind both the ink and the magician's will to the paper, as well as impart some of the magician's yang energy to the creature as well, and the link created by the blood permits the creature to *continue* drawing this energy from the magician. I call it the Blood Thread technique. As you can imagine, this method takes a high toll on the magician, far in excess of the amount of blood used. If you're concerned about an army of these creatures, be comforted—it would take a strong young *onmyoji* to create and maintain even one of them. Any more and the effort would kill them."

"How about over time, could more be created?" Kenji asked.

Master Chang drew a deep breath and then grunted. "No, that's not possible, even for a young, healthy man. As I said, the Blood Thread *continues* to draw the magician's life energy so long as it exists, so the magician has no chance to recover his strength. The longer the creature lasts, the weaker the magician will become. Even two such creations would drain the magician to his death in a very short time, and then the creatures would die as well. They can live only so long as the magician does. It's a powerful—but very dangerous and limited—technique."

I had an inspiration. "But what would happen if the method you just described was combined with the technique you used to create Mitsuko?"

"A continuing supply of living energy fueling a created body with its own volition . . . I hadn't thought of that."

"Yes, you had," I said. "Or you're not nearly as clever as I know you to be. Why you didn't do this with Mitsuko is obvious, but if the idea hasn't occurred to Lord Tenshin, I have badly over-estimated him."

"It's true I'm no longer a young strong man," Master Chang said. "I don't have the living energy to spare. Lord Tenshin, on the other hand . . . yes, it might work. Like Mitsuko, it would have its human memories, perhaps even believe it *was* still human and go on with its perceived life as normal if the transition happened close to death—ghosts tend to be confused, in the first hours of their creation. Yet the link does not simply power the creature, it gives the magician the ability to control the *shikigami*, even at a distance. I would not do such a thing even if I could, but Lord Tenshin might, given the need—in is his own perception of 'need.' I have to say his sense of the ethical balance of the universe is somewhat lacking. Still, he paid well enough."

I grunted. "For the right price, I'm guessing the proper balance of the universe is open to interpretation?"

"Always," Master Chang said without hesitation. "And price doesn't have anything to do with the matter."

"We failed to recognize Mitsuko. Is there a way to identify these creatures? I mean, short of cutting their heads off and hoping they turn into paper?"

The old man grinned. "One such as Mitsuko is sustained by the power of the charm, as I said, and so has no need to eat or drink. More to the point, she *cannot* eat or drink. Her body is real enough, but her reality is a physical manifestation of a charm written on a piece of paper. If she were to have, say, a cup of saké, the contrast between her actual physical reality and the perception she has of herself . . . well, it's like a sleeper being slapped awake. The shock is simply too much and the soul flees, destroying the charm. I discovered this by accident with a previous servant. I have no doubt the same would apply to a creature created by the Blood Thread technique."

"So if we suspect such a one, all we would need to do would be to get it to eat or drink to discover the truth. Which implies we'd first need cause for suspicion, and otherwise these things are indistinguishable from a normal human."

"Just so," Master Chang agreed. "You do see the problem."

Kenji glanced at Mitsuko. "It's not right, Master Chang."

The old man frowned. "What do you mean?"

"A spirit should be exorcised so it may return to the wheel

of death and rebirth to work out its karma. You create a trap for them and turn them into servants. You are delaying their eventual transcendence!"

"It is not a trap, Master Kenji," Chang said. "It's a restoration of balance. I admit what you say might apply if Mitsuko was a confused spirit who was not aware of her situation, but Mitsuko chose this. Like a spirit being reborn into the physical world on the Wheel of Death and Rebirth. She simply doesn't remember doing so."

"How convenient she does not remember," Kenji said.

"For her own sake she does not remember, Master Kenji. It is an act of kindness. No matter, she has little time in any case. I'm sorry, Mitsuko, but as I can see Master Kenji does not believe me, I am commanding you to remember, and answer Master Kenji's questions."

Through all this discussion—the parts which concerned her and the parts which did not—Mitsuko had stood at her place beside the cubbyholes and crockery jars that held Master Chang's wares, and her expression had not changed a flicker. But now as Kenji approached, I saw a touch of fear.

"I want to ask you something," Kenji said. "Will you answer me truthfully?"

"I have no reason to lie to you, sir," Mitsuko said.

"Not even on orders from your master?"

She actually smiled slightly then, and I think that was the last stone in the wall. I was no longer able to think of Mitsuko as an "it" or a created thing. Whatever passed for flesh in Master Chang's creation, I no longer had any doubt he had told the truth about Mitsuko—there was a person in there.

"If so ordered, I would obey," she said, "but how could he have known what you would ask?"

While personally I would not entirely rule out the possibility, I silently conceded it was a bit far-fetched, even for someone as subtle as Master Chang. Kenji apparently came to the same conclusion.

"Master Chang said you chose to come here, to . . . accept, the body you are wearing now. Is this true?"

"Yes," she said softly. "I remember now. It's true."

"May I ask why?"

Mitsuko wasn't smiling now. She looked haunted. "Because it was better."

"Better than what? Being a ghost?"

She bowed her head. "I was always a ghost, sir," Mitsuko said softly. "Even when I was alive. I had no home, I had nothing. I *was* nothing. I died in the street and my body was raked up like a dead leaf. I lingered because I could not believe I had any place else to go."

"Then Master Chang offered you a place," I said.

She looked up then. "More than a place, sir. A purpose," Mitsuko said. "A chance to be something, to someone. Even just as a servant. *Something*. Yes, I chose this. I only wish . . . " She stopped.

"Yes?" Kenji urged.

"I only wish it had lasted longer," she said, and there were tears in her eyes. A moment later her appearance changed. Her shape grew wavy, like someone who had just stepped into a fog. She turned translucent, transparent, and then there was nothing left but a scrap of paper that fluttered to the floor.

Master Chang shook his head. "You may not believe this, gentlemen, but I really will miss her."

Kenji looked grim. "There is a temple nearby, Lord Yamada," he said. "When we leave here, I would like to go there for a while."

Certainly there was a temple nearby. This was Kyoto. There was always a temple nearby. I didn't say this. Nor did I ask why we would be visiting a temple. I had a feeling I knew.

"In which case you'll need this," Master Chang said. He reached behind the table and pulled out a bag of uncooked rice. He offered this to Kenji, who just stared at it.

"For your conscience?"

Master Chang grunted. "Think what you will of me, but my conscience is my own concern. This is for the offering," he said. "And prayers for Mitsuko's soul. That *is* why you're going to the temple, is it not?"

"Yes," Kenji said.

"Then do it properly. Take the offering. For Mitsuko's sake, not mine."

Kenji took the rice, and I followed him back out into the streets of the capital. The temple was a short walk. They always were. Kenji went inside, and I found a spot in the temple garden and waited while the two *bushi* accompanying us tried not to look bored. Temples had never been my favorite places, nor did I usually enter one voluntarily unless there was dire need. I tended to associate them most often with funerals, as that was one of their main functions, and the role they had played far too often in my experience. As for Mitsuko, a proper funeral would have taken days we did not have to spare, but prayers and offerings for the departed were the next best thing. I thought about chiding Kenji for doing this for a person he didn't even know, and without payment, but decided against it.

Kenji was, at least in some regards, as bad an example of the priestly class as one would ever hope to find; he drank, he ignored the dietary restrictions, and even now in his fifties he was a pursuer of women, a surprising number of whom he managed to catch. Yet he was very much a priest in one regard— he had an extremely clear vision of his own moral center, where the line could be drawn, what lay on one side, and what resided firmly on the other. The plight of the unfortunate Mitsuko had clearly crossed that line.

When Kenji emerged from the temple, he joined me on my rock in the garden. "Did you do what you needed to do?" I asked.

"Yes. Did you?"

"What we learned from Master Chang were things we mostly already knew, except for the technique which created—or rather, resurrected—Mitsuko. If Master Chang's description of the process is correct, however, we cannot expect an army of such creatures. But consider, a *shikigami* which can withstand water like a human being, indeed, one which can *pass* as a human being, undetectable by either of us? This concerns me greatly."

"If we'd been dealing with even one such at the Widow Tamahara's, for example . . . " Kenji didn't finish the thought, but he didn't have to.

I had considered that scenario. "Lord Tenshin expected Lord Yoshiie to be indoors at the Widow Tamahara's establishment. His strategy was brilliant, but his tactics were flawed. He considered the chance of rain but fortunately the saké attack didn't occur to him. He's very clever, but not infallible."

"I often say the same of you, Lord Yamada. What do we do now?"

"I intend to stop by my rooms at the Widow Tamahara's establishment and consider if there's anything there I might need to take with me. If you have any immediate unfinished business in the capital, I'd suggest you see to it now. We will be bound for Mutsu province very soon."

"I already have everything I need, so I'll stay with you for now, if you don't mind," Kenji said, looking a bit doleful. "Most of my unfinished business is best settled by me being somewhere else for a considerable amount of time."

"Mutsu does have the advantage of being very far away," I said. "Let's go."

When we arrived at the Widow Tamahara's, we left our escort on station at the gate and went inside. I had been dreading returning to this place, considering the mess we'd made of it the previous evening, but I needn't have worried. Most of the damage had already been repaired, and the Widow Tamahara herself, at least by comparison to her scowling demeanor, was in an almost jovial mood.

"I see your shop has been mostly set to rights," I said.

She grunted. "Thanks to Prince Kanemore. A gang of workmen showed up at my door this morning and said they were hired by His Highness, Prince Kanemore. He even sent payment for the saké your friend there was flinging around the room."

"The waste of it grieved me even more than it did you," Kenji said.

"I would not wager on that," she said.

As for the saké, truth be told I could still smell it clinging to the air of the room, for all that everything had been freshly scrubbed. Since the room always smelled slightly of saké, I had no doubt the intensity of the aroma would fade in time. "Prince Kanemore is the most generous of men," I said. "Is everyone all right?"

"One of my guards has a knot on his head the size of a lantern," she said. "But otherwise everyone escaped unscathed . . . Lord Yamada, first there was my previous guard, and now these things. Am I to expect that such strangeness will continue as long as you are under my roof?"

"It's possible," I said, "but unlikely, as I will not be under your roof for some months. If the place burns down in my absence, it will have nothing to do with me, I swear."

"Hardly comforting." The old lady waved a single bony hand in dismissal. "Fine then. But make sure your rent is paid for the interval before you leave."

"Tamahara-san, before I go—did those workmen go anywhere else on the grounds?"

She frowned. "No, I would have seen. They came in, did as they were directed, and left again. Frankly, I could use more like them. Why, what do you suspect?"

"Oh, nothing at all. Just curious."

Kenji followed me out onto the veranda. "Do you suppose Prince Kanemore really did send those workmen?"

I considered. "It is the sort of thing he might do and fail to mention. And considering Lord Yoriyoshi is more likely to put his son in a cage than to let him come back here, I don't see what an enemy would have to gain by such a deception. And if the Widow Tamahara is correct, they had no opportunity for mischief even if mischief had been the intent. But we had best take a look around the compound while we are here."

We made as thorough a search as we could, and since Kenji was neither drinking nor distracted at the moment, I trusted his heightened sensitivity to the supernatural to detect the things I could not see. Neither of us found anything amiss.

"We can ask Prince Kanemore about it if we get the chance, but I think perhaps we are overly cautious."

"When extremely clever people are trying to kill you? There is no such thing as 'overly cautious,'" Kenji muttered.

I had no disagreement with that. Back to our original mission, we went to my rooms. Referring to them as "rooms" perhaps gave them too much credit: I had one six-mat room and one other, which was little more than an alcove, for extra storage. I had one small chest for brushes, paper, and inkstones. I slept on a cushion on the floor, covered with less or more layers of clothing, depending on the weather. I already carried my dagger and *tachi*. There was little else to consider save some extra clothing, which I began to gather into a bundle while Kenji watched.

"I have not asked how you feel about going to Mutsu," he said.

I knew what he meant. There had been many wars against the Emishi over the years, and one of them had destroyed my father and thus my clan, or rather the scheming of a former Fujiwara official had led my father to be branded a traitor to the Emperor. What had been taken from my father and thus my family would likely never be restored, and while I had gained some measure of revenge long ago, restoration of my father's good name seemed forever beyond my reach. Prince Kanemore had requested we go to Mutsu, and he had done so in the full knowledge of my family's history, friend or no, because he believed it necessary. Considering Lord Tenshin's abilities and the Mutsu Abe's obvious ambitions, so did I. This did not mean I was fond of the idea, and I said so.

"If there were a choice? I would not go. But there is none. For either of us."

Kenji just sighed. "You will do what your friend asks. I will do what the Crown Prince's royal uncle commands. Either way? No choice at all."

When we emerged from my rooms, I was carrying my bundle. We found Kaoru in the courtyard, standing beside the Widow Tamahara's one scrawny *sakura*. Only it was no longer quite so scrawny looking, now that it had begun to bloom. I was a little ashamed to realize I had not even noticed.

She smiled at us. "Isn't it beautiful?"

"Yes," I said but without much enthusiasm. Soon the *sakura* all over the capital would be in glorious bloom, winter would have officially released its grip on the land, and spring would be here again. Time to put the winter clothing away, time for pruning, time for planting . . .

Time for war.

CHAPTER FIVE

FOR SOME REASON I had assumed Kenji and I would be walking with the foot soldiers or, at best, assigned to one of the supply wagons. Prince Kanemore had an entirely different perspective. He had assigned mounts for each of us and a ration of fodder, along with a groom to see to the horses properly. The last bit I considered no more than sensible—Kenji and I both knew how to ride, after a fashion, but that's where our understanding of the beasts ended.

"Highness, you know how I feel about horses," I said.

"I do, but there is something I need you to understand, and this is more from a friend than a prince," he said.

"What is it?"

"You've never taken part in a war. Fighting? Yes, and more than most, but war is a different thing. An *army* is a different thing. The fact you are not there as a *bushi* may not be relevant, since there is a lot of confusion in a battle and you might find yourself in the middle of one, intended or not. You may find it will be necessary to give orders and have those orders obeyed, most likely by men who won't have a clue as to who you are and what your rank may be. Do you see what I mean?"

"You're saying there's a much better chance of being obeyed if I'm on horseback."

He laughed. "I'm saying there's a good chance they won't even *notice* you, let alone obey, if you are not. Mounted archers will make up the majority of Lord Yoshiie's warriors, and anyone who commands them in the field will be mounted as well. They expect this. Granted, in an army of this size not everyone on horseback is important, but everyone who is important is on horseback. In order for you to be effective, it's not enough to *be* important. You have to *look* the role as well. Which is why I have supplied you and Kenji with new clothing. It is also why you will overlook your belief that horses are dumb, skittish beasts, and learn to appreciate them."

I was never inclined to disagree with Prince Kanemore any more than necessary, and especially when he was right. War was his domain, not mine, and I would have been a bigger fool than I usually attempt to be to argue the point. "Thank you. I will do my best not to embarrass you, Highness."

"Bring the horses and my servant back if you can, but mostly try to stay alive and keep Lord Yoshiie in the same condition," he said. "That will be thanks enough. Much depends on this."

By the end of the first day on the road I was not exactly in a thankful mood. My posterior was as sore as it had ever been, including the time I fell off a high wall and landed on a mound of pine cones. Plus, the army had made a temporary bivouac on the shores of Lake Biwa. The place had unpleasant associations for me.

Kenji found me standing in a small clearing not far from

shore. He didn't say anything at first, for which I was grateful. For a while we just looked across the water to the high hills bordering the shoreline.

"This is where it happened," he said finally. It wasn't a question.

I didn't know how much he knew about the death of Princess Teiko. It wasn't something I talked about, but then I wasn't the only one there, and Kenji had a talent for finding out what he wanted to know. It was a useful trait but, from time to time, an inconvenient one.

"There are times," he said finally, "when I wish I was as wise as priests are reputed to be. Maybe then I'd know what to say to you."

"There's nothing to say. I've made peace with my loss."

He grunted. "No you haven't, because no one ever does. You try to accept it. You remind yourself this is a transient world, no more than an illusion, and yet the scar still aches. Personally, I don't mind my own scars. There are worse things than pain."

Sometimes it was easy for me to forget Kenji, in his way, had known loss as great as my own. Yet here we both were, going on with life and doing what needed to be done, partly for duty's sake, but also because we still believed such things mattered. It wasn't healing, exactly, but it would have to do. While we stood in companionable silence, I noticed a patch of white within the woods near the shore.

A ghost?

I looked closer and realized it was not a ghost. It was a fox-demon. "Lady Kuzunoha is here," I said.

Kenji shrugged. "You did say she was planning to accompany

the army, and Lord Yasuna is with our group, not Yoriyoshi's. Do you think she wants to talk?"

"I seldom see her unless she does. I'd better go alone."

Kenji respected Lady Kuzunoha almost as much as I did, but that didn't change the fact she was a fox-demon and he was a priest. Neither was ever going to be completely at ease in the other's company.

"I'll wait here," Kenji said affably. He sat down with his back against an old maple tree and made himself comfortable. I went down into the woods.

Lady Kuzunoha met me in a small clearing on the edge of the water.

"I have heard," she said without preamble, "that you and my lord saved young Yoshiie's life."

"It is true. Lord Yoshiie is very grateful to Lord Yasuna."

"And yet my lord is still a prisoner," she said.

"Lord Yoshiie's personal gratitude does not change the Emperor's orders to take Lord Yasuna to Mutsu, and so he will. But Yoshiie agrees there is little to gain by attempting to use him as a hostage."

Lady Kuzunoha looked disgusted. "I have lived among humans for many years, easily—for the most part—passing as one of them. Yet I admit I still don't understand them."

I couldn't suppress a smile. "Lady Kuzunoha, what makes you think *we* do? I will say Lord Yoshiie is in a very difficult position. On the one hand he must obey his father and the Emperor both, yet he also owes his life to a man they have compelled him to place in harm's way. There is simply no way to reconcile these things, save to do what he must while—to the degree possible—keeping Lord Yasuna from harm. If the worst were to happen—"

"In which case," she interrupted, "I have told you what I will do." For a moment the foxfire glowed brightly around her.

"*If* the worst does happen," I continued, "Lord Yasuna would not want Lord Yoshiie harmed on his account."

"Did he say so to you?" she asked.

"No. But he understands why he's here in the first place. He does not blame Yoshiie for his situation. And if you know Lord Yasuna as well as you should, you would know what I say is true."

The last of the foxfire winked out. Lady Kuzunoha looked as weary as I felt. "I do know that. So tell me, Lord Yamada— what do you propose I do with my rage if I am cheated of my revenge?"

"What are you doing with it now?" I asked.

She frowned. "I don't understand."

"Not too long ago you reminded me of your true nature. Suppose Lord Yasuna had been a fox himself, and another vixen had lured his affections from you. What would you have done then?"

"I would have killed her," she said. "And taken great pleasure in doing so."

"So how is this different? You cannot be with him, and I know that is what you desire above all else, save perhaps reuniting with your son, Doshi. Yet both are beyond your grasp—taken from you not by a rival but by cold circumstance, which feels neither pain nor regret. How do you tear out *its* throat? You have been cheated of your revenge since the day you left Lord

Yasuna's household. Tell me the idea of finally having a target for your revenge doesn't appeal to you."

"At the cost of my lord's life?!"

"Yes," I said. "That is the cost. Whatever you decide to do, please remember this."

I knew I was stepping on treacherous ground, but the rage in Lady Kuzunoha's eyes faded as soon as it appeared. Which was very fortunate for me. I knew very well what she was capable of, and goading her was perhaps not the wisest thing I had ever done. But I had to see if there was a way to change her mind. I did not want Lady Kuzunoha as an enemy, but I knew, if something did befall Lord Yasuna with the current situation unchanged, she would try to do exactly as she had said, just as I would protect Lord Yoshiie at all costs, as *I* had said. If a confrontation came to pass it would mean the death of at least one of us. I hoped there was another way. "If you truly wish to protect your former husband, then help me. There is much we don't know about what forces Abe no Sadato has at his command."

She scowled. "You're not referring to *bushi*, are you?"

"Such things are Lord Yoshiie's concern. Mine is for the *onmyoji* Lord Sadato has at his command. Lord Tenshin, for one. He learned some techniques from Master Chang, but he clearly had another teacher. He is quite skilled, and I don't yet know the extent of his power. It would be to both the Minamoto's and Lord Yasuna's advantage if I did know."

"Lord Yamada, you do have the habit of looking for alternatives, whether they exist or not."

"One usually finds what one troubles to look for."

Lady Kuzunoha smiled then, a wistful smile. It did not last

long. "I have not forgotten my earlier promise, nor will I do so," she said slowly, "but I will think about what you have said."

She took two steps into the trees, and in one moment she was no longer there. I went back to where Kenji was waiting.

"Have you accomplished anything?" he asked.

"I didn't get my throat torn out," I said. "Which feels like accomplishment enough for the moment."

"I haven't sensed anything along the trail," Kenji said, "but I did manage to gather a little more information while you were chatting with Lord Yoshiie today."

"More like trying not to fall off my horse and being chatted *at*. He mostly wanted to talk about Prince Kanemore and why *shikigami* didn't like saké. He at once managed to dominate the conversation and yet clearly didn't attach great importance to it. Whatever his strategies might be, he's keeping them to himself. So. What did you find out?"

"Not a lot," Kenji admitted, "because no one seems to know a lot. As soon as we skirt Lake Biwa tomorrow, we'll pick up the Tōsandō and be on the Eastern Mountain road until it runs out."

"There's a reason Mutsu is often called 'the land beyond the road,'" I said. "Regardless, despite the uproar they caused in the Sixth Ward, this is not a very large force—Yoshiie cannot be planning on taking the fight back to the Abe with no more men than these and the ones under his father's command. I doubt the Kiyohara alone will be enough of an addition."

"A contingent from Kawachi will be joining us in a day or two, I'm told, all Minamoto *bushi*. We'll pass through half a dozen provinces before Mutsu. Yoshiie has the Imperial Writ, so he expects to pick up allies along the way."

"In other words, there will be *bushi* from several different clan branches joining the cause. It will also be a perfect opportunity for agents of the Abe Clan to infiltrate." I said. "No one will think twice of meeting someone unfamiliar to them."

"Yes, and there's nothing we can do about it," Kenji said cheerfully. "Chances are very good we are doomed . . . or Yoshiie is, which is pretty much the same thing. If we reach Dewa at all, it will be a miracle."

"We will not be at full strength until then, and by even approaching the barrier at Dewa, we are practically on the Abe's western doorstep. Do you think for one moment Abe no Sadato and his *onmyoji* don't know we're coming? You heard what Prince Kanemore said—Yoshiie is their prime target. The events of the last two weeks bear this out."

Kenji grinned. "I did mention 'doomed,' did I not?"

In reality it took four more days for the reinforcements from the Minamoto stronghold in Kawachi to arrive. Our path then went beyond Lake Biwa through Mino and then on to Shinano and the mountain road. The governor of the province met us near the border and added two score mounted archers to our number before wishing us a speedy journey. Nor did I blame the man—not all provisions could be brought along, and the required foraging and requisitioning for even a relatively small army was always disruptive and costly for the folk around it. Even if the army in question wasn't an enemy bent on destruction, destruction was going to happen. Lord Yoshiie maintained tight discipline, and I was pleased to see he attempted to keep the worst incidents to a minimum until we reached the mountain road, after which there were very few opportunities for . . . misunderstandings, with the locals. The governor had spread the word of our coming and the road was mostly deserted. However, I wasn't pleased with the notion that every cotter and rice farmer in Shinano knew of our movements. I expressed my concern to Lord Yoshiie, but he just shrugged it off.

"Have you ever tried to hide an army and recruit for it at the same time, Lord Yamada? Because if you know the secret, I'd be pleased to hear of it," he said, and that was the end of the discussion.

While the going was treacherous along the road itself, the scenery was quite striking—we were within view of the peak of Mount Kyodai, and it was hard to keep from being distracted. I imagined it would have been even harder in the fall season, with the leaves of the maple trees turned to flame instead of their current brilliant green. I rode ahead some distance while Kenji, to the degree the narrow trail allowed, rode up and down the sides of the column, his priestly senses searching for danger.

I heard hoofbeats and then Lord Yoshiie was beside me. He was not in full armor, but he was wearing his chest piece and helmet. With his golden half-moon *maedate* on his helmet and his war bow and quiver of yellow-fletched arrows, he struck quite a figure. Not for the first time, I had the feeling I was somehow glimpsing the future, but whether Lord Yoshiie's future or simply something greater than all of us, I didn't know, nor did I concern myself overmuch with the feeling. I did not discount such intuitions, but at the same time I'd never found much practical value in prophecy when all my problems were usually rooted in the here and now.

"I have sent out scouts on the ridge above and in front, Lord Yamada," he said. "And it is my considered opinion no one is going to be climbing the mountainside to attack us."

"With all respect, Yoshiie-sama, a human certainly could not."

"Ah. You're thinking of more of those creatures like we fought in the wine-shop," he said. "They are strong, I will admit, but not so strong."

"Creatures such as those, yes," I said, "and possibly worse things besides. Forgive me, but until I know for certain what we are dealing with, I would prefer to take no chances with your life or the success of the Emperor's edict."

Yoshiie's visage darkened for a moment, and I considered perhaps I had gone too far. I was used to working, if not completely on my own thanks to Kenji, at least with smaller numbers. Except for Prince Kanemore himself, *bushi* were outside my experience, and Yoshiie was a man not used to having his methods questioned even by implication, and certainly not by someone of my insignificant status. But he finally grunted something noncommittal and withdrew back to the column. The message, however, was clear enough—my axis of free action was not to be unlimited, nor was my judgment even in matters of the *onmyoji* to go unquestioned. I was Prince Kanemore's agent, not one of Yoshiie's trusted generals, just as Lord Yasuna was a hostage, despite whatever gratitude Yoshiie may have felt toward us. I knew it would be wise not to forget either. After a good look around, I rode back to the column and found Kenji.

"Nothing?" I asked.

Kenji scowled. "Nothing at all. Not a scent, a feeling, nor a whisper."

"You look disappointed."

"Surprised, rather. For an enemy who could arrange an ambush on a mountainside as easily as a tavern, this place is ideal—there is no room to maneuver, or to bring up aid if needed. Twenty *shikigami* could hide in the ridge above, swoop down and push the vanguard right off the mountain, and Lord Yoshiie with it. If the enemy does not do what you expect, you can take it for granted he will do something you do not."

Kenji's fears echoed my own, but I was trying to view the problem from both sides. "*Onmyoji* are not so common that Lord Sadato could have such agents in every domain we pass. The bulk of them would remain under his physical control, or he's a fool. This was simply one wasted opportunity. Which doesn't mean all such will be wasted."

"You can wager Lord Sadato will give Lord Tenshin free reign to attack at some point, and at the place and moment of his own choosing," Kenji said.

"He will have an advantage no matter what, and he'd be a fool not to use it. I would," I said. "In his place."

Kenji glanced up the trail. "At least we'll be past the larger mountains by the time we approach Shinano's border with Echigo. After which the path to Dewa will be much less rugged."

"Less rugged perhaps, but still mountainous," I said. "And still plenty of places for an enemy to hide. Not to mention it's closer to Mutsu and Lord Tenshin's current base of operations."

"Doomed," Kenji said.

"You keep saying that."

"And I will continue to do so," Kenji said serenely, "until you prove me wrong."

"Or we die?"

"Really, Lord Yamada . . . and you say I'm the gloomy one. I have faith in you."

I'm glad he did. Personally, I wasn't certain I was up for the challenge.

When the *bushi* assigned to scouting returned and reported they had found nothing, I breathed a little easier. There was still the small matter of approaching so close to Mutsu before turning northwest for Dewa, but after observing Lord Yoshiie's precautions, I was certain he was not being careless in the least. I should not have been surprised—he could not have been as reckless as he first seemed, or he wouldn't have lived to see his twenties. He also knew what *shikigami* were capable of, having fought them personally on two different occasions. Plus, he had taken this same road from and to the North more than once. If there happened to be a good spot for an ambush along the road, chances were Yoshiie already knew about it. That he had seen no reason to explain any of this to *me* was a little annoying. I understood his mission was to defeat the Abe, but *mine* was to keep him alive long enough to complete it. I'd have preferred his cooperation, rather than his mere tolerance of my presence. For the moment, it was enough that there had been no attacks, and the army was making good progress through Shinano. At our current rate, we'd reach the Echigo barrier in a couple of days at most, and that province was, if anything, more securely in its local governor's hands than Shinano. Surely there would be no cause for concern there, even if it shared part of its northeast border with Mutsu.

As soon as the notion occurred, I found myself repeating my own advice—"It's not the snake on the rock that kills you. It's the one in the grass you didn't see."

There was a lot of grass still between Lord Yoshiie and Dewa.

In the evening, the moon—a mere crescent when we left the capital—was now in its full glory. I found a spot in a small clump of pines. It was a little too near a sheer drop of several hundred feet to a valley below, but it afforded a marvelous view of the moon floating over the mountains. I was soon joined by Kenji and, somewhat to my surprise, Lord Yasuna. None of us said anything for a good long while. The night had started off clear, but now dark clouds were pushing in and the moon was temporarily shrouded.

"What do you think of Lord Yoshiie, Yamada-sama?" Lord Yasuna asked.

That was a little more deference than I was used to, especially from someone of Lord Yasuna's rank, but the question was one I'd been considering for some time. "He is a skilled warrior and strategist. I cannot imagine him living at Court," I said finally.

Lord Yasuna grunted. "There was a time when living at Court would have been all that mattered. Now I can imagine a time when this will not be the case."

If Kenji understood the reference, he kept it to himself. I was pretty certain I did. "I see you've been speaking with Prince Kanemore."

Lord Yasuna smiled. "Prince Kanemore may be unique among the royal family in that he sees the storm which is clearly coming."

I liked and respected Lord Yasuna, but if there was a more dangerous pastime than discussing politics with a member of the Emperor's Court, I wasn't sure what it might be. Fighting an *oni* probably came closest, but the beauty of such a competition was that the worst an *oni* could do to you would be to kill you.

"What storm are you referring to, Lord Yasuna?"

He smiled then. "Honestly . . . I rather think what Kyoto thinks of any of this is the least of our problems at the moment, Lord Yamada. Wouldn't you agree?"

"For the moment? Certainly. But the moment will pass, bringing another behind it. Even so, yes, I am well aware of Prince Kanemore's opinions. There was a time when emperors led their armies into battle, but those days are long past, and no one expects them to return. If the Emperor's will is to be enforced, then it will be men like Yoshiie who will enforce it."

"There was a time when Lord Sadato did the same. Until he, like his father, realized where the real power lay. It is to the Minamoto Clan's advantage to oppose the Abe. What if it had been to the Minamoto's advantage to join with them? What would the Emperor have done then?"

"Fortunately for all concerned, I am not the Emperor."

Lord Yasuna laughed then. "It is really a pity you left the Court so soon, Lord Yamada," he said. "You would have done well there."

I wasn't certain if I was being complimented or insulted. Knowing Lord Yasuna as I did, I considered it might be a little of both. Kenji, who until now had kept silent, spoke up.

"Rewards and punishments only go so far. If the clans become more loyal to themselves than they are to the Emperor, we could see the situation in Mutsu repeated throughout the land."

Lord Yasuna looked thoughtful. "Shall I tell you gentlemen a secret? It has some bearing on our current situation."

That was the hook, and I rose to the bait, as Lord Yasuna doubtless knew I would, but there was no help for it. I didn't know nearly enough about our situation, and any one of the things I did not know could get Lord Yoshiie and the rest of us killed.

"I am always glad to hear what you have to say."

"The Minamoto have been fighting this war, off and on, for nearly twelve years," Lord Yasuna said. "If the Minamoto and the Taira had joined forces, they would have crushed the Abe long ago. Why has this not been arranged?"

"The Emperor's government has promised the Abe's place in Mutsu to the Minamoto if they succeed, with the promise of the spoils of war to reward those who have chosen to join the Minamoto cause. That is an inducement to ordinary *bushi*, certainly, but hardly an incentive to the great and powerful Taira. What does the Emperor's government have to offer them?" Kenji asked.

"The governorship of Mutsu, for a start," Lord Yasuna said. "The previous holder of the position hasn't demonstrated much aptitude. Remember, the Minamoto will merely be appointed military commanders of the province, just as the Abe were, so there are more rewards available if needed. This alliance could have been arranged."

"And your secret is why it was not?" I asked.

Lord Yasuna shook his head. "The secret is the Emperor himself favored such an alliance. Prince Kanemore was one of those who opposed this idea, and he is primarily the reason it was not implemented."

"Because he knew it was not in the Court's best interests to demonstrate to the Minamoto and Taira such an alliance was possible?"

"Well and discreetly put, Lord Yamada. Aside from loyalty—not to be discounted—the thing which keeps the military families under Imperial control is they distrust each other far more than they distrust the Emperor's government."

Lord Yasuna didn't bother to express the potential consequences should that situation ever change. He didn't need to do so. Instead he apparently turned his attention back to the glorious full moon. I was content to do the same. When Lord Yasuna spoke again, I assumed he would be returning to the previous subject, so I was not prepared for what came next. I don't see how I could have been in any case.

"We'll be passing near the village of Yahiko," he said. "Are you going to visit your sister?"

For a moment I was too stunned to say anything, but Kenji was not.

"Lord Yamada, what is he talking about?"

Lord Yasuna shrugged. "I must apologize, for I assumed you knew. Lord Yamada has two sisters living. One older, one younger. The elder is a nun in the temple complex near Yahiko, Yahiko-ji. Yahiko-jinja, the shrine of the gods, is better known, compared to the temple. Your sister could not have chosen a more obscure place to retire from the world."

"Apparently not so obscure," I observed finally. "Lord Yasuna, how did you know this?"

"Back when I needed your assistance in the . . . domestic, matter, I made it a point to find out as much about you as I could. I am a cautious man, Lord Yamada. Forgive me, but a man in my position has to be so."

Kenji glared at me. "Honestly, Lord Yamada, I thought we were friends."

"We are, not that either of us deserves one," I said. "But look at the matter from my perspective, Kenji-san—my father was executed as a traitor to the Emperor. To this day there are those who believe the charges were true. Plus I have made quite a few enemies all on my own. For their protection, it was best that as few people knew of my siblings' existence as possible. I must commend Lord Yasuna's initiative in discovering them."

"Again, I must apologize to you," Lord Yasuna said. "I should have realized."

"I understand," I said, "yet perhaps now you will not think it strange that I intend to keep my distance from the temple . . . as much as I would like to see Lady Rie again. And Kenji, I will ask your pardon as well and hope you understand."

Kenji's anger hadn't entirely passed, but he managed a grudging, "Well, if *I* had a sister, I probably wouldn't tell me either. Even if she *was* a nun."

I grunted. "Do not think this did not occur to me."

After that, and until the clouds rolled in for good, we concentrated on the moon and said nothing at all. It seemed the safest course for all concerned.

CHAPTER SIX

THERE WERE no incidents in our progress through Shinano. That is to say there were no attacks such as normal travelers might expect on a well-traveled but still isolated roadway, though such an attack certainly seemed less likely on a company as well-armed as ourselves. Any human bandits in the area clearly had the sense to avoid us entirely, but on the night before we were due to reach the Echigo barrier, several ragged thieves were caught attempting to pilfer our supply wagons. Lord Yoshiie had their heads mounted on poles by the roadside, and their bodies unceremoniously dumped over the side of the mountain road. The task was complete before he finished his evening meal. Soon after, I found our young horse groom, whose name I barely remembered to be Taro, losing his own meal by the side of the road in sight of the grim display. He stood up and wiped his chin as I approached. He couldn't have been more than fourteen or fifteen, about the age Lord Yoshiie had been when he first went to war with the Abe. I hadn't paid Taro much attention before, probably because I didn't associate with the horses more than I had to. Now I saw only a frightened young man.

"I gather you've never seen a dead man before," I said.

"My grandfather," he said, "but not . . . "

"Not like this?"

He barely had time to mouth the word "no" before he was bent over again, retching. Apparently the boy had already lost what little was in his stomach, since nothing came out, but I waited until he was finished. "There's no shame in being sickened. It's an appropriate response, but best to get it out now. Since we're going to war, you're likely to see death again, and probably not as tidily as Lord Yoshiie's justice."

He finally straightened again. He still looked a bit greenish in the waning moonlight, but his voice was steady. "Forgive my weakness. I will go see to the horses."

"Yes, since you can be certain I will not. Besides, I've found if there's something I don't want to think about, doing something entirely different tends to help. Or drinking . . . but I don't advise the latter."

Kenji arrived just as Taro was leaving. He went up to the poles where the heads were mounted and took out his prayer beads. I would have joked about his poor choice of clients, unable to pay for his services as they were, but I didn't have the energy to goad him. I felt tired, suddenly, and more inclined to silence. When Kenji's prayers were finished, he walked over to where I was standing.

"I suppose we will see many more like them before this journey is done," he said.

"It was kind of you to pray for them," I said.

"Even though they cannot pay me?" Kenji asked mildly.

"I was thinking that. You have known me too long to doubt it," I said. "And yet here you are, undoing all the good of my restraint."

"Fate has decreed in this life I am to be a priest," Kenji said.

"As for what sort of priest I may be, well, fate is silent on the subject. It may be I do not always remember what the point of being a priest is. Yet I can assure you, Lord Yamada, there are those in some of the richest temples in Kyoto who never do remember. That's assuming they ever knew."

"I need not be persuaded on the point, since I daresay I've met more than a few of them myself," I said dryly. "So why did you pray for those men, Kenji-san? I admit I am curious."

"Because, judging from their ragged and half-starved appearance in life, it was a safe wager no one else would. I make that reason enough."

Now and then Kenji did surprise me. It was part of the reason we'd been able to remain friends. Whenever I was feeling judgmental toward him, I usually managed to remember those times and turn my attention back to my own faults, which, it must be said, were abundant. For example, the reason I'd given for not visiting my sister was it was for her own protection, which was true as far as it went. That did not mean I wasn't afraid to face her.

"I'm not suited for this," he said after a long pause.

"Surely you don't mean travel. You've visited more famous places in the country than I have, including the sea shore at Echigo."

"No. I mean this," he said and waved an arm back to where the army was camped. Their fires were like stars scattered across the mountainside. "So many souls about to be released back to the wheel of rebirth and death, thus to begin all over. And what can I do for them? I suspect the answer is—nothing."

"They're not why you're here," I pointed out. "Lord Yoshiie is our primary concern, and we must assure Lord Yasuna's well-being so Lady Kuzunoha doesn't feel compelled to destroy the

Minamoto . . . and trying not to get young Taro killed so we can return him to his rightful master. I would think they are more than enough to worry about."

Kenji grunted. "Far more than enough to worry about, considering our Lord Yoshiie has to defeat an entire army which can call on supernatural allies, but all the Abe Clan has to do is kill Lord Yoshiie. But none of this alters my other obligations as a priest."

I had no argument worth posing. While Kenji's piety was a sporadic thing at best and usually quite selective as to which tenets it observed, I knew it to be genuine, if often ill-timed and inconvenient. Kenji was what he was, and you might as well argue with a mountain.

During the night I dreamed I was keeping watch on the mountain road. The heads of the executed thieves kept me company.

"You don't suppose you could fetch my body from the ravine?" the leftmost asked. "I was rather fond of it."

"I can't leave my post, and it wouldn't do you any good even if I found the missing parts. Your body is broken beyond repair," I said. "The crows will be along soon, and that will be the end of it."

"Is this what death feels like?" asked the one in the middle.

"Having never died—at least that I can recall—I'm ill-equipped to advise you," I said.

"You two should quit complaining," said the one on the right. "We all knew this could happen."

"It's not a subject on which I'm prepared to be dispassionate," said the first.

"Prepared or not, dispassionate or not, you're all still dead," I pointed out.

The middle thief begged to differ. "The dead don't speak."

"Ghosts often do, but you are not ghosts. You are three severed heads on poles. I would think in your place being dead would be an advantage. I would not want to be in your situation and still live."

"Probably not possible," admitted the third.

"Probably for the best," agreed the second.

"You should go see Lady Kuzunoha," said the first. "She's waiting right up there."

The three heads then fell as silent as the graves they had been denied. I glanced up toward the mountainside and saw the white fox-demon sitting demurely on a boulder not too far from the road. I made my way up to greet her.

"It seems the talking heads were correct," I said.

"As a fox-demon I move between the worlds at need," Lady Kuzunoha said, showing her sharp teeth in something resembling a smile. "Since I grew my third tail, it's even gotten easy to do. The dead thieves could see me clearly. I am curious to know how you could hear them."

"They were speaking to me," I said.

"Yes, Lord Yamada, but how? What breath did they have for speech?"

"I hadn't considered the matter," I said. "It just seemed a natural thing."

"It shouldn't seem so. When great powers are invoked, the

veils between the living and the spirit world can become easily torn. Even in your present situation, you should realize this."

"My present situation?"

She sighed. "Dreaming. Only now you won't be able to hold on to the dream. This is the way of things."

She was right. Already she, the severed heads, the road, and even the mountains were growing less distinct.

"Before you go . . ." Lady Kuzunoha dipped her muzzle to the stone and picked up a small object in her teeth. This she tossed at my feet. It was the remains of a *shikigami*.

"Lord Yoshiie's scouts might miss one or two, as I expected, but *you* really should be more careful," she said, and then the dream dissolved. I woke up, lying on my sleeping mat. Next to me was a battered slip of paper covered in teeth marks.

When I related the story to Kenji over the morning meal, he just shook his head.

"Such creatures were put into this world to trick and mislead the righteous," he said piously. "However . . . if she must be here, I'm glad she's working for us and not against."

"She's working 'for' us, as you say, only because our interests and her own are in harmony. This will likely not always be the case."

"A problem, I hope, for much farther down the road," Kenji said. "Or were you merely reminding yourself of this?"

"It is something best not forgotten," I admitted. "I'll feel somewhat better when both Lord Yoshiie and Lord Yasuna are safely inside Dewa, although 'safely' is probably not the right term to use. Say rather that neither is dead at the time."

"By the way . . . you did say you have no intention of visiting your sister near Yahiko, correct?"

RICHARD PARKS

"I did."

"You may not get your wish. I am reliably informed that, once we cross into Echigo, Lord Yoshiie intends to make a pilgrimage to both the shrine Yahiko-jinja and Yahiko-ji, the temple complex devoted to the goddess Kannon. This is where your elder sister is cloistered, is it not?"

I felt a little chill. "It is."

"Well, you *might* be able to avoid her," Kenji said, grinning. "But since I am also informed Lord Yoshiie plans to stay at the temple overnight, and our writ requires we remain near him, at the moment avoiding your sister does not appear likely . . . unless she is also avoiding you?"

I didn't answer him. I briefly considered attempting to persuade Lord Yoshiie against the pilgrimage, but my own arguments sounded hollow to me. Making a show of piety and respect for the *kami* and the goddess alike before battle and receiving the blessings of both abbots and priests, on the other hand, made perfect sense as reassurance to his troops of the rightness of their cause. Even those who served strictly for the chance of spoils and rewards would expect no less. Plus, the temple compound itself, to my understanding, was walled and far more defensible than a campsite on open ground. Lord Yoshiie knew his business, but that wasn't making mine any easier.

Fortunately, Lord Yoshiie's forces were well on their way to breaking camp, and young Taro came leading our mounts, already saddled and bridled, through the chaos. He gathered up our sleeping mats and cooking utensils and the like and began expertly packing them up.

"Feeling better?" I asked.

He paused in his work long enough to bow. "I am well, Lord Yamada. Please do not concern yourself. I'll see that your bowls are washed before the noon meal."

I held the reins of my horse, a beautiful white mare—yes, I could dismiss them as stupid, obstinate beasts, but I could not ignore their finer qualities on an esthetic level, try as I might—as I watched Taro hurry off. "I'm not used to being waited upon," I said.

Kenji smiled. "I could get used to it very quickly, but I'm trying not to do so. All things are impermanent, and the services of Prince Kanemore's attendant? Doubly so."

The column was soon ready to move, and Kenji and I mounted our horses and took our respective places. We crossed the barrier into Echigo early that same afternoon. Lord Yoshiie met briefly with a courier from the provincial governor, and by dusk in two day's time we were approaching the temple complex at Yahiko. It was my understanding the governor himself would bring another detachment of *bushi* to add to our ranks before we crossed into Dewa.

"Mutsu borders on Dewa to the east, but at Echigo on its southwest corner. The Mutsu barrier is just a few leagues to the northeast," Kenji said when he joined me again near the head of the column.

"Lord Yoshiie knows this. He's sent a dozen or more scouts." As I was riding closer to the head of the column, it was easy enough to observe at least the outward signs of discretion.

"Have there been any reports?" he asked.

"Three by my count, and so far nothing appears to concern

our young leader. Besides, would Sadato risk drawing Echigo into the war directly by an attack across its border? The entire province mobilized to join the Minamoto and Kiyohara is not quite the same concern as the governor volunteering a few dozen *bushi* as a nominal demonstration of loyalty to the Emperor."

"I keep forgetting war is more political than merely strategic or tactical. All I can seem to remember is that it gets people killed. I'm enough of a priest to disagree with this aspect of it all."

I had no real disagreement with him. Personally, I wouldn't give a rat's tail for all of Mutsu province and three more besides. It had already led to the death of my father and the destruction of our family's fortunes. I had long since reconciled myself to this, but that didn't mean I was eager to re-open an old wound. None of which changed the reality that Prince Kanemore was my friend, and loyalties aside, I understood what was potentially at stake should the Minamoto fail. I was no great friend of the Minamoto and neither was Prince Kanemore, but allowing the country to fall into chaos would mean a great many more deaths and great misery besides, and I said as much to Kenji.

"We trade a few lives to save many more. Perhaps it is the right thing to do," Kenji said. "That doesn't mean no one will answer for those lives."

"Then let it start and end with Lord Sadato and his murderous lackey, Tenshin."

Kenji gave me a quizzical look. "I do believe you're taking Lord Tenshin's actions personally."

"Probably much more than he himself is," I admitted. "Maybe it's the treachery against his brother that does not sit well with me. One who has lost most of his family might tend to overvalue them."

Kenji laughed. "Lord Yamada, if you are in need of perspective, please consider I had *three* brothers, and hardly a day went by I didn't want to kill at least one of them. I only meant you should not let your anger interfere with your judgment," he said. "I know you can use the sword you carry and likely will have to do so before this business is over, but your sword is not why you're here, any more than my staff is why *I'm* here. Your talent is your discernment. If that is compromised, you're useless to everyone, including yourself."

I took a long breath, and let it out. "I will keep what you said in mind."

I couldn't help but be annoyed, even though Kenji's words were no more than sense. Neither of us spoke again until the northern barrier was in sight. We had skirted the village of Shirakawa deliberately, as we were well supplied and Lord Yoshiie wished to avoid any potential problems with the townsfolk of the sort that inevitably happened when large bodies of armed men passed through. I'm not sure if his motives were entirely altruistic or whether he simply wished to avoid calling attention to us. I suspected the latter, but regardless of the reason, we had made good time and had crossed Echigo province without incident. There was another messenger from the governor. I had made it a point to remain as close to Yoshiie as protocol and common sense allowed, and so I was able to hear when Yoshiie related the contents. The governor of Echigo would bring his contingent to join us in three days' time. Until then, Yoshiie would be hosted at the temple near the village of Yahiko as he made his promised pilgrimages to the temple itself and the nearby shrine, Yahiko-jinja.

"Yoshiie-sama, pardon me, but how many people know about your plans to visit the temple?" I asked.

"Everyone in our army," he said drily. "That was rather the point."

"Yes, certainly," I said. "But otherwise . . . ?"

"I had to reveal my plans to the governor of Echigo as a courtesy, and to the Shibata Clan chief. I imagine more than a few know by now, but I do know what your concern is. My scouts have reported already—the temple goes about its business as usual, and there is no one in the area who shouldn't be there," Yoshiie said. "The temple walls are strong and easy to defend if needed. I will be quite safe there."

I bowed. "At such times I almost feel as if Prince Kanemore suffers from an excess of caution, to have sent me along. Yet these are the sorts of questions I must ask."

He grunted. "Fail to do so, and I would question the good prince's judgment. You will accompany my party within the walls . . . and your priest as well. Let it not be said I was uncooperative in regard to Prince Kanemore's wishes."

"I am grateful," I said, and bowed again. Yoshiie rode some distance away to confer with the members of his bodyguard. I kept my distance until he returned to the head of the column. I did not want it said that I was overstepping my bounds. Yoshiie was barely tolerating our presence as it was. I didn't entirely blame him—he had his own mission to worry about, just as I had mine.

Kenji rode close. "What are your concerns about the temple?"

"I should have none. It is secure and will be surrounded by loyal *bushi*. It's clearly a much safer encampment than any we've had so far. I don't like that our leader's plans to stay there are so well known, but how could it be otherwise without defeating a large part of the reason for doing it?"

"Obviously, it cannot," Kenji confirmed.

"We will accompany Lord Yoshiie's party within the walls. Be on your guard."

"Why?"

"Because there is absolutely no reason why being on our guard should be necessary."

Kenji smiled. "To someone who knows you, Lord Yamada, that makes perfect sense."

We saw very little on the balance of the journey to Yahiko, neither people nor animals. There were one or two carrion crows shadowing our path. Apparently they had been following us since the incident with the thieves, hoping for another meal, in which case they were disappointed.

We reached the temple compound in good order. I hadn't been certain how much weight to give to the initial reports about the compound's suitability for defense, but I was pleasantly surprised. The temple enclosure was on high ground, using the largest of several wooded hills to best advantage. The walls were of stone with red-tiled pitched roofs to divert the rain, and we could see the tops of the temple structures themselves tiled in the same manner, rather than with the more common cedar shingles. Raised wooden platforms had been spaced at intervals just inside the walls to serve as watchtowers, but as far as I could tell, only the one nearest the gate was currently occupied. While the hillside and even the interior of the temple walls had trees, the approaches had been cleared to give clear lines of site along the road leading to the temple complex.

Kenji and I were riding at the front of the column at Lord Yoshiie's request.

"For a small temple they appear to be well provided for," Kenji said.

"This is the family temple of the Shibata Clan," Yoshiie said, "who are unrelenting in their support. If they were as supportive of the Emperor's will, this war would have ended years ago."

No doubt another reason Yoshiie chose this particular temple to make his pilgrimage. Honoring the Shibata in this manner cannot hurt his cause. My estimation of Lord Yoshiie as a politician as well as a military commander increased.

"It seems strange a nunnery would be included in the temple complex itself," Kenji said.

There were as many reasons for a woman to take holy orders as for a man, but in general the mainline sects were either unconcerned or openly hostile to the idea of a woman achieving Enlightenment. There were exceptions but not many. As often as not, nuns formed their own communities or, when possible, continued to live as they had before, with their families, and continued their spiritual practices in, if not solitude, at least separation from others on the same path. That had not been an option for my sister Rie, who had come here instead.

"The nunnery adjoins but is separate from the main complex and has its own gate, for obvious reasons," Lord Yoshiie said. "The nunnery itself was established many years ago by a member of the Shibata Clan who had taken the tonsure herself, and wanted a safe place for her spiritual practice. Apparently she was afraid, if she remained at home, her father would eventually arrange a political marriage for her, holy orders be sodded. As she was a generous patron, the abbot at the time agreed. Eventually other nuns joined her there and carried on after her death."

"Your pardon, Yoshiie-sama, but I'm surprised you're so well versed in the history of this temple," Kenji said.

Yoshiie just grunted. "I appreciate good strategy, Master Kenji, wherever I find it, and by removing herself from her father's direct control, the Shibata nun achieved her objective. The story speaks to me of someone who understood the value of a strategic retreat. Frankly, gentlemen, I did not wish to return to the capital at all after our last setback—my anger and shame at being defeated pressed me to return to the field, but the example of the Shibata nun allowed me to be persuaded that this was not the wisest course, so I chose to withdraw and regroup. Time will tell if I made the right choice."

While I was listening to Lord Yoshiie tell his story, I could not help but fix my attention, briefly, on the fact there was a wall between the nunnery and the temple proper. I still believed it best that I called no attention to Rie's presence or our relationship. Considering the forces at work against both Lord Yoshiie and me, I did not think this course overly cautious, and the promise of the wall and gate made me believe avoiding contact might be possible.

"More crows," Kenji said.

I had noticed our followers from the execution of the thieves, but there were more of them, as Kenji had just noted. Perched in the trees on the grounds of the temple, a few on the walls and roof peaks. Normally a flock of crows would be a rather noisy thing, but these were almost silent. Lost in my own concerns, I had barely noticed them until Kenji pointed them out.

"There must have been a funeral recently," Yoshiie said.

Death attracted them, and since it was the purview of temples to arrange and conduct funeral rites, a few crows loitering about would not be considered unusual. This was more than a few.

"Lord Yoshiie, would you be so good as to send your guard in first?" I asked.

He frowned. "Might I ask why? This is a pilgrimage, not the investment of a castle."

I smiled. "A humble suggestion, nothing more. For such an important event, perhaps a small display and some pageantry might underscore its significance?"

"I hadn't considered the matter in that way," he admitted. "Very well."

Lord Yoshiie gave the order, and two lines of bushi comprising about thirty men rode ahead of the column. Resplendent in *yoroi hitatare* bearing the Minamoto Clan crest, they did make for an impressive sight. As they approached, the gates to the temple swung open, and they rode inside, half to the left and half to the right, to maintain two separate lines in the inner courtyard. We followed as Lord Yoshiie rode between them to where the abbot of the temple waited to greet him. The monks of the temple lined up behind and in front of Lord Yoshiie's party. We had ridden halfway to where the abbot waited for us when Kenji reined his mount toward me.

"Lord Yamada—" His voice was a harsh whisper. I raised my hand for silence.

"I see them," I said.

The monks clustered close to the rack of spears near the wall was one more piece of the puzzle; if the situation wasn't clear enough already we both heard the creak of the thick temple gates closing behind us and the consternation of the *bushi* behind us who had found the gates shut in their faces.

"I suppose I should have asked what the appropriate greeting to give an abbot might be," Lord Yoshiie said.

"In this particular case? Simplicity itself," I said.

"What is it?" he asked, but I was already drawing my *tachi*.

"Kill him!" I shouted.

To his credit, Lord Yoshiie barely hesitated, but that small delay nearly cost him his life. The "abbot" pulled a long dagger from his robes and sprang forward while Lord Yoshiie was still drawing his sword. I crashed my mount into the false cleric and sent him flying. I hadn't meant to. My intention was to shield Yoshiie and turn my sword on his attacker, but my control of the skittish beast was not as precise as I had imagined. Still, it served the purpose, and while the man struggled to his feet, one of Lord Yoshiie's archers put an arrow through the man's throat. He fell back down and stayed there. Before I could turn back toward Yoshiie, one of the monks rushed me with a long spear, which I barely managed to deflect. The man knew his business, and it was only by reining to the side and spurring my mount so hard it jumped that I dodged the second strike. Another arrow sprouted in the man's leg like a bloody weed, and I cut him down before he'd finished screaming.

By now the remaining archers had dropped their bows and drawn swords for close-quarters fighting. By my quick count, five of them had waited too long and were down, either wounded or dead. As many of the monks were in the same condition, and the fighting was fierce.

Sohei?

It was a reasonable guess, since bandits and rogue *bushi* were not uncommon, and most monasteries kept contingents of armed lay-brothers for self-defense. Then again, they didn't normally disguise themselves as ordinary monks and acolytes— and certainly not as abbots. As much as I wanted to turn my mind to the puzzle, there was no time. We were outnumbered by at least half-again, and the outcome was far from certain. I was relieved to see Lord Yoshiie still in his saddle and fighting with the skill and intensity of a professional warrior. After seeing Yoshiie fight at the Widow Tamahara's, I did not judge him to be quite at Prince Kanemore's level, but then I didn't know anyone who was. He was undeniably more skilled than I was, plus he used his mount to good advantage, keeping it moving, charging and retreating as the situation dictated. I urged my horse forward and managed to cut down another spearman attempting to attack Yoshiie from the rear.

"We have to keep moving," he said, breathing hard.

I understood. We lacked numbers, but our one advantage was we were mounted and our opponents were not. Yoshiie shouted a command I didn't understand, but apparently his guard did. The survivors quickly broke away from whomever they were fighting and rode to his side. There wasn't a great deal of room to maneuver in the courtyard, but they used what space there was to regroup. I was about to join them when I noticed that Kenji wasn't with them.

Has he . . . ?

The thought barely formed before I heard the shouting. While our attackers were concentrated on Lord Yoshiie and his *bushi*, Kenji had made a run for the gate. I could hear the shouts of our soldiers outside the wall, and the door shuddered as they attempted to force it down. Kenji was dismounted now, trying to raise the beam that held the gates closed with one hand while fending off two attackers with his staff held in the other, but the beam was too heavy for one man to lift, and the men pressing against the doors from the other side were not helping. I rode past one spearman and rode over another before my horse stumbled on something I couldn't see and I went flying over its neck. I landed hard, and for a moment could see nothing except an explosion of stars, even as I struggled back to my feet. There was a slim blur on the ground that I prayed was my *tachi* and was rewarded with the familiar feel of its hilt as I reached down. My vision cleared enough for me to realize the only reason I was still alive was the closest monks were intent on stopping Kenji from opening the gate—they hadn't even noticed me. I cut one down just as Kenji released the beam, took his staff in both hands, and cracked the skull of another. Shouts and furious threats came from our attackers as they realized the danger, but it was too late. Together Kenji and I managed to shift the beam, and the remaining troops burst through the gates and thundered into the courtyard just as Lord Yoshiie led his surviving guard in a charge from the opposite direction. I wish I'd had the presence of mind to call for prisoners, because in less time than it would have taken me in my younger days to drain a cup of saké, the fight was over.

Not a single one of the false monks was left alive.

"You're bleeding," Kenji said.

"So are you."

We examined each other's wounds, but neither of our hurts appeared to be serious. Apparently one of the spearmen had nicked my shoulder, and in the heat of the moment I hadn't noticed. Kenji had a shallow cut on his leg but was otherwise unharmed. We were bandaging each other when Lord Yoshiie and several of his retainers rode up. He immediately dismounted.

"How did you know?" he demanded.

I winced as Kenji pulled the bandage tight. "I believe Master Kenji noticed them even before I did. What I saw was the outline of the abbot's dagger in his sleeve. I would often do the same thing, in situations where a sword was too bulky and noticeable, so it was no trick for me to discern. What leader of a temple greets an honored guest armed? Not to mention the rack of spears, which wouldn't be unusual in a training field for *sohei*, but in the temple courtyard? By the time they shut the gate behind us, their intentions were clear."

"As for me," Kenji said, "I've seen careless dress before, even in abbots. But no one had any idea how to wear a surplice correctly. It stood to reason these people were not who they appeared to be."

Lord Yoshiie grunted, which was apparently as close to an acceptance of our reasoning as we were going to get. He turned to his men. "Search the grounds," he shouted and then turned back to us. "Gentlemen, please come with me."

Lord Yoshiie phrased his words politely, but it was not a request. We and two of his guards fell in behind as he entered the main worship hall adjoining the courtyard. We saw the first bodies immediately. They had been stripped of their priestly robes before being killed.

Rie . . .

It was all I could do to concentrate on what we were seeing, but there was no reason to believe the nunnery had been spared and even less when the first reports reached us: more bodies, stripped, apparently the real monks and priests of Yahiko-ji. Besides my concern for my sister, there was something else about the attack which nagged at my mind, but catching it was like trying to grasp a morning mist. For his part, now that the situation was resolved, Lord Yoshiie considered it from the perspective of tactics.

"The Mutsu border is not very far from here. My scouts reported no movement, but that was apparently because these assassins were already in place. It would have been easy enough to slip across the barrier disguised as merchants or refugees from the fighting. But to slaughter priests, to defile this sacred structure . . . Lord Sadato is my enemy, but I have always known him to be an honorable man. I would not have believed him capable of this."

I spoke up. "Your pardon, my lord, but it's possible he didn't even know of it. If someone in his employ was tasked with your destruction, someone with a demonstrated lack of restraint, the precise method of your . . . removal could be a detail such a person might not share with his patron."

Yoshiie scowled. "I assume you refer to Lord Tenshin. Perhaps so, but if it was done in Sadato's name, then he is responsible. Besides, these were not *shikigami* who attacked us."

"True, but *shikigami* would not have been a good choice for this sort of operation. The timing alone . . . " I stopped.

"What is it, Lord Yamada?" Kenji asked.

"There was something about this whole matter that bothered me, I mean aside from the obvious point we could have very easily been killed. Now I know what it is."

"I have you two to thank that we did not," Lord Yoshiie said. "But what are you referring to?"

I took a slow breath, let it out. "The timing of the attack wasn't merely adequate, it was nearly *perfect*. Consider—a temple is a busy place. There was no way such men as we fought could have kept up this pretense for any length of time. This temple receives pilgrims and visits from local people on an almost daily basis, any of whom would have realized something was amiss. No, in order for the attack to succeed, they would have to move their men into a position from where they could overpower the real monks and take their places with only a few hours' notice at *most*. I am guessing we'll find their encampment nearby if we search the woods surrounding the temple. This body," I said, pointing to the corpse who appeared to be the late abbot, "has bled profusely, and yet the blood has barely had time to turn black. I'll wager he was killed no more than an hour or two ago."

"Impossible," Lord Yoshiie said, "my scouts—"

"For all their diligence, are only human. Our every movement has been shadowed and reported hour by hour. I do not as yet know how, but it is the only explanation."

From the look on his face, I knew Lord Yoshiie had reluctantly come to the same conclusion. "The sooner we know the answer to that question, the better. In the meantime . . . " he turned to one of his guard. "Tell Toshiro I need him."

I recognized the name as one of Lord Yoshiie's couriers. The guard soon returned with the man in question, a short and wiry fellow wearing the Minamoto Clan colors, now spattered with blood. He immediately kneeled, but Lord Yoshiie pulled him to his feet. "Go to the Shibata Clan chief," he said. "He'll want to know what happened here."

After the courier withdrew, Yoshiie added, "More to the point, *I* want him to know what happened here."

"Your pardon, my lord," Kenji said, "but unless we get luckier than I expect we're going to, proving that the Abe Clan was behind this outrage will be very difficult. So far we've found nothing to tie this to Lord Sadato."

"You're thinking of the Emperor's justice and courts of law," Lord Yoshiie said, "but I'm thinking I don't have to prove who the culprit is—I know. And so will the Shibata Clan."

I could see his point. If whoever planned this attack hadn't understood or ignored the consequences of failure, they were either far less intelligent or far more desperate than I had believed. I wasn't relieved to know the second possibility was the more likely. A cornered animal was always the most dangerous.

"Lord Yamada, I will need a word in private," Lord Yoshiie said.

Kenji bowed to him. "I have the feeling I am needed elsewhere," he said. "Don't you agree, Lord Yamada?"

"Yes . . . and thank you."

Either I was getting easier to read in my dotage, or Kenji, who had known me longer than almost anyone, was simply developing his skills, but he knew what I wanted him to do, and he immediately left to do it. The guard withdrew to a discreet distance as I bowed.

"I am at your service, Lord Yoshiie."

"Frankly, Lord Yamada, I had my doubts. You are here under Prince Kanemore's auspices, and it is common knowledge Prince Kanemore is no friend of the Minamoto. Yet you have saved my life now on two occasions. My resentment of your presence appears to have been misplaced."

I bowed lower. "As you are carrying out the Imperial will—and that is where Prince Kanemore's loyalties are—I can assure you his offer of my assistance, worthless as it might be, was genuine. As is my determination to help you see the Abe Clan is brought to heel. Prince Kanemore understands the danger they present if Lord Sadato is allowed to consolidate and expand his influence."

"So our interests coincide. For now. Fair enough and properly stated. But I still owe you a debt. What do you wish of me?"

"Only that you accept Kenji-san's and my services, for whatever they might be worth, and place no unnecessary impediments before them. I will consider this gratitude enough."

He almost smiled. "And will your friend settle for so little as well?"

If I had assumed Lord Yoshiie hadn't paid much attention to either of us, the question shattered that assumption. "It is a great deal, in my opinion, but as for Kenji, well . . . if you could spare a token reward of rice and cloth, it would probably help convince him of the sincerity of your gratitude."

Lord Yoshiie did smile then. "Done."

Soon after, Lord Yoshiie recalled his guard and sent him to finish searching the remainder of the building, but he found no other bodies. As the guard finished his report, Kenji returned.

Clearly, and unlike Yoshiie's guard, he had seen more bodies. Many more, from the expression on his face.

"The nunnery?" Lord Yoshiie asked, impassive.

"Yes. Those poor women . . . " Kenji looked as if he wanted nothing more than to be sick, but he took a breath and kept his voice steady. "Lord Yamada, I came to tell you . . . your sister . . . "

I felt my brain and body go numb, and there seemed to be a mist rising around me, so thick and deep that I almost didn't hear what Kenji said next.

"We've found her. She's alive."

CHAPTER SEVEN

My RELIEF at the news of my sister's survival had been near overwhelming. I had always been fond of Rie, but perhaps I had not altogether understood exactly how fond. The fact that neither of us has laid eyes on each other in over fifteen years did not seem to matter at all. Lord Yoshiie's interest was, undoubtedly, of an entirely different nature, and his expression of it, while kind enough, helped bring me back to the task at hand.

"If I know Tomotoki, he'll be here in less than two days with a considerable force behind him—the Shibata will not take an attack on their family temple lightly. It would be best if we have as complete a picture of the events leading up to this sad day as possible," he said.

"With your permission, Yoshiie-sama, I will question my sister in this matter."

"Thank you. While I'm pleased *anyone* survived this abomination, that it was your sister makes it doubly fortuitous. I had no idea any of your kinsfolk were present here."

"Very few did know," I said, bowing low, "or would be concerned at such a trifling matter. But I thank you."

"There were other survivors," Kenji said. "Two others so far, and I still hope for more. Apparently the nunnery was attacked last, giving some of the residents time to either hide or flee. Clearly the attackers did not think they had the time or necessity to be more thorough . . . although they were certainly vicious enough."

"Also with your permission, I will question the other survivors as well," I said.

Yoshiie grunted assent. "Be as gentle as the urgency allows."

I bowed again. "You may depend on it."

Kenji and I took our leave then. Outside, now that the fighting was over, the grimmer work of the aftermath was well under way. The bodies of our attackers were being gathered and carried out the front gates to be deposited in a temporary pile, after first being stripped in search of any identifying marks or items. So far nothing had been found, and I was not surprised— it stood to reason whoever ordered this travesty would not want anything remaining to link them to the sacrilege in any way. If Lord Yoshiie was correct, however, it would scarcely matter so far as his own opinion was concerned. The bodies of the actual priests were being treated with more respect. Cloth taken from the temple's storerooms was being used to make temporary coverings for them. As Kenji and I approached the gate to the nunnery, it was clear a similar procedure was in place there.

"I had to bruise the skull of one of Yoshiie's men who was, shall we say, being disrespectful. You may have to plead my case with his lord."

"Somehow I doubt it. It's more likely any complaint from the fellow would result in one more body on the outside pile, and probably not yours. Yoshiie has no intention of letting this opportunity go to waste. Such a lack of judgment on the part of one his men might endanger this."

Kenji scowled. "Opportunity . . . ? Oh. You mean the Shibata."

"Just so."

Kenji finally sighed. "Well, it stands to reason they'll want revenge. This isn't my temple, and *I* want revenge. Do you really believe Lord Tenshin was behind this?"

"I don't think Lord Yoshiie believes Lord Sadato would have sanctioned the attack if he had known the extent of the plan. Whereas I'm not convinced of Lord Tenshin's scruples about any detail necessary for removing the obstacle Lord Yoshiie represents. Still, so far we have found no evidence of *shikigami*. All our attackers left corpses and thus must have been human. Whatever I may think, there is no proof either way."

"Considering the timing, as you pointed out earlier, and the complexity, I would not have chosen *shikigami* to carry out this attack in the first place. And there are always provincial *bushi* for hire," Kenji pointed out. "Even so, it would certainly take a low or desperate lot to do this."

"All true," I said, but my mind was elsewhere. Perhaps *shikigami* were not directly involved, but Lord Tenshin would not have been taking advantage of all his resources if he had not used them in some capacity. But what? I had the feeling the answer was close by, if only I had the eyes to see it. At the moment, the answer was eluding me.

In some ways, the nunnery attached to the Yahiko temple was a mirror of its larger neighbor—there was a temple proper, plus a lecture hall, storerooms, and barracks for the residents. The survivors had been gathered into the lecture hall under guard, but to Kenji's—and my own—disappointment, no more had yet been located.

"Kenji—" I began, but he anticipated me.

"I understand. I believe I am needed elsewhere."

Kenji took his leave, and I sent the guard outside. I was left alone with the three surviving nuns. There was an old woman, at least in her sixties, with her head bowed, counting her prayer beads. Another was a young girl, perhaps no more than thirteen or so. She did not kneel but was rather curled up in a ball like a cat, slowly rocking back and forth, shivering. Someone had draped a coverlet over her, but it didn't seem to help. The third woman was my sister.

Rie had changed very little. She was a small, delicate-appearing woman. In her forties now, she was still as striking as her mother had been, as best I could remember—she had died when we were both very young. Rie's head was cowled in white cloth like the others, and I wondered how much gray was now in the night-black hair I remembered. I recognized her instantly, and she apparently did the same of me. I heard a faint gasp. In a moment she was on her feet and had grabbed me in what I imagined a bear hug to be like. I was having some trouble breathing.

"Goji-kun! Is it really you?"

"Elder Sister, you had best hope so," I said, attempting to make her ease her grip. "It would be unseemly for one of your station to be embracing strange men. It . . . it is good to see you."

For a moment it was as if we were both twelve again, and the horror that had just occurred was no more than a bad dream. We were the children of the same father but different mothers, and even though she was the elder, it was only by the space of a few months. We had been raised together, and she, like myself, had planned for a very different life before the disgrace and death of our father. When her mother died, Rie had been adopted by father's First Wife, my mother, as if she had been her own. Before my father's death, they had been discussing suitable marriages, but afterward my mother had taken holy orders, and Rie had made the decision to join her. My mother had barely lived another year as a nun before a pestilence took her.

Rie finally let go, and when she did, she staggered. I helped her kneel back down on one of the available cushions.

"Are you injured?"

"No. I'm just . . . ooh, my poor sisters . . . "

The guards had brought water, and I offered some to Rie, but she demurred. "I'm afraid I might not be able to keep it down. Perhaps later. We . . . we understood Lord Yoshiie would be making a pilgrimage here, but I never suspected you would be with him. You should have written me."

"There was no time, and too much chance of any letter being read by the wrong people. Besides, you know why I have kept my distance."

"I've never agreed with your reasoning," Rie said softly. "But I do understand it. Yet danger has found me anyway, has it not?"

I had no reply. Even as a child Rie had a knack for pointing out the obviously true things one might not want to admit. It was clear this was something about her which had not changed. "Lady Rie, we will speak of other matters later, but for right now I need to know what happened here. Anything you can tell me might be useful, however insignificant it may appear to you."

"The prioress sent me on an errand to Yahiko . . . " She paused and looked to the older woman. "Tomoko-ana? Do you know if she . . . ?"

She had addressed the old woman with the honorific for a woman who had taken holy orders, and I wondered if I should be thinking of my sister as "Rie-ana," since she had not adopted a new name for her new life, as so many others did. For her part, the old woman just looked down and continued fingering her prayer beads. She appeared to be weeping. Rie looked away. "I had just returned when the attack on the monastery began . . . and ended very quickly, it seems. The gate was barred, but one of those worthless men must have already been inside, because the next thing we knew, the gate was open and the murderers were among us. I didn't know what to do . . . I don't think any of us had time to really grasp what was happening. Some of the women didn't even run . . . I hid in a storage building, but our supplies were depleted—that's what I went to Yahiko about—and there was no good place to conceal myself. I heard the screams getting closer, I knew they were searching the buildings . . . I was certain I was going to die. But then everything stopped."

"What did you do then?" I asked.

"Nothing," Rie said. "I was too terrified to leave the storeroom, afraid someone would see me. I'm not sure how long I was in there . . . not long, I think, before I heard the fighting start up again. It must have been when Lord Yoshiie's party was attacked. Is he . . . ?"

"Lord Yoshiie wasn't harmed. Fortunately we detected the deception before the trap was fully sprung. But it was a close thing."

"I am grateful for his safety and for your own, brother. At least the cowards didn't get what they came for," Rie said.

While I did not have the greatest respect for our attackers, I would not have described them as cowards. Vicious, certainly, and without scruple or piety, to murder priests and nuns without hesitation, but cowards? They had to know their chances of carrying out their mission and withdrawing safely to Mutsu were slim at best. Even if they'd managed to wipe out Lord Yoshiie's personal guard as well as Yoshiie himself, that still left an entire *army* at the temple gates, most of it mounted and able to move swiftly and dominated by Minamoto loyalists keen on revenge. There was another, smaller gate on the east side, but no northern gate, and the east gate was in full view of the main road, so there would have been no means of escape

Unless . . .

"My sister, you said there must have been someone already inside the nunnery, but no one saw who it was or how they entered?"

"Yes." Rie frowned, and then she sifted positions to place herself next to the old nun. "Tomoko-ana, did you see anything? Please, it's important. Try to answer."

"I-I hid under the guest quarters," the old woman said finally. "When the gate was first barred. I didn't see what happened. I heard . . . oooh." Her voice dropped. "You can ask Mai-chan, but I don't think she's come back to herself yet."

That much was clear. The young nun still lay on her side, holding her knees, making no more sound than the occasional whimper. When Rie tried to touch her, the girl shied away from her, terror in her eyes. Rie sighed. "My brother, I'm afraid you'll learn nothing more from us for now. Perhaps if . . . when, Mai has had time to recover?"

I turned and summoned the guard back into the room. "I am

Lord Yamada, acting on behalf of Lord Yoshiie in this matter. What is your name and what are your instructions?"

The man bowed. "I am Hojo no Toshiro. I was to hold these women until they had been interrogated, and await further orders."

"Just so. Your orders now are simply this—you will continue your duties until you are relieved, but these women are not to be considered prisoners. You are here for their continued protection only. See they are provided with whatever necessities they may require. Understood?"

"Yes, Yamada-sama."

I spoke again to Rie. "I have matters to attend to, but for now I need you and your companions to stay together. Do what you can for Mai-chan, as I would still like to speak to her when possible. I will see you again, soon."

"Until then, go with Amada."

I went, but I wasn't sure if the Buddha had decided to join me or not. Back outside in the main compound, the grim work of gathering the bodies continued. I found Kenji serving in his priestly capacity by a row of draped bodies. "No other survivors among the priests?" I asked.

Kenji looked grim. "If there are, they are well-hidden indeed. Before you ask, I did have the walls inspected. There's no sign of a breach, and if anyone scaled the wall, they did it without so much as breaking a tile."

"Which doesn't mean it did not happen, but whoever did manage to get in was very skilled. I need to look for myself."

"Do you need my assistance?"

"I can see you are needed more here. I will send for you if my situation changes."

The bodies of the real monks were being moved into the main temple to join those of the murdered abbot and the other priest we'd discovered inside. Lord Yoshiie had withdrawn from the first hall and had commandeered the main lecture hall as a temporary headquarters. I presented myself to him there.

"Your men have located no other survivors?" I asked.

"None, I'm afraid. What did you find out from the nuns?"

I summarized what little I had learned from Rie and the elder nun. "The one called Mai is still overcome by the terror of what happened to her. If she comes back to herself, I will question her as well, but it's not likely she knows any more than we've already learned."

He sighed. "I was hoping for more."

I shared his disappointment. "Have your men found where the attackers entered?"

Yoshiie scowled. "I had assumed they came in through the main gate. It's normally not barred, and we know they were in disguise."

"In which case they would have knowingly committed suicide, whether they succeeded or not, as they must have known the only means of escape would be blocked by your army. While certainly conceivable, I think we should check out the alternative—they had another way out."

"Considering how close they came to accomplishing their mission, perhaps I have underestimated them," Lord Yoshiie said. He immediately summoned three of his *bushi* and ordered them to accompany me. I led them toward the rear of the compound where there were no buildings, only the trees which had taken it over. I felt my suspicions intensify.

"Was this area searched?"

"Yes, Lord Yamada," said the leader of the *bushi*, a stolid, forty-ish man named Akimasa. "Lord Yoshiie wanted to be certain we had accounted for all the fallen monks and any attackers who might have hidden themselves."

"And so you concentrated your efforts among the trees then? Not the wall?"

Akimasa frowned. "We did look for a breach, but that was all, my lord."

As I had surmised. "Spread out," I said to all three. "Search the wall and the area just under it."

Akimasa looked puzzled. "Your pardon, Lord Yamada, but what are we looking for?"

"Gentlemen, I promise you will know it if you find it."

It did not take long. One of the *bushi* discovered three long bamboo poles lying on the ground by the side of the wall nearly opposite the main gate. Each had an iron hook affixed to the end. "Does anyone know the purpose of these items?" Akimasa asked.

I picked one up and examined it. The pole was far too flimsy to support the weight of a man, so any idea I might have had of the assassins sliding down on them from the wall was easy to dismiss. Yet the hook on the end was suggestive. I took three steps back from the wall itself and looked up. At first I could see nothing but the tiled roof covering the top of the wall, but then I noticed a piece of rope barely visible above the roofline, I tested the flex of the pole.

"Let's see."

The pole was long enough to reach the top of the roofline,

and when I snapped it forward against the tiles, the hook swung around over it just like a fishing pole. When I pulled it back it was dragging a rope ladder. "There should be at least two more. Find them," I said.

The *bushi* took the other two bamboo poles, and in short order there were four rope ladders hanging down into the compound. I seized the first. "Follow me."

The command was a bit redundant. One of the younger *bushi* had reached the top of the wall before I was barely halfway up. "They were here," he said.

When I reached the top of the wall, I could see what he meant— the assassins had made an encampment within the shadow of the wall itself. While there was no sign of a fire, such proximity seemed rather reckless to me until I realized, judging from the undergrowth and tree litter nearby and the vines on the wall itself, this area of the compound was very lightly patrolled, if at all.

The attackers knew that. I'm beginning to think they knew nearly everything there was to know about this temple. They picked their spot and waited until the time was exactly right.

None of this should have been a surprise to me. It was likely the temple had been visited many times in the past by Abe partisans, and even guileless pilgrims would have had useful information to impart to someone more interested in tactical concerns than in the Yahiko temple's traveler facilities. The question still on my mind was how had they timed the attack so precisely? I had no answer for that.

The ladders had been spiked to the beams beneath the tile roof, but on the outside just past the apex, so they were inconspicuous from inside the compound itself. Clearly, they had used these to gain entry. Concealing them afterwards seemed a bit overcautious to me, but it was always possible that someone might stumble upon them and sound an alarm, plus the ability to hide the ladders after they had completed their mission would have slowed down any pursuers for the time it would have taken them to discover where the assassins had gone. In context, the attempted slaughter of everyone inside the temple compound made perfect sense; locking everyone within the nunnery instead would require posting guards since the gates were designed to be barred from the inside, not the outside, which would have cost them manpower they could not spare. Nor could the victims have been confined inside even the larger buildings, since none of those structures were designed to act as prisons and could be easily escaped, and in any case their shouts almost certainly would have been heard. No, the more I understood, the more it became clear to me the massacre of the priests and nuns had been dispassionately and ruthlessly calculated as the price for achieving Yoshiie's death. As much as I tried not to let my personal feelings intrude, I could see no other hand save Lord Tenshin's at work here.

I turned to Akimasa. "Please report what we have found to Lord Yoshiie. Also, have the walls of the nunnery searched. There should be at least one such ladder there. You two," I said to the other *bushi*, "are to come with me."

"Where are you going, in case Lord Yoshiie asks?"

"Where our would-be assassins intended to go, once they had your master's head."

I reached for the nearest rope ladder and clambered down the far side of the wall, and the other *bushi* quickly followed. After a moment of apparent uncertainty, Akimasa climbed back down into the compound to do as I had asked. Unlike the rope ladders meant to be lowered into the compound side, these had been anchored to the ground with spikes and were thus much easier to negotiate. Doubtless they had planned to leave them in place, as they could not be seen from within, simply pulling up the part hanging down into the compound, just as we had discovered them now.

We stood at the mouth of a deep ravine running through the hills surrounding the compound on the northwest side. We found sleeping blankets and food, and judging from the original size of casks and their remnants, it was clear the assassins had been in place for several days. A quick glance up left and right showed hillsides choked with trees and undergrowth with no paths visible—there was essentially no chance at all someone could have stumbled upon the assassin's encampment by accident.

I had assumed the assassins had planned to descend into the ravine after hiding their ladders again to throw off searchers and, while the Minamoto were still trying to figure out where the attackers could possibly have escaped to, been well on their way to the Mutsu barrier before the Minamoto had the presence of mind to send a force to cover the border. Yet the defile on the northeast side was nearly impassable, and even if the assassins could scale it, chances are they would have emerged into the open too close to the temple to avoid detection.

It's clear they did have a plan to escape, but in order to do so they would have to follow the ravine for some distance, and it's going the wrong way.

The ravine snaked through the trees, following the lines of the hills behind the temple, and that way lead to the northwest, away from the safety of the border. I wanted to know if the ravine changed direction farther on, and there was one quick way to find out.

"We're going hunting," I said to the two *bushi* accompanying me. "Be on your guard—we don't know if any of the assassins escaped the battle."

Not that I considered this likely. If any assassins had managed to escape the carnage, the sensible thing for them to do would have been to throw the bamboo poles back over the wall into the ravine once they had used them to retrieve the ladders. The poles wouldn't have been needed again, and removing them would have been the work of a moment or two at most and would have helped cover their escape. Granted, such a fine detail might have been missed in the heat of the moment by men running for their lives, so it was still best to be on guard.

I led the way along the ravine, looking for any signs of prior travel. I didn't have to look long. Runoff from the surrounding hills left the ravine muddy in some spots and sandy in others, and there were the prints of sandals in many places, all heading toward the temple, but none heading in the opposite direction. We kept moving, but neither the ravine's direction nor the difficulty of scaling its sides changed much, except possibly in the latter's case to become even more difficult, as the ravine began to deepen as we moved through it. Nor had the footprints ceased or shown a point of origin other than the way we were traveling. I became more and more convinced climbing out of the ravine this close to the temple had not been their plan. All that remained was to find where the ravine led and, more to the point, what we might discover there.

In time the wall on the northwest side of the ravine began to slant rather than dropping straight down. It would have been easy for the assassins to climb out now, but they would be on the wrong side of the temple and have to double back across the main road—far too risky an endeavor in such numbers. The trail of footprints we followed still pointed to an origin farther along in the ravine.

The younger of the two *bushi* stopped, sniffing the air like a deer. "Do you smell that, Yamada-sama?"

I did. And of all the things I might have expected to smell in this particular situation, this scent was not one of them. "That's the ocean."

The northwest coast of Echigo, famous in poetry and legend—I had not realized we were so close. We had not gone more than a bowshot farther before we could hear the muffled roar of the waves breaking on sand. Now the assassins' escape plan was suddenly clear. What wasn't clear was if there was anything else to gain from this knowledge.

"Stay here," I said. I went forward alone. The floor of the defile had already started to rise, and I could have climbed out to either side now, but I kept following the footprints. The defile ended on a high bluff overlooking the beach. I slipped forward carefully and kept hidden as best I could as I peered out toward the water. Below me I could see a steep but negotiable path down to the sand. Anchored about three bowshots offshore was a ship in the Chinese style, bearing no *mon* or other markers. On the beach itself, there were five boats, fishing skiffs by the look of them, beached but only enough to keep them from being carried out by a falling tide. It would take the work of only a few moments to get them underway, I estimated.

The sun was getting low in the sky. I heard voices, but at

first I saw no one. Then I realized the voices were coming from almost directly below me. Two men, fishermen from the look of them, had made camp under the lee of the bluff. I breathed a silent prayer of gratitude that I had heard them before they had spotted me, but apparently they had been gathering firewood from farther up the beach. They were an older and a younger man, possibly father and son from the resemblance. Their voices drifted up to me, and I listened.

" . . . how much longer?" said the younger.

"As long as it may take," said his companion. "Have some patience. There's no more reward if we leave without them."

"We should have heard something by now. And I do not trust those pirates," the younger man said, nodding at the ship.

"Perhaps there was a delay. As for the pirates, there's no need. They won't come ashore, and all we need do is see their boats safely launched once those men return. What happens to the fools then is not our concern."

"Likely they'll drown—you saw them when we brought them from the ship, there's not one among them who knows how to handle a skiff. We already have their gold for arranging the boats. I say we leave now and save our heads."

"They promised us double, son. So your father says we *will* wait, and that's an end to it."

So that man is your father. Well, you are wiser than he is, for all the good it would have done you. I do not think those men would have left either of you alive if they had returned.

I carefully pulled myself away from the edge of the bluff and made my way back to where the two *bushi* were waiting. "Gentlemen, bring your bows. Quietly, if you please."

We slipped back to the edge of the bluff. I considered the matter for a moment, then had one of the *bushi* fire an arrow which struck within inches of the older man's feet. Startled, the two immediately glanced up, to find me and my two companions, one of whom already had his second arrow nocked.

"Gentlemen, you may not believe me when I tell you this, but as of now, you are both potentially lucky men. And in case you were thinking of running, I would advise against it. As you've seen, these men are very good archers," I said clearly. "Kindly wait for me."

I made my way down the trail, followed by one of the archers. The second *bushi* remained on the bluff, his bow ready in case the men decided to test us. That proved unnecessary. The two fishermen had immediately kneeled and placed their faces to the sand. The *bushi* with me now had an arrow ready as well.

"Sit up," I said. "I can't talk to you if you're buried in the sand like crabs."

Blinking, they obeyed, and the terror in their eyes would have been proof enough of their fear, even if they were not shaking so. I didn't mind. Fear was sometimes a useful tool, and I fully intended to make use of it now.

"As I see matters, you two have a problem," I said. "If I take you back with me to the temple, the only question in regards to your fate is whether Lord Yoshiie or the Chief of the Shibata Clan or the governor of Echigo will have the privilege of ordering your torture and execution. Any delay would only last as long as it took those three to agree on the matter."

The older man could barely speak. "But . . . my lord, we have done nothing!"

"You mean other than assisting in an attempted assassination of the Minamoto Clan chief's son and the slaughter of priests and nuns in holy orders? You were hired to land those men and then see them safely back to their pirate transport, were you not? If you deny it again, this conversation is at an end."

I was not bluffing about delivering the pair of them to Yoshiie. Distasteful as such an action would be, the slaughter I had witnessed at the Yahiko temple and the near-loss of my own sister had put me in the right frame of mind to carry it out.

"My lord," said the younger man, "What did you say about Yahiko temple . . . ?"

"Slaughter," I repeated, being very careful to enunciate each syllable. "Almost everyone who had resided at the temple is now dead. Murdered by your friends."

"They were not our friends!" the old man said. "We were hired—" he stopped.

I smiled then. "No, please continue."

The old man took a long, slow breath, apparently trying to calm himself. "It's true, we were hired to get several men ashore here, but we did not know who they were or what they intended."

"We had no idea they meant to attack the temple!" the young man said. "We didn't know . . . "

"You land a heavily armed group of men at the back door of a temple with few defenses. What did you think was going to happen? Or were you thinking only of the gold?"

Their silence was answer enough. I was not entirely without sympathy, since I understood what desperation mixed with greed could make a man do. I had only one more question. "The

141

ravine in this bluff isn't visible from the sea. Did you tell them about it? Did you hand them the lives of those innocents?"

"We barely spoke to them, or they to us. They seemed to know exactly where they were going, and they made straight for the path up to the ravine," the younger man said. "Only one man returned, but he ordered us to wait for the rest, which we were doing. My lord, I swear this is true."

"What about the man who returned?"

"He was well-dressed, and thin . . . a bit hawkish about the face. He appeared to be in command. We rowed him back to the ship. I don't remember much else about him, except I had the impression he might have been ill. He seemed a bit feverish."

The possible illness was interesting enough, and the man he was describing certainly sounded like Lord Tenshin, but this was hardly proof. I had clearly learned everything I was going to learn from the fisherman. The only thing I had now to consider was whether I believed him. I decided I did. It would have been easy enough to miss one man's track returning to the sea among so many going the other direction.

In order for the attempt to work, they had to already know about the ravine. All their planning depended upon it.

"Get out of my sight," I said. "If I see either of you again, ever, I will make you wish I'd handed you over to Lord Yoshiie. Do you understand me?"

Apparently they did. They took to their heels and had soon disappeared toward the north. The younger of the two archers frowned. "My lord, was it wise to let them go?"

"Perhaps not," I said, "but killing them would have gained us nothing. We have greater prey to hunt."

Out on the water, the pirate ship was unfurling its sails. If the ones who had planned the attack did not yet know it had failed, they soon would. For the moment there was little to do save to find out if Lord Yoshiie's diplomatic skills were as well honed as the ones he used for fighting the enemies of the Emperor. We made our way back to the temple wall and climbed over the wall to find Akimasa waiting for us.

"I was about to go after you when I heard you returning. Did you find anything, my lord?"

"Just a pair of foolish fishermen and the boats the assassins had planned to escape in. And a Chinese pirate ship."

Akimasa put his hand on his sword hilt as if the pirates were coming up the ladder behind us. "Pirates?!"

"So I surmise, but they were leaving, so of no concern. Have you completed your search of the nunnery walls?"

Akimasa relaxed a little, but he still seemed somewhat nervous. "Yes, my lord. We even had some of our more nimble companions scale the walls and examine every inch of them from the roof itself."

"How many ladders did you find there?"

"There were no ladders, my lord," Akimasa said.

"None? You're certain?"

"Yes, Lord Yamada. As I said, we were very thorough."

That was curious. I had expected the attacker who had opened the gate to the nunnery had used the same method to gain entry as his companions, but apparently this was not the case. Still, the trees did grow close to the wall there. It was entirely possible one had simply climbed over. Most likely it wasn't important, in the scope of things, but it was something which didn't quite make sense, and such things worried me like a splinter one could feel but not quite locate.

"I believe I need to take another look at the gate to the nunnery," I said.

"Forgive me, my lord, but the mention of the pirates distracted me. The reason I was going to follow you is Lord Yoshiie wants to see you."

"Then obviously I must answer his summons before I do anything else." I bowed to all three men. "Thank you for your assistance."

I made my way to the lecture hall as quickly as I could, since I knew Lord Yoshiie was not a man who liked to be kept waiting. On the way there I saw a flash of white in the trees, no more, but I knew, when my immediate business with Lord Yoshiie was done, there was yet another person requiring my presence, but I considered it fortunate. I had questions for Lady Kuzunoha as well, and this way it would not be necessary for me to go looking for her. I just hoped the answers were ones we could both live with.

CHAPTER EIGHT

LORD YOSHIIE awaited me in the lecture hall, and as I expected, he was not alone. I had already seen *bushi* bearing the Shibata *mon* on the grounds assisting Lord Yoshiie's men with the bodies, though there was little left for them to do save stand watch. I got a glimpse of Kenji, but didn't attempt to speak to him. Unless there was another in Lord Yoshiie's levy I didn't know about, Kenji was the only living priest now available, so it would fall to him to see the proper funeral rites were observed until more clerics could be summoned.

Lord Yoshiie and his visitor sat on cushions on the dais, where the former abbot or higher ranking priests would recite the sutras or lecture in happier times. I found a cushion on the floor in front of them, kneeled, and bowed low.

"Lord Shibata no Marumasa, may I present my counselor, Lord Yamada."

I almost smiled. *Counselor?* Well, I had to admit it *was* a far better designation than "unwanted baggage the royal family forced on me," and perhaps indicative of my improved standing in Lord Yoshiie's estimation. I hoped I wasn't about to make him doubt his judgment.

"It is an honor," I said.

The chief of the Shibata Clan was a youthful-seeming man

whom I knew to be in his middle fifties. He had managed to keep the Shibata uninvolved with the struggles against the Abe Clan until now, but I had the feeling the situation was about to change and indeed already had.

"Lord Yamada," he said. "I have heard of you."

I could only imagine what he had heard and how much of it was true. Judging from his expression, very little of it, true or not, appeared to be in my favor.

"Akimasa reported the ladders. Did you find anything else?"

I told them about our trek through the ravine, the boats, and the—likely—pirate vessel in the Echigo coastal waters. "I believe their plan was to skirt the coast past the northern border of Dewa. They could have returned to Mutsu on its northern coast. Or . . . "

Lord Shibata frowned. "Or?"

"Or just as likely the pirates would have murdered the lot of them and claimed any reward for themselves. As the assassins failed in their mission, it is a moot point."

I deemed it prudent not to mention the fishermen. If Lord Yoshiie needed a target for his anger, it was best directed toward his actual enemies.

"Not everyone knew about the ravine," Lord Muramasa said. "Nor was the normal sort of pilgrim who came to the temple likely to discover it. There had been a small gate placed there, but it had been sealed over for many years."

This was something I had not known. "If you will forgive my asking, why was it sealed?"

The older man smiled then. "In my grandfather's time it was planned as a means of escape in case the temple was attacked by bandits or the Emishi, who raided much farther south in those days. Yet the abbot discovered it was mostly being used by priests who wished to avoid their dietary restrictions by buying fish from the locals . . . or for even less appropriate meetings. He had the gate removed and the gap sealed."

"So whoever ordered the attack on Lord Yoshiie had to know about the ravine beforehand. It was a crucial part of their plan."

Lord Muramasa raised an eyebrow. "What are you implying?"

I bowed again. "My lord, no one would either consider or believe for a moment your clan would have any part of an attack on its own holy temple. I merely meant Lord Yoshiie's movements have been precisely tracked, and however this is being accomplished, our enemies were also supplied with the layout of the temple, including the best means of sudden and secret entry."

"I have faith in my scouts, but they have found nothing. How could this be done?" Lord Yoshiie asked.

"This question is puzzling me as well, my lords. I do intend to find the answer."

"Regardless, we know who is ultimately responsible," Lord Yoshiie said.

"I can hardly believe this outrage," Lord Muramasa said, and his anger and bewilderment were both evident. "The Shabata Clan's relation with the Abe have never been warm, but to do this? I would not have believed it possible. Yet the evidence is overwhelming."

Evidence?

Obviously, the arrow of guilt pointed directly at the Abe, but that was only common sense, not proof. I wanted to ask what evidence he was referring to but, as with the fishermen, I considered it best to keep silent, at least until I had the chance to find other sources of information.

"Lord Muramasa and I have much to discuss," Lord Yoshiie said. "Please inform me if there is any change in your understanding."

The dismissal was clear and I took my leave. Outside, now and then one could still hear the crows calling to one another, but the covering of the bodies had seemed to discourage them, and there were fewer in the trees now. I immediately went searching for Kenji. As I did so, I spotted Lord Yasuna some distance away, standing with a group of Shibata *bushi* as if he were just one more member of the honor guard over the bodies. His expression was as melancholy as any I'd ever seen on a human being. Naturally, I would have expected one of his cultured sensibilities to be shocked and outraged by what had happened here, but I saw no sign of it now, just a profound melancholy. I should have taken the time then to speak to him, but I had more pressing business. I found Kenji working among the dead, calmly and methodically washing a corpse.

"If I were a follower of the Way of the Gods, this would render me ritually impure for a month or more," he said. "As it is, this is merely distasteful. But there is no one else, at least for the men."

"What about those unfortunate women in the nunnery?"

"Your sister and the nun Tomoko-ana have assumed this duty . . . for which I owe her a great deal. I'm not sure I could have borne it."

"I'm sure my sister would have preferred an occupation to sitting idle," I said.

"She said the same when she informed me of what she was going to do. Not asked, mind you. Informed. Not that I would have objected. Where have you been?"

I repeated to Kenji what I had told Lord Yoshiie, only this time I didn't leave out the part about the fishermen. He just grunted.

"I don't think they deserved to keep their heads, and such foolish behavior will catch up with them sooner rather than later," Kenji said. "Yet for what little it matters, I agree with your actions."

"Regardless, they are not our concern. We know the Abe, at least indirectly, were responsible for the attack. Yet so far we haven't found any sign that *shikigami* were involved, or indeed anything which would point directly to the *onmyoji* working for Lord Sadato. I had believed there was no proof of the Abe's involvement. Lord Muramasa indicated there was. Do you know what he was talking about?"

"I believe I do. Come with me."

Kenji led me farther into the compound where three bodies lay wrapped in white cloth, and nearby a fourth, only it had been draped over with bloodstained robes, not carefully wrapped in clean cloth like the others. "All the attackers had shaved heads, so with both assassins and priests in a similar state of bloody mess, at first glance it was hard to tell them apart. No one realized this man was in priestly robes. Since the only men who were so garbed were our attackers, by rights he should have been dumped in the pile outside with the other assassins. If this had happened, it is likely no one would have known. I had already started my ritual cleansing when I noticed it myself."

"Noticed what?"

"This."

Kenji uncovered the man's lower half. At first I didn't see anything other than a gaping cut, but then I saw his pubic hair. "It's red?" It wasn't blood, I knew. It was the wrong shade of red, and blood would have turned black by now in any case.

"Red. This man was an Emishi."

The barbarians' hair color varied from very light to dark, but a light red was not uncommon. "Was there just this one?"

"No. Now that I knew what to look for, I did look, and it was clear at least three more attackers were Emishi. Their features are slightly different from the others, but under the circumstances no one noticed. I reported this to Lord Yoshiie."

"So the attackers did come from Mutsu," I said.

"There is no doubt at all. What I still don't understand is why."

"Isn't it obvious? To kill Lord Yoshiie."

He sighed. "That's not what I meant. What I don't understand is why they would risk using Emishi in the first place, even if it was only three or four of the lot. Their presence is a direct link to Mutsu!"

"True," I said. "But think about it—if the attack succeeded? No trace of the attackers to be found, and no one could prove that Mutsu was involved. Even if the Shibata suspected Mutsu and wanted revenge, now they would be on their own. With Yoshiie dead, his father would have had difficulty continuing, and the Emperor's writ would likely be rescinded if the campaign failed. The other *bushi* would have returned to their homes, leaving Mutsu unmolested for at least a year or more. Plenty of time to strengthen their position and work on alliances before a new military governor could be appointed. It's possible the Emperor's government would have been forced to come to terms with the Abe rather than punishing them."

"But the attack did *not* succeed," Kenji pointed out.

"Again true, but the nature of the plan meant the Shibata Clan would be left with a violated clan temple and a strong desire for revenge on whoever was responsible. This would be more than enough incentive to finally join the Minamoto cause, and proof be sodded. That there *is* proof is almost beside the point, and if the *Emishi* warriors were available, no reason not to use them. If the plan failed, it failed utterly, and the presence or absence of the barbarians changes nothing. No, Kenji, what interests me now is the reasoning behind the attempt."

"Other than killing Yoshiie would likely, as you just pointed out, end the war? It has been going on, with minor interruptions, for nearly twelve years!"

"But why take the risk? Lord Sadato has bested Yoshiie in the field before. It's not impossible he might do so again. This possibility had to be weighing on the minds of all *bushi* who have joined the Minamoto. The forces we've picked up along the way have, for the most part, been little more than tokens. This is about to change—drastically, I wager."

"The Shibata?"

"Not just the Shibata. If the governor of Echigo doesn't at least double his intended levy, I'll be amazed. Then there are the temples in Echigo and Dewa. Once they learn of this outrage— and you can be certain Lord Yoshiie will see they *do* learn— likely they will send their lay-brother warriors, the *sohei,* to join us as well. How long will the funeral rites take? The Shibata will insist on a delay until that is done, almost certainly."

"More than a month, under normal circumstances, but Lord Yoshiie has already sent messengers to the closest temples. They will be sending additional priests to handle the prayers and to take over the proper functioning of the temple itself for the time being, so all will be handled appropriately and respectfully enough to satisfy the Shibata, I think. We will be able to continue to Dewa once the initial rites are concluded . . . probably a week or two at most."

"More than enough time for Lord Yoshiie to pick up even more support. This ill-conceived attack is likely to mean the complete destruction of the Abe Clan. There was potential benefit, but nothing compared to what the Abe stood to lose. Lord Sadato, by all accounts, is neither a fool nor reckless. So again I must wonder—why take this risk?"

Kenji rubbed the stubble on his head. "I can't fault your expression of the matter, and if what you say is true, then there are only three possibilities I can see. The first is the Abe Clan's situation is worse than we were led to believe, and this was an act of pure desperation."

"Possible, but unlikely," I said.

"The second is this plan was conceived and carried out without either Lord Sadato's knowledge or approval."

"Possible," I admitted. "Perhaps even likely. What's the third alternative?"

"One which does not necessarily exclude the second, unfortunately. The alternative that concerns me the most—the possibility the plan to assassinate Lord Yoshiie has not failed. Yet."

I frowned. "You suspect other conspirators, unknown to us?"

Kenji sighed. "I suspect nothing. I simply remember

something an occasionally wise man once said to me. He told me to be on my guard. When I asked him why, he essentially said 'because there was no reason to do so.'"

I almost laughed. "I believe I've met the fellow, Master Kenji. But I would never call him wise."

"Be that as it may, we now believe the worst is behind us, Lord Yamada. What if we're wrong?"

I started to argue the point, but it occurred to me my own advice might have some merit. "Then let us be on our guard," I said. "Always."

I left Kenji to his grim duty and crossed into the nunnery, where I found my sister Rie and Tomoko-ana likewise engaged. The first guard was no longer there, but another kept watch at a respectful distance.

"I don't wish to intrude—"

Rie dismissed my remark. "Under the circumstances, we will not ask for your assistance—not out of delicacy, as our sister nuns are no longer concerned with such trivialities—but because I know my brother, even after all these years. You did not come here to assess our progress, did you?"

My sister, as I remembered, was just as blunt of speech as ever, but she wasn't wrong. "I still need to speak to the nun called Mai," I said. "Is she any better?"

"Brother, you will have to judge for yourself, but there was no change when we left her to assume this sad duty," Rie said. "Just so you understand the situation better, Mai-chan has not yet taken holy orders. She was offered to the temple as a servant by parents who could no longer care for her. Such things happen far too often with girls of poor families. She was only fortunate they didn't choose to sell her to a brothel instead. Our prioress took her in with the understanding she would make her own choice when the time came . . . which now, may never come."

I considered this. "Thank you. We will talk later, when both of our obligations allow."

I bowed to the women and proceeded to the building where the three surviving nuns were being housed. The guard acknowledged me and I went inside. I came back out onto the veranda immediately.

"Where is she?"

"Who—" the guard started to ask, but then he hurried past me and peered into the interior. "How did she escape?" he asked.

It took us only a moment more to discover the shuttered window, now closed but unlatched. *Difficult to force from the outside, but simplicity itself to open from the inside.* Any suspicion I'd had that Mai had been taken against her will evaporated. Mai had apparently recovered her senses well enough to work out an escape, but the *how* of it barely concerned me. I wanted and needed to know *why.* When we came back outside, Rie and Tomoko-ana were waiting for us.

"What has happened? Where is Mai?" Rie asked.

"Gone, and apparently of her own volition," I said.

"The child is not in her right mind," Tomoko-ana said. "She must be found before she comes to harm."

I wanted to say she could not have gone far, but in truth she could have vanished the moment Rie and Tomoko left her alone, and they had been at their work, judging from their progress, for hours. "Is there another way out of the compound?"

"We have another door in the wall," Rie said. "We use it for errands."

I had an idea. "Could it have been used to get one of the assassins into the compound?"

Rie was adamant. "No. It was always barred from the inside, the same as the main gate. Since they somehow got our connecting gate open, there would have been no need to unbar both of them."

What Rie said made perfect sense, and there was still no answer as to how the assassin had gotten inside. I put the question aside for the more immediate concern. "Show me."

Rie and Tomoko-ana led me to the far side of the nunnery compound. There was a small but strong door, almost a second gate, set in the wall. Only it was not barred and halfway open. I saw a small footprint in the dirt just beyond it. I looked out. There was a small road going north and south, beyond that wooded hillsides, but no sign of Mai. "Why would she run?" I asked. "The danger is past."

"She may not understand this. It is as Tomoko-ana said," Rie replied. "Her mind is clouded by fear. Who can say what she was thinking? But we need to find her before . . . before anything more happens to the poor girl. She is simply not capable of fending for herself in her current state."

"Leave this to me," I said, as I closed the door and picked up the bar and put it back into place. "For now, keep this door barred and continue with what needs to be done. I will let you know as soon as she's found."

"We must depend on you, brother," Rie said. "Please, find Mai-chan for us."

The sun was getting lower in the sky, which was more than enough reason to hurry. I commandeered two *bushi* who looked as if they needed something to do. I told them who we were searching for and, once the trail from the nunnery had proved impossible to follow, sent one on the road north toward the ocean and the other south toward the town of Yahiko. For myself, I crossed the road and entered the trees of the hillside. I didn't necessarily expect to find Mai there, but I knew I would find someone.

I had barely reached the crest of the first wooded hill when Lady Kuzunoha appeared there. I sometimes forgot just how beautiful she was in her human form. What I never intended to forget was what she really was under the mask of humanity she wore. A mask, I knew, she often wore merely to humor ones such as myself. It was only when she spoke of Lord Yasuna I felt as if she secretly wished with all her heart her human mask was real.

"Lord Yamada," she said without any preamble, "what is the matter with Lord Yasuna?"

"I don't understand what you mean," I said. "I saw your lord just before I left the temple compound. He was in good health and certainly, to my best knowledge, under no threat of any kind."

"Did he not seem . . . disturbed to you? Or did you notice?"

"Actually, he seemed sad. A thing not to be overly wondered at, I would think, considering what happened in the temple, as I'm sure you're aware."

"I know what happened there," she said. "And before you ask me, no, I was not involved in the attempt on Lord Yoshiie's life."

I was about to set foot in dangerous territory, but I didn't see any way around it. "Lady Kuzunoha, surely you cannot be indifferent in this? We both understand it would be to your advantage for Lord Yoshiie's mission to fail. If he falls, the attack against the Abe is thwarted, and Lord Yasuna will be able to return home."

"If Yoshiie succeeds, the result is the same," Lady Kuzunoha pointed out. She smiled then. "Yet my lord returns to the capital much faster and is less exposed to the hazards of war if Lord Yoshiie were to meet with fatal misfortune sooner rather than later, and I will not pretend to weep if it happens, but neither do I seek it. I have been honest with you in this regard, Lord Yamada, and I will continue to be so. I expect the same from you."

"Very well, then I must ask—did you know an attack was planned?"

"I did not. Before today I had not so much as crossed this road. I had planned to avoid the temple altogether. There is something . . . something not right there." She said, hesitantly. I was not used to Lady Kuzunoha being hesitant, and it worried me.

"There would have been a large number of assassins pretending to be priests," I said.

She looked at me with the vaguely pitying look I had seen from her at our first meeting, many years before. "There is no 'would have been,' Lord Yamada. There is nothing 'past.' Whatever was wrong there is *still* wrong. My concern for my lord brought me there so I could see him with my own eyes, and I do not regret that, but I will not go there again except either to save or avenge him."

"What are you talking about? What is wrong?"

"I do not know," she said. "But I should not have to tell you my fox-demon senses are much more refined than your own, and there is something unnatural about the place. If you really want to protect Lord Yoshiie, I'd advise him to continue to Dewa province without delay."

I knew this would not be possible, at least not yet. Decorum and proper respect was crucial when building alliances, which Lord Yoshiie was in the process of doing even as Lady Kuzunoha and I met. There was no chance he would risk failure at such an important task based on what was no more than a suspicion. I would have told Lady Kuzunoha the same, but her attention had already shifted.

"I wanted to see you because of my concern for Lord Yasuna. Something is troubling him. I can sense this, even as I sense what is waiting within the temple grounds now. I would understand anger or fear, perhaps, in this situation, but sadness? This I do not understand. I-I want you to find out what is making him so sad."

It seemed Lady Kuzunoha was as confused by Lord Yasuna's reaction as I was. "He may not confide in me, but I will do my best, I promise. In return, however, I am in need of a favor from you."

She frowned. "What is it?"

"Sometime this afternoon a young woman named Mai disappeared from the community of nuns. I need your help to find her, and before dark if possible. She is . . . confused, somewhat, by what has occurred."

Lady Kuzunoha smiled. "Confused? If she sought escape I'd call her mind clearer than the lot of yours. Regardless, there are *youkai* and worse lurking in these woods, so it would probably be best she is among her own kind. At least they—so far as I know—do not wish to make a meal of her. Show me where I can find her scent."

That wasn't as straightforward a matter as I would have liked. In order to properly catch the scent, Lady Kuzunoha would need to do it in her true fox-demon form without attracting attention, and there was an army camped outside the temple now. Fortunately, decorum—and Lord Yoshiie's orders—had kept the bulk of the men away from the northwest side of the compound where the nunnery was located. We chose our moment and slipped across the road to the back gate.

"There are many scents," Lady Kuzunoha said, her muzzle twitching.

"You'll be looking for the most recent."

I had been careful not to disturb the tracks Mai had left there, and it took only a few more moments before Lady Kuzunoha had isolated Mai's spoor. "This way," she said.

We crossed the road again, and Lady Kuzunoha led us back into the wooded hills, but in a slightly different direction, further north and west than where we had met.

"Why did she flee? Do you know?" Lady Kuzunoha asked. I have no idea how she was able to form human words with a fox's muzzle, but during the time I'd known her, the ability had been apparent.

"I did say she wasn't in her right mind."

The fox sighed. "So you did, which explains nothing. When the rational mind fails, there is still instinct, even in humans. Instinctive reactions are simple and direct, and so are what triggers them—hunger, pain, lust, but most of all, fear."

"Perhaps, but fear of what? The danger was past, so far as she knew."

"She is apparently of a different opinion on the matter, would be my guess," Lady Kuzunoha said. "Ah. This way . . . and you brought your sword. Excellent."

"Excellent? Why?"

"Because we are not the only ones trailing your fleeing maiden. I suggest we hurry if you want her returned alive."

We picked up our pace, but there was a limit to how fast we could move through the woods without risking losing the scent. The trail led into a defile not unlike the one on the opposite side of the temple, only this one led us up into the space between two large hills rather than down into a ravine.

"I hear them," Lady Kuzunoha said. "Follow me!"

That proved difficult, as Lady Kuzunoha in her fox-demon form was faster than the fastest courier who ever ran. But I did manage to keep her in sight until she disappeared into the undergrowth about a bowshot ahead of me. I forced my way through the bushes, getting several scratches on my hands and forearms in the process. When I emerged again into the open, I found Lady Kuzunoha standing stock still just a few paces into the clearing. Just ahead of us I saw Mai with her back pressed against the rocks where the defile dead-ended against a sheer rock wall. Apparently she'd been trying to climb it when her pursuers, including us, had caught up to her. To the left was what appeared to be an elegant lady in long robes. To the right was a stubby little creature, outwardly a man, on all fours and completely naked, with no head. It had what looked like its rear end pointed straight at Mai.

"Why didn't you—" I began, but then I realized why Lady Kuzunoha had not leaped to the girl's defense. "Oh."

"I would just have frightened her more," Lady Kuzunoha said as she reassumed her human form. "You take care of this."

I sighed and calmly walked between Mai and the two *youkai*. It was as I expected—the thing with a woman's form had a face completely blank, as if her eyes, nose, and mouth were covered by skin. The naked torso and legs had a single eye where by rights its arse-hole should have been.

A noppera-bō and a shirime. I drew my sword, but I didn't even bother to swing it. "Shoo. Both of you. Now."

They didn't need much goading. Such creatures lived to startle and frighten the unwary, but Mai was already frightened, and their weird appearance was not having much additional effect. The *youkai* clearly were not getting the reaction they'd expected from me, either, so they emitted chittering laughter as if their tricks had worked anyway and then faded like wraiths into the bushes. I put my *tachi* back in its scabbard. "It's all right, Mai-chan. They're just trickster creatures—a little startling in appearance, but completely harmless. You're lucky it wasn't an ogre."

Mai just pressed her back tighter against the rock face. Her eyes darted left and right, and apparently she decided on right. I barely managed to catch her arm as she tried to dash away. She tried to bite my hand, and I managed to pin her and then hold her at arm's length as I looked directly into the terror in her eyes. "You're *safe* now. Stop fighting me!"

I was a little surprised when she did just that. I felt her relax in my arms. "I'm going to let you go now, Mai. Please don't try to run again."

I did so, and she did not run. She sank to her knees for a moment and then bowed forward, but she wasn't bowing to either me or Lady Kuzunoha, who was merely watching the scene with polite curiosity.

"In case you're wondering, Lord Yamada, the girl is still terrified, I can smell it. She's just given up. Resigned herself to her fate."

"Resigned? To what?"

Lady Kuzunoha looked puzzled. "If I didn't know better, I would think she has resigned herself to death. Lord Yamada, the poor girl thinks you're going to kill her!"

I could hardly believe it, but then Mai reached up and pulled her hair—too long, I finally noticed, for a proper nun's tonsure— to the side, exposing her slim neck, and I knew that Lady Kuzunoha was right. Mai was waiting to die. *Expecting* to die.

"This is very interesting," Lady Kuzunoha said. "Lord Yamada, what did you do to the poor girl?"

I glared at the fox-demon. "Other than chase her through the woods so she doesn't end up as a ogre's dinner? Nothing, I swear."

She smiled then. "Don't swear to me, Lord Yamada—it's none of my concern either way. But if the girl has no reason to be afraid of you, I'd suggest finding out why she is, if you can. It might be important to know."

I kneeled down. Mai shuddered when I took her shoulders, and I raised her up and forced her to look at me. "Mai-chan, I know you have been through a lot, but you are safe now, I promise. I am not going to hurt you, and I'm not going to let anyone else do so."

One thing I realized right away, looking into the girl's eyes, was something I had not understood until then—Mai was no mere frightened animal, with her mind unhinged and unable to comprehend—I knew she heard me and understood what I was saying to her. What she seemed to be having a problem with was in believing what I told her. "Girl, think. If I wanted you dead, you would be dead now. So why are you still alive?"

Her mouth moved then, but no words came out. After a moment she just looked at me. I wasn't sure if what I was seeing then was actual hope, but it was no longer the panic and terror I had seen before. Her mouth moved again, and I could see the struggle on her face, but she still could produce no sound, not even a whimper. She tried once more, and there were tears streaming down her face.

"I hope we can speak later," I said, "but for now, it's all right. You'll speak when you're ready, but it's getting dark. We need to get back to the temple."

She shied away then, briefly. "You are under my protection from this moment on, Mai-chan. Nothing there is going to hurt you, I promise."

"Be certain you keep your word, Lord Yamada," Lady Kuzunoha said. "I don't think you'll get a second chance with this one."

Mai let me lead her out of the woods. Lady Kuzunoha accompanied us to the edge of the trees but no farther. "Remember your promise to me," she said and then vanished into the shadowed forest.

I knew the nunnery gate would still be barred, so I took Mai through the main gate. We got several interested looks from the *bushi* quartered nearby, but no one tried to interfere. I had intended to take Mai back to the nunnery to place her in the care of my sister and the nun Tomoko, but as soon as I started in that direction, she hung back and started to resist me.

"What is it, Mai? What's wrong?"

Again, silence, but now the girl was pressed against my back, holding on to my *hitatare* as if I were the only thing to cling to and there was some abyss waiting to swallow her below. "Oh. You remember what happened there, don't you? It's all right now, the assassins are dead. You're safe."

Mai clearly wasn't convinced, and the more I tried to take her in toward the nunnery, the more panicked she became. I finally gave up and accepted the inevitable. I moved again, this time toward the lecture hall, and Mai followed me without resistance. I found Kenji resting under a tree. He looked as drained and weary as I felt.

"Who is your charming shadow?" he asked.

"Her name is Mai. She is a survivor of the massacre in the nunnery. It would appear her memories of that tragedy are too vivid to allow her to return there, at least for now."

"Hello, Mai-chan," Kenji said. Mai just moved a little closer behind me and Kenji grunted. "A shy one. What do you plan to do about her?"

I'd been giving the matter some thought as well and could manage just one conclusion. "The only thing I can do, I'm afraid."

I saw one of Lord Yoshiie's messengers nearby and called him over. "As I am otherwise obligated, I need you to deliver a message to Lady Rie in the nunnery. Can you do this for me?"

"I am at your service, Lord Yamada. What is the message?"

"Tell my sister that Mai has been found and is safe," I said, "but for the time being, she must remain under my protection."

Kenji raised an eyebrow, but the courier merely bowed and left to deliver my message. "Now then, before you say anything on the matter, this is strictly until Mai-chan has recovered from her trauma. Once she's feeling better, I expect her to return to the nunnery, or possibly to another such establishment, I suppose, depending upon what the Shibata decide about the further operation of the temple."

"I have no direct information," Kenji said, "but if they do not re-establish Yahiko-ji as it was, perhaps with the addition of a large contingent of *sohei*, I will be surprised. But the three of us will be in close quarters in the rooms Lord Yoshiie has allocated to us. What shall I say if anyone asks about Mai?"

"Say she's my servant. There is a small storeroom off the same corridor, no more uncomfortable than our own arrangements. Mai can sleep there."

"You've never taken on a servant in your life, Lord Yamada."

"And I haven't now, but I need an excuse to keep the girl close to me until this . . . situation, is resolved."

I told Kenji what Lady Kuzunoha had said. "You're sure you haven't sensed anything?"

"Nothing at all," Kenji said. "It's possible the spiritual defilement of this place is dulling my senses . . . either that, or I am very tired. We will start the funeral fires soon, and I have some assistance arriving tomorrow, I am informed. If they are priests attached to the Shibata Clan, likely they'll just take over, so perhaps I can start looking for this *wrongness* Lady Kuzunoha spoke of. But at the moment I need sleep. Badly."

"Let's find something to eat first. I'm sure Mai is as famished as I am."

"No problem there. I received a large gift of rice and two bolts of silk from Lord Yoshiie today."

I was not surprised. Lord Yoshiie was not one to overlook a detail. Neither, I hoped, was I. "By the way, on the subject of Mai-chan, Master Kenji . . . "

He just grinned. "I know what you're going to say, Lord Yamada. Do not worry—Mai-chan is safe with me. Or safe *from* me, however you choose to look at it."

I smiled then. "I'm glad we understand one another."

"How could it be otherwise?" Kenji asked. "We know each other too well."

CHAPTER NINE

THE NUN TOMOKO appeared by the screen which led to our quarters the next morning. She was holding a small bundle tied up in a square piece of blue cloth. "I've brought some things for Mai-chan," she said. "Would . . . would it be possible to see her?"

I saw no reason to object, but considering Mai's reaction to returning to the nunnery, I wondered if her reluctance might extend to anyone who had shared the ordeal with her. As we opened the sliding door, I soon learned this was not the case.

Mai awoke, but rather than shying away, she seemed genuinely happy to see the old woman. Even so, Tomoko-ana had no more luck drawing speech from the girl than I did. The old woman kept her visit short, but just before Tomoko-ana left, she took me aside.

"Perhaps Mai would like to send Lady Rie a written message?" I asked. "I can find some ink and paper." I had planned to do so anyway, on the assumption Mai would perhaps be able to answer some questions if she could write her answers rather than trying to find her voice.

Tomoko-ana smiled her gap-toothed smile. "I'm afraid Mai's parents were illiterate, and she never learned to read or write. We had planned to teach her, but she hadn't been with us for very long. I understand from Lady Rie that Mai must remain here for now, but perhaps your sister can visit Mai-chan later, when her duties permit. While—praise to Buddha—the new priests the Shibata sent are beginning to arrive, there is still much for us to do."

"I'm sure Mai would like to see her whenever it is convenient. Until then, rest assured that I will be watching over her."

The old woman smiled again. "Just so you know, Lady Rie said if it had been any other man on earth, she'd have gotten Mai away from him if she'd had to beat him to death with a club. As it is, she may want to have a serious talk with you."

"I have no doubt of it. While I welcome her conversation, please assure my sister violence will not be necessary. I will gladly return Mai-chan to your care as soon as she is ready and willing to go."

"I must admit the change of residence seems to agree with her," Tomoko-ana said. "She seems much calmer. Perhaps you were right in that her memories of the attack on the nunnery are too vivid. Maybe it is for the best she is here with you for now."

The old woman took her leave then. Kenji left as well, only to return shortly carrying our breakfast of rice and broiled fish. "Usually an army knows no better arrangement than to strip the surrounding countryside bare, but this is undoubtedly not an option here. The Shibata and, as I understand it, the governor of Echigo are both funneling supplies through the town of Yahiko, and Lord Yoshiie had the temple's own kitchens pressed into service, in addition to dispersing cooking stations within the camps. I'm rather impressed by his level of organization."

"Lord Yoshiie knows what he is about, so far as armies are concerned. I'm surprised the Abe have lasted this long, even with magical assistance."

I was going to fetch Mai then, but there was no need. I heard the door to her room slide open and she emerged, apparently drawn by the heady scent of food. While it was not customary for noble-born men and women to eat together under most circumstances, the folk of the countryside observed no such niceties, and I had lost enough of my pretensions—Rie would perhaps say "culture" instead—over the years not to care about such things. The three of us ate together in silence, and I noted that, whatever else might have been amiss with Mai, her appetite was very healthy indeed. I took this as an encouraging sign.

We had just finished our meal when a courier arrived from Lord Yoshiie, and I was summoned to the main hall of the temple. I was more than a little concerned about leaving Mai in Kenji's care, not because I believed he might go back on his word, but because of Mai's reaction. But when I simply told her I had to leave for a while and she was to remain with Kenji until I returned, she took the news very calmly and merely bowed to me when I finished my instruction.

"Your best behavior, Kenji-san," I said.

"Whatever it is you think I might do, taking advantage of the helpless is not among them," he said stiffly.

"I know. I just felt the necessity of needling you a bit."

I left them and went to the main temple building, where I found Yoshiie and the Shibata Clan chief pouring over a map spread across the hall floor. So intent were they upon the map it was a few moments before they noticed my presence.

"Lord Yamada, I am concerned about Abe no Yasuna. He has not been seen since last evening. Did you speak to him, by any chance?"

"No, my lord, although in truth I had planned to before . . . before I was needed elsewhere. I did see him in the compound just before dusk, however."

"As did several people, but not since. I would like for you to search for him, if you would indulge me. I would send scouts, but as you can imagine, they are all rather occupied currently. If you cannot find him, I need to know this as well."

"Certainly, my lord," I said, and quickly withdrew.

I knew the possibility of another sneak attack, this time probably from Abe *bushi* striking across the border, had to be on Lord Yoshiie's mind, so his scouts would be occupied indeed. The possibility Lord Yasuna might seek to slip away and return to the capital was one which had never occurred to me. The man had given his word, and I knew him to be the sort of man who did not break his oath, once given. Besides, if he did return without permission, there would be consequences, even for someone as highly placed and influential as Lord Yasuna. There would be much more severe consequences to the Emperor's mission and Lord Yoshiie personally if anything had happened to him.

If he has come to grief, I shudder to think what Lady Kuzunoha will do.

She had been very plain about her intentions, and I knew her to be one who kept her word, as well. The situation could be far worse than I had imagined. I wondered if the best I could hope for would be Lady Kuzunoha had appeared to him and persuaded him to flee, but there were two strong arguments against such optimism. The first was she had told me she did not intend to enter the temple compound again, and I believed her. The second was she would not show herself to her former husband unless the situation was dire indeed. If Lady Kuzunoha had been a human woman instead of a fox-demon, I had no doubt she and Lord Yasuna would have gladly grown old together. This became impossible once it was clear to Lady Kuzunoha she would not be able to live as a human without the chance of her true nature being discovered, thus bringing shame on her husband's clan. I had been of some assistance to both Lady Kuzunoha and Lord Yasuna during that difficult period, and no one understood their sad situation better than I. A meeting would do nothing but tear open old wounds.

I considered other possibilities. One was that he had decided to escape and join his distant relations in Mutsu, but the northeast countryside was crawling with Minamoto scouts. There was simply no way he could evade them. Southwest to the capital? More likely, but there were pickets on all the roadways now, and someone would have seen him. Besides, it would have been extremely foolish to attempt the roads alone, and I knew Lord Yasuna to be no fool. But just to satisfy myself, I left the temple grounds long enough to confer with the guards and anyone present who might have noticed a lone nobleman wandering about. As I expected, no one had seen him.

Strange. How could he have left without being caught or seen?

When the answer came to me, I could have cursed myself for a fool. I ran to the back wall of the temple compound, leaving several startled priests in my wake, only to find one of the rope ladders hanging down over the wall. Either someone from the outside had entered, or someone had left. I made an educated guess as to which, and made a note to ask Yoshiie to either destroy the ladders or post a guard, but that last had to wait. I climbed up and over and back down into the ravine. I moved as cautiously as I dared, but there was no sound except the occasional call of a crow. There were fewer of the birds now, but they were still a common sight around the unfortunate temple. I looked but could not see where the call had come from. I kept moving all the way to the end of the ravine, and I was back at the beach.

Lord Yasuna was there.

He had found a rock to sit on about twenty feet from the surf and was staring out over the sea. The waves were steady and calm, but there were dark clouds on the horizon. I made my way down to the beach and walked up beside him, making no effort at stealth. He kept looking out over the water.

"It seems we may have a storm coming," I said.

"If I were a braver man," he said, "I would be gone before it arrives."

I took a slow breath, wondering how much honesty this conversation was capable of sustaining. There was no choice except to find out. "I don't believe we're speaking about the same thing, Lord Yasuna."

"Living is one storm after another, and as long as one *does* live, one cannot avoid them all," he said

"There are those," I said, "who are concerned for your well-being."

"Why should they be? I am not. If I were a braver man . . . " He didn't finish.

"You would have walked into the sea by now?" I asked.

He finally looked at me. "Have you ever done something you've regretted, Lord Yamada? I mean truly regretted, to the core of your being?"

I didn't even need to pause to think. "Yes, Lord Yasuna. I have."

"How do you live with it? How do you make it *right*?"

I considered all the things I could have said to him, all platitudes and hollow things I didn't believe. When they were all dismissed, the only thing I had left to say was the risky, dangerous truth. "You cannot make it right, Lord Yasuna, because such things can never be undone."

"Then my only choice is to die," Lord Yasuna said. "This was my own conclusion."

"And take your regret to the grave? How many more ages in hell would this require? No, Lord Yasuna, one has to live as deeply and as long as one can. It's true the past cannot be changed, but the future is like blank paper and it lets you create something closer to your heart. You can work to lessen the suffering you have caused, heal the injuries you created. I do not know what your regret may be or how deeply you feel the weight of it, but I tell you this, as one with more regrets than I can count—whatever it is, you must find ways to make certain that as few people as possible pay the price for your mistake from this day forward. Only the living can do this. The dead have no part to play."

"You are very kind, Lord Yamada," he said, after a few moments' silence.

I quickly dismissed the notion. "Lord Yasuna, there is no kindness in anything I have said to you, for I personally know how difficult such a path is to walk. Telling you to let the ocean tides take you would have likely been kinder."

He kept his silence for a while, and I kept my own. He finally turned to me again. "I will think about what you have said. For now, perhaps it would be best to return to the temple."

We walked together up the bluffs to the ravine and back toward the temple. I heard the crows calling again.

"Don't you think it's strange?" Lord Yasuna asked.

"What is strange?"

"The crows," he said. "Following us the way they have. Surely you noticed?"

"I have," I said. "Does the smell of death cling to us?"

"Likely so," he said. "Sometimes I think I can sense it upon me. Still, it is unusual behavior, don't you think?"

I did indeed. And with just a little more reflection, I was pretty certain I knew what Lord Abe no Yasuna's regret was. I sincerely hoped I was wrong. When the time came, that idea would need to be tested, but now was not the time. I saw Lord Yasuna safely back into the temple compound and then climbed the rope rungs again myself, only this time I was very careful to cut each ladder loose and leave them all in a pile down in the ravine. No one else would be coming or going from that direction for the immediate future. That left only three gates to watch, which, in my current circumstances, were still far too many.

I found the proof of this when I returned to our quarters to find Kenji and Mai both missing. A courier soon directed me to the main hall, where I found Kenji placing wards on all the doors and windows.

"The guards would likely suffice, but it's best to be safe," he said.

"Kenji-san, what's happened?"

"I destroyed a *shikigami* inside the compound not more than an hour ago. It had disguised itself as an abnormally large *mamushi*, but I knew what it was the moment I saw it."

I remembered to breathe again. "Well . . . a strange choice of disguise considering where we are—I've never seen many snakes this far north myself—but we've been expecting something of the sort, and a venomous snake is a natural for a *shikigami* assassin. Is Lord Yoshiie all right?"

"Quite all right," Kenji said grimly. "It seems the snake wasn't after him in the first place."

"Not . . . ? But who was it after?"

He looked at me. "Mai-chan."

For a moment I felt dizzy. "But . . . that makes no sense! Is she . . . ?" I couldn't finish.

"She is alive and lucky to be so," Kenji said. "And you are right—it makes absolutely no sense. What would any of the *onmyoji* or Lord Sadato have to gain by harming Mai? I'm astonished they even know of her existence, but obviously one of them does."

At this point I was not surprised at anything Lord Sadato and his minions knew, but what did surprise and puzzle me as much as it did Kenji was why an attempt had been made on Mai's life in the first place. "Can you tell me what happened?"

"After you left, Mai followed me as I assisted the Shibata priests, but there was less that needed doing now, and we returned to our quarters. I don't think Mai slept well last night, since she started yawning and withdrew to her room. Just as she did, I felt the presence of one of these creatures and started after her, but no sooner had she closed the screen than she screamed and threw it open again and ran into the hallway with this thing close behind her. It looked like a *mamushi*, as I said, but it was bigger than any such snake I've ever seen. Its fangs were as long as my thumbs! It ignored me and chased after her, but fortunately I was able to catch up and brain it with my staff before it caught the poor girl." He pulled a battered piece of paper from a pouch on the ties of his robe. "Look at this."

It was clearly the remains of a *shikigami* but relatively crude compared to most of the ones I had seen lately. I studied the calligraphy carefully. "This reminds me of Lord Tenshin's work, but it's far too crude. Possibly one of Abe no Sadato's lesser minions is responsible, or an apprentice to Tenshin."

Kenji nodded. "That was my impression as well. The snake, not even considering its abnormal size, wasn't very convincing as a living creature, but I have no doubt, if it had managed to bite Mai, she would be dead now. She's under guard in one of the outbuildings until I'm done; then she'll be returned to our quarters."

"I'll need to report to Lord Yoshiie now, but as soon as we're both able, we'd best check on her."

"Agreed."

It was only the work of a few moments to gain admittance to the temple hall and inform Lord Yoshiie that Lord Yasuna had been found and where. He accepted my explanation, which was the man had shown poor judgment in going off alone but had not intended to leave. Which, I knew, was not *completely* true but close enough to the truth to fit the situation. For my own part, I was relatively certain Lord Yasuna was no longer a threat to himself or others. Which did not mean the matter was entirely closed.

"I can understand his melancholy," Lord Yoshiie said. "One such as Lord Yasuna is a creature of the capital. This must all be very strange and unsettling to him. I do regret the necessity of his presence, but perhaps it will not be for very much longer. I have reliable reports from my father that the Abe are in some disarray."

"Forgive my asking, but do you have any indication as to what caused this disturbance among the Abe?"

"Apparently an internal matter of some sort, yet I do not believe for a moment that Lord Sadato is ready to submit to the Emperor's will."

Neither did I. The history of this conflict was one of pain and loss on both sides, and I fully expected it to end in the same manner, but that was mostly Lord Yoshiie's concern. He personally, Lord Yasuna, my sister, and the surviving nuns were mine, and they were more than enough. I took my leave then and found Kenji again. "Let us go see Mai."

I hoped she would not blame me for not being there when she had been in danger, but she seemed genuinely glad to see both of us. She had been brought her mid-day meal under Kenji's instructions, but there were portions waiting for us as well. Mai herself served us with very passable skill. Considering what had happened, she seemed remarkably undisturbed. I did notice her face seemed to grow more animated when Kenji spoke to her. Kenji noticed my noticing.

"This started even before the snake," he said. "I think I remind her of someone, someone who she considered a kindly and harmless old man Actually, Lord Yamada, I find her attitude a bit insulting."

"You'd best hope she keeps it, for your sake. Otherwise my sister will be after both of us with a very large cudgel. Regardless, you do realize Mai-chan can hear you?" I asked. "I wonder if she understands your implication."

Kenji grunted. "I know she can hear me, and I'm sure she does understand. She thinks it's funny."

I was astonished to see Kenji was correct—Mai was smiling, although she'd clearly learned enough decorum from the nuns to hide her mouth with her hand as she did so. I hoped this was an indication of her further recovery, but time would tell.

"I need to know more about the snake. I assume it got into her room through the shutters?"

"There's no other way it could have. I'm a fool for not warding our rooms yesterday, but it never occurred to me someone would send an assassin after us, with Lord Yoshiie the person here who matters."

"Not 'us.' Mai specifically. Besides, Lord Yoshiie has very loyal and dedicated guards both around the perimeters of his quarters and within. A *shikigami* so crudely made would have been spotted by any of them, especially since most of Yoshiie's men have some experience with the creatures. I am forced to the conclusion this construction was never a serious threat to Lord Yoshiie, and therefore Lord Yoshiie was not its intended victim. Mai was. You said as much yourself."

"It could just as easily have entered our quarters as Mai's, but it did seem focused on her completely. But kill Mai? Why?" Kenji asked. "Can you tell me what possible reason there might be?"

Mai's cheerful mood had naturally gone more somber as we spoke, but I didn't feel comfortable leaving her alone again, and there were things Kenji and I needed to discuss. Since most of it concerned her, I couldn't deny Mai had a right to know.

"The only reason Mai is here in the first place is because I planned to question her about the day of the attack, once she regains her voice, and this was only for the sake of being thorough. If someone else knew this, one could deduce this someone does not wish me to discover what Mai might know. Yet what could she possibly have seen that would make a difference now? For all that I do want to talk to her, I'm not sure what she could add we don't already know."

"She might not know anything," Kenji said, and then turned to the girl. "But obviously there is someone working in the shadows who thinks—or fears—otherwise. Mai-chan, I know you cannot talk yet, but perhaps you can tell us this much somehow—did you see something during the attack? Something unusual, something that perhaps an enemy would not want known? Please think carefully."

Simple and direct. The response was the same—Mai began to weep. Then her mouth moved. No sound came out of it, but the shape it made as Mai tried to push out a word with her breath was very familiar.

"*Hai.* That's what she's trying to say, Kenji."

There was no doubt in my mind, now. Mai did see something, and for this, someone among our enemies wanted her dead.

Kenji was livid. "How? How did they know? Do they have eyes in every tree?"

"Remember what I had said about our enemies tracking our every move? *They are still doing it*, and so they know about Mai. It's the only explanation which makes any sense to me."

"Again, how?"

" 'Eyes in every tree,' isn't that what you said? You may be closer to the truth than you know. I think it's time we found out. Mai? We need to go outside, and I want you to come with us."

The girl obeyed, but she and Kenji both appeared puzzled as I led the way out into the temple courtyard. There were still a few crows about but, as I had observed earlier, far fewer of them now that the bodies had been removed. I found Akimasa with his contingent of men on guard duty near the main gate. "Master Akimasa, who is your best archer?"

Akimasa didn't even hesitate. "Tokisuge, my lord," he said.

"If you don't mind, I'd like to see a demonstration."

Akimasa seemed a little bemused but quickly agreed. "As you wish, Lord Yamada. What is the target?"

"Let's clear this section here," I said, indicating the right side of the courtyard. The few people there were quickly relocated. I took a bamboo pole and used my dagger to score one section until I was able to break it off, yielding a piece about five feet long. "We can use the wall itself as a berm to make certain no arrow goes astray."

I found a soft patch of ground near the wall and pushed the pole in until it could stand upright. On top of it I place a small piece of melon rind which some careless diner had discarded in the temple garden. I then paced off a distance of eighty feet while Akimasa brought his archer forward, a lean young man I'd guess to be in his mid-twenties, with long fingers and a rather sharp nose

"You are Tokisuge-san?" I asked.

"Yes, my lord. You wanted me to see me shoot?"

"I do. Can you hit that bit of melon?"

He frowned. "At this distance, my lord? Any of us could hit it."

"I will require you to prove this, in your own case, but a demonstration will be enough. Please take your position."

Tokisuge took his place at the mark I had defined, but before he took his arrow to draw, I leaned forward and whispered "Forget the melon rind. Your real target is perched at the top of that maple tree behind us. You will have to shoot quickly, and I do suggest you use a line-cutter. Clear?"

"Yes, my lord."

I stepped back. "Whenever you are ready," I said aloud.

Tokisuge selected a different arrow than the one he had intended and drew. He held the draw for a moment or two and then pivoted smoothly in place, raised his bow and let his arrow fly.

"Craaww . . . !"

The creature's scream was almost like a real crow as the arrow cut through it. As I had suggested, Tokisuge had used a type of arrow commonly called "the frog's crotch," an inverted point with two blades sharpened on the inside edges which could cut a ship's lines or a man's throat, depending. In the case of the false crow, it cut it nearly in half, but what fluttered to the ground was no more than a piece of paper.

"A fine shot indeed," I said. "Thank you for the demonstration."

"What was . . . ?" Tokisuge began, but it was clear he already knew.

"You were with Lord Yoshiie on the previous campaign, weren't you?"

"Yes, my lord. We lost several good men to those . . . are there any more of those things about?"

"If you see any, you have my permission to treat them the same way."

Tokisuge looked grim. "With pleasure, my lord. With pleasure."

Word spread through the camp quickly, as I had expected, but the summons to Lord Yoshiie's presence came almost sooner than I believed it would. Since both my and Kenji's attendance was required and I wasn't about to leave Mai alone, she came along, kneeling at a discreet distance. Lord Yoshiie sat on a folding chair on the dais as Kenji and I kneeled before him.

"Lord Yamada, we knew we were being spied upon, but when did you discover I was being spied upon by *crows*?"

"Only today, my lord, and it wasn't a crow, as I'm sure you realize. It was a *shikigami* in the form of a crow. Your experience of them is in an approximation of the human form, but they can take almost any shape the *onmyoji* desires. I apologize for not realizing what they were sooner, but under our current circumstances, a few crows are to be expected, and since they kept their distance, as a crow normally would, it made their true natures difficult to detect."

"Then what aroused your suspicions?"

"I owe this to Lord Yasuna. He noted a few of the crows were acting strangely, which in hindsight had also occurred to me. So I asked one of Akimasa-san's archers to help test the idea. As you noted, we already knew our movements were being shadowed. Now we know how. Since some of the archers have scores to settle, I think it unlikely there will be a crow that dares show itself for the balance of our journey, *shikigami* or otherwise."

"Which cannot begin soon enough, to my way of thinking. My father waits for us in Dewa, but he has sanctioned the delay under the circumstances." Yoshiie looked grim. "No wonder my scouts found nothing. How much do you think the spies discovered?"

"Other than our precise movements, and numbers? More than enough to plan the initial attack. Since that failed, we can expect either Lord Sadato or those acting in his name to try again."

"Another reason we should be on the move, Lord Yamada. How can we be sure there are no more of these things lurking within the camp itself?"

"Your pardon, my lord," Kenji said, "but I would have detected any such if I even came near it, as would any priest worth his training. As Lord Yamada said, it was only the distance which kept either of us from detecting these crow-things from the start. A creature within the compound would be easier to conceal, true, but also much easier to detect."

I hope you're not forgetting about Mitsuko, I thought, but I knew he wasn't. There was no point in going into such matters with Lord Yoshiie, but it was of great concern to me. While I was good at recognizing the normal run of *shikigami* and Kenji could sense them even in the dark, neither Kenji nor I could spot such a one as Mitsuko by sight or proximity, unlike the *mamushi*.

Yoshiie scowled. "I feel like the target on an archery range sitting here, yet circumstances will keep us at Yahiko-ji for at least another week. The governor of Echigo arrives day after tomorrow with additional men, so he in turn must pay his respects to the fallen, and there will be a feast in their honor which will take time to organize properly. After which we can in good conscience leave the balance of the funeral rites to the priests. For my father's sake and the good of the Minamoto Clan, I need to live to fight Lord Sadato one more time, so I will continue to depend on you gentlemen in this matter."

"We remain at your service, but may I make a request, Lord Yoshiie?"

He frowned. "What is it?"

"When the time comes to have your feast, would you order each member of your personal guard drink a cup of saké beforehand? If it is your command, no one will refuse."

"I do not think refusal their possible refusal would be an issue," he said, almost smiling. "But why?"

"You do remember what defeated the *shikigami* at the Widow Tamahara's?" I asked.

"Ah. Indeed."

"If it humors my lord to give a reason, say it is in honor of Tokisuge's fine shot today."

"One cup will impair no one—certainly not those men. Easily done. Also, I will require Master Kenji's and your own presence."

We bowed. "It will be an honor."

Also, I realized, an opportunity to ferret out a soul-created *shikigami*, if any were present. At a feast, everyone would be expected to eat or drink, thus making it very easy to discern someone who was not doing either, other than the guards. Thus the honorary cup of saké. It was clear to me now the forces which had made more than one failed attempt on Lord Yoshiie's life were a long way from giving up. The crow and the snake had proven it. Then there was the failed attempt at the temple—it had raised the stakes considerably. If Lord Yoshiie lived to bring his new, larger army to bear on the Abe Clan, it was hard to see how Lord Sadato could avoid his clan's destruction. Under such circumstances, I was not about to forget the example of Mitsuko. Master Chang had handed Lord Tenshin a very powerful weapon. It defied common sense to believe for a moment he would not attempt to use it. Which left three questions I needed to answer before it was too late: "When," "how," and—perhaps most of all—"who."

"The sooner we are away from this place, the better," Kenji said after we were dismissed. We were walking back to our quarters, with Mai dutifully following. "There is something not right here, and I think Lord Yoshiie's chances of survival improve if he's a moving target."

"I think he is of the same opinion. Have you sensed anything?"

"Nothing definite. Nothing clear. It's just a feeling, but it's getting stronger. I don't like it."

"That's close to what Lady Kuzunoha said."

"Lady Kuzunoha is a fox-demon, and you know my opinion of such creatures," Kenji said, then sighed and continued. "That doesn't mean she's wrong."

We walked in silence for a bit, but then something occurred to me. "Have you seen Taro in the last two days?"

"Not since he led your mount away after the fight with the assassins," Kenji said. "The beast had been slightly injured, and I imagine he is tending it. The horses are being stabled in a temporary paddock outside the south wall, and there you will likely find him. After all, the horses are his primary responsibility, not you and I."

"I understand that. He's just a detail I've overlooked. I don't want to make a habit of such things. It could cause a lot of people to die, not just Yoshiie."

"Then visit him, if you are concerned. Personally, I'm not going near those creatures until it is time to ride again."

I made a mental note to do that very thing, but I had other matters to see to first. I judged there to be a few hours of daylight left, and I wanted to make use of them. I stopped and beckoned Mai forward. "Mai, I'm going to need to leave for a little while. I want you to stay close to Master Kenji. Do you understand?"

" . . . ai."

"She spoke!" Kenji said. "Well, almost."

It was a sound. Interpreted as a fragment of a word, it was a reasonable response to my instructions. Perhaps it would not be so much longer before Mai could reveal what shock and terror had buried within her. Until then there was much to do. I smiled. "Oh, and Kenji—not too close. Clear?"

"Do not worry. Just do not be gone any longer than you can avoid. After all, I am just a kindly old man. I may need help with the next snake."

"Don't pout, Kenji-san. It's not dignified."

I took my leave before Kenji chose to explain his opinion of "dignified," as I was certain this was not the sort of language a young woman like Mai should hear, peasant farmer's daughter or not. I made my way across the compound and passed through the gates to the nunnery. I found my sister and Tomoko-ana arranging bundles on the veranda of the nunnery's lecture hall.

"Kind of you to visit again," Rie said. "Or have you forgotten about your sister already?"

"I never did forget about you," I said. "Even if it's true I never expected to see you again in this life. What are you doing?"

"Gathering the personal belongings of our fallen sisters. As you might expect, none of them owned much, but perhaps their families would want such mementos as there are. Our prioress was the sister of the Shibata Clan chief, Muramasa."

"I didn't know."

"It's not something she herself made much of, but he did visit from time to time. I had met him before on one of those visits, so I presumed to bring her belongings to him. Poor man, I think there was a tear in his eye."

"He's lost his sister. It doesn't follow they were close, but his visits suggest he might have been so."

"Or he was trying to get her to renounce her vows and become a marriage asset to the Shibata."

"Was that what he was doing?"

She smiled a little ruefully then. "I have no idea. I really do not think so. Once she had renounced the world, had Lord Muramasa not already lost his sister? The world had no more claim on her, any more than it does with me."

"Attachments are not so easy to sunder. Even for those whose will is strong and whose oaths are sincere. I still believe I *do* still have a sister, and care for her welfare, is why I kept my distance, until circumstance forced our reunion."

"That was almost sweet, but let us not speak of what is past, brother. Our first parting was painful enough. I expect our next one to be no easier," she said softly.

"Is there anything you need?"

She laughed then, covering her mouth with the sleeve of her robe. "The supplies I had gone to Yahiko to buy were delivered this afternoon. Considering that now they are merely needed for Tomoko and myself . . . and possibly Mai, later, I expect them to last for some time. Was this why you came here? I know it wasn't just to see me, or you'd have managed to do so before now."

My sister's perception was as sharp as ever. "It's true. I wanted to look around some more, if you don't mind."

She shrugged. "Certainly not, but what is the point of it?"

"Perhaps none, but I think it is odd that Mai is so frightened of this place. She refuses to go near it."

Rie frowned. "You didn't tell me this before, you just said you needed to talk to her. Her fear is very strange. Has she said anything?"

"Not yet, but she's beginning to recover her voice."

"I am pleased to hear it. Perhaps she can rejoin us soon, if this is her wish."

I frowned. "Why wouldn't she return?"

"Brother, were you not listening to me when I first spoke of her? She is not a nun, she was designated as a novice for convenience sake. Who can say? She may decide to remain with you, however I would attempt to dissuade her, for her own sake. You can barely look after yourself."

"I should want to dissuade her as well, but I am taking better care of myself these days than I once did. At least now I'm making the effort."

"From all I have been able to gather of you over the past several years, this is indeed a change. May I walk with you as you poke about? Tomoko-ana, can you handle this on your own?"

"There's little enough to do," the old woman said. "And I gather your brother will be leaving soon. I don't mind doing the rest."

Rie seemed to consider. "How soon?" she asked as she fell into step beside me.

"Perhaps a week, possibly a little longer. It depends on so many things."

"I will be glad enough to see the backside of Yoshiie's army. I can hardly pass by the gate without drawing leers. Imagine, at my age . . . They do not seem to be discouraged by the cowl I wear."

"I know that if one attempted more, Lord Yoshiie would spike the man's privates on a pole as a warning to the rest. Still, one cannot fault their taste. I remember your mother, possibly as well as you do. She was a beauty, and you did inherit much from her."

Rie sighed. "Since the time our father died, I think I have learned possibly one new thing at most, which is simply this—detaching yourself from the world is easy. Persuading the world to detach itself from you? That is the hard part. Obviously, I have failed. Still, it was good to see you again, brother."

I'm not sure what broke the final barrier. Perhaps it was the way my sister smiled at me, but the torrent was suddenly unleashed, and I could not stop it. "I'm the one who failed," I said. "When our father died. If only . . . "

She looked at me. "If only what?"

"If only I had not let myself fall to pieces the way I did. All those years . . . It was my responsibility to hold the family together. I failed. I wasn't strong enough."

"I do know a little about what inner devils you were fighting, brother, never think otherwise, but this one is strictly your own illusion. There was nothing left to hold together—Michiko's marriage was already formalized. My mother had already left this sad world; your own mother was not long behind. The strongest man in the world could not have done better."

"But you—"

Rie looked confused for a moment, and then she laughed at me. She stopped where she stood and nearly doubled over. It was neither dignified nor refined behavior in one such as my sister, but she did it anyway.

"What is so humorous?" I asked.

She regained control, but it clearly took an effort. "It—it was wrong of me to laugh at your pain, brother, and I do apologize, but for all this time did you actually blame yourself for my taking holy orders, believe that circumstances forced me to this?"

"Well . . . didn't they? When our father was executed, and I was so useless . . . "

Rie sighed. "Dear Goji-kun, do you really think you're so grand that you are responsible for everything? Shall I now burst your illusions for you? I consider this important for your eventual salvation, but do you want to know the *real* reason why I took the tonsure?"

There was a faint roaring sound in my ears, and I felt dizzy. I waited a moment for the feeling to pass. "Yes. I would like to know."

"There had been discussion of a marriage for me. I wasn't against the idea by any means, but do you remember what happened when our father was ordered to Mutsu to assist Lord Sentaro? Just before he left? Think."

"We wanted a game of *shogi* but couldn't find the pieces. We finally located them on the veranda outside my mother's apartments. Our father was visiting her at the time, and we . . . overheard them talking," I said.

"Rubbish. We eavesdropped, and what we heard was our

father promising to retire from public life once he had returned from his assignment in Mutsu. Retire and never leave her alone again. She always hated his frequent absences."

I remembered. "I wasn't surprised. I had expected something of the sort."

"So did your mother. The next morning and for weeks afterward she was as happy as I'd ever seen her. But then our father did not return, and we soon learned he never would. That's when I knew what I had to do."

"I don't understand," I said.

"Is it so difficult? Our father loved your mother. I know what they felt for each other was very powerful. And still it was for nothing. Do you understand now? I knew then that, whatever attachments I made—even if they found me a husband I cared for as much as they cared for each other—sooner or later we would part. Losing our father destroyed your mother. She was never the same after his death, and so far as I'm concerned, she died long before her body succumbed. Her attachment to this world, embodied in our father, was what really killed her. It seems so silly, even now—an attachment to the world so strong that it took her from it! I vowed I would never be so foolish."

"You—you had already decided?"

She smiled then, but it was a sad smile, and she did not bother to cover it. "You were too deep in your own despair at the time to consider my decision might have nothing to do with what you did or didn't do. Your absence helped ease me into the life I chose, and I have been very happy in it, but I did not know you blamed yourself or indeed that you thought there was anything in my decision which called for blame."

"I guess there wasn't," I said.

She sighed again. "None at all. I celebrate my choice and give thanks every day of my life. Honestly, brother . . . for someone with such a reputation for cleverness, in some matters you are a bit of a dolt."

"That much I did know," I said, "but thank you for enlightening me."

This smile she did hide. "Oh, you are still a long way from *enlightenment*, I assure you. So. I do not suppose we will see each other again, once you leave this place. And it is probably best for both of us that we do not, so think of this as a last gift to my dear fool of a brother."

I smiled. "What will you do when we are gone?"

"There is still myself and Tomoko-ana . . . perhaps Mai as well, perhaps not, but as long as there remains one of us, our community will survive. Others will join us in time, and the Shibata priests will tolerate us for their lord's sake until we are re-established and self-sufficient again. Those murderers will not destroy what we have built here."

I had already been feeling like an old wound had finally been washed clean, and now I also had my sister to thank for reminding me why I had come to the nunnery in the first place. "I almost forgot why I came here—I need to walk the around the walls of your compound," I said.

"And I am happy to walk with you, for now. But whatever for? Did you not send those men already to examine our walls?"

"I did. I was thinking that, perhaps, I might notice something they had missed."

She frowned. "What sort of thing?"

"I couldn't possibly know until I see it."

"Fine, but honestly now—at this point, does it really matter how they got in?"

"Perhaps not, but I can't know *that* either, until I know how it was accomplished."

Rie had no answer. She merely followed me as I slowly walked the limits of the nunnery compound. By the time I'd reached the back wall, I had to confess myself defeated—there was simply no way an attacker could scale the wall without leaving some evidence behind: a ladder, a rope, perhaps even a climbing pole, but there was nothing. I did not question Akimasa's thoroughness—he knew what to look for and where, but there was no sign. I had placed my wager on a scaling ladder, something discarded into the underbrush on the outside of the wall where Akimasa's men might have overlooked it, but the height of the wall dictated one on *both* sides of the nunnery's wall. Unlike many temple compounds, the wall at Yahiko-ji was not merely for show. It had been built with defense in mind and stood higher than four tall men. Scaling the top of that wall with no way down would have gained an attacker nothing but a broken ankle.

"Any conclusions?" Rie finally asked.

"None which make any sense."

"That would be 'no' then," she said.

I had to admit she had it right. "By everything I have seen, it is simply not possible one of the assassins gained entry. Yet we know this did happen."

"Our dead sisters are proof enough of this. I don't know how they did it, but I confess I do not care. The 'how' of it makes no difference to the ones we mourn now."

Nor should it, I though, *but it still does to me.*

"I'm going to ask you a question, sister, and I need an honest answer."

"Brother, do you think I am inclined to lie to you?" she asked mildly.

I sighed. "I merely meant the question is a bit . . . indelicate."

Rie raised an eyebrow. "Oh?"

"We all know monks and priests are not always in full accord with the vows of their orders, especially in, shall we say, matters of the heart?"

"You mean priests and monks sometimes take lovers? Yes, brother, I was aware of this. Some abbots are more tolerant of this behavior than others, but it does happen, as witnessed by the sealing of the back gate to the temple compound. Are you about to suggest my sister nuns might have been guilty of the same behavior?"

"Is it possible?"

"Honestly, brother. If you're suggesting one of my sisters opened the gate for a lover who proved to be an assassin . . . well, yes, it's possible. But consider how improbable it is! Such relationships do not develop without time and the right set of circumstances. Yet the attack on the nunnery could not have been more than a precaution to quell possible alarms, so why go to the trouble? Besides, quarters for the prioress and the senior nuns were always set closest to our rear gate by design. So the chances of anyone using the gate in such a manner—ever—without being discovered are remote at best."

"Was that by design?" I asked. "You're saying your prioress did not trust either the monks or the nuns under her supervision?"

Rie laughed. "I'm saying, brother, she trusted human nature to do as human nature often does. Honestly, aren't you being far too clever? One set of rope ladders such as you discovered on the monks' compound would have served just as well to get the enemy inside the nunnery with far less left to chance. Yet you find nothing."

I clearly had been grasping at straws, and my sister had ably demonstrated how flimsy this particular straw was. I was at once chagrined and frustrated, but even a flimsy possibility was better than none. Except for the undeniable fact the nuns had been slaughtered, one would be forced to conclude the assassins could not have gained entry. I was baffled, and there were few conditions I hated more.

"You could be right," I said. "Painful as it is to admit."

"I *am* right," she said. "And it won't be the first time, brother. You'll survive it. You always did."

CHAPTER TEN

I'VE NEVER HAD the knack of just letting go of something puzzling me. Rie knew this. So it would have been no surprise to her, had she known, that I took it upon myself to make a circuit of the nunnery walls from the outside. All I had to do was go out the main gate, walk back to the small outside gate which marked the northernmost point of Yahiko-ji, and walk the boundary, all the way to where the nunnery compound ended and the main temple compound began, just short of the ravine.

This did not teach me anything I did not already know from my examination of the inside wall, but at least I was able to eliminate the idea of a discarded scaling ladder, improbable as it was. There was no sign. No footprints, no out of place indentations in the ground along the perimeter, not even an animal trail Nothing.

The assassin did not scale the wall. The assassin did not break through the wall. If the assassin did not have a mistress on the inside, how had the breach occurred? The answer I kept coming back to, time and again, was that it was impossible. Yet it had happened, so it clearly was *not* impossible. Somewhere there was another possibility I had overlooked, and all I had to do now was find it. So far I had considered every possibility that made any sense whatsoever—

Perhaps it is time to consider a possibility which makes no sense at all.

Which turned out to be easier than I had believed it would be.

What if I was right about the method but wrong about the reason? Suppose one of the nuns had indeed opened the gate, not for a lover, but for the assassin, knowing all along what he was, what would happen?

The idea made me shudder, but once the possibility was considered, I realized there need be no assassin. Someone in league with the temple's attackers would simply have opened the nunnery's main gate to the temple compound directly and let the attackers who were already inside the walls into the nunnery itself. The small outside gate need never have been opened at all, not for a lover or anyone else. So . . . if not a lover, then why? Money? A nun grown tired of the ascetic life of contemplation in alliance with her sister nuns' murderers for gold? As distasteful as such a possibility remained, I now had to consider it. I also considered it just as likely the corrupt nun was immediately cut down for her pains, since from the reports of both Tomoko and Rie, who had seen the attack from different positions, it was clear the attackers did not plan to leave anyone within the nunnery alive, and thus she would have become the very first victim . . .

I went back into the temple compound. My sister had gone into the village of Yahiko on an errand, but I found Tomoko. The old nun was praying and lighting incense in their temple. I waited until she was done.

"Tomoko-ana, I need to ask you something."

"Certainly, Lord Yamada. How may I be of service?"

"I apologize for raising such a painful issue, but you and my sister were the primary attendants for the fallen nuns, yes?"

"Primary and only, my lord," she said.

I took a breath. "Can you tell me whose body was found closest to the main gate?"

Tomoko frowned. "Let me think . . . oh. There were several near to the gate, but the closest was our late prioress, the Shibata nun."

I thanked Tomoko and made my way back to our quarters. I found Kenji and Mai engrossed in a game of *shogi*. "I didn't realize Mai-chan knew the game," I said.

Kenji grunted. "She didn't before I taught her. She even beats me now and again."

No small feat in itself. If Kenji was not a *shogi* master, he was certainly the closest to one I had ever met. I could not beat him in more than a third of our matches, and I was a better than decent player in my own right. "Mai-chan, please excuse us for a moment. There is something I need to discuss with Kenji-san."

Mai bowed and withdrew to a discreet distance, although she never left our sight. I kept my voice low as I related what I had found—or rather not found—in my examination of the nunnery walls. I then related my theory on the traitor nun. Kenji listened very attentively and withheld all comment until I had finished. Then he just sighed deeply.

"Lord Yamada, have you lost your mind?"

"I'm beginning to wonder this myself."

"Considering this is the Shibata family temple, it should not be too surprising the prioress, by tradition, is recruited from that family. While there was some reluctance at the time of the nunnery's founding, the position is now deemed a great honor. Why would she betray it?"

"I agree, it makes little sense," I said. "Unless, painful as this is to consider, Tomoko, Mai, or my sister Rie were somehow involved?"

"You do realize this makes even less sense?" Kenji said. "Knowing what we know now about the nature of the attack, that those three survived attests more to their innocence than any suspicion of complicity."

"I thought so as well, but my judgment where my sister is concerned cannot be dispassionate. Still, everything that *does* make sense has proved impossible, and I'm left with almost nothing. Regardless, the Shibata nun was closest to the gate at the time of the attack, which is suspicious, but even if she were responsible I cannot prove anything, and even if I could, doing so would not be . . . wise."

"By which you mean you'd be dropping a steaming pile of nightsoil directly into the Minamoto/Shibata alliance?"

While I did not like Kenji's choice of metaphor, I had to admit he had summed up the situation accurately. "Yes."

"So—even if you are correct, you cannot prove it. If you *could* prove it, you would not because doing so would compromise Lord Yoshiie's mission, and thus our own. Nor would proving anything explain why the Shibata nun would commit such a despicable act, because the only one who could shed any light on the question is dead. Is this about right?"

"You're forgetting about Mai. We know she saw something. Perhaps it was the sight of the Shibata nun opening the gate that has so overwhelmed her."

"Perhaps, but even if she did see exactly that and was able to say so, the reality of the situation is that she must keep silent. So. Is there a point to this line of inquiry?"

"Kenji-san, something is still not right here. I may not have Lady Kuzunoha's instincts, but I do have my own. The danger is nowhere near past."

"I agree, and so we must concentrate our efforts on keeping Lord Yoshiie safe until we can depart this place. You cannot do this by chasing ghost-lights through the forests of Echigo, can you?"

"One would not think so," I said, "except I—at this moment— feel fairly useless in any other capacity. Perhaps chasing ghost-lights is all I *can* do for Lord Yoshiie."

I had not realized what I said to Kenji might prove to be literally true—the guards on the road spotted the ghost-lights that very evening. Apparently not knowing what else to do, Master Akimasa had sent for me. Fortunately, Kenji and I had not yet retired, although we were near to it. We were forced to rouse Mai as well, since after the *mamushi*, neither of us was willing to risk leaving her alone and unguarded.

We left the compound by the main gate. To the left I could see where a new meadow was being created. Woodcutters from Yahiko and the surrounding area had been recruited to clear a large section of forest for both space and wood to fuel the funeral pyres that would be lit soon. It was not yet summer, but the corpses could not be left as they were for much longer without very unpleasant consequences. For the moment they remained guarded by both *bushi* and priests to keep scavengers—and worse—at bay. Tomorrow, if all went well, the bodies would be given up to the flames and their souls hastened to whatever awaited them beyond this world. Kenji, naturally, had his certainties about what that would be. I could never be so sure, until perhaps my own time to take my leave of the world had come. I had long since chosen not to consider the matter overmuch beforehand.

Master Akimasa met us there on the road, together with two of his archers. "This way, Lord Yamada."

I had expected him to lead us in the direction of the shrouded bodies, but instead he proceeded north on the road toward the outer wall of the nunnery. We hadn't gone very far before I could see what he was talking about. Kenji had already taken out his prayer beads and began to mumble something I recognized as part of the Diamond Sutra. Frankly, I was surprised he hadn't already started a full exorcism, as his first instinct when confronted with a ghost was to banish it from this world. He considered doing so an act of kindness, but at the moment he just looked puzzled.

"Why just the *onibi*? And so few?"

I understood what he meant. There were ghost-lights hovering at the edge of the wooded hillside on side of the road opposite to the nunnery gate. Not ghosts themselves, or at least not full-blown ones, the small blue orbs danced in the air almost like fireflies. They were indications of the presence of a ghost, but their number suggested we were dealing with one ghost only, not a horde.

"What did you expect, Kenji-san? An invasion?"

"Weren't you? Have you forgotten what happened here? What lies back down the road waiting on their funeral pyres?" he asked.

"Sudden and violent deaths may produce confused spirits," I said. "But you know as well as I do this isn't enough to produce a ghost. Ghosts linger in this world for their own reasons, and we don't always understand what those reasons are."

"Anger and revenge are powerful incentives for a ghost," Kenji said dryly. "I would have expected more than one. No matter, and no matter their reasons, this one must depart. We must see to it."

Kenji had his perspective. I had mine. "If this is the ghost of a nun, I need to talk to her."

Akimasa turned about as pale as I've ever seen a living human being. "Talk . . . ?"

I smiled then. "Master Akimasa, despite what you may have been told, most ghosts aren't especially dangerous. Startling, yes, even frightening, but seldom harmful unless one remains too close to one for an extended period. They feel the lack of living energy, and they tend to take it into themselves from whatever sources are handy—food, plants, and even people. With the proper precautions, I'll be fine. Kenji?"

Kenji produced a paper spirit-ward from a pouch he kept tucked into his robes. This he gave to me. "Just keep it on your person. It will prevent the ghost from draining you like a wine gourd. Otherwise, be careful. We don't yet understand what sort of ghost we're dealing with."

I took the ward and tucked it into my *hitatare*. "Master Akimasa, Kenji and I are going forward. Please look after Mai-chan until we return." I turned to Mai and told her to wait there with Akimasa and his men, and she bowed to let me know she understood.

"We'll remain here, but please don't get yourself eaten," Akimasa muttered. "Lord Yoshiie will blame me for it."

"I will do my best to avoid such an unfortunate outcome," I said.

As I drew closer, it was easier to count the precise number of *onibi*, but I still did not see the ghost. Kenji was barely a pace or two behind me. "It's strange," he said.

Many things were strange, so I had to ask, "What in particular?"

"Ghosts are many things, but one thing they are *not* is capricious. They are very specific about what they want and where they abide, though as you say, it's not always clear to mortals why they do what they do. Yet you and I have both been on this road as night falls, and neither of us has seen anything here before. Why now?"

"A new manifestation, possibly, and its location which would suggest this was, indeed, one of the unfortunate nuns. Or it could be a monster of some deadly sort *pretending* to be a ghost, specifically to lure you and me in close."

"Oh, fine," Kenji said, "so many *other* people had been the targets of assassins lately. I was beginning to feel unwanted."

"Don't fret. I'm sure there are multitudes who would wish you dead. Probably the husbands and fathers and estranged lovers of your many inappropriate liaisons."

"There are more than a few of those," Kenji conceded. "But I'm doubtful . . . ah. I see our ghost now."

So did I. The ghost hadn't moved, but our angle of vision through the trees showed a gap, and there was the ghost, kneeling on the ground. I had seen ghosts manifest as giant lanterns, skeletons, floating heads, and in one case, a large fish, but this image was strictly human. A dignified-looking older woman in a nun's robe and cowl, kneeling in prayer under the trees while the *onibi* swirled around her, blue flames in thrall to an elegant moth. I knew the ghost's appearance was a nothing but memory and could change at any moment depending on the situation, but right now the spirit either perceived itself as a human being or merely wished to give that impression to observers. Either way, I hoped she would be in the mood to talk—or was even still capable of speech. I had known ghosts who could converse like any living person and others who were little more than a remembered purpose, and woe to any who were perceived as an obstacle to that purpose, whatever it might be.

"Do you think it is the prioress?" Kenji asked. "I never saw the body, so I don't know what she looked like . . . assuming her attackers left her corpse in a recognizable state."

"Let us find out."

I approached cautiously, for all that I was reasonably certain the ghost was already aware of our presence. Even so, she appeared to take no notice. I realized, even as she prayed, her eyes never closed. They were fixed on a point across the road, and the intensity of the spirit's gaze made me tremble a little. I tried to look in the direction she did, but all I could see was the wall of the temple and the rear gate to the nunnery. When I looked back at the ghost, I finally did notice something else.

The ghost-lights were disappearing.

I stopped where I was, just past the edge of the woods, and counted. Then I waited for a moment and counted again. There were definitely fewer of them the second time, and this was one more matter of the last several days that didn't make any sense. *Onibi* were not spirits themselves but more like moths drawn, for whatever reason, to the spiritual flame that was a ghost. For the *onibi* to be disappearing meant either the ghost was losing coherence as an entity and was about to dissipate, or—

She's eating them!

The glow surrounding the ghost had been growing in intensity but so slowly I hadn't even noticed. It was the disappearance of the ghost-lights that finally helped me make the connection and showed me what I should have been looking for. I took another step forward, and now I could feel it—the sensation was like standing on the edge of a cliff, only you knew the cliff wanted to pull you down. I felt light-headed and sick at once. It took a great effort to move back.

"My name is Yamada no Goji," I said. "I wish to speak to you."

The ghost turned to me, and her face changed. There was nothing about the serenity of praying nun about it then. Her visage was monstrous.

"Kenji, move toward the wall," I shouted, just as the creature began a low growl in the depths of its throat.

"Why?" he asked.

"The ghost is gathering strength, and it would have taken mine except for your ward. That tells me it is planning something. I have the distinct feeling that whatever it is will not be pleasant."

I circled the ghost until I was between it and the gate, with Kenji a few paces behind me. The ghost finally stood and approached the road, and there were no ghost-lights to be seen. I spoke to the creature directly. "Again, I would speak to you. I am Yamada no Goji. Are you the Shibata nun?"

There was no growl. This time the creature smiled at me. The smile grew wider and wider, and it was nothing but a show of long, pointed teeth. The ghost reached out toward me with arms grown long and taloned like a demon's.

"Kenji, ward the gate!"

The ghost's manifestation had moved beyond the ethereal and was rapidly approaching the demonic. I had let her seeming serenity lull me into misunderstanding the situation—rage and hatred were evident in the creature's countenance now, and I knew these two powerful forces were in the process of transforming the creature into an ogre. I had seen that happen once before and only now understood how much trouble I was in. I scarcely had time to glance back at the nunnery to see Kenji placing a spirit ward on the gate before I drew my *tachi* and settled into a swordsman's stance. Kenji began chanting behind me. The tone and inflections were familiar, but I couldn't understand the words. Whatever they were, they appeared to have no effect on the ghost, who had now turned the entirety of her attention on me.

"I can see that you are not in the mood for conversa—"

She struck so fast I almost didn't see it coming. I barely deflected her blow as she aimed the talons of her left hand like a spear. I heard a shriek from where we had left Akimasa and Mai but didn't dare turn my attention away from the ghost. It had grown powerful enough to attack with physical force, and I knew it was only Kenji's talisman in my robe that kept the creature from draining my life-force like a leech. As matters stood, its direct attacks were more than enough to concern me. I dodged another—by a hair's breadth—and the third time its talons struck sparks from my *tachi* as if we'd clashed metal on metal.

Whatever questions I'd hoped to ask the prioress—if indeed this ravening monster before me was once that person—were now moot. The creature was now little more than a purpose given form and power, and I still did not know what that purpose was. Nor could I take the risk of stepping aside to find out. Allowing such a thing in its current state and temper into either the nunnery or the temple compound was unthinkable.

"Kenji-san, I can't hold it off forever!"

Kenji barely paused in his chant to shout the word "Stall!" before resuming his chant with redoubled fervor. I understood. Whatever he was attempting might take more time than either of us had, but it was the only chance. It wasn't as if I could slay the thing with my sword—it was already dead.

There was a blur on my left, and then a spear struck the creature with a sound like an ax on wood. Akimasa held onto the other end with grim determination.

"Get back!" I shouted, but it was too late. The revenant merely clutched the spear shaft in its talons, trapping the weapon as it struck with its other hand, rather more a swat than a focused blow, but the impact sent Akimasa spinning back into the darkness. The ghost plucked out the spear like a splinter and then snapped the shaft in its talons. In its renewed rage it seemed to grown even larger. A few more moments and its transformation into an *oni* would be complete. If there remained any chance of stopping the thing, it had to be now. I swung my sword at the creature in the hope of driving it back a step or two, but I failed to consider how completely unconcerned the thing was with me and my sewing-needle of a weapon. It merely flicked the blade aside with one talon and then slashed across my chest. I felt a deep burning in my flesh, and suddenly my legs failed me. I found myself sitting on the ground with my sword beside me with no clear memory of how I'd gotten there. The creature raised one taloned paw to finish me off; there was nothing I could do about it. I tried to prepare myself for the blow, but it never came.

I heard the sound of running feet, and then someone was standing between me and the ghost. It was Mai. She stood, trembling, with her arms outstretched as if to shield me; it was like watching a rabbit try to face down a bear.

"Mai-chan, run! She'll kill you!"

Mai did no such thing.

Neither did the ghost. It just stared at the girl, a quizzical expression on its face as if it could not quite understand what was happening. Mai slowly lowered her arms and bowed to the monster. Much to my shock, the creature returned the gesture. Then it began to shrink and transform back into its original appearance. When the transformation was complete, it smiled a sad smile and turned back in the direction it had come, now fully in the form of a human woman. In another moment it had disappeared into the wooded hillside, and Kenji and Mai both were kneeling at my side. I heard shouts from up the road and more running.

"I'm all right. See to Akimasa," I said.

"You are most certainly *not* all right," Kenji said, after giving me a quick going over. "But you'll probably live. Mai-chan, please stay with him." Kenji left, and I tried to get up, only to realize that, no, I was most definitely not all right. After a moment or two I found even sitting up was entirely too much effort. I let Mai half-lower, half-drop me the rest of the way to the ground, where I was content to lie while the girl fussed over me. She pulled a cloth from her *obi* and pressed it against my chest. I could still feel the sting of the ghost's talons, but I was reasonably certain the scratches were not deep, despite the blood. I was only mildly interested when I noticed the corner of a piece of paper sticking out of my now-ragged *hitatare*. I managed to pull it out and realized it was Kenji's spirit-ward. Its condition was somewhat shredded and blood-spattered, not unlike my chest.

"That's it," I said to Mai or possibly no one in particular, "It wasn't the blow itself. When she disabled the talisman she drained my strength, but I will recover."

Mai made a face and continued trying to press the cloth firmly against my wounds. The bleeding had already subsided.

"Thank you," I said. "I think you saved my life but, honestly, I do not understand why *either* of us is still alive."

Mai let out a small sigh, but that was her only response. I persisted. "You saw her face . . . her original face, didn't you? Was she the former prioress? The one they called the Shibata nun?"

Mai still didn't speak, but the answer was clear in her eyes as she began to weep.

Mai knows even more than I once believed. But what has locked her tongue, and why will it not release?

I yawned. I probably didn't mean to say what I said next aloud, but I was having some trouble telling the difference between my voice in the world and the voice in my head. "Such silence may get us all killed."

The last thing I remembered was Mai smiling at me, but the tears had yet to stop. When I awoke again it was daylight—I could tell by the way it filtered into the room through the cracks in the walls and the tears in the screens. I was back in our quarters. My robe was open and Mai was very gently washing my chest. It hurt, regardless of how gentle she was. I must have moaned, because she hesitated a moment before continuing her work.

That will be a scar . . . or rather, several.

I heard the screen slide open.

"About time you're awake. I was beginning to doubt my estimate of your condition." Kenji stood there, looking disapproving. "Honestly, Lord Yamada, you'll wear the poor girl out. She's hardly left your side."

"How long was I asleep?"

"The balance of last night and most of this day. I've arranged some food. If you can stand, let's get you cleaned up."

After washing and dealing with more pressing bodily functions, I felt somewhat better, for all that I still felt very unsteady on my feet. "Did you see what happened?" I asked.

"You mean aside from the ghost knocking you on your arse?"

"I mean when Mai-chan saved my life."

"I did, yes. I was sure I'd lost both of you. The rite of exorcism is a delicate one and can only be hurried so much. As it was, I never got to finish it."

"Meaning the ghost will be back."

"Perhaps," Kenji said. He looked thoughtful. "Yet how can we be certain? We don't even know why it left in the first place. I doubt it was the exorcism rite—the creature hardly knew I was there."

"It apparently recognized Mai-chan and didn't wish to harm her."

"So much so it turned from its purpose? Granted, we don't know what its purpose *was*, but whatever its goal, that goal was clearly on the other side of Mai. So why did the thing stop?"

"I don't know. But I'm beginning to think Mai does."

Mai kept still as if she hadn't listened to a word we'd said, but I knew better. The puzzle of Mai was no longer a less-pressing concern. I was coming to believe Mai was perhaps the key to everything. If nothing else, the Shibata nun had driven that particular lesson home.

"Oh, I remember now . . . Akimasa? How . . . how is he?"

"Better than you, I think," Kenji said. "Bruised and sore, but the blow was almost an afterthought. She didn't drain him the way she did you . . . yes, I found what was left of my talisman when Akimasa's *bushi* carried you back here. Lord Yamada, I saw the thing's face when you spoke your name. If I didn't know better, I would think the ghost was angry at *you* personally."

"But why? I never met the woman before her death, nor have I had any dealings with the Shibata Clan until now. She certainly had no reason to dislike me."

"That is just how it appeared," Kenji said, also clearly at a loss. "It makes no sense, I do admit."

"I'm getting very weary of matters which make no sense. We need to find some answers soon. I have the feeling Lord Yoshiie's life may not be the only one in the balance."

"Speaking of whom, I was instructed to say he is very cross with you. He does not wish to have to explain himself to Prince Kanemore if you were to get yourself killed."

"Coming from Lord Yoshiie, that almost sounded like concern. Regardless, we need to prepare for the ghost's return . . . if it does return. I still wish to speak to it."

I was watching for Mai's reaction, but there was none. She merely rose and removed the bowl with its tainted water she'd used to wash me earlier. Kenji just sighed. "Lord Muramasa has ordered his chief priests to assist in the exorcism, should that be required," Kenji said. "With their help I believe I can conclude the exorcism quickly, but probably not in time to save your life if the ghost returns and is determined to kill you. Perhaps you should bring Mai for protection."

In my weakness and to my shame I actually considered this, but only for a moment. "No, Mai is too valuable to risk, so I'm afraid I'll have to take my chances. Just be certain that Lord Yoshiie keeps the balance of his priests around himself in case we fail."

"Already arranged as a precaution, but do you really think the Shibata nun would harm Lord Yoshiie?"

"At this point, Kenji-san, I do not know what to think."

THAT EVENING, as I stood at the nunnery's north gate, the situation was somewhat different than the night before. Kenji stood in a semi-circle of monks and priests, all with prayer beads out and ready. Two score of Lord Yoshiie's *bushi* stood with their bows at the ready. I, however, was not even carrying my sword. Master Akimasa and myself were not the only ones battered and bruised from the previous evening. My *tachi* was also in need of tending and was currently in the care of a Minamoto sword polisher, which I considered to be just as well, as I was still too weak to use it effectively and doubted it would be of much use in any case. As a rule, swords were not very effective against a creature already dead, even if it was manifesting physically. Regardless, it was all I could do to walk, even leaning on the priest's staff Kenji had loaned me. He had taken care to weave talismans into the brass rings on its top, and they muffled the jingling of the rings as I walked.

Akimasa stood in command of the archers, and he appeared unharmed save for a dark bruise under his right eye. I had already formally thanked him for his bravery, which he dismissed as merely part of Yoshiie's directive to "keep Yamada out of trouble." Mai was back in our quarters, under guard. Other *bushi* were in the nunnery itself, as a precaution in case the ghost managed to elude us, though if matters went badly, I wasn't sure what use they would be. I had forewarned my sister and Tomoko-ana, and if they did hear the exorcism rite begin from outside the walls, they promised to join in immediately, and I certainly hoped they would do so. It might be their only chance.

"It's begun," I heard Kenji say.

I spotted the *onibi* even as Kenji spoke. "If I'm going to make another attempt, it has to be now, before it gathers too much strength," I said. "Stand ready."

Slowly, because indeed I could move at no other speed, I made my way through the edge of the forest on the far side of the road. I hadn't noticed how quickly the land began to rise the night before, probably because I had been much more steady on my feet then. I had to move carefully, placing the tip on the staff on the next bit of clear pathway and taking each step in turn. Even so, it did not take very long to reach the ghost.

Just as on the night before, she kneeled in prayer in a small clearing with the ghost-lights swirling about her head. There were more of them this time. I shuddered to think what she would be like once she had begun to absorb them all.

"You are the Shibata nun," I said.

For a moment I wondered if she had heard me, but then she slowly turned in my direction, and I heard my name, clearly spoken. "Yamada."

"You remember me." We had only "met" the night before, but she had been far from being human then. I was a little surprised she did remember.

"I am sorry," she said.

I blinked. I don't know what I had expected from her, but this certainly was not it. "For trying to kill me? That no longer matters now. I need to ask you—"

"You don't understand," she said. "But you will. I am so sorry."

She was right. I did not understand, but I tried to take the first step toward understanding. "I need to ask you—did you open the gate to your attackers?"

"The one who betrayed us is dead," she said softly. "The one who killed us still lives. See to it. Take care of Mai."

"It was not you?"

"No," she said, and I don't think I've ever seen a look of greater sadness on anyone's face in my life, alive or dead.

"Why did you attack the nunnery?"

She shook her head slowly. "Take care of Mai," she repeated. I could already see the distance in her dark eyes. "Help me," she said. "I must go."

"Help you . . . ?

"Please. Help me . . . go."

I looked up. There were fewer ghost-lights than there had been. The transformation would soon be happening again. The puzzling thing was I had come to the opinion the Shibata nun did not wish to become the creature that nearly destroyed me and Akimasa, but it was clearly beyond her power to prevent the transformation would happen with or without her consent. The purpose chaining her soul to this world had not changed and so would act on her even if she no longer wished it. But I still did not know what that purpose was, and the ghost was telling me what she wanted to tell me or what she *could* tell me, which was not what I wanted to know.

Is it, perhaps, what I need to know?

I hoped so, because I was out of time. I called out to the priests, "Master Kenji, Gentlemen—please proceed."

The droning chants of the rite of exorcism began immediately, this time echoed by a dozen voices. Even so, I was afraid I'd started too late. One by one I watched the *onibi* disappear like dying fireflies, but still the ghost of the Shibata nun did not rise nor change appearance. I did see her hands clench so tightly that phantom blood began to trickle onto her robes, but still she did not move.

She is fighting the transformation with all of her strength.

"You do not wish to leave this world as a monster, do you? Please keep trying. It won't be much longer."

I hoped I was right, but my words did seem to steady the ghost a little, and even though she could no longer truly breathe, I saw her chest rise and fall slowly as someone trying to enter a meditative state. Then her entire body trembled, and the transformation began, slowly enough, but the change was definite. Her fingers elongated into talons, her white hair escaped the cowl and turned wild and flowing as if blown by an unseen wind. I don't know what reserves of spiritual strength the Shibata nun summoned, but she pushed the monster her nature was trying to make of her back into whatever dark recesses from which it had emerged. Her hair fell to her shoulders, her fingers were just fingers again, her hands a delicate woman's hands.

Her image began to fade. The exorcism was working. She looked at me. "Thank you."

Her words were so soft on the wind I wasn't entirely sure I'd heard what I thought I heard, and then she was gone. The exorcism was over. The remaining ghost-lights milled about overhead for a little while as if lost, then drifted away. The timbre of the chant was different now. Kenji and his fellow priests were praying. It was over.

I heard the sound of the nunnery gate being thrown open, then a babble of voices jarred against the prayers. I hobbled out of the woods just in time to see one of the *bushi* assigned to guard the surviving nuns come speeding past the priests.

"Lord Yamada! Please come quickly . . . " The man paused to catch his breath.

"What is the matter?"

"Your sister, Lady Rie. She has collapsed."

CHAPTER ELEVEN

"I am sorry if I worried you."

Rie kneeled on the bedding on the floor of her quarters. She was pale but otherwise appeared her normal self. Tomoko-ana, clearly relieved, kneeled a short distance away.

"What happened?" I asked.

"We had joined in the exorcism," Tomoko said. "We were near the end when Lady Rie fainted."

Rie sighed. "Again, I must apologize. There has been so much . . . I-I guess I'm not as strong as I sometimes like to believe I am. Is—is it done?"

"Yes, the ghost has been banished. She will not return."

Tomoko-ana frowned. "One of the priests said it was the Shibata nun."

"Yes," I said.

"I don't understand," Tomoko said. "Why would she wish to harm us?"

"We don't know that she did," Rie said. "She met with a sudden and violent death. Such an end could prompt one to focus their anger on the place where it occurred, perhaps believing those who had harmed her were still present. We don't know what would have happened had she reached this place."

"I suppose that is true," Tomoko admitted. "She was such a

gentle, brave soul. I remember . . . I heard her shouting, ordering them to stop—"

Tomoko swayed briefly, and now Rie was on her feet, with her arms around the old woman. "She is at rest now, thanks to my brother and our brother priests," Rie said. "Please do not dwell upon her death. I want to remember her life and what it meant to us. Surely she would want us to do the same."

Tomoko shuddered, and wiped her eyes with her sleeves. "Forgive a foolish old woman."

"There is nothing to forgive," Rie said. "You've said no more than I have thought myself these past few days. The fires will be lit tomorrow, this place will be cleansed, and we will start again." Rie turned to me. "I am told there is to be a banquet and ceremony to honor and re-dedicate Yahiko-ji. Our attendance has been requested by Lord Yoshiie himself, excepting Mai who is excused due to her . . . condition. May I assume you will be there as well?"

I took a slow breath. "It rather depends on what strength is left to me. The way I feel at the moment, I might sleep through the entire affair. But perhaps you should consider doing the same? I know this time has been very hard on you."

Rie demurred. "We cannot dishonor our fallen brothers and sisters by being such layabouts. I will be there. I will not hold it against you if you are not, Goji-kun, and Lord Yoshiie has more guards than the Emperor. You have done more than enough already."

"Not yet I haven't," I said. "But I do hope to. Until then, I have matters to attend."

"You still haven't gotten your color back," Tomoko said to Rie. "I will bring some of the *daicon* soup you like so much."

"I had two bowls at the evening meal as it is," Rie said, "but if you insist . . . ?"

"I do," Tomoko said.

"I leave my sister in your capable hands, Tomoko-ana," I said.

Kenji was waiting for me outside. "You didn't need to wait here," I said. "But since you have done so, walk with me."

The night had turned clear, with almost no clouds. Also no moon, but the stars were bright. The haze of summer had not yet come to obscure them. We started back to our quarters. I paused for a moment at the gate separating the nunnery from the main compound. The wooden beam was very thick and heavy but had been arranged to pivot on the left side so only one end needed to be raised to unbar the gate. Even so, I tried it and could raise the beam only with great difficulty. I had the Shibata nun's own word, but now I knew the Shibata nun could not possibly have unbarred the gate, or at least not alone, as I would have realized if I'd examined the gate more thoroughly. It was clearly designed so no single one of them could open it. I had wasted a question unless, perhaps, the Shibata nun had actually answered the question I had not asked.

"I was foolish to think the Shibata nun opened this gate."

Kenji grunted. "Not unless several of the nuns as well as the prioress were complicit in their own murders, which—yes—is nonsense on the face of it," Kenji said, then he went on, "I do not wish to intrude in family matters, but how is your sister now?"

"Much better. Apparently the recent unpleasantness was catching up to her. With a little food and rest, she should be fine."

"I am pleased to hear it. Now then—did you learn anything from the Shibata nun?"

"Nothing but more questions, I'm afraid." I related what the ghost of the Shibata nun had said, slowly and carefully going over the meeting in my mind to make sure I had omitted nothing.

"She apologized to you? Twice? Well, she did almost kill you, but that's not the sort of regret one normally expects from a ghost."

I thought about it. "Kenji-kun, what worries me is not the apology, but the expression of it. I do not think she was apologizing. I think she was expressing sympathy, perhaps even pity."

Kenji frowned. "Pity? To whom?"

"To me."

Kenji looked at me. "Lord Yamada, while I confess I myself have felt that particular emotion towards you from time to time, it was not under such circumstances and certainly not lately. It's true your time on this earth has not been without tragedy, but I do not see you as pitiable and fail to see why anyone else would."

"I think the Shibata nun did."

"Considering the Shibata nun never met you in life, I find it doubly strange that this would be the case. Unfortunately, and assuming you are correct, the only person who could tell you *why* she felt this way is now beyond this world. 'The one who betrayed us is dead. The one who killed us all still lives.' Is it a riddle? What does it mean?"

"I do not know, but I think there is yet someone living who might be able to shed some light on this."

Kenji frowned. "Are you referring to Mai?"

"Before Mai stood in her way last night, the ghost wanted nothing more than to kill me. My name alone seemed to enrage her, as if she knew who I was. After that, the spirit felt sorry for me. Consider this for a moment, Kenji-san. I have, and I find her sorrow even more puzzling than her rage."

"You think Mai knows what this means?"

"We've known from the start Mai saw *something*. At first I believed the information might simply be useful in piecing together the full story of the attack. Since then I've come to believe her information might be even more important than I am yet capable of understanding."

"She still can't speak, except in fragments," Kenji pointed out.

"She managed to tell the ghost something all the same. I don't know what or how, but it was enough to turn the ghost aside when that was beyond the power of both of us to do. More to the point, we assumed Mai's mind had been temporarily unhinged by the massacre, and she was still in the grip of remembered terrors. Placing herself between me and the ghost of the Shibata nun was one of the bravest acts I have ever seen. That was not the action of a person in the grip of unreasoning fear. If she's still afraid, she's afraid for a reason."

"The attempted *shikigami* attack would seem to bear this out," Kenji said dryly.

I had almost forgotten . . .

"Kenji, by any chance do you still have the remnants of the creature?"

The priest frowned. "I think so. I normally keep such things for later study, when possible."

Kenji pulled out a pouch and began rummaging through it. "I keep my wards close to hand, but this . . . ah! Found it."

He handed a battered piece of paper to me. Kenji had not been gentle with the creature's snake-form, and it showed in the remnants of the paper. A second look told me pretty much what my first look had told me, back on the day of the attack. It was a crude script, obviously not what I would have expected from Lord Tenshin, but then I knew there were *onmyoji* in the Abe Clan's employ other than Tenshin, and it could have been created by any of them. Crude and apparently done in haste as it was, there was still something familiar about the script.

Curse me thrice for a fool . . .

"Kenji, do you have an example of Lord Tenshin's work in there?"

"Probably, though most were thoroughly destroyed. None from the rain of saké have survived, I know that much. Ah, yes, here's one."

The side-by-side comparison was all it took. "Look here, Kenji—the way the *kanji* for *hi* is rendered. Check the separation of the first two strokes."

"It's identical," Kenji said, "but this could be coincidence."

"Then check the proportion on *mizu* and *shin* as well."

Kenji studied the paper. "Also identical . . . so we were wrong. Lord Tenshin did do this . . . but why would he disguise it? It's not as if we didn't already know his murderous intent nor suspect his involvement in this desecration. For his service to an outlaw clan, he is already under sentence of death. Adding this abomination to his crimes would not change that."

"True, Lord Tenshin attempting to conceal his involvement is yet one more thing which makes no sense, unless he wasn't doing anything of the sort."

"Then, pray, what was he trying to do?"

"Make a *shikigami* to attack whatever threat Mai represents to him, which is what he did do. As for the crudeness and apparent haste of the spell . . . what if, rather, this is the best he could do under the circumstances?"

"What circumstances, Lord Yamada?"

"This is, I think, the real question."

Kenji looked grim. "If there is a danger here, and it's clear to us both now there is, it must act soon. Tomorrow the Echigo governor arrives with additional archers, and the temple will be rededicated. Once that happens, Lord Yoshiie will have discharged his diplomatic obligations to the Shibata and be free to take his now very considerable force of allies north into Dewa, join his father and the Kiyohara forces assembled there, and march directly through the mountain passes into Mutsu, still far in advance of the winter snows. Any further attacks on Lord Yoshiie will have to be direct, and he is more than capable of meeting them. Whatever evil has managed to insinuate itself within Yahiko temple will be left thwarted, and Lord Sadato and the Abe Clan will be the ones in peril."

"So whatever trap Lord Tenshin has managed to set in place will have to be sprung soon. I think we both know the consequences if he succeeds."

Our quarters were in sight now. Guards patrolled the perimeter and were placed at the entrances, as we'd requested.

"Let's go check on Mai. She's probably worried."

"You go ahead. I need to think for a bit. The night air is good for this."

Good the night air might have been, but my thoughts refused to clarify anything. The worst part was I firmly believed the answer was dancing in plain sight of me and I simply could not see it. No, a nun did not open the main gate—it was impossible.

Did a nun let a lover in the back gate? Almost—but not quite—equally impossible. Nor, as Rie and my own common sense told me, would such a ploy even be necessary. The assassins always had the means to enter the nunnery, just as surely as they had the means to enter the main compound—the same technique would have worked easily. Why didn't they use it?

Because they knew the gate would be opened. The enemy was already within the walls.

It was the only answer that made any sense at all, so therefore it was not impossible. I merely did not understand how it was done, which was not the same thing. Every method I was able to think of until now had already been considered and then discarded. However the breach at the gate had been achieved, the method was one I had not yet considered. But what was left?

If Mai does know, I'm running out of time to solve the puzzle. If she does not . . .

It occurred to me, in such a case, I might be out of time, period.

For want of a better idea, I left the night to the stars and guards and went inside to find Kenji shaking his head in exasperation. "For a moment I believed Mai had run away again."

"Where is she?"

"Hiding in a clothes trunk. I considered hauling her out, but that seemed a little harsh."

I frowned. "What clothes trunk?"

"The one Lord Yoshiie sent over. There's one in our room, as well."

I went to see what Kenji was talking about, and there was, indeed, a lacquered trunk of considerable size. Neither I nor

Kenji would have fit in it, but if the one in Mai's rooms was the same, she'd have little trouble. I opened the lid.

"There's a new *hitatare* in here."

"Also new sandals, leggings, and robes appropriate for a priest," Kenji said. "I already looked. Lord Yoshiie apparently heard about the sad shape of your current clothing after the ghost's attack."

"Either that or he did not wish us to dishonor our company in the rededication ceremony and feast," I said, "but it was considerate of him all the same."

More than considerate. The new clothes were of far better quality even than the ones he had first provided, which, by comparison, were probably not much good now for anything but rags. I was suddenly in the mood for a bath, but first things came first. I went into Mai's room, announcing myself before I entered, and saw another similar trunk. The lid rose just enough for her to peek out at me.

"There is no *mamushi*," I said. "The Shibata nun will not be returning. But she was not what you were worried about, was she? No. Come on out, Mai-chan. It's only Kenji and me. You're safe. Please get out of there before you rumple your new clothes."

The lid slowly raised, and then Mai stood up. I noted then there was no chance that she'd put her new garments in disarray, as they had already been removed and placed neatly across her bedding. It was a fine new set of robes, three layers not counting a Chinese-style jacket in summer green. Such garb wouldn't have been out of place for an Imperial servant, though a noblewoman would have had to wear many more such layers to get the proper effect. I sometimes wondered how they managed to move at all.

"So it appears you will be going to the feast after all," I said, whereupon Mai sunk herself back down in the trunk and closed the lid.

I sighed. "Never mind. If you don't want to go, you don't have to go, but I understood from my sister that you had been excused."

The lid dropped the last few inches with a resounding thump.

"Mai, I meant what I said to you. I will make excuses if necessary, but you will not be forced to attend if you don't wish it. But why not? Tomoko-ana and Lady Rie will be there. I also understand a new prioress has been chosen. Don't you wish to meet her?"

Apparently not. The lid remained firmly closed.

"I'm tired of talking to a clothes chest, Mai-chan. Come out of there before you suffocate."

For a moment or two I wondered if she was going to ignore me, but the lid finally opened again. Mai stood up, but not before taking a long look around.

"I said it was just Kenji and me. Who did you think would be here?"

To no one's surprise, she didn't answer me. She simply stepped out of the clothes chest, kneeled in front of me, and bowed low. I took a long breath. "Mai-chan, do you remember the Shibata nun? How you saved my life?"

She simply bowed lower, which I took for a "yes." "You weren't afraid of her, were you? I have to say I certainly *was* afraid of her. Very afraid. Terrified. But you were not. I wish you could tell me why that was."

Mai looked up at me. Her mouth moved as if she wanted to say something, but then it closed again, and her face went as stony as a statue of a Buddha.

"You're not ready," I said. "I know, but I think it's really important you tell me what is frightening you. How I can I protect you—or any of us—if I don't know what I'm protecting you from? Do you see my problem? I'm afraid something very bad is about to happen and I'm not going to be able to stop it."

Mai looked directly at me then, and her face was a little less stony. I recognized the look in her eyes. It was the same one I had seen in those of the Shibata nun's ghost—pity.

Oh, Mai-chan. What do you know that I do not, and will you tell me before it is too late?

MY DREAMS that night were troubled. I dreamed I was back at Lake Biwa watching Princess Teiko, the woman I loved, about to step off into space from a high cliff. I was too far away and my legs moved so slowly I felt as if I were running through mud. I would be too late again, and there was nothing I could do except to watch her die. But then the figure I believed to be Princess Teiko changed, and now it was Mai-chan about to step off the cliff, and I was no closer to stopping it. Then Akimasa and Taro and Lord Yoshiie, then Kenji, then Tomoko-ana, and finally Rie, my sister. One by one I watched them all fall and die, and I could do nothing because the ground *was* mud, and I sank deeper into it with each step.

Rie died last, and it was she who rose as a rotting corpse from the water of the sacred lake to stare at me accusingly with her hollow eyes. "You couldn't save me, you know," she said. "You're always too late when it really matters."

"It's not too late! This isn't real!"

The same look, then, from the Shibata nun and Mai-chan and now on my sister's rotting face—pity.

"You're not as clever as you think you are," my sister's corpse said as it sank back into the water. "You never were."

Never . . .

The morning dawned clear and bright. Kenji, not known as an early riser, was already dressed and gone. This was the day of the rededication ceremony, and I knew, hedge priest that he was, his association with Lord Yoshiie had given him a bit more prominence than he was used to, and so he had duties. I did not, save for the usual one of trying to keep Lord Yoshiie alive, and right now I considered his bodyguards of much more use than I was. Fortunately, Lord Yoshiie's bounty included a less formal set of clothing for daily wear. The *hitatare*, although very fine, was suitable for formal banquets and such but not for much else. I got dressed and looked in on Mai, who was not in her quarters. I felt a moment of panic before I realized she was sitting in plain sight on the veranda. The guards had changed, but she was still under protection to the extent that someone, including Lord Yoshiie, could be protected from a threat without shape, form, or name.

"Come with me," I said to her, and she immediately fell into line behind me as I spoke to the guard, "Let no one save Master Kenji enter while we are gone."

"Understood," he said.

We went to where breakfast was still available and, once we'd eaten, I considered what to do next. "Shall we visit Lady Rie and Tomoko-ana? I'm sure they'd like to see you.

I took a step in the direction of the nunnery, but Mai hung

back, and I saw the fear return, sudden and fierce, to her eyes. *The nunnery still frightens her. I wondered. Yet she didn't seem to mind being outside its walls . . .*

"Never mind. Let's go somewhere else . . . I know! Let's visit the horses."

The fear receded as quickly as it appeared. Mai seemed almost cheerful as we left the main gate and proceeded south on the road to where Kenji's and my mounts were corralled. Mai barely glanced at the funeral pyres, their preparation complete and soon to be set ablaze. I knew one of the carefully wrapped corpses was that of the Shibata nun, but I also knew just as certainly her spirit had already departed the earth, and in an hour's time those of her sisters and brother monks would be sent on their own journeys. I saw Kenji with other priests conducting funeral rites. It had not been possible to conduct a proper funeral with each ritual done at the appropriate time, but under the circumstances no one was being terribly stringent about such matters. What could be done was being done.

The sight of the bodies does not bother her. I did not know if that was strange or not. I knew that Mai had been a peasant farm girl and as such was not terribly sheltered. Her compromised mental state seemed more related to the attack itself, but wouldn't this stark reminder of the aftermath drag up frightening memories? Yet Mai was smiling as we approached the paddock, the charged funeral pyres apparently already forgotten.

"Were there horses where you came from?"

She nodded absently. Her attention was on the horses milling about the enclosure. I could not have picked out the mounts Kenji and I had ridden if my life had depended on it, but I quickly found Taro, who was working with the other servants to bring in fodder. Suddenly the horses were far more alert as they were given breakfast.

"This is Shiroirei," he said, patting the neck of a white mare, "and this is Neko." He pointed to a black-maned horse several feet away." Only now I recognized them as our mounts.

"You're taking good care of them," I said.

"It is my duty . . . and I love horses," he said, though he was looking at Mai, who was now running her fingers through Shiroirei's mane.

"This is Mai," I said. "She might be traveling with us for a time. I'm not certain at the moment."

"Do you like horses?" Taro asked.

She smiled at him, then went back to playing with the horse's mane. "She doesn't talk," I said. "But I hope she will soon."

Taro shrugged. "It's all right. The other grooms talk all the time . . . about things. Sometimes it's better to be quiet. And she does like horses, I can tell."

I didn't ask what things the grooms talked about. I was fairly certain they were subjects unsuitable for Mai's hearing.

"She used to live on a farm." I said. While horses as draft animals were rare on a typical farm, it was not beyond possibility Mai had come in contact with the beasts before now, either through travelers or one of the horse breeding operations. She seemed at ease while petting Shiroirei's neck. Neko approached from the other side and nudged Mai with her muzzle, and soon Mai was petting both, who seemed to appreciate the attention. She barely reached either horse's shoulder, and she had to reach up to scritch them. Either of them could crush her in an instant, but she didn't seem the least bit concerned to have such massive beasts so close. She was far more at ease in their presence than I would probably ever be.

This doesn't fit.

As with the ghost of the Shibata nun and the presence of the funeral pyres, I was reminded again Mai was not nearly so timid and delicate a creature as she sometimes appeared. This was not the first time this had occurred to me, but now it was almost as if it was being emphasized. Yes, she had been genuinely frightened, so much so she'd risked an escape into monster-haunted forests rather than remain at the temple. But the sort of mindless terror I'd seen in her on the first day when she'd been little more than a quivering heap, the mindless terror which had robbed her of her capacity for speech, it simply did not fit the young woman I was coming to know.

She isn't afraid of returning to the nunnery because of bad memories. She's afraid because the danger is still there!

I could have kicked myself for a fool. Aside from Lady Kuzunoha's warning, I already knew something was still not right, and my instincts had pointed me at the nunnery, but try as I might, I had been unable to locate the danger. I and others had searched it repeatedly and found nothing, though a great part of the difficulty was none of us understood what we were looking for. Mai did know, I was as certain of it now as I had ever been. Yet if the danger remained, my sister and Tomoko-ana were in the thick of it. Neither had been harmed, but I was certain neither of them was the target. Lord Yoshiie was, and perhaps this was the only reason either of the surviving nuns was still alive. In attacking them, whatever it was would reveal itself, perhaps too soon. I now realized both women should be removed to safer quarters as soon as possible. There were still outbuildings within the main temple compound not in use and would be relatively simple to secure, at least from human interference. With the gates to the nunnery barred and guarded, whatever was within it could damn well stay there until the ceremonies were over and it could be searched even more thoroughly, not excluding tearing everything down until we found . . . what? I still didn't know, and I couldn't escape the feeling I damn well should know.

I left Mai briefly in the care of Taro, Shiroirei, and Neko while I found one of Lord Yoshiie's couriers. We would need Lord Yoshiie's permission, but I did not think this would be an obstacle. I gave him instructions and sent him off. When I returned to the paddock, Mai was singing to the horses. I didn't recognize the tune, but it was probably a traditional peasant song, one of a sort you'd likely not hear in the capital. Her voice, clearly untrained, was lovely.

She saw me then, and she stopped singing and went back to petting the horses as if nothing at all had happened.

"Mai-chan—"

She turned away from me, and I stopped to take a long breath. I knew that a song, something remembered, repeated, was not the same as speaking, but why had she reacted as if she'd been caught doing something she shouldn't? Like so much else, Mai's affliction simply no longer made sense to me. Fear? Yes, and likely justified. But mindless horror, terror? It did not fit the Mai I had come to know, and so her affliction of speech did not fit either.

What if the truth is Mai most certainly can speak, but refuses to do so?

Which also didn't make sense. Unless . . .

I finally thought of a reason. A silly, unbelievable reason. I couldn't even hold on to the idea at first. I could see it but not quite grasp it, like a bright minnow in swiftly moving waters. So I refused to grasp it, to understand it the way a fuller comprehension would eventually require. Perhaps I didn't need to think about the implications, for now. I considered it a puzzle, like one of those clever wooden boxes which appeared to have no hinges, no latch—indeed appeared to be nothing more than a simple block of wood—but opened easily once you knew the trick. All I had to do was not think too much about what I was going to find inside.

"Mai-chan, I think we need to return to the compound. Say goodbye to your new friends."

I'm not sure who was sadder for her to leave then: Mai, Taro, or the two horses, since all three of the latter walked with us as far as the makeshift fence as we headed back to the temple compound. We had barely returned to our quarters when I received word that both Tomoko-ana and my sister had adamantly and very vocally refused to leave the nunnery. I wasn't terribly surprised. Both Tomoko-ana and Rie had made their determination to preserve their community very clear, and I think they were afraid their relocation would prove to be the first step in their order's dissolution. I accepted the inevitable, but did order a rotation of guards be placed within the compound at all times. The nuns could protest *that* if they wished, but I was certain they would not. I wanted to take the news in person to Lady Rie and Tomoko-ana before the ceremony began, but there was no time. As things stood, I had to leave Mai in the care of two rather stolid Minamoto *bushi* with strict instructions she was to have no visitors save for myself and Kenji.

I was then present along with Kenji, Lady Rie, and Tomoko-san when the funeral pyres were finally lit. The two nuns concentrated on their prayer beads as the smoke from the dead rose into the sky. Lord Yoshiie, Lord Muramasa, and the Echigo governor sat in state on a raised dais on the far side, ringed by *bushi*. I was pleased to see Lord Yoshiie had not lowered his guard, but after so many failed assassination attempts, he didn't seem likely to forget the dangers. Once the burning was well under way, they withdrew along with the Shibata priests to the temple proper. I saw a veiled woman among them who had not been in evidence during the lighting of the funeral pyres themselves.

"Who is that?" I whispered to Kenji. "The new prioress? I had heard she was here."

"Just so," he said. "Lady Shibata no Akiko, Lord Muramasa's first cousin? Second? I'm not sure. She will be formally presented at the feast tonight, but the actual investiture is taking place now, along with the rededication."

"Aren't you going?" I asked.

"I'm no longer needed," Kenji said. "The Shibata priests have made it clear this is their responsibility now, and for my part they are welcome to it. I'll be glad when we're gone from here."

"As will I. But we're not marching on Mutsu just yet."

As the fire grew, I fancied I could feel the flames of hell on my skin, and there was a smell like burning feathers. "Kenji-san, do you have a spare set of prayer beads?"

Kenji looked at me. "Do you even know how to pray?"

"It has been a very long time, but I think I can remember."

Rie had shown me once. How to count the beads, what the number of them meant. I watched the two nuns work through their prayers with practiced ease. Kenji just shrugged. "Use mine. I'm through with them for the moment."

He handed me the necklace of large wooden beads that he wore, so thick and uncouth-looking compared to the delicate *malas* in use by the women, but they did make a satisfying *click!* as I snapped each bead into place, one after the other. I prayed for the fallen. I prayed for Mai. I prayed for my sister and Tomoko-ana, and Lord Yoshiie and Kenji. I did not pray for myself, with two exceptions—I prayed I was right, and I prayed I was wrong.

I leave that in your hands. Whatever Buddhas or gods might be listening will just have to sort this out for yourselves.

When the prayers were ended and the pyres were burning down to ash, I returned the beads to Kenji. Neither Tomoko nor Lady Rie protested when I had guards escort them back to the nunnery, nor had I really expected them to, since I was no longer insisting they leave the compound, though Rie could not resist needling me a little.

"Honestly, brother, if something within the nunnery wished us harm, would we not already be dead?"

I knew this was not necessarily the case, since the situation within Yahiko-ji had finally taught me common sense was not giving me the solution I needed. Regardless, and since both Tomoko-ana and my sister were to be honored guests at the feast, the guards' simple task was to remain close but outside their quarters, and then escort them again to the feast when the time had come.

"How long before the rededication ceremony is concluded?" I asked Kenji.

"The new abbot likes to hear himself talk, so it will take a little while. Why?"

"Because we need to use this time to make ourselves a bit more presentable. We're going to request a private audience with Lord Yoshiie."

"Very well, but would you mind telling me why we are doing this?"

I glanced back at the funeral pyre. "For the only reason that matters now—to save Lord Yoshiie's life and so fulfill our sworn oath. At whatever the cost."

THE MAIN LECTURE HALL at Yahiko temple had a different look that evening—the stone lanterns were all lit, and extra lanterns were hung from the trees and on twine strung from the eaves of the verandas out to the first tree limbs. They glowed red and yellow and plum-colored. If I didn't know otherwise I'd think it was *matsuri* time and I'd walked into a festival. The funeral rites for those murdered at Yahiko temple were not yet concluded and wouldn't be until we were already in Dewa province, but this one exception to welcome the new Shibata abbot and prioress was, all agreed, appropriate for the occasion. Whereas quite often I felt as if I'd been in mourning for most of my life. The reminder that this was not necessarily our natural condition did little to lighten my mood.

The feast was well begun before Kenji found me alone on the veranda by the main entrance. "Your sister has been asking for you."

"Please tell her I'll be in soon—it's almost time to begin. How are they arranged?"

"The new prioress is in the middle, just in front of the dais. Tomoko-ana on the left and Lady Rie on her right, from where you enter the hall. The new abbot will be seated on the dais, per protocol. You and I are to flank the dais, me on the left, and you on the right, plus the guards on either side of us. That was the seating Lord Yoshiie specified."

"It is an honor to be allowed so close," I said. "Let us do our best not to abuse his trust."

Kenji went back inside, and I settled in to wait. I did not have to wait for very long. I heard the voices coming from the adjoining meditation hall where Lord Yoshiie had taken residence in our time at the temple. He was preceded by the abbot in full regalia, then Lord Muramasa, and the man I assumed to be the Echigo governor. It was hard to tell who was who, since they were all resplendent in full armor, with their *menpo* covering their faces and their *maedate* crests slicing the night wind. I bowed as they approached and then hurried to take my place on the right side of the dais, as instructed. Kenji was already kneeling on a cushion to the left. Lady Rie gave me a disapproving look for my late arrival, though the prioress and Tomoko-ana hardly looked at me. They were seated at a centrally placed low table no more than a bow's length from the dais itself, as testament to the honor they were being afforded this night. The rest of the tables were further away, now filled with Minamoto and Shibata *bushi*, other priests, and a rather uncomfortable group I took to be the headman of Yahiko village and his guests. I turned my attention back to the procession entering the lecture hall from one of the side entrances, which placed them behind a line of *bushi* as they approached the dais from the left.

Since they were in armor, their campstools had been set on the dais, except for the abbot, who had a fine silk cushion awaiting him. We all touched our foreheads to the floor as the lords took their places on the dais.

Lord Muramasa rose then. He had his war-fan in his hands and waved it once like a baton over the assembly. "Lord Yoshiie has requested the honor of proposing a toast to the fallen but especially to those who are with us tonight, joined by our cousin prioress of Shibata."

The pages and other servers were already quickly moving through the assembly, filling their cups. One of them brought a clay pitcher and set it before me.

"Lord Yoshiie, with your permission?" I asked.

The central figure nodded slightly, and I quickly moved to place three saucer-like cups in front of Tomoko-ana, the new prioress, and my sister. Kenji himself presented saucers to the lords on the dais. As one they raised them to their lips and drank, and Tomoko-ana and the prioress quickly followed their example.

"Brother, what is the meaning of this? You know I cannot drink rice wine," Rie said, her voice a harsh whisper.

"Nor do I expect you to, nor either of your companions. This is nothing but pure water. Drink it."

Rie just stared at her saucer as if she could not quite comprehend what she was seeing. "I-I cannot."

I think, perhaps, I had held on to just a sliver of hope, right up until that moment. "Sister," I said, "I really must insist."

What happened next happened in almost less than an instant.

Rie shot to her feet, sending the table flying. In one step she was across it, a formerly concealed dagger in her hand, racing toward Lord Yoshiie. Despite the fact I was ready for her, she almost made it, but I threw myself at her from the side and managed to bring her down. I felt a hot sting in my arm as she slashed with the dagger. I did my best to trap it, but with her flailing sleeves and non-human speed I couldn't even see it. She struggled to her feet, despite my best efforts, to be greeted by a ring of *bushi,* who, fortunately, had remembered their orders and kept their swords sheathed. She hesitated, and I used the chance to seize her wrist and twist her arm behind her back. It took all my strength to hold her.

"Take her," I shouted, and the ring of *bushi* closed in. By then the rest of the company were on their feet, and many had their daggers drawn, though only the guards had been allowed to bear swords in the hall itself.

"Sheathe all weapons," Lord Yoshiie commanded. The *real* Lord Yoshiie, who appeared now at the main doorway. The man on the dais removed his face guard to reveal himself as the man we had chosen to play the part, a Minamoto *bushi* of a similar height and build to Lord Yoshiie. A very brave man whose bravery, thanks to my clumsiness, had almost cost him his life.

"We have her, Lord Yoshiie," Akimasa announced, as Rie was tied with ropes that even she, in her altered state, could not break. "What are your orders?"

Lord Yoshiie stared at me. "Lord Yamada, are you certain about this?"

"Yes, my lord. We need her alive and unharmed. For now."

Lord Yoshiie grunted. "Take her away."

CHAPTER TWELVE

THE FEAST, as one might expect, ended rather abruptly. Now Kenji and I kneeled inside the mediation hall while Lord Yoshiie paced. Lord Muramasa and the Echigo governor, whose name I had finally learned was Mitsutaka, sat on stools nearby studying Kenji and myself as if we were some strange creatures that had never seen the light of day before. My arm was bandaged where the creature which was now my sister had slashed it. The wound wasn't deep.

"You were right, Lord Yamada," Yoshiie said finally. "How did you know?"

"I only suspected, my lord," I said. "The ceremonial toast was the true test. A *shikigami*, even one of this advanced type, cannot eat or drink, nor do they need to do so. We must be careful this one does not have the chance, as it would destroy her."

I was still having a great deal of difficulty trying not to think of the creature as Rie. This was made harder by the sure understanding that part of it, perhaps even the greater part, was indeed my sister. That was the cruelest thing of all—my sister was dead. And yet, here she was, by all appearances every bit my sister, Rie. Perhaps the worst part was that Rie herself likely did not understand what had happened to her, and when the time came, I would need to be the one to tell her.

"What I still don't understand is why we haven't executed the creature already," Lord Muramasa said. "The thing is clearly dangerous!"

I was quickly running out of whatever reserves of strength I had used up until now. "Very dangerous," I said. "The only thing more dangerous would be to destroy it. Perhaps Master Kenji can explain this better than I can."

Kenji shot me a look that clearly said he didn't appreciate being thrown into the glare of such men, but he seized the role and made it his own. "I was there when Lord Yamada learned of these special kind of *shikigami*, and there were two types—one can operate under its own volition without constant directives from the *onmyoji* and another sort, which does not depend on the fading power of the spell itself to draw its life-force but is supplied by a direct connection to the *onmyoji*. It literally draws its strength from the magician who created it, and can only live as long as the magician himself does."

"Which sort is the creature with Lady Rie's form?" Lord Mitsutaka asked.

Kenji took a deep breath. "Both, my lords. It was Lord Tenshin's genius to combine the two forms in the same creature. Only it seems unlikely he used a voluntary soul." He looked at me then, and I nodded.

"My sister was murdered deliberately and for a purpose," I said. "The false body to receive her spirit was already prepared. Normally, a willing spirit would be summoned to take up residence there. Instead, I believe a confused spirit who did not yet understand what happened to her was tricked into the false body. I have no doubt now the man who escaped on the pirate ship was Lord Tenshin. He used the very link that even now gives her sustenance to control her. The nuns let Rie back into the compound when she returned from her errand; no one could possibly detect the change. It was this *shikigami* who opened the gate to let the assassins in. This is the reason so many of the nuns were cut down at the gate itself—they were trying to stop her."

"Are you saying Lord Tenshin's servant created this . . . abomination, merely to have a second chance of success if the first attack failed?" Lord Muramasa asked.

"No, my lord Shibata. He had two reasons, only one was the murder of Lord Yoshiie. The other was Lord Tenshin has a personal grudge against me. There was a reason my sister was chosen and not, say, the Shibata nun, who in some regards would have served the purpose better. I think he had planned Rie would carry out the assassination so I would have to watch my own sister executed, and only then with her true nature revealed would I understand the full depth of his revenge."

"Is this why the creature still lives?" Lord Muramasa asked. "I still do not understand it."

"If I may, my lords," Kenji said. "I mentioned earlier the creature draws its strength from the magician who created it. A great deal of strength, as the creature demonstrated tonight. So long as the creature with Rie's soul is not destroyed, the link remains, and Lord Tenshin cannot create another—to do so would kill him. So long as the creature lives under our control, he is powerless, and grows weaker by the day."

"I see the advantage," Lord Yoshiie said. "But you still did not answer my question—how did you know?"

I looked at the floor. "When the ghost of the Shibata nun returned, she was headed for the nunnery. She only attacked me when I spoke my name. I did not understand at first—we had never met in life, and she had no reason to dislike me. So why attack me? *Because I was her murderer's brother.* She would have attacked the nunnery itself because she knew my sister—or what she believed to be my sister—was still inside. Perhaps she sought revenge, or perhaps she wanted to protect those, like Mai and Tomoko, who remained. We will never know. The point is, her anger at me made no sense, unless I was connected somehow with what had happened to the nunnery. Plus, in order to open the gate to the nunnery, the enemy had to be already inside, yet lifting the bar required the strength of at least two people . . . or one *shikigami*. The only answer left was that one of the nuns was not what she appeared to be. The Shibata nun's reaction to me, plus Lady Rie's collapse during the exorcism ceremony when she should not have been affected, made my sister, unfortunately, the likely choice. I must beg your forgiveness that it took me so long to put the pieces together."

"What must be done with the creature?" Lord Muramasa asked.

"We must keep her . . . it, safe. Under close guard and confinement but safe. Now that Lord Tenshin's plan has failed, he will want to destroy it so he can recoup his strength for another attempt. I doubt he expected his creature to survive your guards once it had managed to kill you. This was an error on his part, and now he cannot break the link so long as we don't allow it. He would have done so already if he could."

"Then we will use it to our advantage," Lord Yoshiie said. "How long must we keep the creature confined?"

"With your permission, until I kill Lord Tenshin," I said. "Only then will the spell be safely broken."

"Permission is granted, but if I understand what you and Master Kenji are telling me, the moment Lord Tenshin falls, your sister—or what remains of her—will die," Lord Yoshiie said gently. "Is this not true?"

I bowed. "My lord, what you saw today was a creation with my sister's likeness and memories. Lady Yamada no Rie is already dead."

Kenji held his peace until we had been dismissed and were walking across the compound. The funeral pyres were almost out, but there was still the glow of embers to the southwest. "I could hardly believe it when you told me about Rie, but I know you didn't grasp the answer and stage this successful charade just because the Shibata nun attacked you," he said. "I know you, and that's not the sort of conclusion you'd draw on such flimsy evidence. Those people may accept it, but I do not. There has to be more to it."

"You are right. What I said to Lord Yoshiie was true but not complete. If you want to know the rest, then come with me."

"Where are we going?"

"I think you know."

We went back to our quarters. I dismissed the guards there and went inside. Mai kneeled in the hallway outside of our room. I think she was waiting for us. I fetched two cushions from our quarters and put them down for Kenji and myself.

"Let's get comfortable," I said.

Kenji just frowned and sat down, but Mai sighed. I followed Kenji's example. Even now I wasn't entirely sure how to proceed, but it was past time to find out if my understanding had any basis in the truth. "Now then, here is our enigma. Mai-chan, a girl so terrified, a mind so unhinged, she lost the power of speech. A girl so brave she risked the mindless wrath of the Shibata nun to save my life. A girl who could walk past the funeral pyres of all the women who had taken her in, given her a home, without shedding a tear. What are we to make of her, Kenji-san?"

"When you put it like that, it doesn't make a lot of sense, does it?"

I nodded. "And this is precisely the problem. The two people I've described don't belong in the same body. Yet here she is. So what conclusion must we draw from this?"

Mai wasn't yielding an inch, but Kenji was starting to put it all together. "The conclusion is one face we are seeing is a mask."

"I believe this to be true, and the only question really left is which one is the true Mai, and which one is the false? I will tell you my opinion of the matter, Mai-chan. Perhaps you will choose to enlighten me if I go astray. Now then—when I first saw you, it was on the day of the massacre. I think the fear I saw in you then was real enough, but I was wrong as to the reason for it. You had seen who let the assassins into the compound, just as the Shibata nun and those nuns who had died at the gate did. Only you, my sister, and Tomoko-ana lived, and none save the Lady Rie herself was supposed to do so. It was of no consequence in Tomoko's case—she had obviously seen nothing. But Rie wasn't certain about you, and your fear of returning to the compound had surely raised her suspicions—or rather, Lord Tenshin's—and this uncertainty meant your death at the first opportunity."

Kenji frowned. "Wait a minute. Why didn't Mai just

tell . . . oh." He stopped suddenly, understanding dawning in his eyes.

"Who first appeared as Lord Yoshiie's representative, aside from the inconvenient guards? *Lady Rie's own brother*. At this point, Mai had to assume we were working together, and even if we were not, how did she think I'd react if she'd said Lady Rie was the traitor? No, Kenji—she pretended to be mute to buy time to escape, because she saw escape as her only chance of survival. That's when she fled the nunnery and got lost in the woods."

"Where you and Lady Kuzunoha found her."

"Another of the many things that made no sense to me—Mai believed I was hunting her to kill her. When I not only spared her life but chased away a couple of *youkai*, she came to understand I was *not* working with my sister. More, I promised to keep her safe. She took the chance I was telling the truth. After all, I could have murdered her in the woods as easily as saved her and no one would have been the wiser."

"And she'd clearly learned the woods were more death trap than refuge."

"Just so. But her problem remained—Lady Rie. Mai needed to tell someone, but who would have believed her? I admit I wouldn't have, at least not then. The assumption would have been the poor demented child was imagining things. No, it was only over time that I came to realize Mai was faking her condition in order to have an excuse not to reveal what she had seen, and I simply could not understand why. It only began to make sense when I forced myself to think the unthinkable—that Rie was the one who let the murderers inside the nunnery."

"That is suspicion, not proof. What if Lady Rie had accepted the toast at the feast?"

"I knew she would not. You see, once my mind was on this path I realized I had never seen Lady Rie eat or drink, not once since the massacre. I saw Tomoko-ana do so, and we've both seen Mai-chan's appetite."

"Wait . . . didn't you tell me that Tomoko-ana was bringing your sister food?"

"True, but I had assumed Tomoko-ana had seen Lady Rie eat. She had not. A woman of my sister's class would never eat in front of others, as a rule, even if she had taken holy orders. When the food disappeared, Tomoko-san took for granted it had been eaten, as anyone would."

Mai smiled then, but it was a sad smile.

"Shall I continue to speak for you, Mai? I think you are more than capable of doing so yourself."

She bowed. "I deceived you and Master Kenji. For what little this may be worth, I am truly sorry."

"So the *shikigami* I killed . . . ?" Kenji asked. "The *mamushi*?"

"Lord Tenshin, working through my sister. Mai-chan was still a loose end, but that failure must have convinced him further attempts would draw attention to Mai's importance, which is the last thing he wanted. Besides, Lady Rie's nature had not yet been revealed, so his plan was still on target. He took the chance we would not learn the truth in time to save Lord Yoshiie."

"Then he was wrong. But Lord Yamada . . . your sister."

"Yes. My sister."

"I loved Lady Rie," Mai said softly. "She was a kind and gentle person, and I didn't understand what had happened to her. She wouldn't have hurt anyone. I think . . . at first I really was a little mad, but as for what you say . . . it is true. I believed you were my only chance to survive. Which is why I threw myself between you and the poor prioress. I did not think she would harm me, but I was certain she would kill you . . . and I needed you. I was able to make her understand I knew what she knew, that was all. She trusted me to find a way to uncover the truth, but I let her down. I could not find a way to tell you so you would believe me. I failed her and I failed you."

"Failed?" Kenji said, "Hardly. You could not have chosen better—you told Lord Yamada by *not* telling him. By being a puzzle he needed to solve, you led him to the answer, and in the only way he could accept—by coming to it on his own, however reluctantly."

I pondered what my friend had said, but not for long. "I'm afraid Kenji-san is quite correct. You were right to think I would not have believed you, at first. I doubt I would have."

"But your sister—" Mai began.

"My sister's soul," I said, "Is still in that creature. Which is why I would not have believed you. I *knew* I was speaking to my sister, Rie, all this time. I never doubted it, not for an instant. Not even when I realized the truth. And so Lord Tenshin has his revenge after all."

Kenji frowned. "How could he have known about Rie? Very few people knew she was your sister. I didn't even know myself until we arrived, remember?"

"I believe Lord Tenshin did know," I said. "*How* he knew is not important at the moment. For right now, there is still a great deal to do. We will be leaving soon, and the *shikigami* that is my sister will be coming with us."

"Wouldn't it be better to leave her here?" Kenji asked.

"How long do you think it would be before she persuaded some ignorant novice to bring her water to ease her suffering, or perhaps a randy priest sees no harm in a brief liaison with a winsome prisoner? No, Kenji. I need her where I can keep an eye on her. She must not be allowed to harm anyone nor destroy herself. When the time comes, I must be the one . . . to end it."

"Lord Yamada, surely—" Kenji began, but I cut him off.

"No, Kenji. It has to be me. I can trust no one else with this. Not even you. Mai, you will return to the nunnery for now. Kenji and I will see you there safely and place you in Tomoko-ana's care."

"For now?" she repeated.

"For now. Lady Rie once said you still had not decided on the path you would take, and I can see she spoke truly in this. Kenji and I will be away for a while, and this cannot be helped. If we live, we will return. I owe you a debt, Mai-chan, and as a rather disreputable woman known as the Widow Tamahara could tell you, I always pay my debts. Eventually."

"My parents promised me they would return," Mai said softly. "And they did not, so I will not ask it of you."

I grunted. "I've come to mistrust promises myself, but I will make this one just the same—you will have a chance to make your own choice. The Rie I knew would have insisted upon it. Until then, try to be of use to Tomoko-ana and the new prioress. They are going to need what assistance they can find."

We helped Mai gather her things and escorted her back through the gates of the nunnery. There was no hesitation or fear on her part this time. We found Tomoko-ana weeping, and it wasn't hard to guess why. When we finally took our leave, I think the old woman was more in Mai's care than the reverse. I looked back at the main hall of Yahiko temple. The festivities had apparently resumed, no doubt on Lord Yoshiie's insistence, and why not? The danger was, for the moment, past, and this was likely the last such chance the Minamoto *bushi* and allies would have before their real work began.

"Shall we join the others?" Kenji asked.

"I am going to take a walk," I said. "But you go. It would perhaps be rude if at least one of us doesn't put in an appearance. I think, under the circumstances, Lord Yoshiie will forgive my own absence."

"You're going to speak with the *shikigami*, aren't you?" he asked.

"Oh, yes," I said. "But not just yet."

Kenji went back to the lecture hall, and I left through the main gate. The guards gave me curious looks, but no one challenged me. I crossed the road then and entered the wooded hillsides. "I know you're here, Lady Kuzunoha. I would speak with you for a moment."

I wondered if she would bother to put on her human appearance for me, but that was the form she took as she emerged behind a briar thicket. I remembered her face, and while I could not explain why, there was some comfort in seeing its familiar outlines. Even after so many years I would not say Lady Kuzunoha was my friend, but it was fair enough to say we understood one another, which was close enough to friendship most of the time. I wasn't certain if this would be one of those times or not.

"How much do you know about the situation in Yahiko temple now?" I asked.

"The scent has changed, Lord Yamada. Which is very strange. The evil is present even now, but the fear and sense of impending danger is gone. I do not understand."

I told her about my sister. Lady Kuzunoha pondered the matter. "I have never been human," Lady Kuzunoha said, "but I lived among them for several years, and I do know what loss is, perhaps even better than most humans do. Lord Tenshin has much to answer for."

"And he will answer," I said. "I will see to it. Yet I must ask you to amend our agreement."

She raised an eyebrow. "Oh? In what regard?"

"I need you to remain near Yahiko temple while we continue north into Dewa."

"While Lord Yasuna rides off into peril? Why should I do this?"

"Because of the debt you owe me now, the one you don't even know about yet."

"Which is?"

"Lord Yasuna's life is in my hands. And if I followed my instincts now, I would kill him myself."

The transformation was immediate. Lady Kuzunoha stood before me now on four legs in her full fox-demon form. Blue foxfire surrounded her like a glory. "You dare—"

"Yes, I do." I said, and then I told her why. It took a few moments, but Lady Kuzunoha resumed her human form. Even so, the scowl on her face could have curdled milk.

"I don't care about Lord Yoshiie or the Minamoto or even

that fool Abe no Sadato," she said. "I believe I have made this clear enough. I care only about Lord Yasuna."

"And how did you plan on protecting him, since the true danger now will be from arrows and spears? It is one thing to slip silently through the woods tracking down *shikigami* and human assassins but quite another to enter a battlefield. More, you cannot allow him to see you or suspect for even a moment you are nearby. You need to let me handle this. In return, I will protect Lord Yasuna, just as I have before, but I need you to remain here and protect the human girl named Mai."

"If you're taking the evil with you, what is her danger?"

"The same one which has existed since we arrived—that Lord Tenshin would find a way to strike yet again. Out of spite, if for no other reason."

"If you fail me, I will kill her myself," Lady Kuzunoha said.

"No, you won't. You will kill me."

The scowl deepened. "We have shared much over the years, Lord Yamada, but do not think for a moment I would hesitate."

"I know you wouldn't. Which is why, if needed, you will take your revenge on me, for it will be my fault if Lord Yasuna dies. It is *I* who own Lord Yasuna's life now. Not Mai and not the Minamoto."

"Don't let him die," she said. "I have your word?"

"You have my word."

"Then you have mine. May we both prove trustworthy."

"Thank you. There is, however, one more thing."

I didn't think it was possible for her scowl to deepen. I was wrong. I also caught a flash of foxfire dancing across Lady Kuzunoha's shoulders. "I would be careful about making demands, Lord Yamada."

"Not a demand. Say rather a favor from one old associate to another. In which case I will be in your debt again."

"What is it you wish of me?"

"Before my sister—or rather the creature bearing her soul—returned to the nunnery, she was last seen alive in Yahiko village. Which leads me to believe she was ambushed and murdered between there and here. Would . . . would you help me find her body?"

For a moment Lady Kuzunoha simply stared at me, but her expression slowly softened and the foxfire winked out. "Lord Yamada, it would be my honor."

We went to search the gullies and ravines between the temple and the village, aided by my best guesses and Lady Kuzunoha's sensitive nose. We searched until the first stray arrows of dawn crossed the horizon, but in the end we found nothing.

"I must say, if Lord Tenshin's henchmen sought to hide Lady Rie's body, they did a very good job of it," Lady Kuzunoha said. "I can detect nothing larger than a dead rat."

"Then, when the time comes, I will politely request Lord Tenshin himself inform me as to where my sister's mortal remains may be recovered."

"If he refuses?" she asked. Her tone was even, but I saw the traces of a grim smile on her face.

"The result will be the same whether he tells me or not. I'm going to kill him. His part will merely be to decide how quickly."

CHAPTER THIRTEEN

KENJI FOUND ME the following morning in the Minamoto encampment, watching the sword polisher put the finishing touches on my *tachi*. When all was done, I could not even tell the blade had ever been damaged. I accepted the weapon and rewarded the man, if not handsomely, at least as generously as I was able.

"A fine job," Kenji admitted. "But considering the service you have already rendered to Lord Yoshiie, it would not be out of place to request a reward. Possibly a new blade?"

I sheathed the sword in its *saya* and fastened the rings on my sash. "This one suits me," I said. "Besides, I have already made a request of Lord Yoshiie, which he kindly granted."

Kenji frowned. "That was remarkably quick, considering your usual unconcern in such matters. What did you ask for?"

"It should be ready by now. Come see."

The armor was mounted on a wooden form built for the purpose. It was rather simple compared to what was worn by Lord Yoshiie and his generals, but I was pleased. The plates of the chest piece were made of layers of leather laminated together and heavily lacquered, with a thick cloth covering of black laced with red. There were similar pieces made to cover my arms and lower legs. A long, divided skirt also of lacquered plates belted at the waist covered the outside of the upper thighs, the inside of which were left bare to aid in riding. The helmet was of iron plates skillfully joined, with articulated metal scales hung from the back to protect the nape and sides of the neck. The *maedate* on the helmet was covered in gold leaf and molded into the shape of a hornet.

The armorer greeted us. "As Lord Yoshiie directed," he said, and bowed.

"A very fine job, thank you," I said.

Kenji waited until the armorer was out of earshot. "Lord Yamada, would you mind telling me what you think you're doing?"

"Isn't it obvious, Kenji-san? I'm going to war."

"We are all going to war. Our mission has been to make sure Lord Yoshiie lives to fight that war. Joining the *bushi* was not our mission."

"I swore I would see Lord Yoshiie safely to Dewa. I will fulfill my vow. If possible, I will even keep him alive until this matter is settled. Yet this is no longer my only purpose. It is Lord Yoshiie's remit to punish the Abe for disobedience to the Emperor. Punishing Lord Tenshin for the murder of my sister is mine. Besides, do you really think it is possible to keep Lord Yoshiie safe without going into battle? That is where he will be, and in such a circumstance, I would rather be in armor than out of it."

Kenji took a slow breath. "I do concede your point, but you've known all this from the beginning. Tell me you had this part planned as well."

"No."

"I thought not. I have lost people dear to me as well, Lord

Yamada, and you know this to be true. I do understand how you feel. You have cause to assume Lord Tenshin chose your sister as revenge, which leads you to reply in kind. Yet what we learned of Lord Tenshin while chasing him was that the man is a ruthless plotter of the first order. I wouldn't hesitate to say he probably never so much as went to the latrine without at least one ulterior motive in his lifetime. But didn't the fact Rie was your sister *make* her the logical choice for his hidden assassin? The closer the association to Lord Yoshiie, the closer his assassin would be as well."

I studied the lacings on the *sode*. "Did you honestly think this had not occurred to me? Let us, for the moment, suppose it is true. Am I supposed to feel better if the murder of my sister was *not* personal, merely tactical? No, Kenji. I need my anger. I plan to put it to good use."

"I merely suggest you do not use it to get yourself killed."

"Ah, you think I'm seeking my own death for failure to protect what is left of my family? For what little this may be worth—that is not my plan."

"Fair enough, but now what?"

"Well . . . you could help me carry this equipment back to our quarters. There's a lot of it."

Kenji sighed. "Do you even know how to wear this?"

"No, but I'm hoping Taro can help. He's seen it done more than I have."

In the end I considered it prudent to enlist Akimasa's aid. He had likely forgotten more about the proper use and wearing of armor than I would ever learn, but for the most part he approved of my choices.

"Not so heavy as some," he said, "and a good helmet such as this is worth more than all the rest together if you ever find yourself on your feet against a swordsman on horseback. Your armor will be hot, and you will always be aware of its weight whether you're used to it or not, but properly laced and fitted, it will not interfere with your movements. Just keep in mind the best armor is the sort that's never needed."

"Meaning it is better to avoid the spear or arrow in the first place. I quite agree."

"For someone who has never been at war, you're a quick study," Akimasa said. "However, there will be a great many spears and arrows. If you do find yourself in the thick of things, avoiding them all is unlikely."

Akimasa repeated his demonstrations and instructions until he was satisfied I knew how to wear the armor properly, then he took his leave. Kenji took a long, slow walk around me. "Lord Yamada, if I didn't know you . . . well, I wouldn't know you."

"I'll never be a proper *bushi*, and if Prince Kanemore could see me now, he'd laugh himself sick. But I think I very well may have to depend on the armorer's craft before all this is over and done. Now . . . help me out of this thing. I need to go speak to my sister."

Kenji began to unravel the knots. "May I go with you? I still think there should be some way to detect the presence of one of these creatures. I wish to test my senses at close range."

"Very well, but please leave the talking to me. And if I ask you to forget whatever you may hear, you will never speak of it again. Is this understood?"

Kenji barely hesitated. "It is."

After I was out of the armor, we stowed it carefully in our quarters. When the time came to move out, it would be entrusted to the supply carts until needed. I merely hoped those instances would be under Lord Yoshiie's control and not the Abe Clan's. We walked from main temple to the storage building where the creature that was and yet was not my sister had been confined. The guards lifted the bar, and Kenji and I proceeded cautiously into the gloom.

"Strange. I don't feel dead."

Rie—for I was still having trouble thinking of her as anything else—kneeled on a floor cushion in a room that was otherwise empty, head bowed as one in prayer or awaiting execution.

"Lady Rie, I must ask you some questions. Answer me if you are able."

She looked up at me then. "Brother, what will it change now, even if I can tell you what you want to know?"

"It may prevent anyone else from suffering your fate," I said. "And bring justice to those responsible."

She smiled then, and I thought for a moment I would go mad. Fortunately I went numb instead. I think this was all that saved me.

"Justice? Brother, there is no justice, only the workings of *karma*. I am told Rie is dead. I am Rie, so if I have been told the truth, then I am dead. Am I dead, brother?"

"Your body is dead," I said. "Your soul lives in this shell created for you by our enemies, and it remembers what it was to be Rie. That is all. You are trapped here."

"The living are trapped for their lifetimes, and then they are sent back to the wheel of death and rebirth. How am I different?"

"You have no mortal weaknesses," I said. "You do not and cannot eat or drink. You have no desires, only the impulse to do as the one who created you dictates. It was he who instructed you to kill Lord Yoshiie."

"It sounds splendid," Rie said. "Except for the part about being at the whim of this silly magician. That will not do. I wish Lord Yoshiie no harm. I wish no one harm."

"Do you remember attacking Lord Yoshiie?"

"Yes. I had hoped you would come to see me. I was going to tell you I don't understand why I did such a thing, but apparently you already know."

"What about the *shikigami* you sent after poor Mai? Do you remember that?"

"It's strange about those things. When you remind me of them, suddenly I do remember. Without the reminder, they slip away, like images from a dream. Before you came, I remembered going to the feast, but no more of it."

I held onto my numbness as I hoped later I would be able to hold on to my anger. "Sister, do you remember when you died?"

"Yes," she said, so softly I almost didn't hear.

"Forgive me, but I must ask you to tell me what happened."

"I suppose you must . . . I was returning to the nunnery from town, alone. I had no reason . . . the roads are safe, they've always been safe. There's nothing between Yahiko and the temple save the Shrine of the Gods. I was just past that place . . . it happened there. I heard a hum, like a wasp, then an excruciating pain in my chest, but only for an instant. The next thing I remember, I was walking back to the nunnery, just as before. I felt no pain . . . I felt wonderful."

"Was there anyone around you, did you see anyone?"

"No, brother. I thought I heard voices from the woods, but I didn't turn to see. Yahiko-ji was already in sight, and I was expected back. I hurried home."

"When you let the attackers into the nunnery, when you attacked Lord Yoshiie and created the *mamushi* to send after Mai, what did you feel then? Did you hear anything? What prompted you?"

"I heard no voices. I was simply overcome with an impulse, as if someone was directing my movements. Like now."

She sprang forward. Fortunately, my instructions had been carried out, and Rie was only able to move half her length toward us when the chain binding her to the floor snapped to full extension. Such was her momentum that she fell at our feet.

"Kill me," she said. "Destroy this thing that ties me to the world, brother."

"I cannot," I said. "Not yet. I am sorry."

"If I am told to kill you or someone else and I find a way, I will do it. I would kill you now if I could reach you. My own dear brother . . . but I would have done it."

"I know," I said. "I promise I will not prolong this false existence a moment longer than necessary, but you cannot ask this of me. Not yet."

"I can ask, and I will," she said. "That, too, is an impulse. Meaning someone else wants you to kill me, maybe even more than I do. For this reason, if no other, perhaps it is best I live . . . well, remain, perhaps, a little longer. But I will beg to die, and you will have to refuse me. I believe . . . I believe someone finds this amusing. I do not."

"Nor I, sister. Nor I." I turned to go.

"Brother, there is something else. You may not want to believe me, since apparently I can be forced to lie, but I can feel a difference now, in this . . . thread of *karma* or magic which binds me to this other person—it is getting weaker. Before now, I didn't even know it was there. It was hidden from me. I am aware of it now, even beyond simply knowing of its existence. I know it for what it is, and it is getting weaker."

"Let us all hope," I said, "that this is so."

When we were back outside, Kenji spoke again. "Do you think she is telling us the truth?"

"About some things . . . I do hope she's telling the truth about the link itself, because her information agrees with what we expected. Rie is sustained by Lord Tenshin's life force, and to feed her strength and speed she requires a lot of it. Which is why he cannot create another such creature so long as Rie—his first creation—survives."

"What if he can break the link himself? We don't know for certain he cannot, after all," Kenji asked.

"Then why hasn't he done so already? No, Kenji-san—succeed or fail, he expected Rie to be destroyed, and if I hadn't explicitly prevented it, this would have happened. He combined Master Chang's soul-ridden *shikigami* technique with the Blood Thread method to create a sustained creature, controllable, but still with its own volition when required. A master stroke to be sure, but as we saw with the first attack on Lord Yoshiie at the Widow Tamahara's, he overlooked something, something which, in hindsight, now appears obvious. He is very clever, but one thing he is not is *thorough*. To be blunt, he started this fire but he does not know how to put it out. Which is why we have to prevent Rie from harming herself. So long as we do this, Lord Tenshin is a *mamushi* with its life bleeding away and its fangs pulled."

"Not entirely," Kenji said. "Whatever else this wretched creature is, she's still Rie, and every moment she survives as she is, that is his twist of the dagger in your heart. You do know this, don't you?"

I had come to welcome the numbness which came over my spirit at certain times. It allowed me to respond without screaming. "You do pick the most inconvenient times to remember you are a priest, Kenji-san. I know precisely what I am doing," I said. "I am keeping my sister's soul imprisoned in that abomination. I know what pain it is creating for her and for me. I can't let either stop me."

"I knew you were already suffering, Lord Yamada. I wanted only to make certain you understood why. Confusion leads to bad decisions, and that armor worries me."

"Probably not nearly as much as it worries *me*," I said. "But I will keep it all the same."

The next morning I checked on the vehicle being modified for my sister's transport. It was the sort of two-wheeled covered cart often used for the travel of highborn women. In this case it was being adapted for use as a mobile cage. Shackles were attached, two on the roof and two on the floor, to restrict Rie's movements. There would be enough slack for her to kneel or sit, but not enough to loop around her neck and choke herself. I knew it was not possible to account for every contingency, but the modifications appeared serviceable. The workmen assured me the cart would be ready before Lord Yoshiie's army was ready to move. Then I sought out Taro.

"It will not be possible for me to keep watch every moment," I said. "So there will be times when I must depend on you to keep an eye on the prisoner. Do you understand her nature?"

"I have heard something of it," the boy admitted. "I do not pretend to understand it. This is apparently some magical creature who appears to be your elder sister."

"You are correct. I will only tell you this once, Taro-san, and it is very important—no matter what happens, you are not to let her out, bring her food or water, or otherwise allow anyone else to do so. No matter how she pleads or how harmless she appears. It is an act. She does not require food or water, and in truth such things will kill her. If you release her or let her harm herself by your actions, pray she does kill you first, because I will if she doesn't. I will regret this, as I have become rather fond of you. But I will do it and make whatever restitution Prince Kanemore requires of me. Am I clear?"

"Yes, my lord. I will not fail you."

I did not like to see the fear I placed in Taro's eyes, but better some fear now than death later, and I already had enough to answer for. I went looking for Kenji, whom I found studying a scroll in the main lecture hall. He didn't even bother to look up as I approached.

"I had always suspected the copy of the Diamond Sutra I had studied on Mount Oe was imperfect. Some of the passages did not appear to be in their correct sequences. This is a far older manuscript, in worse condition but far better order. No wonder my talisman against nightmare goblins had never worked right. Sometimes it even manages to summon the little buggers."

"Good. I'll probably require a working talisman sooner rather than later."

Kenji carefully re-rolled the scroll and placed it back in its ornate cover. "You are not alone. We depart tomorrow for Dewa. Lord Yoshiie received messengers from both the governor and his father early this morning."

I took it upon myself to scout our path from the temple complex to the north road leading to Dewa, with Kenji for reluctant company, even though I knew Lord Yoshiie's scouts were scouring the countryside daily. Apparently the Minamoto archers had taken my advice to heart. There wasn't a crow to be seen and very few birds of any kind.

"The crows will know to avoid the road. I hope the other birds have as much sense."

"Do you detect anything?"

"Nothing. Not so much as a flea-demon."

"How about when you were near my sister's *shikigami* earlier?" I asked.

"I had intended to mention that, Lord Yamada—also nothing. Even knowing what I know now . . . nothing at all, save for your sister's living spirit. It is quite strong, even now. I confess myself at a loss at this point—I react to her as I would react to any human. She sets off no alarms, raises no questions, suggests nothing masked or hidden. Lady Kuzunoha or one of her ilk, on the other hand, I would notice in a second."

"I should hope so. Lady Kuzunoha knows what she is and takes pride in it. She only humors us by wearing the form of a mortal woman now and again. That she fell in love with a human she considers her great misfortune, but she doesn't deny it happened."

Kenji said, "I consider it her misfortune to be what she is, as it is so much harder for a demon to achieve enlightenment. Regardless, my point is any normal spirit activity in this place is something I would recognize in a heartbeat. There is none."

"But wouldn't you expect some?" I asked. "It's not as if such things are uncommon."

"Lord Yamada, you know very well Lord Yoshiie has protectors besides ourselves looking out for his welfare, and not all of his scouts are simple *bushi*. If there's so much as a *kappa* between here and the Dewa barrier, I will be amazed. He is, as you well know, a fast learner."

"Likely the only reason he's still alive, our own efforts not to the contrary. I move we go back to our quarters and rest. Tomorrow promises to be a busy day."

The army departed Yahiko-ji early the next morning. Rie was securely confined within her cart, managed by Taro. I was riding Shiroirei, and Kenji was on Neko. I had to admit it was harder to think of the animals as simply brute beasts now that I knew their names. There was a magic in names, or perhaps they reflected what lay within. Artists seldom worked under the names they were born with, and often a man's name might be changed upon coming of age, or a woman would adopt a use-name as the women of Court did, so their birth names would not be known, sometimes even to their closest associates. Lady Rie had considered such things frivolous even before taking the tonsure, and had not followed the custom of adopting a new name for her new status. She was always Rie, and yet Lord Tenshin had taken this from her. Rie was no longer Rie, or at least not completely herself, and now never would be again. I considered this alone was crime enough to merit the most severe punishment, without even considering the massacre and desecration brought to that holy place.

As the column rode away, I noticed a large contingent, possibly several hundred, Shibata Clan archers separated from the column and gathered to the side. They watched us ride out, impassive.

"Has something gone wrong with the alliance?" I asked Kenji. "Have you heard anything?"

"No. Perhaps Lord Yoshiie left them here to watch the Mutsu barrier in case a force tries to flank us from there."

"Perhaps," I said. I glanced at Lord Yoshiie, who did not seem to be in the mood for questions or to take any notice of the apparent defection. I shrugged and let the matter drop.

We crossed the Dewa barrier the next afternoon and were immediately joined by a mounted contingent from the Kiyohara Clan, led by the clan chief's younger brother. They held a brief conference with Lord Yoshiie, still on horseback. What I could hear of it involved the numbers of *bushi* that Yoriyoshi had mustered at the provincial capital for the march on the Abe. Yoshiie apparently found the information satisfying—I heard him grunt approval. We were, by all indications, in extremely friendly territory, but I couldn't forget the same had allegedly applied when we were ambushed at Yahiko-ji. Yet despite any concerns I might have had, within a few days the combined army was safely encamped within a few leagues of the Kiyohara stronghold. Kenji and I were careful to—discretely—examine Lord Yoshiie's quarters within the stronghold itself and as much as we could inspect of the immediate surroundings, but we found nothing of concern.

"Strange," I said.

Kenji didn't bother to ask what I meant. "Strange? I say rather a pleasant change. It's not as if the area has been purged of all supernatural influences. I've detected two moth demons and a ghost, but it is my considered opinion all are harmless."

"No *shikigami*." I said.

"Well, not now. I am told there were a few rooted out in the last month, but nothing since."

The Kiyohara themselves had gained first-hand knowledge of the existence of *shikigami* and had taken appropriate measures. Yet all they had found had been of the low quality sort, no more than a step or two above the crude *mamushi* that had tried to poison Mai. All it took was an awareness of what to look for to spot them. Yet if there were any more like Rie . . .

"There won't be any more Ries to be found, will there?" I said. I'm not certain if I was really speaking to Kenji or not, but he heard me.

"Lord Tenshin certainly isn't capable of creating more. And even if he had passed on the technique to any other *onmyoji* in Lord Sadato's employ, they have his example to make them reconsider."

"I know enough of Lord Tenshin to doubt he would share such a powerful technique with anyone," I said. "Despite its drawbacks."

"I agree. I merely point out it probably wouldn't make any difference if he had done so."

I didn't argue, for I had come to the same conclusion. I still considered it likely we would face at least some of the creatures when the attacks came in earnest, but another nearly perfect assassin like Rie? No. Especially considering it was easy enough to find a human assassin to make the attempt, and engaging such would be far less subject to unpleasant repercussions, except for the assassin. Knowing what I did of Lord Yoshiie's personal guard, I wouldn't have bet a bowl of bad rice on an assassin's chances. The failed ambush at Yahiko-ji and the unsuccessful attempt by the Rie-creature each represented a special opportunity for Lord Sadato and Lord Tenshin. Now those opportunities were gone. No, Lord Yoshiie's greatest threat now came from the thousands of Abe Clan *bushi* who would be quite openly and honorably and, yes, *enthusiastically* trying to kill him. A man who could bring Lord Yoshiie's head to Abe no Sadato could doubtless name his own reward.

Yet, despite all this, I still expected the Abe to try to assassinate Yoshiie, because they simply had too much to gain by doing so and not a great deal to lose. Thus I could not understand why there was no sign, none at all, of any such attempt. I said as much to Kenji.

Kenji looked thoughtful. "You're right. It does seem a little strange. Perhaps they've done their worst," he said.

"What if they have? That doesn't mean they wouldn't try again. Lord Sadato has enough spies and scouts of his own. He must know what he is now up against. Desperate measures, I would think, would be in order. Yet they don't appear to be in process. Does he know something we do not know?"

Kenji took a long breath and let it out. "Perhaps he does. But what if the thing he knows has nothing to do with Lord Yoshiie's desired demise?"

"I don't understand," I said.

"We've assumed to this point Lord Sadato had sought out *onmyoji* on an unprecedented scale to attack his enemy or rather his main threat—Lord Yoshiie. What if it was Lord Tenshin who, acting as a mercenary, presented the idea to Lord Sadato who, perhaps in a moment of desperation as you described, consented. And then there was Yahiko-ji."

"You're saying Lord Sadato did not approve the attack?" I asked.

"The plan speaks far more of Lord Tenshin that Lord Sadato. I'm saying it's unlikely he would have done so if he'd known all of what Lord Tenshin had in mind. If Yoshiie had fallen at the temple, the massacre would have simply been a detail, and who was to say the Minamoto did not slaughter the priests and nuns themselves out of revenge? If the plan had worked—"

"Yes, but it didn't."

"And Lord Sadato was left with the knowledge—and there's no chance he doesn't know now, if he didn't before—that an agent acting on his behalf slaughtered dozens of clerics and nuns? What if you, an honorable man, discovered what horror had been committed in your name? What would you do then?" Kenji asked.

"I'd punish those responsible severely, but we know Lord Tenshin is still alive."

" 'Severely' doesn't rule out confining such people while you dealt with more immediate matters, say, an invasion," Kenji said.

"Which Lord Sadato will fight on his home territory, from fortified positions, but you might be right about the *onmyoji*. Lord Tenshin, bless the man, quite likely has proven to Lord

Sadato that the magicians, Tenshin especially included, cannot be trusted."

"I believe this to be so, but I don't think there's any way to be certain," Kenji said.

"Actually, there might be a way. I will show you, but first you have to swear to me that you will tell no one. I mean this, Kenji-san. You cannot reveal what you will see or hear to anyone."

"Very well, I do so swear. Now, what is this mysterious thing?"

"Not a thing, Kenji-san. A man."

"I HAD EXPECTED you to come," Lord Yasuna said. "Sooner or later. How is my execution to be carried out?"

Lord Yasuna was still technically a prisoner, but an honored one. Not only did he have spacious quarters within the Kiyohara stronghold, but he was attended by servants from our hosts' personal household. I was, naturally, careful to dismiss them to a discreet distance upon our arrival.

Kenji just stared. "Execution?"

"Lord Yasuna is referring to my understanding it was he who was passing very specific information about Lord Yoshiie's plans to the Abe Clan, using the *shikigami* cleverly disguised as crows," I said. "We did know our movements were being monitored, but clearly Lord Tenshin needed more information than *that* to plan the temple attack. He had to know Lord Yoshiie planned to visit there. Unless there's some other offense against the Emperor's writ I am unaware of?"

"That's more than enough," Lord Yasuna said.

"Especially when you add that he also told Lord Tenshin about my sister. You did, didn't you? It had to be someone in contact with the Abe who knew my sister was cloistered here. You were the only one who met both conditions."

"Yes, Lord Yamada, but I swear—"

"Please don't," I said.

"You mean, it's true?" Kenji asked.

"It is," Lord Yasuna said. "Much to my shame."

"But . . . why?" Kenji asked.

"Lord Yasuna is the only one who can answer that in full, but my guess is the Court branch and the provincial branches of his family were in closer association than any of us guessed."

"Also true," Lord Yasuna said. "I had fostered Lord Sadato's nephew for some years—he wanted the boy to become accustomed to the ways of Court life. I'm afraid I grew rather fond of him in the time he was with me. I did not wish to see his family brought to ruin. In my foolishness, I have ruined my own."

"Your sister . . . the temple at Yahiko-ji . . . ? Lord Yamada, why is this man still alive?" Kenji asked.

"Because he has been foolish, but it is Lord Tenshin who bears the responsibility for what happened both to Yahiko-ji and my sister, not Lord Yasuna. He did not know and likely never imagined what Lord Tenshin had planned. That is why he has been so despondent. I know this to be true."

"How do you know that?" Kenji asked.

"Because it was Lord Yasuna who brought the crows to my attention, and thus, himself as well. I had suspected they were there because of all the death, but I had noticed how some of them seemed to be following us. Lord Yasuna mentioned it as well, which led me to speculate, which led me to testing Akimasa-san's archer. The only reason I can think of for such an action was that he regretted any part he may have played in the murders. So we have him to thank that the worst of the spying was ended, if for nothing else."

"I couldn't believe it," Lord Yasuna said. "I was naïve not to think I was endangering Lord Yoshiie directly, but the slaughter . . . Lady Rie. For that I deserve to die."

"I agree," Kenji said.

"Whether you agree or not, you are sworn to silence, and I will hold you to your oath," I said.

"Lord Yamada, you cannot—" Kenji looked me in the eye then, and he didn't bother to finish. "All right, I've sworn. But what do we do about this?"

"We don't do anything about this. My lord, you will need to come to terms with your guilt on your own, but I would advise against self-destruction. If you kill yourself, I will inform Lord Yoshiie of your involvement, and that will be the end of the court Abe and the ruin of your son's future."

"I had reconciled myself already to the destruction of my family," Lord Yasuna said, but I could clearly see an echo of hope on the man's face. It wasn't much, but it was something I could use.

"You can spare yourself that, if you choose, for your son's sake if not your own, but do not think for an instant I am bluffing. As I said before, one can only atone while one is living. That is what I expect from you. I think you should expect it of yourself."

"I-I will consider what you have said."

"Then I will keep my silence. Come, Kenji-san. We have other matters to attend."

Kenji waited until we were well away from Lord Yasuna's quarters and any possibility of being overheard before he spoke again.

"If Lord Yoshiie finds out about this—"

"He is not going to, nor does he need to do so. Lord Yasuna is not a man to repeat a mistake. And before you ask . . . I have my reasons."

"Lady Kuzunoha," Kenji said. He wasn't asking a question.

"Think what you want. Our priority is Lord Yoshiie. If I can best honor Prince Kanemore's trust in me—and us—by allowing a traitor to live, then that is what I will do."

"You're not the only one in need of revenge, Lord Yamada," Kenji said.

"Then focus your rage where it should be focused, Kenji-san, and that is not Lord Yasuna. Your anger rightly belongs in the same place as my own."

"I will consider what you have said," Kenji replied, echoing Lord Yasuna. "If you leave me any part of Lord Tenshin still capable of feeling pain. Now then—what are these 'other matters' we need to attend?"

"Actually, that's mostly for me. I'm going to visit my sister."

"Do you want me to come along?" Kenji asked.

"Thank you, but no. This time it is something I need to do alone."

I found Taro at his post guarding my sister's prison, and I offered to relieve him for a while. He gratefully turned the matter over to me, and no sooner than I was alone with her, Rie spoke to me.

"You shouldn't have come," she said. Since she was still, at least in part, my sister Rie, it was the sort of thing I expected her to say.

"Would it be better if I stayed away and simply imagined your suffering?" I asked.

There was one small window cut into the front of the cart. It was barred with iron strapping, but I could see her pale face in the gloom. "That's just the problem—I am not suffering. I am sealed into this hot, airless conveyance, no food, no water, no place to . . . to relieve myself, and yet . . . " Her voice trailed away.

"And yet you are not hot, nor hungry, nor thirsty, and you have no need to relieve yourself. Even after three days."

"I don't think I really believed it, but it's true, isn't it?" she asked. "My memory of dying. My memories of what I was made to do. I'm not alive, am I?"

"No. At least, not in the way you once were."

"Will I have to remain like this?" Rie asked.

"For now, yes—I hope it will not be for much longer."

Rie looked away into the darkness. "When the time comes, will you be the one to destroy me?"

"I will destroy the one who made your false body and trapped your soul within it. When that happens, you will be released."

"In telling me this, haven't you also told him . . . the one I feel connected to me?"

"Yes. I want him to know."

"Ah. I think I do understand now," Rie said.

I frowned. "What do you understand now, sister?"

"Why you come to see me, even though I know it grieves you. You come *because* it grieves you. Because it reminds you of why

274

you will seek revenge for me. Brother, the part of me that is still Rie does not want this."

"I know," I said. "But I do. The revenge I seek is on my own behalf, not yours. I do not claim to be as enlightened a being as I know you are. I am a creature of this world as it is, sister. I want revenge for what has been taken from me."

"Brother, I renounced this world over twenty years ago. We have hardly spoken to each other for fifteen of those years. How could I be taken from you, when I was already gone?"

"But you weren't," I said. "At least, not until now."

"What difference does death make?" Rie asked. "It is the same."

"No. Before Yahiko-ji, I knew you were alive and safe. When I came to the temple, I learned more than that. I learned you were *happy* and doing what you felt called to do. You cannot imagine what this meant to me, Elder Sister. Renouncing the world is not the same as leaving it, for as I well know the world is far more tenacious than that. The work you were doing might have been in preparation for the next world, but it was done within *this* one, the one I shared with you. All this is what Lord Tenshin has taken from me."

Rie sighed. "And what has Lord Tenshin taken from me? My life, my work, my sister nuns whose deaths I brought about through his direction? I would have added poor Mai-chan and Tomoko-ana as well if he had so ordered. Who has the greater cause for revenge, brother?"

I didn't have to think about the question for very long. "You do," I said.

"Which I hereby forswear."

I almost smiled then. "As I said, sister—I never claimed to be as enlightened as you are."

"I am no saint, brother, but I do understand something you do not—a sword of revenge always has two edges, and if one tastes blood, so will the other."

"I will take the risk."

"I will not," she said. "Kill me."

"I promise, you will be released when Lord Tenshin dies. Until then, the bond between you keeps him weakened. He will do greater evil if he has the chance, and I do not intend to give him that chance."

"I am not asking you to spare his life, brother. I am asking you to destroy me now. What Lord Tenshin does then is his affair and on his own head. Deal with him as you see fit. But when the time comes, let there be no connection between myself and Lord Tenshin. Do not tell yourself you take your revenge to earn my release. Release me yourself. Let me go, brother."

"T-that is Lord Tenshin speaking," I said.

She smiled at me through the gloom, and she didn't bother to cover it. "Goji-kun, you know this is not true. Whatever part of Rie remains now is speaking to you, and it is your sister who asks this of you—kill me, or rather destroy this thing I have become."

"You cannot ask me . . . "

"I can," Rie said. "I do."

"I must go," I said then. I didn't wait to hear anything else she might say. I stumbled away, not really caring about direction or how far I had walked until I felt a tug at my sleeve.

"Lord Yamada?"

It was Taro. I looked up and realized I was near where the horses had been corralled. I even recognized Shiroirei and Neko quietly chewing their fodder. "Don't worry about what she said to you," Taro said. "She said many things to me, but I didn't listen, just as you instructed. Whatever she said to you, it wasn't real."

Yes, it was. That is the problem.

"You did well, Taro-san," I said. "I should have taken better heed of my own instructions. Thank you for your concern. I am all right."

Which wasn't true at all. But hope I might eventually be so. "We're leaving tomorrow, I am told. Is all prepared?"

"Yes, my lord. I've seen to your armor. You'll need to wear it through the mountain pass."

"Why? Do you think the Abe will ambush us there?"

"No," he said. "They will not be able to bring enough force to bear. More likely they will contest our passage on the other side. I am told the outlet will be relatively narrow, and thus the Minamoto won't be able to bring their full force into use. If the Abe can hold the passes, they can delay us for weeks, possibly months, even until winter. This is what I would do."

"I'm sure Lord Yoshiie has considered this," I said.

"That may be," Taro said, "but I don't know what he plans to do about it."

Neither did I, but it made an interesting question to ponder while I tried my very best not to think of what Rie had said to me.

CHAPTER FOURTEEN

IN ANOTHER WEEK, young Taro's grasp of tactics was fully validated. When our vanguard reached the end of the mountain passage, they were greeted with a rain of arrows. Six or seven *bushi* were killed or wounded immediately. While the passage itself was not blocked, the Abe had fortified positions controlling the exit. Lord Yoshiie ordered a halt, and I heard the command echoed up and down the line. It was impossible to retreat quickly, as our column was spread out for some distance through the mountains, and as it was, we were barely out of arrow range ourselves, and every now and then one would skip past our horses' hooves like a dying hornet.

Kenji managed to thread his mount through the confusion to where I was. "Is the war over before it even began? How are we supposed to get out of this?"

"That is a good question. Let us hope our young general knows the answer."

Lord Yoshiie seemed completely unconcerned. He gave orders to two of his scouts, who immediately moved forward to positions that, while not out of danger, were out of the direct line of fire of the archers, even though the archers were doing their best to kill them anyway. I could see sparks from the steel arrowheads striking the rocks providing the scouts cover.

"What are they going to accomplish there?"

We didn't have to wait long to find out. Suddenly there was the sound of drums and a great shout from outside the passage. The order was relayed to stand ready for a charge. Then one of the scouts, after a quick look around the rock shielding him, struck sparks to a fire arrow and launched it high over the mouth of the passage.

"Forward!"

I didn't have time to think about what was happening. Our column, narrow as it was, thundered down the last several hundred feet to the passage end, and then we were riding toward what looked like a forest of pointed stakes. Just as I was certain we were about to be impaled, the entire column wheeled to our left, punched through a line of mounted archers before they could nock another arrow, and then fell upon the Abe right flank. I felt a sting at my shoulder and another across my forearm, but I drew my sword and cut down a man trying to spear someone next to me.

I now had a better idea of the forces arrayed against us and had thus started to wonder why we all hadn't been killed in the first few seconds of our charge, but a glance toward the Abe left flank gave me my answer. At least half of the opposing force had not been able to concentrate their arrows on us because they were already under attack. I saw *bushi* bearing the Shibata Clan colors firing into the massed Abe archers who were quickly falling into disarray.

Where did they come from? I thought, before I remembered the Shibata force which had remained behind. They weren't to guard the border, as I had first believed; they were to enter Mutsu in enough force to make their way west and then north to meet us upon our entry into the province. It was clear they had taken the Abe by surprise, and their attack was what the scouts were waiting for and what the fire arrow signal had meant.

I had hoped that Kenji had been sensible and hung back, but I saw him dodging a spearman in order to knock an Abe archer from his saddle. I rode to his side as soon I managed to disentangle myself from a knot of riders that was half Abe, half Kiyohara, though I knocked an Abe *bushi* from his saddle in the process. I found myself hoping I hadn't ridden over the man, then remembered this was war and to do so would be a desired outcome. I was still having trouble grasping what I was doing. I had fought for my life on more than one occasion and against multiple opponents, but there was always a more personal element to it. The kill or be killed dynamic was the same, but I personally bore no ill will to anyone I was fighting. I wondered if it was the same for them, even as they did their best to kill me.

I reached Kenji only to have him take a hard swing at my head, which I barely dodged. Even so, his glancing blow made my ears ring. "Stop, you idiot! It's me!"

"Lord Yamada? Sorry, I forgot about the armor."

"It is fortunate for me I didn't. What about you? You're not supposed to be here!"

Kenji didn't look happy. "When the order came, I didn't have much choice! It was either flow with the river or be drowned!"

"As long as you're here, let's find Yoshiie . . . and try to stay alive."

"You do the same!"

It was the place of a general to direct his forces from a secure position, but there was no secure position on that first battlefield. While Lord Yoriyoshi directed forces from the rear, we found Lord Yoshiie in the thick of the fight, surrounded by his personal guard, but even so two arrows were lodged in his armor. He was taking no notice of them that I could tell. Kenji and I joined the perimeter *bushi*. The greatest danger was arrows, but every now and again a foot soldier or unhorsed *bushi* would try our line. At first I had thought it reckless for Lord Yoshiie to lead the charge, but now I was starting to understand his strategy. While the Shibata charge had allowed the vanguard to get through, the balance of our forces were still in the passage, leaving us heavily outnumbered, and Lord Yoshiie had made himself a target. Yet the longer he remained alive, and the longer the Abe warriors concentrated on attacking him, the fewer there were to contest the mountain pass. Every minute brought hundreds of Minamoto and Kiyohara *bushi* through the pass in a flood that showed no signs of abating.

One of Yoshiie's guards went down with an arrow piercing his throat. I goaded Kenji's horse through the gap and then took my place in the defensive circle. One of Yoshiie's personal attendants ran to my side and handed me a long spear. I could see the advantage, as I really had no room to swing my *tachi* now, and I sheathed the blade and took up the spear instead. The weapon was unfamiliar, but the principle of it was simple enough—use the pointed end, which I did several times in quick succession. Sweat was running into my eyes now despite the helmet's padding, and it was getting harder to see. I used a lull to wipe my eyes, and then I realized it wasn't a lull. The reinforcements streaming through the mountain pass had finally broken the Abe center, and those Abe who had survived were in orderly retreat. Lord Yoshiie immediately called off any pursuit and began to roam the field to arrange his forces in formal battle order while his father led our remaining forces out through the pass. I rode with Lord Yoshiie's bodyguard while Kenji separated himself to perform priestly duties.

There was a great deal for Kenji to do in the aftermath, but it had to be done quickly. Lord Yoshiie soon ordered the advance, and we pushed on toward the heart of Mutsu until evening. There was a considerable force of Abe *bushi* still in our vicinity, but we didn't stop until Lord Yoshiie and his father found what they considered an adequate defensive position to make camp. I didn't see Kenji again until nightfall. By then the wagons and servants had caught up. I was relieved to see Taro, leading Rie's cart. He in turn seemed very relieved Kenji and I had not managed to get ourselves killed but perhaps more so that Shiroirei and Neko had come through unscathed.

"You'd best have someone look at that arrow, Lord Yamada," he said as he led our mounts away to be tended.

Arrow . . . ?

It wasn't until I was standing on the ground again that I began to realize just how weary I was and remember I had not come through the battle untouched. I found a campstool and Kenji helped me peel the armor off. When we were ready to remove the chest and back pieces, we realized doing so wouldn't be possible until the arrow was removed.

"Brace yourself," Kenji said, barely giving me time to do anything before he yanked the thing out.

"Chie . . . !"

"Language, Lord Yamada." Kenji held up the arrow. "Fortunately for you it wasn't the barbed sort, or it would have hurt a lot more."

The arrowhead looked like a miniature of my spearhead. There was a bit of blood on it, but only a bit. Kenji lifted the body armor over my head and dropped it unceremoniously on the ground with the arm and leg pieces. I had already removed my helmet.

"I was too old for this when I started," I muttered, giving my weariness full rein. The rush of battle was long over, and whatever mixture of excitement and terror that had kept me going until then was quite used up. Kenji examined my wounds. Aside from the arrow in my shoulder, there had been a glancing strike on my left forearm that had drawn blood, but neither was serious. Without the armor it would have been a tale with a different ending.

"Kenji—" I began, but he interrupted me.

"Before you say anything, I promise to stay out of the next one if at all possible. I am a priest, and that's a warrior of a different sort. And you should do the same. You didn't dishonor yourself by any means, but this is not your element."

"I know, but until our business is concluded, it will have to be. Lord Yoshiie remains our priority, with or without magical attacks. Speaking of which, did you see any signs of *shikigami* back there?"

"Nothing at all," Kenji said, "which you must admit is strange, considering the number of warriors assigned to prevent our passage. Clearly Lord Sadato understood the importance of containing us there, and a fight with such a limited tactical goal would have been a natural fit for the use of *shikigami* . . . if the word 'natural' can be used at all when referencing such an unnatural creature."

I considered. "Maybe you were right about Lord Sadato. Have we seen any *shikigami* at all since Akimasa's archer destroyed that one in crow form?"

Kenji grunted. "No, but it doesn't matter if I am right or not," he said. "The danger from human beings is real enough."

I entrusted my armor to the supply wagons, and Taro promised to look after it. Fortunately it needed no patching, so it would be ready for my use whenever required, which I hoped would not be for a while yet.

"I still have some of Lord Yoshiie's gift of rice," Kenji said. "Let's make a fire and have something to eat."

"I like your idea," I said, but we were immediately interrupted by a messenger in Minamoto colors.

"Gentlemen, Lord Yoshiie requests you attend him."

Kenji and I glanced at each other, but there was nothing to do but follow the messenger back to where Lord Yoshiie was quartered. A *maku* of cloth bearing a design of the Doves of Hachiman, which Yoshiie sometimes used as a crest, had been erected in a circle near the hilltop, essentially no more than a privacy curtain, and we were ushered inside. As camps went, it was not especially luxurious. There was a pavilion that could possibly keep the rain off, but otherwise the cook fires, pots, and racks of weapons were little different than one would have found in any *bushi* encampment. I didn't see Lord Yoriyoshi, but Lord Yoshiie was out of his armor now, which had been stored on a special rack made for it, and I noted bandages on his right arm and chest. Kenji and I presented ourselves and kneeled.

"You summoned us, my lord?" I said.

"I did. First I must scold Master Kenji a bit for taking the field, first as a priest and second without proper armor. That was brave, but also both foolish and inappropriate."

I was sure Kenji was smiling, or wanted to, but he didn't raise his head. "My lord, I heartily agree with you. It will not happen again."

Lord Yoshiie grunted. "Then we need not speak of it again. As for you, Lord Yamada—thank you."

I almost looked up then. "I am your servant, but may I ask what I am being thanked for?"

"For taking the field, even though it was not your responsibility to do so. For joining my guard when it was necessary to hold the line until the rest of our troops could join us. For deflecting at least one arrow meant for me."

I had absolutely no memory of that last incident, but I had to admit it was quite possible. There had been a lot of arrows.

"Your life is also my responsibility, my lord, in order for the Emperor's will to be carried out, but I admit I am no *bushi*."

"Just so," he said. "Which makes your behavior and effectiveness in today's engagement all the more surprising. It has yet again been made clear to me that Prince Kanemore did me a great service in securing your involvement in this matter."

"I am honored."

And I *was* honored. I was also worried. Lord Yoshiie, whatever else he might have been, was a practical man. If he was praising me now, he certainly meant what he said, but I had the distinct feeling there was more to this than I had yet heard.

"Gentlemen, please raise yourselves. My father needs rest and has retired early, but you will be dining with me this evening, and there is a matter I would discuss with you."

We sat up then and were served by members of Lord Yoshiie's personal guard, men I had fought beside that day. The fare wasn't much different than what Kenji and I would have managed on our own—rice, of course, and the added luxury of broiled fish and a bit of radish. There was also rice wine. Kenji shot me a questioning look, which did not go unnoticed by Lord Yoshiie.

"I have heard something of your reputation, Lord Yamada," Lord Yoshiie said. "If the wine is inappropriate, I apologize."

"Not at all, my lord. It is very true there was a time in my life when I was more likely to be drunk than sober on any given day. Yet it is also true drink was never my master. I had hoped to turn rice wine into a servant and bend its effects to my will. That did not happen, but nothing prevents me from drinking to your continued fortune and good health."

I took the cup and drained it with one gulp. The fire in my throat was familiar but faint, almost ghostly. In a moment or two it had faded completely. I set the cup aside. "We are at your disposal. What did you wish to discuss with us?"

"This does concern both of you, but specifically you, Lord Yamada." His attendants brought up a low table on which had been placed a map. "Now then. You can see this river here . . . " Lord Yoshiie indicated the map. "Lord Sadato's primary castle lies on the Kuriya River just to the north of us. There are smaller hill-forts and such scattered around, but the ones that really matter are located where the Koromo River meets the Kitakami River . . . here, then again where it meets the Kuriya . . . here, and one closer to the headwaters of the Kitakami . . . here." He touched the points on the map where the locations of the forts had been marked. "Each is well stocked and garrisoned, and the retreating forces from our battle today will likely be used to reinforce all of them. If we attack one at a time, even with such a large force as ours, we risk flanking attacks from the other forts in relief. If we proceed directly to Lord Sadato's stronghold, we place large and active forces on our rear and right flank. Unacceptable, and Lord Sadato would be a fool not to take advantage. Yet the number of our forces gives us another option—we are going to ignore Lord Sadato's main fortress and attack all three supporting fortresses at once, with myself and my father keeping a large enough force in reserve to move against Lord Sadato if he attempts to relieve any of them."

I had to admit there was a simple elegance to the plan. If each and every fort were under siege, there would be no possibility of any of them coming to the others' aid. Lord Sadato alone would be free to move and in so doing risk an open field battle against a still formidable army or face the possibility of losing the better part of his forces when the forts were reduced. The danger was two-fold: splitting the Minamoto forces meant any one contingent was more vulnerable to an attack from the Abe main force, assuming it managed to evade Lord Yoshiie's reserve. The second was the forts in question might prove strong enough to withstand our separate assaults and delay the Minamoto advance until winter, when the weather itself would force our withdrawal.

"I am no strategist," I said, "but I certainly see the advantages."

"And the disadvantages?" he asked.

I told him what had occurred to me, and he nodded with satisfaction. "You are more of a strategist than you admit, Lord

Yamada. Yes, I would judge a possible delay as our greatest danger. All three forts must fall and quickly. If we achieve this, then there is nothing save hard fighting between ourselves and Kuriya Castle, where open battles will be to our advantage. This is where I require your assistance."

"What can I do?" I asked.

"I want you to lead the attack on the northernmost fortress."

For a moment or two I was too stunned to speak. "My lord . . . I am willing to do whatever you need of me, but surely there are men under your command with much more experience in these matters?"

"Oh, many indeed. Akimasa for one. He will be accompanying you as your second in command, and I would strongly advise you to listen to him, but he is not of sufficient rank to command such a force on his own. While you are—to be blunt—barely acceptable, acceptable you are. You will be in nominal command, but I expect Akimasa to take care of the details, one of which is the eventual surrender or destruction of the fortress. Now, if you were one of my *bushi*, that would rightly be the end of our discussion, as you have your orders. But I do understand you're going to wonder about this arrangement, yes?"

"The question did cross my mind, my lord," I said.

"It is simple—after my father and I had chosen among our generals to lead the assaults on the central and the southern fortress, we were left with two—the heir to the Shibata Clan and the heir to the Kiyohara. Both are green and a bit headstrong, but even allowing for that, to give the command to one of them is to slight the other, which I cannot afford to do. A joint command would be a disaster, as I do not believe them capable of working together. So instead they will have the 'honor' of remaining with me as personal counselors, and I will pretend to listen to them while you and my other generals go do what really needs to be done."

"I understand your dilemma," I said, "but you did say this concerns Kenji as well?"

"Say rather his special talents, in addition to your own. We know a considerable number of Emishi were involved in the massacre at the temple. Their presence suggests the northernmost fortress, which is in closer proximity to the barbarians' allotted territories, was used as a recruitment and staging site. Therefore, if my information is correct, this fortress was the base from which the attack on Yahiko-ji originated."

"You believe the *onmyoji* involved were once based there?" I asked.

"Not 'once.' I believe they still are," he said. "Which very much includes Lord Tenshin."

My expression must have been clear to read, because this time Lord Yoshiie did smile. "Yes, Lord Yamada. I knew this would get your attention. I believe my information to be reliable, though you must discover this for yourself. If he is captured alive, Lord Tenshin belongs to you, as I have said, so do as you see fit. As for the other *onmyoji*, if any are present, they are already guilty of disobeying the Emperor. Akimasa has my orders concerning them."

After we were dismissed, Kenji and I walked back to our encampment. Taro had built a fire for us and arranged for bedding, which was fortunate because such practical matters as where we were going to sleep that night hadn't had a chance to cross my notice.

"Thank you," I said, but Taro just shrugged.

"Prince Kanemore was explicit that I look after you gentlemen to the best of my ability—after the horses, no offense meant. I am only carrying out his wishes."

"As are we, Taro-san. And, none taken."

I had already resolved to have a very serious discussion with Prince Kanemore about this very matter upon our return to the capital, assuming we did return. For now there was little more to do save to try to survive as we saw our mission to its end.

"I don't like this," Kenji said as we settled in for the night.

"What part?" I asked. "I'm not very fond of this entire enterprise, considering what it has cost me so far."

"Fate is what has already happened, so clearly it was meant to be so," Kenji said, "which is not to diminish your loss, Lord Yamada. My concern now is for what is to come. You do know the *onmyoji* loyal to Lord Sadato are to be summarily executed?"

"That was my assumption," I said

"This does not bother you?"

"Does it bother you? You said yourself you wanted revenge for Yahiko-ji, whereas I think of Rie and my cup of empathy is quite drained. I also think of the innocents who will inevitably suffer in war regardless of what happens at the north fort. At least the *onmyoji* have the advantage of deserving death, and I daresay a great many more will have death whether they deserve it or not. Let us change what we can change, Kenji-san, and leave the rest to whatever gods or Buddhas seem inclined to help. Frankly, both have been rather scarce lately."

"I hear what you say, Lord Yamada. Next I will see what you do. Good night."

Kenji rolled over and that was the end of the conversation. I must have sensed I had somehow not suffered enough during the day's events, so I went to talk to Rie. I found Taro nearby. His blankets were unrolled under the cart itself, but he was not in them. Rather, he was standing some distance from the cart, a look of fear and confusion on his face.

"Lord Yamada! I was just about to come for you."

"What's the matter?"

"I don't know, but something is wrong with Lady Rie . . . I mean, something new. She said some things to me, but it was different this time—none of it made any sense, and her face was strange-looking."

I followed Taro to where my sister was confined. She sat in the middle of her cart, her shackles in place, looking exactly as I would have expected her to look.

"I want to die, but we have already discussed that," she said. "So, brother, what have you come to talk about instead?"

Taro looked puzzled, but I had my suspicions and merely waited. We did not have to wait for very long. Suddenly the corners of Rie's mouth began to twitch, and when she spoke again she neither looked nor sounded like the Rie I knew.

"Insufferable!" she said, in a voice both thick and hoarse. "Free me at once!"

"You know that is not going to happen," I said.

She frowned. "Who are you?"

"I am a friend of Lady Rie's. Who are you?" I asked. "No, don't bother—you are Lord Otomo no Tenshin, yes?" I didn't need the confirmation by this point, but the stunned look on what should have been my sister's face was validation enough.

"Who are you? What have you done to me?"

"Far less than you have done to me and mine, Lord Tenshin."

"Where am I?" the creature asked.

"That is a good question. Where do you think you are?"

"Do not trifle with me! I am an *onmyoji* of great power!"

"I know what you are, Lord Tenshin. I know what you have done and can do. Answer my question, if you know the answer."

"I—I am dreaming. I must be dreaming!"

"Then it's time to wake up," I said.

There was no way for me to be certain, but I believe he did just that, for in a few more seconds the strangeness left my sister's face, and she was Rie again, or as close to Rie as was possible under the circumstances. "Brother? Where did you go?"

"I have not moved from this place, sister. I think you were the one who left us for a while. Where did *you* go? Do you remember?"

She frowned. "All I can remember is a prison. A little larger than this one, but only a little. Was it a vision of hell?"

"I do not think so. Listen to me very carefully, sister—I believe Lord Tenshin is beginning to lose control of the link between you, and rather than simply manipulating you like a puppet, his will is actually manifesting within this constructed body. This time it happened while he slept, but if I am correct, it may begin to happen when he is awake. When—if—that happens, he will take control of you, speak from your tongue, see what you see, possibly without even meaning to do so. When that happens, you may, as just now, see through his eyes, *be* where he is. I need you to let me know what Lord Tenshin sees."

"How can you trust me to relate it? Is he not still in control of me?"

"I'm not even certain he is in control of *himself* at this time, and the issue of trust I will leave to whatever judgment remains to me. I know you have no reason to do so, but despite what I must do to you when the time comes, I would like your help."

She shook her head, looking disgusted. "Certainly there's a reason, you dolt! You are my brother. Even as I am, whatever karma has brought us to this, you remain my brother."

"I know, but thank you."

"Whatever for?"

"For helping me remember. When the time comes, I will need you to remember as well."

"What do you mean? Of course I will," Rie said.

I wish I could be as certain as you are, sister. But we shall see.

CHAPTER FIFTEEN

KENJI WAS RIGHT.

But then, so was I. We crossed the Kitakami River in good order, and by the time our forces reached the northern Abe stronghold from the eastern side, the periods when the spirit I knew as Lord Tenshin took over Rie's constructed body had become more and more frequent and, as was quickly apparent, beyond his control. Fortunately, Akimasa took charge of arraying our forces to conduct the siege itself, for even if I had possessed the skill, my mind was focused on a separate problem: the increasingly erratic link between my sister and Lord Tenshin. If I was present during one such interlude, he would appear to gloat, but I saw the fear in his eyes—and it was his eyes, not my sister's, looking at me then, and I had no doubt I was looking into a soul which was not that of my sister. The difference was subtle but beyond mistaking. When the manifestation ended and Rie returned, she always spoke of being confined, and there were others there, but she could relate little beyond that.

Kenji, never one to accept validation—or anything else—at face value, remained skeptical. "Even if Rie isn't lying to you under Lord Tenshin's direction—which is still quite possible— how do we know Lord Tenshin and the other *onmyoji* are confined *here*? Their prison could be anywhere."

"In our last conversation, Rie spoke of much confusion and noise beyond the place where she—I mean he—is being held. That is likely our siege."

"Or the siege of either of the other two Abe strongholds," Kenji pointed out.

"Very true. We won't know for sure if Lord Yoshiie's information is correct until this castle falls," I said.

As the nominal leader of the siege, my accommodations had changed somewhat since the Minamoto had forced their way into Mutsu. Kenji, myself, and Akimasa shared a camp *maku* bearing the Minamoto crest, as Lord Yoshiie had directed. There was to be no question as to who was responsible for its downfall when the fort did fall. Also, so far as the defenders knew, Lord Yoshiie himself was present, and so I gathered it was at the other two sieges as well.

The Abe fortress was solidly built, with a foundation of stone that raised it several feet above the banks of the river. There was higher ground nearby, which had made me wonder why the fort had not been built there instead, but Akimasa had the answer.

"There is only one decent crossing point on this part of the river, and the fortress commands it. Any further away from the river and they would be out of bowshot and unable to contest an enemy's crossing. Here, they can thwart any attempt to cross the river."

Which explained why we actually crossed the river at a point not too far from the central fortress with the forces assigned to its destruction, then immediately separated to ride north so we could approach our own goal from the land side. Even so, the fortress was strong, and so far we had been able to do little save exchange arrows with the defenders. Akimasa had said nothing on the matter as of yet, but I could tell that he was worried.

"Time," he muttered.

"Eventually we must win," I said. "And I am guessing this is the problem?"

"You heard Lord Yoshiie," he said. "We can wait them out, since Lord Yoshiie has the men he needs to hamper any relief, but they would have been expecting us. If they don't have sufficient supplies to last at least two months, Lord Sadato is a fool. And I happen to know the Abe Clan chief is not a fool. There's glory in a direct assault—"

"And a lot of men will die," I said.

Akimasa smiled. "What I was *about* to say, was pretty much the same thing. Lord Yamada, I am here to do whatever it takes, and if a direct assault is our only option, it will be costly and possibly futile, but we will attempt it. I would like another option, but I—that is, we—cannot wait forever to find one."

What Akimasa said was no more than sense, for which I was grateful. Not every general in the field, by all accounts, was as careful with the lives under his command. While it was true I did not have a great deal of experience at this sort of thing, it was not true I had none. I had once been part of a force consisting only of myself, Kenji, a master demon queller, and a handful of *bushi* who had managed to root out a mountain fortress full of *oni*. The main difference, so far as I could see, was that, in the previous case, we had been able to break through the main gate with relative ease. Here, this would be a lot harder.

"Suppose we manage to open their gate?"

"The fort has a lot of manpower," Akimasa said, "but once we can bring our own force to bear against them, I have no doubt of the outcome. We will have to break through the gate to do that. My idea is to find a suitable tree and make a battering ram, which would be part of a direct assault and also quite costly, even assuming we succeed. How do *you* propose to break their gate?"

"I said 'open,' not break. At the moment, I don't have a notion. I would like a little time to consider the matter."

"That is fortunate," Akimasa said. "For a little time is all we have."

I left Akimasa making his plans for the direct assault he believed would be necessary. I was hoping it would not, or at least not in the way he expected. While I was not overly concerned about the safety of the Abe Clan *bushi*, I had become somewhat fond of Akimasa himself and many of the men I had come to know within our own forces. More, I was worried, in the chaos of such an attack, something might happen to Lord Tenshin before I had my reckoning with him, and this was simply not acceptable. We did need an alternative strategy, but just then I was completely in the dark as to what the alternative might be. I needed to take a look at our situation, and, while I was still used to walking, I had too much ground to cover in a short time. I had Taro get Shiroirei ready to ride, and I made a circuit around the fortress, being careful to stay out of bowshot. Which is not to say that now and again an archer on the walls wouldn't try his luck, but I had judged accurately, and the few arrows loosed at me fell short.

On the inland side of the fortress, I didn't see anything I didn't already know about. Our forces were deployed in a ring, with improvised wooden walls and portable woven bamboo shields as protection against the arrows. There was one very formidable-looking gate on the south side of the compound, covered by archer towers and in a position where defenders could also rain stones or anything else down on any attackers from the walls themselves. Akimasa knew his business, and if he thought the gate could be breached, then it probably could be. But the price would be very high.

The design of the fortress didn't vary until I was past the south gate and looking at the west side of the fortress, facing the river.

What is that?

I rode as close as I dared, almost to the point where I had to be more concerned about the Abe archers' accuracy than their range, but on the river side I saw a gap in the foundation, about ten feet across, where the water flowed into the fort itself. There appeared to be some sort of piercework gate there; it would have blocked a person or a boat from entering, but was no barrier to the water. As I turned back, I noticed a dark shape under the water near shore. I judged its size and shape and how it moved and quickly ruled out the creature being a fish. I rode back to our camp, surrendered Shiroirei to Taro, and went to see Akimasa.

"Certainly I knew about it," he said. "It was built so the fortress can be resupplied from the river. Assuming the craft could evade the enemy, a boat could easily enter there, once the defenders unbarred the water gate. I don't know what you are thinking, Lord Yamada, but it was well designed. Its position makes it easy to cover from the walls, and even if we could get men to it, even if they could get the water gate open, we wouldn't be able to bring any sufficient force to bear from the river—it would be a useless attack."

"I wasn't thinking of an attack. I was thinking of sabotage."

Akimasa frowned. "I don't understand."

"I need a little more time to see if what I have in mind is even possible. Give me until tomorrow. Surely we can delay that long."

"Well . . . " he hesitated. "All right—tomorrow morning. It's likely Lord Abe will try to relieve at least one of his fortresses, and Lord Yoshiie cannot be everywhere. The longer we sit here, the more likely we'll be inviting a flank attack, which we may not have the strength to repel. Once the garrison joins in—and they will—our force would be caught between them. We have to begin our main assault tomorrow. I don't dare wait any longer, Lord Yamada."

"Understood."

I went to fetch Kenji and Taro. When I told Taro what I wanted of him, he turned a little pale. Kenji's reaction was a bit more explicit. "Lord Yamada, are you *trying* to get the boy killed?"

"I will do my best to prevent it. But yes, Taro-san, what I am asking of you is very dangerous, and I doubt Prince Kanemore would approve. If we succeed, however, the Emperor's will is carried out, the war ends sooner, and fewer people die in the process. I do know I am asking a great deal, and you have the right to refuse."

Taro blinked. "I do?"

"I have more than enough to answer for already," I said, "and will likely have more sins on my head before the day is over. I have the power to force you, but I do not have the right. Nor will I think less of you if you were to refuse. In your place, I might do the same."

"I will do it," he said, finally. "But I have one request."

"Name it," I said.

"Apologize on my behalf to Prince Kanemore if I do not return to the capital. I would not want him to think I had sought to escape my obligations to him."

"I promise," I said. "Now, then—let us go over again what you need to do, so perhaps such an apology may not be necessary."

We chose a spot where the undergrowth was thick and ran nearly to the water's edge. We were too far from the fortress to worry about arrows but also too far from the river ford. The shallows there were no wider than my own height before they dropped off into deep water well over a man's head, and doubly so for someone of Taro's stature. Kenji and I took cover in the undergrowth as Taro stripped down to his loincloth and waded slowly into the river.

That's it, Taro. Well in, but not too far. Make it come to you.

There was a roil on the surface of the deeper water, and as we watched, we could see an arrowhead-shaped wake quickly moving closer. Taro almost took a step back, but he stopped himself. Kenji was fingering his prayer beads, and I breathed a silent prayer to whatever gods of the river might be listening.

The creature was quick. It emerged from the deep water onto the sand bar by shore and headed straight for Taro. The boy did take a step backward then and almost died for it, but he remembered his instructions and bowed low.

The creature stopped in its tracks. I could see it a little better now and saw that my original inference was correct—a *kappa*. The thing was ugly, as one might expect—beaked mouth, scraggly hair, scaly green skin, and what appeared to be a turtle's shell on its back. It stood perhaps a head shorter than Taro did, but I had no doubt the creature had several times my own strength, and Taro would not have had a chance, except for the weapon of knowledge I had given to him.

Kappas were monsters. But they were *polite* monsters.

Faced with the courtesy of Taro's bowed greeting, the *kappa* had no choice but return it, and when he bowed, we could see the bowl-shaped indentation on the top of his head, and the river water that gave the creature its strength spilled out. Before Kenji and I could even move, Taro reached out, grabbed one of the creature's scaly arms, and pulled.

I think the *kappa* was more startled than we were, but in the next moment, two things happened: Taro and the creature fell onto the riverbank in a tangle of arms and legs, and Kenji and I tore through the underbrush. Before it could wrestle itself away from Taro, we grabbed the creature by both arms. Now I could see the thing's wicked-looking claws, each the length of one of my fingers.

I think they will serve nicely, I thought. Still, I was careful to hold him by the forearm so he didn't have room to use the claws on me, and Kenji quickly followed my example.

"Let me go! Humans will suffer if you do not release me!"

Its voice was raspy and harsh, the words tentative as if the creature didn't have a lot of chance to practice speaking.

"Actually," I said, "*Kappa* will suffer if it does not behave itself. You were going to devour our friend here, but now you have lost your strength and the vital essence of the river that gives you life. You know what is about to happen, don't you?"

Fear was in the creature's large eyes now, but I knew it wasn't us he was afraid of. The change had already begun. I could see wrinkles appearing on the creature's face, soon spreading to its arms and legs. It was literally drying out before our eyes."

"Have you ever seen a dried fish? That is what you are about to look like," Kenji said. Taro had simply withdrawn out of the *kappa*'s reach and was staring at the creature, fascinated.

"A river goblin. They're real," he said. "I mean, I believed you, but—"

I almost laughed. "But you weren't certain. No matter, you did what you needed to do, and I am grateful. Now then, monster—I'm going to ask you for a favor. You can refuse, but if you do, you will turn into a dried-up husk that we will probably use to fuel our campfire. What say you?"

"Let me go!" The thing was practically begging, but I had come too far and risked a boy's life to capture the creature, and it was going to help us whether it wanted to do so or not.

"You don't have a lot of time, so I would save your breath for the oath you're about to swear to us. Kenji?"

Kenji took a set of prayer beads from around his own neck and muttered a prayer before he placed it around that of the river goblin. "You will swear by the Buddha to do as we ask. You will be compelled to keep your oath, so do not swear lightly." Kenji touched the beads one more time and spoke a word I didn't understand.

"The time has come," I said. "Do you swear to do as we shall instruct, to the limits of your strength and life? Once this is accomplished, you will be free of the oath, but not until then."

The wrinkles stopped spreading and were now deepening. We could feel the thing shrinking as we held it. If the creature proved too stubborn, all would be for naught, but it finally opened the beak not really suited for human speech and rasped out the words. "*Kappa* swears!"

"Excellent," I said, and we tossed the creature back into the river like an unwanted fish. As might be expected, the first thing it did once it surfaced, was try to remove the prayer beads, most likely hoping to throw them at our heads and laugh at us for fools. The beads would not come off. As the river goblin struggled against them, they began to tighten.

"Being strangled to death is really not much better than drying out," Kenji pointed out. "But it's your choice."

The thing finally gave up, and we could hear its sigh across the water. "Had to try," the creature muttered. "What is *kappa* to do?"

The simple beauty of my plan was that it required no alterations at all to Akimasa's. By mid-morning he had our forces arrayed. There was some grumbling, as a large contingent of our archers were being forced to dismount and fight on foot, but I could see the advantage from Akimasa's point of view—the archers, rather than racing about the fortress firing at random, would be firing in formation. While it was true they would also be in range of the archers on the wall, our archers would be shooting from behind a barrier of large bamboo shields arranged in front of them, which at least gave them equivalent protection to the men on the walls.

RICHARD PARKS

"The goal is not necessarily to kill their opponents," Akimasa said. "But rather to limit the Abe archers' ability to shoot at will while we attack the gate."

We were both mounted and in place with a large force of spearmen and archers just out of bowshot. I had kept the spear Lord Yoshiie had given to me at that first skirmish, and I was grateful for it now. We watched as the ram approached the gate, advancing slowly under the cover of another line of the bamboo shields. At one point the defenders opened a smaller door in the overhang around the gate and attempted a sortie against the ram, but our archers were easily able to drive them back, killing several. One of the men carrying the ram fell, but the remainder pressed on.

My armor was not the most comfortable clothing I had ever worn, but as I watched events unfolding before me, I was again grateful for it.

"You heard the complaints from the archers now on foot," Akimasa said. "War was different in our fathers' time—you had two groups of mounted archers who would essentially ride around and shoot at each other. Sometimes I think the goal was as much to return home alive with the most arrows in your armor as win the battle."

"This," I said, "is not like that."

Akimasa grunted. "No, it is not. Perhaps our fathers had the right idea . . . stand ready."

Despite our archers' best efforts, the men supporting the ram were taking losses, and this included the men deploying the shields. I knew Akimasa had sent twice as many as would be needed to operate the ram, but now I was beginning to think this might not be enough. Now the ram was at the gate. I held my breath. The sound of the first good strike against the gate would be our signal to charge. And I think this, as much as my eagerness to free my sister's spirit, was why I had taken my place with Akimasa and the spearmen, rather than taking the proper place of a noble commander, on a campstool out of arrow range, directing the battle with couriers and signal fans as Lord Yoriyoshi quite sensibly was prone to do.

If the gate isn't breached quickly, this day will not go well for us.

The gate to the fortress shuddered, and our line shot forward as one, charging at the gate, which was still standing.

One more . . .

The ram struck the gate again, but it still held. At the rate we were covering ground, it looked like we would ride directly into it and smash ourselves like fishing boats driven onto the rocks.

One more. That's all you have.

The gate groaned with a sound that cut through the shouts of the men and the screams of the arrow-bitten horses and then the gate swung inward. By this time I was close enough to see the defenders fall back as the gate swung in unexpectedly on them. They knew the gate should never have failed after three blows, but we knew something they did not know—our *kappa* had kept his word, slipped over the water gate in cover of darkness, evaded the guards who were watching our camp, not their own compound, and used its great strength and iron-like claws to weaken the beam holding the gate. The first line of defenders were simply ridden down, and then we were within the fortress, our archers now firing on the *bushi* manning the walls from within and without, our spearmen engaging those *bushi* pouring into the compound from the surrounding buildings before they could position themselves effectively. I killed two men who were trying to kill me and managed to wound a third severely enough he could not continue to fight. My helmet deflected one arrow, another lodged itself in my saddle not a finger's breadth from my leg. I kept pressing forward until I had reached the far side of the compound, and only then wheeled Shiroirei for another pass. Our men riding through the breached gates were a tide that could not be stemmed.

In the end, very few of the defenders were left to surrender to us. The couriers reporting our victory to Lord Yoshiie departed before the last of the garrison was captured. I left it to Akimasa to complete the securing of the fortress and see to the disposition of the prisoners. Lord Yoshiie had instructed him to show mercy where possible, no doubt primarily because he expected to remove the Abe as rulers of the province and not all of the *bushi* in their employ had ties of blood loyalty, and so were potentially useful to him. I knew Lord Yoshiie was not especially bloodthirsty as war leaders went, but he was, as I'd realized more than once, practical above all else. There would be no revenge killing, I was certain, but it would not stop him from taking Lord Sadato's head if and when the opportunity came. I was simply grateful any such decisions on this day were Akimasa's, not mine. Except for one. I dismounted from Shiroirei to look for whatever prisoners the Abe might have been holding, but first I sent two of our *bushi* to fetch my sister.

"Still alive, I see."

Kenji came through the gate at the head of the contingent of priests and healers assigned to our forces. They all set to work immediately, except for Kenji, who walked over to me first.

"I was fortunate. Or not, as the day may prove."

"Even so, let's have a look at you."

I unfastened my helmet and attached it to Shiroirei's saddle, after first determining the arrow that had struck the saddle earlier had not penetrated through to the horseflesh beneath it. I wouldn't have liked to see the expression on Taro's face if that had happened. Meanwhile Kenji inspected me.

"Not so much as an arrow cut, this time. And now?"

"Now I will do what I really came to do."

"Certainly. Storming the fortress and turning Taro into *kappa* bait was simply a distraction."

It didn't take a great deal of sensitivity to know Kenji was not happy with me at the moment. I cannot even say I blamed him. I wasn't entirely happy with myself. I even felt a shade of guilt on behalf of the water goblin. Not that this would have changed one thing I had chosen to do. I did hope one day he would pardon me. I was not sure I would be able to do as much for myself.

"I will not ask you to help me with this," I said.

"You could try forbidding me, but that won't work either. If it must be done, then let us see it done. There is still the matter of settling accounts with Lord Tenshin."

Neither of us spoke again until the two men I had sent to bring Lady Rie into the compound appeared, leading the image of my sister on chains. They seemed wary, as if she had resisted, and as they approached, she resisted again, but they held firmly to her chains. I had hoped the *shikigami* would not force me to bind her, but this was not to be the case. Yet it was soon clear I had been right about the continued degradation of Lord Tenshin's control—I saw her face change before each and every struggle, and knew it was Lord Tenshin who was blindly fighting, not my sister. I wasn't sure what difference it would make, but I took careful note.

Kenji and I took my sister's chains in our own hands, and I dismissed the *bushi*.

"Brother, why have you brought me here?" she said, in one of the times when she was Rie again.

"To face your tormentor. I believe I owe you that much, sister."

"My death is already a fact, brother," Rie said. "His is not, nor will it change what has happened to me. You must destroy what is left of me, you know this to be true. Where that man is concerned, you still have the choice of mercy, so think carefully on what you do."

"As I told you before—I am not as enlightened as you are. What I will do now is on my own head, for you have instructed me better at every opportunity."

"I am very fond of you, brother, but you really are a fool."

I had no argument with that. We had not even begun our search when one of Akimasa's subordinates ran up to tell us the garrison's prisoners had been found, and would I come to pass judgment? I let the man lead us down to the rooms—or rather pits—cut into the foundation itself. They had no doors but only a grillwork covering the top of each of them. We went by them one at a time, and for the most part we simply saw frightened, miserable faces looking up at us.

"Please examine the prisoners. Akimasa-san said you would

know which fell under Lord Yoshiie's directive toward the magic workers."

"I will need some time," I said. "Please, check back in a little while, and I will have a proper answer."

We watched the man disappear from earshot before Kenji spoke. "These are the *onmyoji*. I recognize some of them."

So did I. Over the years I had been in contact, amiably or less so, with several of them but not all. Judging from the numbers, I rather doubted all or even most of the prisoners fell into that category. There weren't that many magicians in all of Kyoto.

"What are you going to do about them?" Kenji asked.

"At the moment, nothing. Help me find Lord Tenshin. I know he is here."

"He is," Rie said softly. "I remember this place."

Kenji gave me a questioning glance then, but I just shook my head. "Later. First, Lord Tenshin."

We found him in a cell all his own, whether to honor him with some distinction or for special punishment, I neither knew nor cared. The face looking up at me from the filth of that pit was not the one I had seen in Kuon Temple, in what now seemed a thousand years gone, but I did recognize the man. I fixed Rie's chain to a supporting post, and together Kenji and I slipped the bolt and hauled the man out of his cell. He could barely stand, so I let him kneel. It was a more appropriate position for what was to follow, regardless.

Lord Tenshin spoke then. His voice was thready and weak. "Aren't you going to gloat, even a little? I would."

"I would not hold yourself as a proper standard of behavior, my lord," Kenji said. "You are nothing but a common murderer."

"Revenge is an occasion to gloat, Lord Tenshin," I said. "Justice, on the other hand, is a more serious matter."

The man laughed then. It came out more of a cackle. "Justice? What do you know about it? The leeches at Court draw their power and wealth from the provincial nobles, who gain nothing but disdain in return. The Court is decadent and weak. I should know—I was part of it for long enough. The Abe Clan and those like them are the future. I have seen it."

"The Abe who locked you away in this place to rot?" I asked.

"Lord Sadato is . . . confused, but great rewards call for great sacrifices, and he will realize this in time. If my plan had worked, the war would have been over! Yoriyoshi is too old to advance his cause now, and without his son he would have been forced to surrender his claim. And then who would dispute the Abe rule? The Heike? Feh. They have no interest in this part of the country, and no one else is strong enough. The Emperor would have been forced to accept the Abe Clan's rule by default. How long do you think it would have taken for the other great lords to see the future as Lord Sadato does?"

"Lord Sadato understood perhaps the cost of the war had become too high. At least so far as you are concerned," I said.

He giggled, and it was easy to see the madness in him. "You call that gloating? It is nothing. Here, since *I* am the one who has his revenge, *I* will gloat! Your sister is dead, even as she stands there next to us. For the difficulty you have given me, for your clumsy interference, I gladly admit to what I have done. I have killed your sister, and so you must kill me now, but you know this will surely destroy what is left of her as well. You will have your 'justice,' Lord Yamada, but it is *I* who will have revenge!"

It took every ounce of control left to me not to strike down Lord Tenshin where he kneeled. It would have been easily done. My sword had remained sheathed throughout the battle, and was sharper than a shaving razor. The time had almost come to use it, but not just yet. I heard my sister's chains rattle. There was a little slack in the reach of it and she used that to approach Lord Tenshin, and then kneel in front of him, no more than three feet away. She looked into the man's face, and Lord Tenshin fell silent while she studied him.

"You're the one," Rie said. "I have seen through your eyes."

He looked away. "Stupid woman. You are nothing. You failed me."

"You failed yourself," she said then. "You compelled me, but I never served you. The soul that is Rie had no part of it. My death, my sister nuns' deaths, even your own death . . . all for nothing. You're a far greater fool than my own sweet brother, and that is saying a great deal."

Rie looked up at me then. "I could wish you spare this man's life, even now, but whether that is within you or not, I must ask you to destroy me first. I do not wish my final destruction linked to him in any way, do you understand? If you must kill him, then do so, but let my death be my own. Kill me first, brother."

"He cannot kill you, as I have already done that. Destroy you? Pointless!" Lord Tenshin said. "I am the one who matters, here, and he must kill *me*. That is the way it must be done. Or how else may justice be served?"

I drew my *tachi* then. "It seems that I have two mutually exclusive requests, and obviously I cannot honor them both." I turned to Kenji then. "In my place, old friend, what would you do?"

For a moment Kenji just stared at me, then he looked away. I nodded. "Do not worry—I did not expect an answer, for I am the only one who can or should answer this question. But before I do, Lord Tenshin, I have a question for you—what did you do with my sister's body? Her real body, that is?"

He grinned his mad grin. "Couldn't find her, eh? Fool, you should have counted your nuns."

"You had Rie bring her own dead body into the nunnery after the slaughter. She was tending the fallen, so it would have been simple to wrap it for cremation like one more murdered nun, and no one the wiser."

Rie shuddered. "Yes. I remember now."

Lord Tenshin hugged himself, barely able to contain his glee. "Clever, yes?"

"Very clever. I admit I never suspected that." I looked at them then, my sister and the man who murdered her, both kneeling before me. "Lord Tenshin, prepare yourself."

"Brother—" Rie began, but the change happened before she was even able to speak. I saw the gleam of triumph in her eyes, and the sad calm in Lord Tenshin's, and with one sure stroke, without even pausing to think about what I was doing, I cut off my sister's head.

They both fell as one, but no sooner had Rie's head touched the stone floor than her outline wavered and became just one more battered piece of paper, only this one was spattered with the dark stains that indicated blood. Even so, there was not so much as a mark of any kind upon my sword.

I sheathed my *tachi* and went to Lord Tenshin's side. He groaned and I helped him to sit up. For a moment he just stared at me, then stared at his hands as if he had never seen them before, and then, with a surprisingly gentle touch, ran his hands over his face.

"What have you done?" he asked, and his voice was strange.

"Justice," I said. "The rest is *karma*, and none of my doing."

Kenji looked from one of us to the other. "Lord Yamada, what in the blazing of the Firejar Hell is going on?!"

"I'm not yet sure," I said. "But I think perhaps something I did not expect. Lord Tenshin?"

"Lord Tenshin . . . " He frowned as if he'd never heard the name before. Then he looked at me. "'Even as I am, whatever karma has brought us to this, you remain my brother.'"

"So I suspected. You are in great need of a bath," I said.

"And food," he said, and he sounded surprised. "I am hungry."

Kenji finally understood, and his voice was barely above a whisper. "Buddha have mercy."

"Yes," I said. "Sometimes."

It was then that Akimasa's subordinate returned, looking rather officious. "Are you prepared to identify the *onmyoji* now?" he asked.

"I'm afraid they're not here," I said. "This is just a pack of common thieves and whatnot, but their crimes were against the Abe, not us, and not worth the time to sort out. You may as well let them go."

CHAPTER SIXTEEN

MINAMOTO NO YOSHIIE: "The weaving of your sleeve has come undone."

Abe no Sadato: "It pains me, yet it cannot be mended."

That is one variation of the exchange. The encounter was less than two weeks old, and already I had heard at least five different versions. I wondered what news of the event would be like by the time it reached the capital, but the basic details of the matter were not, to the best of my understanding, in dispute— Lord Yoshiie's forces had routed Lord Sadato's in one of their few open battles, and Lord Yoshiie had personally given pursuit when he spotted Lord Sadato fleeing the field. Lord Sadato was close to escaping, but Lord Yoshiie called out he had something to say to him. I have no idea why Lord Sadato would fall for such an obvious ploy, but it did lead to the exchange of verses, as laden with symbolism as any at Court. The "weaving of your sleeve" reference was to Lord Sadato's fortresses, which were either in dire straits or already fallen to the Minamoto and their allies. Lord Sadato's poetic response, in that context, is plain enough. From that point, the story made less sense. Supposedly Lord Yoshiie had prepared to fire an arrow at Lord Sadato, but changed his mind and let the man escape to fight again.

I resolved to ask Lord Yoshiie what *really* happened, if I ever had the chance, but such things did not have my highest priority. What was already clear enough was the encounter was well on its way to becoming the sort of thing legends were built upon. Considering he was already informally known as "Hachimantaro," or the Son of the God of War, I didn't think the legend had far to go.

All this had happened even before our own forces rejoined the main army, minus a substantial number to re-garrison the fortress with *bushi* loyal to the Minamoto cause. Unless any force Lord Sadato could muster was able to enlist the aid of a reluctant *kappa*, I did not think the stronghold was in much danger of changing hands again.

That only left Kuriya Castle, which was already under siege. Lord Yoshiie had cleverly diverted the Kuriya River itself to flood the area immediately around the castle, making either escape or relief much more difficult. I pondered looking for more *kappa* at that point, but I couldn't quite bring myself to put young Taro through the ordeal again. I had already tested my own luck and that of those around me far more than even I considered wise. My armor was now packed away in the supply wagons, and so far as I was concerned, it could stay there. My last act before departing the northern castle was to set fire to the cart that had been my sister's prison and watch it burn. We made new travel arrangements, as was necessary.

There was little for Kenji and me to do, except to wait on Lord Yoshiie's pleasure. After another week Lord Yoshiie summoned me. I found him seated on a campstool on a hill near the river that had a commanding view of the siege. I kneeled, but he motioned me to sit on the empty stool beside him. At his nod, his guards and other counselors withdrew out of earshot.

"I have Akimasa's report," he said without preamble. "He apparently credits you for keeping our losses much lower than expected on the northern fortress, the details of *why* this is so remain a bit hazy, however. Could you enlighten me?"

"I . . . persuaded, for want of a better word, someone in a position to sabotage the gate to do so in our behalf. That was all. Most of the credit must go to Akimasa and the *bushi* under his command. He is a very capable person."

"You were one of the first through the gate, according to Akimasa."

"I had business within the fortress, my lord. Some of which you knew about."

"And Lord Tenshin?"

"Lord Tenshin is dead. I killed him."

"And the person you have been seen with who strongly resembles the dead man?"

"Is someone else, someone to whom I owe obligation. You have my word on this, my lord. The man responsible for the slaughter at Yahiko-ji is dead."

Lord Yoshiie grunted. "Well, then . . . we will consider the matter closed."

I bowed. "Thank you, my lord. And I was in earnest when I said most of the credit must go to Akimasa-san. It is a pity he is not of higher rank. He would make an excellent general."

"That he would, I believe."

"As for the issue of his rank . . . someone, perhaps, in a position of power could do something about this."

"True," Lord Yoshiie said. "Perhaps someone will, at the proper time." He didn't say anything else for a while. I simply waited.

He finally grunted. "Lord Sadato cannot hold out much longer. The castle will fall soon, and whether he surrenders or not, I must take Lord Sadato's head back to the capital. There are no more *shikigami*, nor will there be. Is this not correct?"

"It is, my lord."

"My father told me he saw a sign of our impending victory in the clouds while he was traveling to Dewa and arranged for a small shrine to the God of War to be built near Kamakura. I think I will visit it, on my way back to the capital. Perhaps I will take the time to enlarge it, if I may. My father is a great man, but he is always . . . circumspect, where his gratitude is concerned. My own is less constrained."

"I am sure Hachiman-sama would look on such an act with approval," I said, mostly because I wasn't sure what else to say, but Yoshiie just ordered one of his attendants forward, who kneeled in front of me.

"You may consider your obligation to my welfare as requested by Prince Kanemore to be faithfully discharged, Lord Yamada, but I would ask a favor of you."

The attendant produced two scrolls from a silk bag and presented them to me. Both were sealed with the Minamoto crest. Yoshiie went on, "I will supply a suitable escort for you and your associates to return to the capital. I would ask only that you personally deliver these two scrolls to Prince Kanemore, with my compliments."

I—we, were going home. I considered it far past time. "I will be honored to do so," I said, "but if may I be so presumptuous as to ask a favor of you in return?"

He frowned. "What is it?"

"Please release Lord Yasuna into my custody, so he may return to the capital as well. His presence or absence can make no difference to your enterprise now."

"Except he has become a rather morose fellow these days," Lord Yoshiie said. "Considering the matter, I do think it best for all concerned that he is returned home. You will actually be doing *me* another favor to take charge of him."

"And I will be honored to do so."

Once I was dismissed, I went to find Kenji. "Lord Yoshiie has discharged us, as our mission is complete," I said. "We are going home. Lord Yasuna as well."

He yawned. "Finally. It has been a splendid adventure indeed— if you can call chancing death most days of the week splendid— but I am weary of the provinces, and I am sick to death of cleaning up the human wrecks these *bushi* leave behind. Worse, I was beginning to think you were going to turn into one of them."

I sighed. "Do not worry. While I am as uncertain of my place in the world as any man may be, I know the profession of warrior is not my path."

"You should consider holy orders," said Lord Tenshin, for I was, for the moment, still thinking of him in those terms. "Sister" was no longer appropriate, but "brother" was still too far away for me to grasp, as a concept and a reality both. Still, as confused as I was, I could only imagine it was worse for the one who had once been my sister, and yet she—he—had apparently accepted the change as the working of *karma* and was dealing with the matter probably far better than I was. I could see he had shaved his head and wore the garb of simple monk now. The clothes did not fit him well, but for now they would have to do.

Kenji snickered. "Please, if there was ever a man *least* suited for the monastic life—"

"—you mean aside from yourself?" I asked.

"Cruel, yet accurate," Kenji said. "My point, however, stands."

"Aside from *myself*," Lord Tenshin said. "But that is the road fate and *karma* have left to me, so it is the one I will take. I fear we will soon be parting again, brother."

"How are you . . . I mean, really? I was telling the truth; I did not plan what happened. How could I?" I asked.

"Honestly, I do not know how you men manage it," he said as if he hadn't heard a word I'd said. "Such obvious vulnerabilities and spiritual disadvantages . . . seriously, I had no idea. Yet if you can cope with what you are, then so can I. It may, however, take some time to adjust. I cannot be Rie, but I am certainly not Lord Tenshin. I will need time and solitude to figure out who and what I am."

"Where will you go?" Kenji asked.

"I considered Yahiko-ji," he said. "But it occurred to me to do so would mean I was punishing myself, which is not the path to enlightenment. Perhaps Mount Oe. Master Kenji, you yourself spoke of being trained there. It sounds wonderful."

"Wonderful? It was hell on earth," Kenji muttered.

"All the better," said Lord Tenshin, looking serene. "I do think it best that I not remain in the north or in the capital where he—I mean I—might be recognized. I think my path must be west."

"I think that would be wise. Yet our path home is through Yahiko-ji and on to the capital," I said. "For now, let us go and give Lord Yasuna the good news."

OUR PARTY increased by one before we returned to Kyoto. I think I had half-expected Mai to choose to remain at Yahiko-ji after all, but no sooner had we arrived than she presented herself to me, her spare clothes and everything else which belonged to her gathered into one bundle and ready for travel.

"Mai-chan is a fine young woman," the old nun Tomoko said to me. "But she is not ready for holy orders, and so I must trust her to your care, Lord Yamada. The Lady Rie I remember would approve, I think."

I was less certain of this, myself, but it did occur to me all I had to do to answer the question was to ask. I decided to let it lie. Once we left Yahiko-ji behind, our escort also increased by one. Several times I saw a flash of white in the hills and forests along the road. No more than that and no opportunity for a meeting. I considered the possibility Lady Kuzunoha had not yet forgiven me for our confrontation over Lord Yasuna and perhaps never would. Even so, I still believed it was a very good idea to be traveling in Lord Yasuna's company. Our *bushi* might have been overwhelmed by a large enough force of bandits, but I pitied any such group thinking of attacking us so long as the fox demon was our shadow.

By the time we returned to Kyoto, I was still of uncertain mind where Mai was concerned. I felt it obviously inappropriate for her to stay in my rooms, yet I was afraid if she were lodged anywhere else at the Widow Tamahara's establishment, the poor girl might assume I had sold her to a brothel. Fortunately, Kenji was able to arrange for her lodging at a nearby temple. Not that this prevented her from coming to my rooms on a daily basis to fetch and carry and clean and in all things behave as my servant. I wanted to tell her this was not necessary, but it also occurred to me, if she was not my servant, then what was she? Everyone needed a place in the world, so what would hers be? I did not know, and yet I had made a promise to her, and I was determined to keep it, yet I was far from certain as to how this would be accomplished.

Kenji was aware of my dilemma and, if anything, less sanguine on the subject than I. "I have said this before, Lord Yamada, and your situation has hardly changed since—you can barely take care of yourself. How will you look after Mai as well?"

"I can't turn her out on the streets, Kenji-san."

He looked affronted. "Did I suggest such a thing? No. The simplest solution would be to marry her, not that I believe this would be a great improvement to her situation."

"Don't be absurd. How fares my . . . your brother monk?"

"He left for Mount Oe yesterday. I wrote a letter of introduction to the abbot. Unfortunately my name will likely get him soundly beaten and left in a ditch rather than welcomed."

I had met the abbot in question, and I did not consider this a likely outcome, but even so—"He left without saying goodbye?"

"I am rather certain he does not consider this 'good-bye.' So. Have you heard from Prince Kanemore yet?"

I had not, though we had been in the capital for over a week. Another passed before I finally received a summons, and when I did, it was to the Sixth Ward mansion where our journey had first begun. I arrived to find the place almost deserted, but to my surprise I was met by Taro.

"It is good to see you, Taro-san. How fares Shiroirei and Neko?"

"Considering their hardships, quite well."

I almost laughed. "*Their* hardships? As I recall, Taro-san, they were looked after even more diligently than *we* were."

"That is possibly true," Taro said. "And I must ask your pardon for it, even as you must remember you chose to be where you were. They did not."

I still did not laugh, but I could not keep from smiling. "That is a good point."

"And now I am neglecting my duties once again. Prince Kanemore wants to see you, as you already know. I will take you to him."

Prince Kanemore was waiting in the audience hall, but the feeling of being nearly alone in that great echoing building had not diminished. He was by himself by all appearance, though I knew two or three trusted guards and attendants aside from Taro must have been near. He wasn't on the dais, he wasn't even sitting in state. He merely stood in the middle of the room, waiting for me.

"It is very good to see you again, Lord Yamada," he said.

I bowed and made as if to kneel, but he grabbed my hand and pulled me back upright. "For now it is just you and I," he said. "We needn't be so formal and correct. First, I must apologize for making you wait for so long. It was not my intention."

"You are a prince of the royal line," I said. "I do not feel slighted if, as I suspect, you had higher priorities."

"Higher? I would not say so. Yet I suppose you have heard the news by now."

Indeed I had. We had not been in the capital more than a few days when word of the fall of Kuriya Castle reached Kyoto. The entire city was buzzing like a nest of hornets at the news.

"I suppose we must expect a triumphal return of the Minamoto heir?" I asked.

"Just so. There have been preparations and plans from dawn to dusk, but now there is just you and I, and I want to know what happened. More to the point, I would hear your opinion of Lord Yoshiie."

"He is a good, honorable, and brave man; a gentleman, an inspired leader and a skilled diplomat. In the long run I think he will prove far more dangerous than Lord Abe ever dreamed of being."

"Do you question his loyalty to the Emperor and his government?" Kanemore asked.

"Not in the least, not even for a moment."

"Then why do you believe he is dangerous?"

"For the same reasons you do—doubtless this understanding was part of why you wanted me to accompany the army to Mutsu in the first place. Yoshiie was already a hero, and this campaign will solidify that reputation—and deservedly so. But it remains that the Abe do not rule in Mutsu now because the Minamoto chose to oppose them. They may have done so on behalf of the Emperor's government, but Yoriyoshi accepted the commission primarily to advance the Minamoto Clan. You know this to be true, and through his brilliant son, he has succeeded. The Emperor's will is law, but the Emperor's power is what the military families choose to give. That was clear to the Abe Clan. It will be even clearer to others."

Prince Kanemore's brow darkened. I merely waited.

"You are right," he said finally. "The Kiyohara and the Shibata saw how much could be accomplished, with or without the direction of the Emperor's government. What we saw in Mutsu, we will see again, I fear. And again. This cannot be helped, but for now, the Emperor's will is upheld. That is what I needed to accomplish, as surely as Lord Yoriyoshi himself did. We will welcome the young hero now called 'Hachimantaro' back to the capital, old friend, but we will do it with our eyes open."

I did bow then. "Let us always have honesty between us, Highness. I do treasure politeness, but given the choice, I've always found honesty more useful. Except, perhaps, in the case of water goblins."

Prince Kanemore laughed. "Water goblins? Lord Yamada, on another day I am going to ask you to tell me that story. For now, it will have to wait. I am neglecting other duties simply by being here."

"Then let me do this quickly." I produced the two scrolls that had been entrusted to me. "Lord Yoshiie requested I bring these to you personally. With his compliments, he said. I do not know what he meant by this."

Prince Kanemore frowned, but he took the scrolls from me and broke the seal on the first one. Whatever was in the first scroll, no hint of its contents came to Prince Kanemore's face. I believed the scroll to be readable, but Prince Kanemore was not. After studying the first scroll for a few moments he broke the seal on the second. When he looked up again, he was smiling like a man who had seen some wondrous object and didn't quite know what to make of it.

"This always feels strange," he said finally.

"Your pardon, Highness, but what feels strange?"

"Knowing something concerning you that you yourself do not know. You haven't the vaguest notion of what is in these scrolls, do you?"

I frowned. "No, they were sealed. I certainly wasn't going to open them simply to satisfy an idle curiosity."

"There would have been no blame, as they both refer to you. The first is a declaration from Lord Yoshiie. As part of his reward for pacifying the Abe, he is formally requesting the Emperor posthumously exonerate and promote three degrees in rank a disgraced noble, namely one Yamada no Seburo."

"My . . . ?"

"Yes, Goji-san. Your father. I can tell you right now His Majesty will likely grant this request, partly because it will cost the Emperor nothing to honor it, but mostly because it will be difficult to refuse the young hero anything. I had requested as much myself and was refused, as our friendship is well known, and my judgment in the matter is considered suspect. I had hoped the next Emperor would be more flexible, but likely that is years away still."

I had not known *that*, either, but Kanemore, being Kanemore, had never told me.

"As for the second . . . " Prince Kanemore paused to study the second scroll even more closely, as if there was something difficult contained therein and he wanted to avoid mistakes. "Yes. Twenty thousand. I knew I had read it correctly."

I had a very odd feeling then. "Twenty thousand, Highness? Twenty thousand what?"

"*Koku.* In rice, as is the custom. That is the value of your new estate near Kamakura."

I couldn't believe what I was hearing. A *koku* was enough rice to feed a grown man for a year. Twenty thousand amounted to—

"That is correct, Lord Yamada. As of now, you are a wealthy man."

"But . . . it is too much!"

"Lord Yoshiie would seem to disagree," Prince Kanemore said. "And, as it is his estate to give, I rather believe he knows what he is doing. More to the point, by giving the news through me, he made sure *I* knew what he was doing. Rewarding my friends is not a poor way to get into my good graces. Which, for the moment and for whatever reason he desires this, I must consider Yoshiie to be."

"You are the uncle of the Crown Prince," I said.

"A good enough reason, I would think," Prince Kanemore said. "This one I must take to the Emperor," he said, referring to the first scroll. "This one belongs to you." He handed me the second scroll, the one giving me title to the estate. A quick look was enough to tell me it was a clear grant, not a simple stewardship arrangement as I had thought at first—the estate was mine. All taxes owed, all income produced. With, it was clear to see, the latter far exceeding the former.

"What must I do?" I asked.

"It is a gift, and you must accept it graciously," Prince Kanemore said. "Unless you wish to insult Lord Yoshiie and, by extension, the entire Minamoto Clan. You do not want to do that. He has also, intentionally I would imagine, placed your fortunes within the Minamoto sphere of influence. Regardless, and the diplomatic aspect aside, Lord Yamada, you're going to need the income. Your family name will soon be rehabilitated, and in addition, you will inherit a higher rank than your father held in life. When that happens, it will be incumbent upon *you* to rebuild your clan. Doubtless you will have responsibilities, in due course. Responsibilities are expensive. Believe me, I know, but it is of no consequence. As I said, you are now a wealthy man."

I wasn't dismissed. Prince Kanemore simply bid me farewell and left, and I heard the sounds of his attendants and guards rejoining him once he had left the audience hall. Kenji had once said that life was an illusion, but never just one illusion, at least not for long. It never quite remained the same. I'm not sure he was talking about such a thing as this, but the illusion, if so it was, had definitely changed. In a moment or two, Taro appeared to escort me out.

"Taro-san, what do you want?"

He blinked. "Want, my lord? I don't understand."

"I mean in years to come. You are in the service of a prince, and that is a fine and envious thing by most opinions, but is it all you desire in this world?"

He hesitated. "I would not say anything against Prince Kanemore. He has been very kind to me."

"Certainly not, nor am I asking you to do so. I merely asked if what you are doing now is what you always wish to do."

He hesitated once more but finally replied in a low voice, "I want to breed and train horses, not merely groom and attend them. I think I have the knack for it, but there's little use for such skills in the capital. Perhaps one day . . . "

"I came to appreciate the creatures a bit more during our time together," I said. "Yes. I can imagine you doing just that. I understand such things are more common around Kamakura."

"And further west and east," he said, "but yes, that is my understanding. I have never been there."

I could see another conversation in the future with Prince Kanemore. The illusion, if I had anything to say of it, would change for more people than myself. When I left the Sixth Ward mansion, I made my way north to the Demon Gate. Kenji was there, plying his trade in spirit wards and exorcisms as I had expected. I sat down beside him and told him what had happened. He seemed rather less surprised by the turn of events than I was.

"You will accept," he said. "Don't try to wiggle out of it."

"I don't appear to have a great deal of choice in the matter."

"Good, for *despite* your best efforts, you have finally become the rich friend I have always wanted. I was beginning to think it would never happen."

"There is one stipulation, however—I will be in Kamakura. At least until I am established in my new estate. This may take a while."

He frowned. "You're not serious! Leave the capital? What matters besides this place?"

"The entire country matters, and this is only going to become more clear in time. Prince Kanemore knows that, even if most of the Court nobility does not. Yet."

"I cannot fathom it," Kenji said. "The provinces are either deadly dull or at war—deadly, period. They are best avoided."

"Will this prevent you from visiting me?"

"Certainly not. Do you think I would break ties with a man who could endow my own temple? I've always wondered what it would be like to be an abbot."

"A small temple," I said. "Perhaps even tiny. Perhaps the size of a small privy."

"A matter for later discussion," he said, all serenity. "After all, Lord Tenshin—no, I have to stop calling him that. He is going to choose a new name for his new life, and as soon as he lets us know what that is, I will refer to him as such. Regardless, after Mount Oe . . . ?"

I could see Kenji's point. Perhaps a larger temple. But, as he had said, this was a matter for later discussion.

"What about Mai?" he asked then.

"Oh, she will go with me."

"Then are you going to marry her, as I suggested?"

I frowned. "Certainly not. The idea is ridiculous."

Now Kenji looked puzzled. "She will remain your servant?"

"Remain? She is not my servant *now*, even if the poor girl seems to think otherwise."

"Not a wife and, by extension I would suppose, not a concubine either. Not a servant . . . Lord Yamada, I am running out of potential relationships."

"Isn't it obvious? I will need to re-establish the Yamada Clan, so as my first act as clan chief, I'm going to formally adopt her."

Kenji glanced toward the heavens. "Of course you are, because you are that kind of fool. You do realize she is already of marriageable age, don't you?"

I demurred. "A little young, to my way of thinking, and she will need time for her education as a lady, but yes, if and when this happens, it will be the Yamada Clan's first alliance since my father's time. I am rather looking forward to it, but I will not force her. I have seen where such things lead."

"This is all very well, but sooner or later you are going to require a son, or hadn't you considered that? Lord Yamada, you really must think about finding a proper wife before you're too old for such things to matter to you. As a friend, I'm telling you this sad day is probably a lot closer than you'd care to admit . . . no offense intended."

"Possibly a little offense intended, "I said. "Yet I do see your point. I am not ruling the possibility out, understand, but I cannot leave my clan's future to the winds of chance. So, concerning a son, I have a plan for this, too."

"A *plan*? Oh, you mean Taro," Kenji said. It wasn't a question.

"Why not? I have seen enough children of the nobility and otherwise to know the results of any union can be . . . unfortunate. With Mai and Taro I know *precisely* what I am getting. The resurrected Yamada line will be off to a fine start."

"I would argue with you on some general principle or other, but I know there is no point. Besides," he said, "you are right. They will certainly be an improvement on *you*."

"You think so?" I smiled, but it was mostly a show of teeth. "Now then, sir monk, let us discuss that temple."

GLOSSARY OF TERMS

baka – A general insult. Usually translated as "idiot," but with connotations of being uncouth and wild, like an animal.

boushi – A hat.

bushi – A warrior. Later this would refer to samurai specifically.

-chan – Honorific connoting a familiar person. It is a diminutive indicating the person is endearing. In general, used for babies, children, grandparents, and teenagers.

chie (or *che*) – An expletive.

daikon – Literally "big root"; white radish.

Emishi – An indigenous people usually identified with the modern Ainu.

hai – Yes.

hakama – Loose-fitting trousers.

hi – The *kanji* character 火.

hitatare – A two-piece outfit consisting of a large-sleeved tunic and divided trousers.

hojo – The abbot or chief priest of a Buddhist temple.

kami – A divine spirit, roughly equivalent to a god.

kampai – Equivalent to "cheers!" before a drink.

kanji – Chinese logographic characters, used for formal documents in the Heian period.

karma – The sum of a person's actions in this and previous states of existence, viewed as deciding their fate in future existences. Informally: destiny or fate, following as effect from cause.

koku – A unit of volume; one *koku* was considered sufficient to feed a single man for a year. Wealth was determined by the number of *koku* in a lord's landholding. Taxes and salaries were denominated in koku.

-kun – Used for those of junior status; can also be used to name a close personal friend or family member.

kuge – Court nobility; an aristocratic class that emerged in the Heian period and held high posts and considerable power at the Imperial Court in Kyoto.

maedate – A frontal decoration for a helmet.

maku – On the battlefield, a curtain enclosing a space reserved for commanding officers.

mala(s) – Buddhist prayer beads.

mamushi – *Gloydius blomhoffii*, A venomous pit viper found in japan, China, and Korea.

matsuri – A festival or holiday.

mizu – The kanji character 水.

menpo – Facial armor that covered all or part of the face and provided a way to secure the helmet.

mon – A family crest or symbol.

noppera-bō – A faceless ghost.

obi – A sash worn with a kimono.

oni – A specific type of dangerous monster, equivalent to the Western ogre.

onibi – Ghost lights. Small will-o'-wisp-type flames that signify the presence of ghosts.

onmyoji – A magician and diviner whose practices are derived from yin-yang. In the Heian period, *onmyoji* gained influence at Court as they could protect against vengeful ghosts and divine auspicious or harmful dates; they could also call and control *shikigami*.

sakura – The cherry blossom tree and its blooms.

-sama – Honorific, usually reserved for someone of high social status.

saya – A scabbard.

samuru – A servant. Thought to be the word from which the later *samurai* is derived.

-san – Honorific, showing respect to the person addressed.

shi – In the context used, a word meaning both "four" and "death."

shikigami – Artificial creatures created by magic to do the magician's will.

shin – The kanji character 心.

shirime – A *youkai* with an eye in the place of his anus.

shogi – Literally: "general's board game." A two-player strategy board game in the same family as Western chess.

sode – Large shoulder guards made from leather in the early Heian period, later of iron

sohei – A warrior attached to a Buddhist temple. Possibly a monk, but more likely a lay-brother, or even a mercenary.

tachi – A long, thin sword originally designed for use on horseback.

yin-yang – A philosophy rooted in both the balance between and interconnectedness of all things: light/dark, male/female, life/death, etc. Probably derived from Daoism via China.

yoroi hitatare – *Hitatare* and *hakama* in matching fabric.

youkai – Generic term for a monster, or pretty much any supernatural creature.

ABOUT THE AUTHOR

Richard Parks has been writing and publishing science fiction and fantasy longer than he cares to remember . . . or probably can remember. His work has appeared in *Asimov's, Realms of Fantasy, Beneath Ceaseless Skies, Lady Churchill's Rosebud Wristlet,* and several "year's best" anthologies. Other adventures featuring Yamada no Goji were collected in *Yamada Monogatari: Demon Hunter* (Prime Books, 2013). A novel, *Yamada Monogatari: To Break the Demon Gate,* was published in 2014, and a fourth novel concerning Lord Yamada, *Yamada Monogatari: The Emperor in Shadow,* will be published by Prime in late 2016. Parks blogs at *Den of Ego and Iniquity Annex #3,* also known as richard-parks.com.